THE BOURBON KINGS

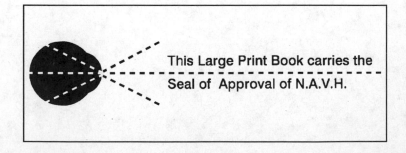

This Large Print Book carries the
Seal of Approval of N.A.V.H.

THE BOURBON KINGS

J.R. WARD

THORNDIKE PRESS

A part of Gale, Cengage Learning

GALE
CENGAGE Learning·

Farmington Hills, Mich • San Francisco • New York • Waterville, Maine
Meriden, Conn • Mason, Ohio • Chicago

Copyright © 2015 by Love Conquers All, Inc.
Thorndike Press, a part of Gale, Cengage Learning.

Thorndike Press® Large Print Romance.
The text of this Large Print edition is unabridged.
Other aspects of the book may vary from the original edition.
Set in 16 pt. Plantin.

LIBRARY OF CONGRESS CATALOGING-IN-PUBLICATION DATA

Ward, J. R., 1969–
    The bourbon kings / J. R. Ward. — Large print edition.
    pages cm. — (Thorndike Press large print romance)
    ISBN 978-1-4104-8343-0 (hardback) — ISBN 1-4104-8343-6 (hardcover)
    1. Families—Kentucky—Fiction. 2. Family-owned business enterprises—Fiction. 3. Bourbon whiskey—Fiction. 4. Large type books. 5. Domestic fiction. I. Title.
    PS3623.A73227B68 2015b
    813'.6—dc23   2015028112

Published in 2015 by arrangement with New American Library, an imprint of Penguin Publishing Group, a division of Penguin Random House LLC

Printed in the United States of America
1 2 3 4 5 6 7 19 18 17 16 15

Dedicated to my beloved
Southern Gentleman,
John Neville Blakemore III,
without whom this, and so much else,
would not be possible.

You are cordially invited to
A Derby Brunch
in celebration of the
One Hundred and Thirty-Ninth Running of
The Charlemont Derby
Saturday, May the Fourth
Ten o'clock
Easterly
RSVP: newarkharris@gmail.com

ONE

Charlemont, Kentucky

Mist hung over the Ohio's sluggish waters like the breath of God, and the trees on the Charlemont shore side of River Road were so many shades of spring green, the color required a sixth sense to absorb them all. Overhead, the sky was a dim, milky blue, the kind of thing that you saw up north only in July, and at seven-thirty a.m., the temperature was already seventy-four degrees.

It was the first week of May. The most important seven days on the calendar, beating the birth of Christ, the American Independence, and New Year's Rockin' Eve.

The One Hundred Thirty-ninth running of The Charlemont Derby was on Saturday.

Which meant the entire state of Kentucky was in a thoroughbred racing frenzy.

As Lizzie King approached the turn-off for her work, she was riding an adrenaline high that had been pumping for a good three weeks, and she knew from past experience that this rush-rush mood of hers wasn't going to deflate until after Saturday's clean-up. At least she was, as always, going against the traffic heading into downtown and making good time: Her commute was forty minutes each way, but not in the NYC, Boston, or LA, densely packed, parking-lot version of rush hour — which in her current frame of mind would have caused her head to mushroom cloud. No, her trip into her job was twenty-eight minutes of Indiana farm country followed by six minutes of bridge and spaghetti junction delays, capped off with this six- to ten-minute, against-the-tide shot parallel to the river.

Sometimes she was convinced the only cars going in her direction were the rest of the staff that worked at Easterly with her.

Ah, yes, Easterly.

The Bradford Family Estate, or BFE, as its deliveries were marked, sat high up on the biggest hill in the Charlemont metro area and was comprised of a twenty-thousand-square-foot main house with three formal gardens, two pools, and a three-hundred-sixty degree view of Washington County. There was also twelve retainer's cottages on the property, as well as ten outbuildings, a fully functioning farm of over a hundred acres, a twenty-horse stable that had been converted into a business center, and a nine-hole golf course.

That was lighted.

In case you needed to work on your chip shot at one a.m.

As far as she had heard, the enormous parcel had been granted to the family back in 1778, after the first of the Bradfords had come south from Pennsylvania with the then Colonel George Rogers Clark — and brought both his ambitions and his bourbon-making traditions into the nascent commonwealth. Fast forward almost two hundred fifty years, and you had a Federal mansion the size of a small town up on that hill, and some seventy-two people working on the property full- and part-time.

All of whom followed a feudal rules and rigid caste system that was right out of Downton Abbey.

Or maybe the Dowager Countess of Grantham's routine was a little too progressive.

William the Conqueror's times were probably more apt.

So, for example — and this was solely a Lifetime movie conjecture here — if a gardener fell in love with one of the family's precious sons? Even if she were one of two head horticulturists, and had a national reputation and a master's in landscape architecture from Cornell?

That was *just* not done.

Sabrina without the happy ending, darlin'.

With a curse, Lizzie turned the radio on in hopes of getting her brain to shut up. She didn't get far. Her Toyota Yaris had the speaker system of a Barbie house: there were little circles in the doors that were supposed to pump music, but they were mostly for pretend — and today, NPR coming out of those cocktail coasters just wasn't enough —

The sound of an ambulance speeding up behind her easily overrode the haute pitter-patter of the BBC News, and she hit her brakes and eased over onto the shoulder. After the noise and flashing lights passed, she got back on track and rounded a fat curve in both the river and the road . . . and there it was, the Bradfords' great white mansion, high up in the sky, the dawning sun being forced to work around its regal, symmetrical layout.

She had grown up in Plattsburgh, New York, on an apple orchard.

What the hell had she been thinking

almost two years ago when she'd let Lane Baldwine, the youngest son, into her life?

And why was she still, after all this time, wondering about the particulars?

Come on, it wasn't like she was the first woman who'd gotten good and seduced by him —

Lizzie frowned and leaned forward over the wheel.

The ambulance that had passed her was heading up the flank of the BFE hill, its red and white lights strobing along the alley of maple trees.

"Oh, God," she breathed.

She prayed it wasn't who she thought it was.

But come on, her luck couldn't be that bad.

And wasn't it sad that that was the first thing that came to her mind instead of worry over whoever was hurt/sick/passed out.

Proceeding on by the monogrammed, wrought-iron gates that were just closing, she took her right-hand turn about three hundred yards later.

As an employee, she was required to use the service entrance with her vehicles, no excuses, no exceptions.

Because God forbid a vehicle with an

MSRP of under a hundred thousand dollars be seen in front of the house —

Boy, she was getting bitchy, she decided. And after Derby, she was going to have to take a vacation before people thought she was going through menopause two decades too early.

The sewing machine under the Yaris's hood revved up as she shot down the level road that went around the base of the hill. The cornfield came first, the manure already laid down and churned over in preparation for planting. And then there were the cutting gardens filled with the first of the perennials and annuals, the heads of the early peonies fat as softballs and no darker than the blush on an ingenue's cheeks. After those, there were the orchid houses and nurseries, followed by the outbuildings with the farm and groundskeeping equipment in them, and then the lineup of two- and three-bedroom, fifties-era cottages.

That were as variable and stylish as a set of sugar and flour tins on a Formica counter.

Pulling into the staff parking lot, she got out, leaving her cooler, her hat and her bag with her sunscreen behind.

Jogging over to groundskeeping's main building, she entered the gasoline- and oil-smelling cave through the open bay on the left. The office of Gary McAdams, the head groundsman, was off to the side, the cloudy glass panes still translucent enough to tell her that lights were on and someone was moving around in there.

She didn't bother to knock. Shoving open the flimsy door, she ignored the half-naked Pirelli calendar pinups. "Gary —"

The sixty-two-year-old was just hanging up the phone with his bear-paw hand, his sunburned face with its tree-bark skin as grim as she had ever seen it. As he looked across his messy desk, she knew who the ambulance was for even before he said the name.

Lizzie put her hands to her face and leaned back against the doorjamb.

She felt so sorry for the family, of course, but it was impossible not to personalize the tragedy and want to go throw up somewhere.

The one man she never wanted to see again . . . was going to come home.

She might as well get a stop watch.

New York, New York
"Come on. I know you want me."

Jonathan Tulane Baldwine looked around the hip that was propped next to his stack

15

of poker chips. "Ante up, boys."

"I'm talking to you." A pair of partially covered, fully fake breasts appeared over the fan of cards in his hands. *"Hello."*

Time to feign interest in something, anything else, Lane thought. Too bad the one-bedroom, mid-floor, Midtown apartment was a bachelor pad done in nothing-that-wasn't-functional. And why bother staring into the faces of what was left of the six bastards they'd started playing with eight hours ago. None of them had proved worthy of anything more than keeping up with the high stakes.

Deciphering their tells, even as an avoidance strategy, wasn't worth the eye strain at seven-thirty in the morning.

"Helllllloooo —"

"Give it up, honey, he's not interested," someone muttered.

"Everybody's interested in me."

"Not him." Jeff Stern, the host and roommate, tossed in a thousand dollars' worth of chips. "Ain't that right, Lane?"

"Are you gay? Is he gay?"

Lane moved the queen of hearts next to the king of hearts. Shifted the jack next to the queen. Wanted to push the boob job with mouth onto the floor. "Two of you haven't anted."

"I'm out, Baldwine. Too rich for my blood."

"I'm in — if someone'll lend me a grand."

Jeff looked across the green fleet table and smiled. "It's you and me again, Baldwine."

"Looking forward to takin' your money." Lane tucked his cards in tight. "It's your bet —"

The woman leaned down again. "I love your Southern accent."

Jeff's eyes narrowed behind his clear-rimmed glasses. "You gotta back off him, baby."

"I'm not stupid," she slurred. "I know exactly who you are and how much money you have. I drink your bourbon —"

Lane sat back and addressed the fool that had brought the chatty accessory. "Billy? Seriously."

"Yeah, yeah." The guy who'd wanted to go a thousand dollars into debt stood up. "The sun's coming up, anyway. Let's go."

"I want to stay —"

"Nope, you're done." Billy took the bimbo with the self-esteem inflation problem by the arm and escorted her to the door. "I'll take you home, and no, he's not who you think he is. Later, assholes."

"Yes, he is — I've seen him in magazines —"

Before the door could shut, the other guy who'd been bled dry got to his feet. "I'm out of here, too. Remind me never to play with the pair of you again."

"I'll do nothing of the sort," Jeff said as he held up a palm. "Tell the wife I said hello."

"You can tell her yourself when we see you at Shabbat."

"That again."

"Every Friday, and if you don't like it, why do you keep showing up at my house?"

"Free food. It's just that simple."

"Like you need the handouts."

And then they were alone. With over two hundred and fifty thousand dollars' worth of poker chips, two decks of cards, an ashtray full of cigar nubs, and no bimbage.

"It's your bet," Lane said.

"I think he wants to marry her," Jeff muttered as he tossed more chips into the center of the table. "Billy, that is. Here's twenty grand."

"Then he should get his head examined." Lane met his old fraternity brother's bet and then doubled it. "Pathetic. The both of them."

Jeff lowered his cards. "Lemme ask you something."

"Don't make it too hard, I'm drunk."

"Do you like them?"

"Poker chips?" In the background, a cell phone started to ring. "Yeah, I do. So if you don't mind putting some more of yours in —"

"No, women."

Lane shifted his eyes up. "Excuse me?"

His oldest friend put an elbow on the felt and leaned in. His tie had been lost at the start of the game, and his previously starched, bright white shirt was now as pliant and relaxed as a polo. His eyes, however, were tragically sharp and focused. "You heard me. Look, I know it's none of my business, but you show up here how long ago? Like, nearly two years. You live on my couch, you don't work — which given who your family is, I get. But there's no women, no —"

"Stop thinking, Jeff."

"I'm serious."

"So bet."

The cell phone went quiet. But his buddy didn't. "U.Va. was a lifetime ago. Lot can change."

"Apparently not if I'm still on your couch —"

"What happened to you, man."

"I died waiting for you to bet or fold."

Jeff muttered as he made a stack of reds

19

and blues and tossed them into the center. " 'Nother twenty thousand."

"That's more like it." The cell phone started to ring again. "I'll see you. And I'll raise you fifty. If you shut up."

"You sure you want to do that?"

"Get you to be quiet? Yup."

"Go aggressive in poker with an investment banker like me. Clichés are there for a reason — I'm greedy and great with math. Unlike your kind."

"My kind."

"People like you Bradfords don't know how to make money — you've been trained to spend it. Now, unlike most dilettantes, your family actually *has* an income stream — although that's what keeps you from having to learn anything. So not sure it's a value-add in the long term."

Lane thought back to why he'd finally left Charlemont for good. "I've learned plenty, trust me."

"And now you sound bitter."

"You're boring me. Am I supposed to enjoy that?"

"Why don't you ever go home for Christmas? Thanksgiving? Easter?"

Lane collapsed his cards and put them face-down on the felt. "I don't believe in Santa Claus or the Easter Bunny anymore, goddamn it, and turkey is overrated. What *is* your problem?"

Wrong question to ask. Especially after a night of poker and drinking. Especially to a guy like Stern, who was categorically incapable of being anything but perfectly honest.

"I hate that you're so alone."

"You've *got* to be kidding —"

"I'm one of your oldest friends, right? If I don't tell you like it is, who's going to? And don't get pissy with me — you picked a New York Jew, not one of the thousand other southern-fried stick-up-the-asses that went to that ridiculous college of ours to be your perpetual roommate. So fuck you."

"Are we going to play this hand out?"

Jeff's shrewd stare narrowed. "Answer me one thing."

"Yes, I am seriously reconsidering why I didn't crash with Wedge or Chenoweth right now."

"Ha. You couldn't stand either of those two longer than a day. Unless you were drunk, which actually, you have been for the last three and a half months straight. And that's another thing I have a problem with."

"Bet. Now. For the love of God."

"Why —"

As that cell phone went off a third time, Lane got to his feet and stalked across the room. Over on the bar, next to his billfold, the glowing screen was lit up — not that he bothered to look at who it was.

He answered the call only because it was either that or commit homicide.

The male Southern voice on the other end of the connection said three words: "Your momma's dyin'."

As the meaning sank into his brain, everything destabilized around him, the walls closing in, the floor rolling, the ceiling collapsing on his head. Memories didn't so much come to him as assault him, the alcohol in his system doing nothing to dull the onslaught.

No, he thought. *Not now. Not this morning.*

Although would there ever be a good time?

"Not ever" was the only acceptable timetable on this.

From a distance, he heard himself speak. "I'll be there before noon."

And then he hung up.

"Lane?" Jeff got to his feet. "Oh, shit, don't you pass out on me. I've got to be at Eleven Wall in an hour and I need a shower."

From a vast distance, Lane watched his hand reach out and pick up his wallet. He put that and the phone in the pocket of his slacks and headed for the door.

"Lane! Where the fuck are you going?"

"Don't wait up," he said as he opened the way out.

"When're you going to be back? Hey, Lane — what the hell?"

His old, dear friend was still talking at him as Lane walked off, letting the door close in his wake. At the far end of the hall, he punched through a steel door and started jogging down the concrete stairwell. As his footfalls echoed all around, and he made tight turn after tight turn, he dialed a familiar phone number.

When the call was answered, he said, "This is Lane Baldwine. I need a jet at Teterboro now — going to Charlemont."

There was a brief delay, and then his father's executive assistant got back on the connection. "Mr. Baldwine, there is a jet available. I have spoken directly with the pilot. Flight plans are being filed as we speak. Once you get to the airport, proceed to —"

"I know where our terminal is." He broke out into the marble lobby, nodded to the doorman, and proceeded to the revolving doors. "Thanks."

Just a quickie, he told himself as he hung up and hailed a cab. With any luck, he would be back in Manhattan and annoying Jeff by nightfall, twelve midnight at the very latest.

Ten hours. Fifteen, tops.

He had to see his momma, though. That was what Southern boys did.

Two

Three hours, twenty-two minutes, and some number of seconds later, Lane looked out the oval window of one of the Bradford Bourbon Company's brand-new Embraer Lineage 1000E corporate jets. Down below, the city of Charlemont was laid out like a Lego diorama, its sections of rich and poor, of commerce and agriculture, of homesteading and highway displayed in what appeared to be only two dimensions. For a moment, he tried to picture the land as it had been when his family had first settled in the area in 1778.

Woods. Rivers. Native Americans. Wildlife.

His people had come from Pennsylvania through the Cumberland Gap two hundred and fifty years ago — and now, here he was, ten thousand feet up in the air, circling the city along with fifty other rich guys in their various aircraft.

Except he was not here to bet on horses,

get drunk, and find some sex.

"May I refresh your No. Fifteen before we land, Mr. Baldwine? I'm afraid there's quite a queue. We could be a while."

"Thank you." He drained what was in his crystal glass, the ice cubes sliding down and hitting his upper lip. "You're timing couldn't be better."

Okay, so maybe he would be doing a little drinking.

"My pleasure."

As the woman in the skirt uniform walked away, she looked across her shoulder to see if he was checking her out, her big blue eyes blooming underneath her fake lashes.

His sex life had long depended upon the kindness of such strangers. Particularly blond ones like her, with legs like that, and hips like that, and breasts like that.

But not anymore.

"Mr. Baldwine," the captain said from overhead. "When they found out it was you, they bumped us up, so we're landing now."

"How kind of them," Lane murmured as the stewardess came back.

The way she reopened the bottle gave him a clue to how she'd take down a man's fly, her full body getting into the twist of the cork and the pop free. Then she leaned into the pour, encouraging him to check out her

La Perla.

Such wasted effort.

"That's enough." He put his hand out. "Thanks."

"Is there anything else I can get you?"

"No, thank you."

Pause. Like she wasn't used to being turned down, and wanted to remind him that they were running out of time.

After a moment, she kicked up her chin. "Very good, sir."

Which was her way of telling him to go to hell: With a whip around of the hair, she hipped her way off, swinging what was under that skirt like she had a cat by the tail and a target to hit.

Lane lifted his glass and circled the No. 15. He'd never been particularly involved with the family business — that was the purview of his older brother Edward. Or at least, it had been. But even as a company outsider, Lane knew the nickname of the Bradford Bourbon Company's bestseller: No. 15, the staple of the product line, sold in such tremendous numbers that it was called The Great Eraser — because its profit was so enormous, the money could eclipse the loss from any internal or external corporate misstep, miscalculation, or market share downshift.

As the jet rounded the airstrips for the approach, a ray of sunshine pierced the oval window, falling over the burled walnut folding table, the cream leather of the seat, the deep blue of his jeans, the brass buckle of his Gucci loafers.

And then it hit the No. 15 in his glass, pulling out the ruby highlights in the amber liquor. As he took another pull from the crystal rim, he felt the warmth of the sun on the outside of his hand and the coolness from the ice on the pads of his fingers.

Some study that had been done recently put the bourbon business at three billion dollars in annual sales. Of that pie, the BBC was probably upward of a quarter to a third. There was one company in the state that was bigger — the dreaded Sutton Distillery Corporation, and then there were eight to ten other producers — but BBC was the diamond among semi-precious stones, the choice of the most discriminating drinkers.

As a loyal consumer, he had to concur with the zeitgeist.

A shift in the level of the bourbon in his glass announced the descent to the landing, and he thought back to the first time he had tried his family's product.

Considering how it had gone, he should have been a teetotaller for life.

■ ■ ■ ■

"It's New Year's, come on. Don't be a wuss."

As usual, Maxwell was the one who started the ball rolling. Out of the four siblings, Max was the troublemaker, with Gin, their little sister, coming in at a close second on the recalcitrant Richter scale. Edward, the oldest and the most strait-laced of them, had not been invited to this party — and Lane, who was somewhere in the middle, both in terms of birth order and likelihood to get arrested at any early age, had been forced into the excursion because Max hated to do bad without an audience — and girls didn't count.

Lane knew this was a really poor idea. If they were going to hit the alcohol, they should take a bottle from the pantry and go up to their rooms where there was zero chance of being busted. But to drink out in the open here, in the parlor? Under the disapproving glare of Elijah Bradford's portrait over the fireplace?

Dumb —

"So y'all saying you aren't going to have any, *Lame*?"

Ah, yes. Max's favorite nickname for him.

In the peachy glow from the exterior security lights, Max looked over with an expression of such challenge, the stare might as well have come with sprinter blocks and a starting gun.

Lane glanced at the bottle in his brother's hand. The label was one of the fancy ones, with the words "Family Reserve" in important lettering on it.

If he didn't do this, he was never going to hear the end of it.

"I just want it in a glass," he said. "A proper glass. With ice."

Because that was how his father drank it. And it was the only manly out he had for his delay.

Max frowned as if he hadn't considered the whole presentation thing. "Well, yeah."

"I don't need a glass." Gin, who was seven, had her hands on her hips and her eyes on Max. In her little lace nightie, she was like Wendy in *Peter Pan;* with that aggressive expression on her face, she was a straight-up pro-wrestler. "I need a spoon."

"A spoon?" Max demanded. "What are you talking about?"

"It's medicine, isn't it."

Max threw his head back and laughed. "What are you —"

Lane slapped a palm on his brother's mouth. "Shut up! Do you want to get caught?"

Max ripped the hold away. "What are they going to do to me? Whip me?"

Well, yes, if their father found them or found

30

out about this: Although the great William Baldwine delegated the vast majority of fatherly duties to other people, the belt was one he saved for himself.

"Wait a minute, you want to be found out," Lane said softly. "Don't you."

Max turned to the brass and glass beverage cart. The ornate server was an antique, as most everything in Easterly was, and the family crest was etched into each of its four corners. With big, spindly wheels and a crystal top, it was the hostess with the mostest, carrying four different kinds of Bradford bourbons, half a dozen crystal glasses, and a sterling-silver ice bucket that was constantly refreshed by the butler.

"Here's your glass." Max shoved one at him. "I'm drinking from the bottle."

"Where's my spoon?" Gin said.

"You can have a sip off mine," Lane whispered.

"No. I want my own —"

The debate was cut short as Max yanked the cork out and the projectile went flying, pinging into the chandelier in the center of the room. As crystal chattered and twinkled, the three of them froze.

"Shut up," Max said before there was any commentary. "And no ice for you."

The bourbon made a glugging noise as his

brother dumped it into Lane's glass, not stopping until things were filled as high as the milk was at the dining table.

"Now drink up," Max told him as he put the bottle to his mouth and tilted his head back.

The tough-guy show didn't last but a single swallow as Max barked out a series of coughs that were loud enough to wake the dead. Leaving his brother to choke up or die trying, Lane stared down into his glass.

Bringing the crystal lip to his mouth, he took a careful pull.

Fire. It was like drinking fire, a trail blazing to his gut — and as he exhaled a curse, he half expected to see flames come out of his face as if he were a dragon.

"My turn," Gin spoke up.

He held onto the glass, not letting her take it when she wanted to. Meanwhile, Max was having a second and a third go of it.

Gin barely drew from the glass, doing nothing more than get her lips wet and recoil in disgust —

"What are you doing!"

As the chandelier was turned on, the three of them jumped, Lane catching the bourbon that splashed out of his glass down the front of his monogrammed PJs.

Edward stood just inside the parlor, a look of absolute fury on his face.

"What the *hell* is wrong with you," he said, marching forward, grabbing the glass out of Lane's hands and the bottle out of Max's.

"We were just playing," Gin muttered.

"Go to bed, Gin." He put the glass down on the cart and pointed with the bottle to the archway. "You go to bed right now."

"Aw, why?"

"Unless you want me to kick your ass, too?"

Even Gin could respect that logic.

As she headed for the archway, shoulders hunched, slippers sloppy over the Oriental, Edward hissed, "And use the staff stairs. If Father hears anything, he'll come down the front."

Lane's heart went into full-thunder. And his gut churned — although whether it was the getting caught or the bourbon, he wasn't sure.

"She's seven," Edward said when Gin was out of earshot. "Seven!"

"We know how old she is —"

"Shut up, Maxwell. Just shut up." He stared down Max. "If you want to corrupt yourself, I don't care. But don't contaminate the pair of them with your bullshit."

Big words. Cusses. And the demeanor of somebody who could ground the both of them.

Then again, Edward had always seemed like a grown-up, even before he'd made the leap into the teenage world.

"I don't have to listen to you," Max shot back. But the fight was already leaving him, his tone going weak, his eyes dropping to the rug.

"Yes, you do."

Things got quiet at that point.

"I'm sorry," Lane said.

"I'm not worried about you." Edward shook his head. "It's him I worry about."

"Say you're sorry," Lane whispered. "Max, come on."

"No."

"He's not Father, you know."

Max glared at Edward. "But you act like it."

"Only because you're out of control."

Lane took Max by the hand. "He's sorry, too, Edward. Come on, let's go before anyone hears us."

It took some tugging, but eventually Max followed along without further comment, the fight over, the bid for independence dashed. They were halfway across the black and white marble floor of the dim foyer when Lane caught sight of something way down at the end of the hall.

Someone was moving in the shadows.

Too big to be Gin.

Lane yanked his brother into the total darkness of the ballroom across the way. "Shh."

Through the archways into the parlor, he

34

watched as Edward turned to the cart to try to find the cork, and he wanted to yell out a warning for his brother —

As their father entered, William Baldwine's tall body blocked the view of Edward.

"What are you doing?"

Same words, same tone, deeper bass.

Edward turned around calmly. With the liquor bottle in his hand and Lane's nearly full glass front and center on the cart.

"Answer me," their father said. "What are you doing?"

He and Max were dead, Lane thought. As soon as Edward told the man what had been going on down here, William was going to go on a rampage.

Next to Lane, Maxwell's body trembled. "I shouldn't have done this," he whispered —

"Where's your belt," Edward countered.

"Answer me."

"I did. Where is your belt."

No! Lane thought. *No, it was us!*

Their father strode forward, his monogrammed silk robe gleaming in the light, the color of fresh blood. "Goddamn it, boy, you're going to tell me what you're doing here with my liquor."

"It's called Bradford Bourbon, Father. You married into the family, remember?"

As their father lifted his arm across his

chest, the heavy gold signet ring he wore on his left hand glinted like it was anticpating the strike — and looked forward to making contact with skin. Then, with an elegant, powerful slice, Edward was struck with a backhanded slap that was so violent, the cracking sound ricocheted all the way out into the ballroom.

"Now, I'll ask you again — what are you doing with my liquor," William demanded as Edward stumbled to the side, clutching his face.

After a moment of heavy breathing, Edward straightened. His pajamas were alive from his body's shaking, but he remained on his feet.

Clearing his throat, he said thickly, "I was celebrating the New Year."

A trail of blood seeped down the side of his face, staining his pale skin.

"Then do not let me ruin your enjoyment." Their father pointed to Lane's full glass. "Drink it."

Lane closed his eyes and wanted to vomit.

"Drink it."

The sounds of choking and gagging went on for a lifetime as Edward consumed nearly a quarter of a bottle of bourbon.

"Don't you throw that up, boy," their father barked. "Don't you dare . . ."

As the jet bumped down on the tarmac,

Lane jolted out of the past. He was not surprised to find that the glass he was holding was shaking, and not because of the landing.

Putting the No. 15 on the tray table, he wiped his brow.

That hadn't been the only time Edward had suffered for them.

And it wasn't even the worst. No, the worst one had come later as an adult, and had finally done what all the lousy parenting had failed to do.

Edward was ruined now, and not just physically.

God, there were so many reasons Lane didn't want to go back to Easterly. And not all of them were because of the woman he loved but had lost.

He had to say, however . . . that Lizzie King remained at the top of that very long list.

THREE

The Bradford Family Estate, Charlemont

The Amdega Machin Conservatory was an extension of Easterly's southern flank, and as such, no cost had been spared when it had been added back in 1956. The construction was a Gothic-style masterpiece, its delicate skeleton of white-painted bones supporting hundreds of panes and panels of glass, creating an interior that was bigger and more finished than the farmhouse Lizzie lived in. With a slate floor and a sitting area with sofas and armchairs done in Colefax and Fowler, there were hip-height beds of specimen flowers down the long sides and potted greenery in each of the corners — but that was all just for show. The true horticultural work, the germination and the rehabilitation, the nurturing and pruning, was done far from the family's eyes in the greenhouses.

"Wo sind die Rosen? Wir brauchen mehr

Rosen . . ."

"I don't know." Lizzie popped the top off another cardboard box that was long as a basketball player's leg. Inside, two dozen white hydrangea stalks were wrapped individually in plastic, their heads protected with collars of delicate cardboard. "This is the whole delivery, so they've got to be in here."

"Ich bestellte zehn weitere Dutzend. Wo sind sie — ?"

"Okay, you need to switch to English."

"This can't be everything." Greta von Schlieber held up a bundle of tiny, pale pink blooms that was wrapped up in a page of Colombian newspaper. "We're not going to make it."

"You say that every year."

"This time I'm right." Greta pushed her heavy tortoiseshell glasses up higher on her nose and eyed the stack of twenty-five more boxes. "I'm telling you, we're in trouble."

Annnnnd this was the essence of her and her work partner's relationship.

Starting with the whole pessimism/optimism routine, Greta was pretty much everything Lizzie wasn't. For one, the woman was European, not American, her German accent cutting into her pronunciation in spite of the fact that she'd been in the States for thirty years. She was also married to a great man, the mother of three fantastic children in their twenties, and had enough money that not only did she not have to work, but those two boys and a girl of hers didn't have to, either.

No Yaris for her. Her ride was a black Mercedes station wagon. And the diamond ring she wore with her wedding band was big enough to rival a Bradford's.

Oh, and unlike Lizzie, her blond hair was cut short as a man's — which was something to envy when you were stuck pulling your own back and tying it with whatever you could get your hands on: trashbag twist ties, floral wire, the rubber bands off bunches of broccoli.

The one thing they did have in common? Neither of them could stand to be immobile, unoccupied, or unproductive for even a second. They had been working together at BFE now for almost five years — no, longer. Seven?

Oh, God, it was close to ten now.

And Lizzie couldn't fathom life without the woman — even though sometimes she wished Greta could be a half-full, instead of half-empty, kinda gal.

"Ich sage Ihnen, wir haben Schwierigkeiten."

"Did you just say we're in trouble again?"

"Kann sein."

Lizzie rolled her eyes but fell into the adrenal trap, glancing over the assembly line they'd set up: Down the sixty-foot-long center of the greenhouse, a double row of folding tables had been lined up, and on them were seventy-five sterling-silver bouquet bowls the size of ice buckets.

The gleam was so bright, Lizzie wished she hadn't left her sunglasses in her car.

And she also wished she didn't have to deal with all this in addition to the knowledge that Lane Baldwine was probably landing at the airport at this very instant.

Like she needed that pressure as well?

As her head began to pound, she tried to focus on what she could control. Unfortunately, that only left her wondering how she and Greta were going to manage to fill those bowls with the fifty thousand dollars of flowers that had been delivered — but that still needed to be unpacked, inspected, cleaned, cut and arranged properly.

Then again, this was the crunch that always happened forty-eight hours before The Derby Brunch.

Or TDB, as it was called around the estate.

Because, yup, working at Easterly was like

being in the Army: Everything was shortened, except for the work days.

And yes, even with that ambulance this morning, the event was still going on. Like a train, the momentum stopped for no one and nothing in its path. In fact, she and Greta had often said that if nuclear war happened, the only things left after the mushroom cloud dissipated would be cockroaches, Twinkies . . . and TDB.

Jokes aside, the brunch was so long-standing and exclusive, it was its own proper name, and slots on the guest list were guarded and passed down to the next generation as heirlooms. A gathering of nearly seven hundred of the city's and the nation's wealthiest people and political elite, the crowd mingled and milled around Easterly's gardens, drinking mint juleps and mimosas for only two hours before departing for Steeplehill Downs for thoroughbred racing's biggest day and the first leg of the Triple Crown. The rules of the brunch were short and sweet: Ladies had to wear hats, no photographs or photographers were allowed, and it didn't matter whether you were in a Phantom Drophead or a corporate limousine — all cars were parked in the meadow at the bottom of the hill and all people filed into vans that ran them up to the front door of the estate.

Well, almost all people. The only folks who didn't have to take the shuttle? Governors, any of the Presidents if they came — and the head coach of the University of Charlemont's men's basketball team.

In Kentucky, you were either U of C red or Kentucky University blue, and basketball mattered whether you were rich or poor.

The Bradfords were U of C Eagles fans. And it was almost Shakespearean that their rivals in the bourbon business, the Suttons, were all about the KU Tigers.

"I can hear you muttering," Lizzie said. "Think positive. We got this."

"Wir müssen alle Pfingstrosen zahlen," Greta announced as she popped the top on another carton. "Last year, they short-changed us —"

One half of the double doors that opened into the house swung wide, and Mr. Newark Harris, the butler, came in like a cold draft. At five feet six inches, he appeared much taller in his black suit and tie — then again, maybe the illusion was because of his perma-raised eyebrows, a function of him being on the verge of uttering "you stupid American" after everything he said. A total throwback to the centuries-old tradition of the proper English servant, he'd not only been born and trained in London, but he had served as a footman for Queen Elizabeth II at Buckingham Palace and then as a butler for Prince Edward, Earl of Wessex, at Bagshot Park. The House of Windsor pedigree had been the linchpin of his hiring the year before.

Certainly hadn't been his personality.

"Mrs. Baldwine is out at the pool house." He addressed only Lizzie. Greta, as a German national who still rocked that Z-centric accent, was *persona non grata* to him. "Please take a bouquet out to her. Thank you."

And *poof!,* he was back out the door, closing things up silently.

Lizzie closed her eyes. There were two Mrs. Baldwines on the estate, but one only of them was likely to be out of her bedroom and down in the sunshine by the pool.

One-two punch today, Lizzie thought. Not only was she going to have to see her ex-lover, she was now going to have to wait on his wife.

Fantastic.

"Ich hoffe, dass dem Idiot ein Klavier auf den Kopf fallt."

"Did you just say you hope a piano falls on his head?"

"And you maintain you don't know German."

"Ten years with you and I'm getting there."

Lizzie glanced around to see what she could use of the massive flower delivery. After the boxes were unpacked, the leaves needed to be stripped off the stalks and the blooms had to be fluffed one by one to encourage petal spread and allow for a check of quality. She and Greta hadn't gotten anywhere close to that stage yet, but what Mrs. Baldwine wanted, she got.

On so many levels.

Fifteen minutes of choosing, clipping, and arranging later and she had a passable bunch shoved into wet foam in a silver bowl.

Greta appeared in front of her and held out her hands, that big mine-cut diamond ring flashing. "Let me take it out."

"No, I got this —"

"You aren't going to want to deal with her today."

"I never want to deal with her —"

"Lizzie."

"I'm okay. Honest."

Fortunately, her old friend bought the lie. The truth? Lizzie was so far away from "okay," she couldn't even see the place —

but that didn't mean she was going to wimp out.

"I'll be right back."

"I'll be counting the peonies."

"Everything's going to be fine."

She hoped.

As Lizzie headed for the double doors that opened into the garden, her head really started to thump, and getting hit with a solid wall of hot-and-humid as she stepped outside didn't help that at all. Motrin, she thought. After this, she was going to take four and get back to the real work.

The grass underfoot was brush-cut cropped, more golf-course carpet than anything Mother Nature dreamed up, and even though she had too much on her mind, she still made a mental To Do list of beds to tend to and replantings to be done in the five acre enclosed garden. The good news was that after a late start to spring, the fruit trees were blooming in the corners of the brick-walled expanse, their delicate white petals just beginning to fall like snow on the walkways beneath their canopies. Also, the mulch that had been laid down two weeks before had lost its stink, and the ivy along the old stone walls was sprouting new leaves everywhere. In another month, the four squares marked with Greco-Roman sculptures of robed women in regal poses were going to be all pastel pinks and peaches and bright whites, offering a contrast to the sedate green and gray river view.

But of course, it was all about the Derby right now.

The white clapboard pool house was in the far left corner, looking like a proper, doctor/lawyer/family-of-four Colonial as it sat back from an almost Olympic-sized aquamarine body of water. The loggia that connected the two was topped by a controlled wig of wisteria that would soon enough have white and lavender blooms hanging like lanterns from the green tangle.

And beneath the overhang, stretched out in a Brown Jordan recliner, Mrs. Chantal Baldwine was as beautiful as a priceless marble statue.

About as warm as one, too.

The woman had skin that glowed, thanks to a perfectly executed spray tan, blond hair that was streaked artfully and curled at the long ends, and a body that would have given Rosie Huntington-Whiteley an inferiority complex. Her nails were fake, but perfect, nothing Jersey about either their length or color, and her engagement ring and wedding band were right out of *Town & Country*, as white and blinding and big as her smile.

She was the perfect modern Southern belle, the kind of woman that people in the Charlemont zip code whispered about having come from "good stock, even if it's from Virginia."

Lizzie had long wondered if the Bradfords checked the teeth of the debutantes their sons went out with — like you did with thoroughbreds.

"— collapsed and then the ambulance came." That heavily diamonded hand lifted to that hair and pushed the stuff back; then brought the iPhone she was talking into over to her other ear. "They took her out the *front* door. Can you believe it? They should have done that around the back — oh, aren't those lovely!"

Chantal Baldwine put her hand in front of her mouth, all geisha-demure as Lizzie schlepped over to the marble-topped bar and set the blooms on the end that was out of the direct sun. "Did Newark do that? He is *so* thoughtful."

Lizzie nodded and turned back around. The less time wasted here, the better —

"Oh, say, Lisa, would you —"

"It's Lizzie." She stopped. "May I help you with something else?"

"Would you be so kind as to get me some more of this?" The woman nodded to a glass pitcher that was half full. "The ice has melted and the flavor's become watered down. I'm leaving for the club for lunch, but not for another hour. Thank you *so* much."

Lizzie shifted her eyes over to lemonade — and *really* tried, honest-to-God tried, not to imagine dousing the woman in the stuff. "I'll have Mr. Harris send someone —"

"Oh, but he's so busy. And you can just run it in — you're *such* a help." The woman went back to her iPhone with its University of Charlemont cover. "Where was I? Oh, so they took her out the main front door. I mean, honestly, can you imagine . . . ?"

Lizzie walked over, picked up the pitcher, and then strode back across the gleaming white terrace to the green grass. "My pleasure."

My pleasure.

Yeah, right. But that was what you were supposed to say when the family asked you to do something. It was the only acceptable response — and certainly better than, "How 'bout you take your lemonade and shove it where the sun don't shine, you miserable piece of veal —"

"Oh, Lisa? It's a virgin, okay? Thank you."

Lizzie just kept on going, tossing another "My pleasure" grenade over her shoulder.

Approaching the mansion, she had to pick her point of entry. As a member of the staff, she wasn't allowed to enter through the Four Mains: front, side library, rear dining room, rear game room. And she was "discouraged" from using any other doors but the kitchen's and utility room's — although she got a pass if she was delivering the three-times weekly house bouquets around.

She chose the door that was halfway between the dining room and the kitchen because she refused to reroute all the way around to the other staff entrances. Stepping into the cool interior, she kept her head down, not because she was worried about pissing someone off, but because she was hoping and praying to get in and out without getting caught by —

"I wondered if you'd be here today."

Lizzie froze like a burglar and then felt a sheen of tears prick the corners of her eyes. But she was not going to cry.

Not in front of Lane Baldwine.

And not because of him.

Squaring her shoulders, she kicked up her chin . . . and started to turn around.

Before she even met Lane's eyes for the first time since she'd told him to go to hell when she'd ended their relationship, she knew three things: One, he was going to look exactly the same as he had before; two, that was not going be good news for her; and three, if she had any brains in her head at all, she would put what he'd done to her almost two years ago on auto loop and think about nothing else.

Leopards, spots, and all that —

Ah . . . crap, did he have to *still* look that good?

Lane couldn't remember much about his walking into Easterly for the first time in forever.

Nothing had really registered. Not that grand front door with its lion's-head knocker and its glossy black panels. Not the football-stadium-sized front foyer with that grand staircase and all of the oil paintings of Bradfords past and present. Not the crystal chandeliers or the gold sconces, nor the ruby-red Orientals or the heavy brocade drapes, not even the parlor and the ballroom on either side.

Easterly's Southern elegance, coupled with that perennial sweet lemon scent of old-fashioned floor polish, was like a fine suit of clothes that, once put on in the morning, was unnoticeable throughout the rest of the day because it was tailor fit to your every muscle and bone. For him, there had been absolutely no burn on reentry at all: It was immersion in ninety-eight-point-six-degree calm water. It was breathing air that was perfectly still, perfectly humid, perfectly temperate. It was nodding off while sitting up in a leather club chair.

It was home and it was the enemy at the very same time, and very probably there was no impression because he was overwhelmed by emotion he was shutting out.

He did, however, notice every single thing about seeing Lizzie King once again.

The collision happened as he was heading through the dining room in search of the one who he had traveled so far to see.

Oh, God, he thought. *Oh, dear God.*

After having had to rely on memory for so long, standing in front of Lizzie was the difference between a descriptive passage and the real thing — and his body responded instantly, blood pumping, all those dormant instincts not just waking up but exploding in his veins.

Her hair was still blond from the sun, not some hairdresser's paintbrush, and it was pulled back in a tie, the blunt ends thick and sticking straight out like a nautical rope that had been burn-cut. Her face was free of makeup, the skin tanned and glowing, the bone structure reminding him that good genetics were better than a hundred thousand dollars' of plastic surgery. And her body . . . that hard, strong body that had curves where he liked them and straightaways that testified to all that physical labor she did so well . . . was exactly as he remembered. She was even dressed the same, in the khaki shorts and the required black polo with the Easterly crest on it.

Her scent was Coppertone, not Chanel. Her shoes were Merrell, not Manolo. Her watch was Nike, not Rolex.

To him, she was the most beautiful, best-dressed woman he'd ever seen.

Unfortunately, that look in her eye remained unchanged as well.

The one that told him she, too, had thought of him since he had left.

Just not in a good way.

As his mouth moved, Lane realized he was speaking some combination of words, but he wasn't tracking. There were too many images filtering through his brain, all memories from the past: her naked body in messy sheets, her hair threaded through his fingers, his hands on her inner thighs. In his mind, he heard her saying his name as he pumped into her hard, rocking the bed until the headboard slammed against the wall —

"Yes, I knew you'd come," she said levelly.

Talk about different wavelengths. He was off-kilter down to his Guccis, in the midst of reliving their relationship, and she was utterly unaffected by his presence.

"Have you seen her yet?" she asked. Then frowned. "Hello?"

What the hell was she saying to him? Oh, right. "I hear she's already home from the hospital."

"About an hour ago."

"Is she okay?"

"She left here in an ambulance on oxygen. What do you think." Lizzie glanced in the direction she'd been headed in. "Look, if you'll excuse me, I'm going to —"

"Lizzie," he said in a low voice. "Lizzie, I'm . . ."

As he trailed off, her expression became bored. "Do us both a favor and don't bother finishing that, okay? Just go see her and . . . do whatever else you came here to do, all right? Leave me out of it."

"Christ, Lizzie, why won't you hear me out —"

"Why should I, is more the question."

"Because civilized people give others that common courtesy —"

And *BOOM!* they were off.

"Excuse *me*?" she demanded. "Like just

54

because I live over the river and I work for your family, that makes me some kind of an ape? Really — you're going to go there?"

"That is not what I meant —"

"Oh, I think it is —"

"I swear," he muttered, "that chip on your shoulder —"

"Is what, Lane? Showing again? Sorry, you're not allowed to twist things around like I'm the one with the problem. That's on you. That has *always* been on you."

Lane threw his hands up. "I can't get through to you. All I want to do is explain —"

"You want to do something for me? Fine, great, here." She shoved a half-full pitcher of what looked like lemonade at him. "Take this to the kitchen and get someone to refill it. Then you can tell them to take it back out to the pool house, or maybe you can deliver it yourself — to your *wife.*"

With that, she spun around and punched out the nearest door. And as she strode off across the lawn toward the conservatory, he couldn't decide what held more appeal: putting his head into the wall, throwing the pitcher, or doing a combination of both.

He picked option four: "Goddamn, moth-er*fucking, shit . . .*"

"Sir? May I be of service?"

At the British accent, Lane glanced over at a fifty-year-old man who was dressed like he was the front house of a funeral parlor. "Who the hell are you?"

"Mr. Harris, sir. I am Newark Harris, the butler." The guy bowed at the waist. "The pilots were kind enough to call ahead that you were en route. May I attend to your luggage?"

"I don't have any."

"Very good, sir. Your room is in order, and if you require ought further than your wardrobe upstairs, it will be my pleasure to procure any necessaries for you."

Oh, no, Lane thought. Nope, he was not staying — he knew damn well what weekend was coming up, and the purpose for his visit had nothing to do with the Derby social circus.

He shoved the pitcher at Mr. Dandy-man. "I don't know what's in here and I don't care. Just fill it up and take it where it belongs."

"My pleasure, sir. Will you be requiring —"

"No, that's it."

The man seemed surprised as Lane pushed past him and headed in the direction of the staff part of the house. But, of course, the Englishman didn't question him. Which, considering the mood he was in? Not only was that proper butler etiquette, but it would fall under a self-preservation rubric as well.

Two minutes in the house. Two damn minutes.

And he was already nuclear.

FOUR

Lane marched his way into the massive professional kitchen and was immediately taken aback by both the olfactory "noise" and the auditory silence. Even though there were a good dozen chefs bent over the stainless-steel counters and the Viking stoves, none of the white coats were speaking as they labored. A few of them did look up, however, recognized him and stopped whatever they were doing, he ignored their OMG! reaction. He was used to that double take by now, his reputation having preceded him across the nation for years.

Thank you, *Vanity Fair,* for that exposé on his family a decade ago. And the three follow-ups since. And the speculations in the tabloids. And don't get him started on the Internet.

Once that lowest-common-denominator, media-packaged celebrity status sucker-fished you?

No getting it off.

As he went over to a door marked PRIVATE, he found himself retucking his shirt, pulling up his slacks, smoothing his hair. Now he wished he'd taken time to shower, shave, change.

And he really wished that meeting with Lizzie had gone better. Like he needed another thing on his mind?

His knock was quiet, respectful. The response he got was not:

"What are you knocking for," barked the Southern female voice.

Lane frowned as he pushed open the door. And then he stopped dead.

Miss Aurora was at her stove, the hot-oil smell and snare-drum crackle of chicken frying in a pan rising into the air in front of her, her weave done in a short bob of super-tight black curls, her housecoat the same one he'd seen her in when he'd left to go up north.

All he could do was blink, and wonder whether someone had played a sick joke on him.

"Well, don't just stand there," she snapped at him. "Wash y'all hands and get out the trays. I'm five minutes out."

Right, he'd expected to find her laying in bed with a sheet up to her chest and a fad-

59

ing light in her eyes as her beloved Jesus came for her.

"Lane, snap out of it. I'm not dead yet."

He rubbed the bridge of his nose as a wave of exhaustion sand-bagged him. "Yes, ma'am."

As he closed them in together, he searched for signs of physical weakness in those strong shoulders and those set legs of hers. There was none. There was absolutely nothing about the sixty-five-year-old woman to suggest that she had ended up in the emergency room that morning.

Okay, so it was a toss-up, he decided as he eyeballed the rest of the food she'd prepared for him. A toss-up between him being relieved . . . and him feeling furious that he'd wasted the time coming down here.

One thing he was clear on? There was no leaving before he ate — partially because she would hog tie him to a chair and force feed him if she had to, but mostly because the instant he caught that scent, his stomach had gone hollow-pit hungry on him.

"Are you okay?" he had to ask.

The glare she sent him suggested if he wanted to continue that line of questioning, she'd be more than happy to spank him until he shut his piehole.

Roger that, ma'am, he thought.

Crossing the shallow space, he found that the TV trays the two of them had always eaten off of were exactly where he'd seen them last — over in the corner, propped up between the entertainment console and the bookcase that was set at an angle. The pair of Barcaloungers were the same, too, each one in front of a tall window, crocheted doilies draped over the tops where the backs of heads went.

Pictures of children were everywhere and in all kinds of frames, and amid the beautiful, dark faces, there were pale ones, too: There was him at his kindergarten graduation; his brother Max scoring a goal in lacrosse; his sister, Gin, dressed up as a milk maid in a school play; his other brother, Edward, in a tie and jacket for his senior picture at U.Va.

"Good Lord, you are too thin, boy," Miss Aurora muttered as she went to stir a pot that he knew was filled with green beans cooked with cubes of ham. "Don't they have food up there in New York?"

"Not like this, ma'am."

The sound she made in the back of her throat was like a Chevy backfiring. "Get the plates."

"Yes, ma'am."

He discovered his hands were shaking as he took two out of the cupboard and they rattled together. Unlike the woman who had birthed him, who was no doubt upstairs "resting" in a medicated haze of I'm-not-an-addict-because-my-doctor-gave-me-the-pills, Miss Aurora had always seemed both ageless and strong as a superhero. The idea that the cancer was back?

Hell, he couldn't fathom her having had it in the first place. But he wasn't fooling himself. That had to be the reason for the collapse.

After he'd gotten the silver and napkins on the trays and poured them both a sweet tea, he went over and sat on the chair on the right.

"You shouldn't be cooking," he said as she started to plate up.

"And you should'na been gone so long. What's wrong with you."

Definitely not on her deathbed, he thought.

"What did the doctor say?" he asked.

"Nothing worth hearing in my opinion." She brought over all kinds of heaped-to-Heaven. "Now be quiet and eat."

"Yes, ma'am."

Oh, sweet Jesus, he thought as he stared down at his plate. Fried okra. Chitterlings. Potato cakes. Beans in that pork boil. And the fried chicken.

As his stomach let out a roar of starvation, she laughed.

But he didn't, and abruptly, he had to clear his throat. This was home. This food, prepared by this specific woman, was home — he'd had exactly what was on this plate all of his life, especially back in the years before his mother had retreated from everything and she and his father had been out five nights a week socializing. Sick or well, happy or sad, hot or cold, he and his brothers and sister had sat in the kitchen with Miss Aurora and behaved themselves or risked getting swatted on the back of the head.

There were never any troublemakers in Miss Aurora's kitchen.

"G'on now," she said softly. "Don't wait to where it gets cold."

Talk about digging in, and he moaned as the first taste flooded his mouth. "Oh, Miss Aurora."

"You need to come on home, boy." She shook her head as she sat down with her own plate. "That northern stuff is not for you. Don't know how you stand the weather — much less those people."

"So you going to tell me what happened?" he asked, nodding at the cotton ball and surgical tape in the crook of her elbow.

"I don't need that car you bought me. That's what happened."

He wiped his mouth. "What car?"

Those black eyes narrowed. "Don't you try to play, boy."

"Miss Aurora, you were driving a piece of — ah, junk. I can't have y'all like that."

He could hear the Southern creeping back into his voice. Didn't take long, did it.

"My Malibu is perfectly fine —"

Now he held her stare. "It was a cheap car to begin with and had a hundred thousand miles on it."

"Don't see why —"

"Miss Aurora, I'm not having you in that junker no more. Sorry."

She glared at him hard enough to burn a hole in his forehead, but when he didn't budge, she dropped her eyes. And that was the nature of their relationship. Two hard heads, neither of whom was willing to give an inch about anything — except to the other one.

"I don't need a Mercedes," she muttered.

"Four-wheel drive, ma'am."

"I don't like the color. It's unholy."

"Bull. It's U of C red and you love it."

As she grumped again, he knew the truth. She adored the new car. Her sister, Miss

Patience, had called him up and told him that Miss Aurora had been driving the E350 4MATIC all around town. Of course, Miss Aurora never dialed him to thank him, and he'd been expecting this protest: She'd always been too proud to accept anything for free.

But Miss Aurora also didn't want to upset him — and knew he was right.

"So what happened this morning with you." Not a question on his part. He was done with that.

"I just got a little light-headed."

"They said you passed out."

"I'm fine."

"They said the cancer's back."

"Who is they."

"Miss Aurora —"

"My Lord and Savior has healed me before and He will again." She put one palm to Heaven and closed her eyes. Then looked over at him. "I'm going to be fine. Have I ever lied to you, boy?"

"No, ma'am."

"Now eat."

That command pretty much shut him up for twenty minutes.

Lane was halfway done with his second plate when he had to ask. "You see him lately?"

No reason to specify who the "he" was: Edward was the "he" everyone spoke of in hushed tones.

Miss Aurora's face tightened. "No."

There was another long period of silence.

"Y'all gonna go see him while you're here?" she asked.

"No."

"Somebody's gotta."

"Won't make any difference. Besides, I should get back to New York. I really came here only to check if you were okay —"

"You're gonna go see him. Before you go back north."

Lane shut his eyes. After a moment, he said, "Yes, ma'am."

"Good boy."

After a serving of thirds, Lane cleared their plates, and had to ignore the fact that Miss Aurora appeared not to have eaten anything at all. The conversation then turned to her nieces and nephews, her sisters and brothers, of which there were eleven, and the fact that her father, Tom, had finally died at the age of eighty-six.

She was called Aurora Toms because she was one of Tom's kids. Word had it in addition to the twelve he'd had with his wife, there were countless others outside the marriage. Lane had met the man at Miss

Aurora's church from time to time, and he'd been a larger-than-life character, as Deep South as Mississippi, as charismatic as a preacher, as handsome as sin.

Not that he was being arrogant, but Lane knew he had always been her favorite, and he figured that father of hers was the reason she indulged him so much: Like her dad, he'd also been called too handsome for his own good all his life, and he'd sure done his share of womanizing. Back in his twenties? Lane had been right there with good ol' Mr. Toms.

Lizzie had cured him of all that. Kind of in the way an embankment would stop a speeding car.

"You go up and greet your momma before you leave, too," Miss Aurora announced after he'd washed and put away their dishes and silverware.

He left the frying pan and the pots on her stove. He knew better than to touch them.

Pivoting around, he folded the dish towel and leaned back against the stainless-steel sink.

She put her palm out from her Barcalounger. "Y'all need to save it —"

"Miss Aurora —"

"Do *not* tell me you flew over a thousand miles just to look me over like I'm some kind of invalid. That don't make no sense."

"Your food is worth the trip."

"That is true. Now go see your momma."

I already have, he thought as he stared across at her. "Miss Aurora, are you going to get help for the Derby?"

"What do you think all those fools out in my big kitchen are for?"

"It's a lot to manage, and don't tell me you aren't ordering them around."

That infamous glare shot his way, but that was all he got and it scared him. Normally, she'd be up from her chair and muscling him out her door. Instead, she stayed sitting. "I'ma be fine, boy."

"You better be. Without you, I got no one to keep me straight."

She said something under her breath and stared off over his shoulder — while he just waited in the quiet.

Eventually, she waved for him to come over, and he did right away, striding across the linoleum and getting down on his knees by her chair. One of her hands, her beautiful, strong, dark hands, reached out and ran through his hair.

"You need to get this cut."

"Yes, ma'am."

She touched his face. "You're too handsome for your own good."

"Like I said, you gotta stick around and keep me right."

Miss Aurora nodded. "Count on it." There was a long pause. "Thank you for my new car."

He pressed a kiss to her palm. "You're welcome."

"And I need you to remember something." Her eyes, those ebony eyes he'd stared into as a child, a teenager, a young man . . . a grown man, roamed around his face, like she was taking note of the changes that gathering age was bringing to the features she had watched for over thirty years. "I got you and I got God. I'm wealthier beyond means — we clear, boy? I don't need no Mercedes. I don't need a fancy house or fancy clothes. There is no hole in me that needs filling — you hear me?"

"Yes, ma'am." He closed his eyes, thinking she was the single most noble woman he'd ever met.

Well, she and Lizzie, that was.

"I hear you, ma'am," he said hoarsely.

About an hour after the lemonade-Lane run-in, Lizzie left the conservatory with two large arrangements. Mrs. Bradford had always insisted that fresh flowers be in the main public rooms and all of the occupied bedrooms — and that standard had been preserved even as she had retreated to her suite about three years ago and essentially stayed there. Lizzie liked to think if she continued the practice, maybe Little V.E., as the family called her, would once again come down and be the lady of the house.

Easterly had a good fifty rooms, but many of them were staff offices, staff quarters and bathrooms, or places like the kitchen, wine cellar, media rooms, or empty guest rooms that didn't require flowering. The first-floor bouquets were in good shape — she'd already done a run-through and pulled out the occasional withering rose here or there the night before. These new ones were for the second-story foyer and Big Mr. Baldwine's room. Mrs. Bradford's vase wasn't due to be refreshed before tomorrow, as were Chantal's and . . .

Would Lane be staying in his wife's room?

Probably, and didn't that make her want to vomit.

Heading up the back staffing stairs, the two sterling silver fluted vases strained her hands and wrists and tightened up her biceps, but she toughed it out. The burn wasn't going to last long, and taking a time out somewhere along the way just prolonged things.

The main hallway upstairs was long as a racecourse, bifurcated by an upper level sitting area, and the conduit to a total of twenty-one suites and bedrooms that opened off on either side. Big Mr. Baldwine's quarters were next to his wife's, with both sets of rooms overlooking the garden and the river. There was a connector that linked their dressing rooms, but she knew it was never used.

From what she understood, once the children had been born that part of the relationship had not been "resumed," to use the old-fashioned verbiage.

When she'd first started working at Easterly, she'd been confused by the names — and had slipped up and called Mrs. Bradford by her legal name of Mrs. Baldwine. No go. She'd been firmly corrected by the head of staff: The lady of the Bradford house was going to be a "Mrs." and a "Bradford" no matter what the last name of her husband might have been.

Confusing. Until she'd realized that that husband-and-wife team had no more overlapping lives than their separate sleeping accommodations. So it was Mr. Baldwine in the suite with the navy blue accents and the heavier mahogany antiques and Mrs. Bradford in the ivory, cream, taupe,

71

and blush suite with the Louis XIV furniture and the canopy bed.

Actually, maybe the pair of them did have something in common: He hid in his office in the business center, she in her bedroom.

Crazy.

Lizzie proceeded down to the curving formal stairs and swapped out the bouquet on the coffee table in that sitting area. Then she went over and stopped at Mr. Baldwine's suite. Knocking twice on the broad panels, she waited even though there was no way he was on the other side. Every morning, he left for his business center next door on the property and he did not return until the seven o'clock dinner hour.

Putting the old foyer bouquet on the floor, she cranked the ornate doorknob, pushed inside, and strode over to an antique bureau that belonged in a museum. There wasn't anything hugely wrong with the flowers already in place, but nothing was allowed to fade at Easterly. Here, in the cocoon of wealth, entropy was not permitted to exist.

As she switched the vases, she heard voices in the garden and went to the windows. Over a dozen men had arrived and were carting in the huge white canvas rolls and long aluminum poles that, with enough manpower and some hydraulics, were going to be The Derby Brunch's eighty-by-forty-foot tent.

Great. Chantal was probably calling up Mr. Harris right now and complaining that the no-fly zone had been violated: If a member of the family or a guest were using the pool, the pool house, or any of the terraces, all work had to cease in the garden and all workmen had to beat feet out of the area until their royal highnesses were finished with their enjoyment.

The good news? Greta was out there already, corralling the men. The bad news? The German was probably telling them to set it all up right next to where Chantal was sitting.

Deliberately.

Fearing that confrontation, Lizzie wheeled —

She froze as a flash of color caught her eye. "What the . . . ?"

Leaning down, she wasn't sure what she was looking at. Like everything at Easterly, William Baldwine's room was spotless, all objects and belongings where they should be, the masculine accoutrements of a powerful businessman in drawers, tucked away in shelves, waiting for him in that walk-in wardrobe.

So what was a piece of peach silk doing

between the back of the headboard and the wall?

Well, she could guess.

And the lingerie sure hadn't been taken off Virginia Elizabeth Bradford Baldwine.

Lizzie couldn't wait to get out of the room, going across to the door fast, opening it —

"Oh, I'm sooooooo happy to see youuuuuuuu!"

The Southern drawl was like fingers on a blackboard, but worse was looking down to the right and seeing Chantal Baldwine throw her arms around Lane's neck and hang off his body.

Fantastic. The two of them were between her and the staff stairs.

"I can't believe you surprised me like this!" The woman took a step back and posed, like she wanted him to have a good look at her. "I was just down at the pool, but came up because the tent people are here. I decided to remove myself so they could be on that part of the grounds to set up."

Well, don't you deserve the Purple Heart, Lizzie thought. *And weren't you heading to the club soon, anyway?*

Lizzie turned around to go for the main stairs to escape. Even if it was against

74

regulation, it was better than having to pass by —

As if on cue, Mr. Harris came up onto the landing with Mrs. Mollie, the head of housekeeping. The English butler was running his fingertip over the top of the balustrade and holding it out for her inspection, shaking his head.

Great.

Her only exits were either over hot coals or through a bonfire. Or ducking back into Mr. Baldwine-who-was-cheating-on-his-wife's room.

Oh, the choices.

She just *loved* her job sometimes.

FIVE

Bradford Bourbon Distillery, Ogden County

Edwin "Mack" MacAllan Jr. walked along the forty-foot-tall stacks of bourbon barrels, his handmade leather boots clapping against the ancient concrete floor, the scent of a hundred thousand planks of hardwood and millions of gallons of aging bourbon as good as the perfume of a woman in his nose.

Too bad he was too pissed off to enjoy it.

In his fist, a memo from corporate was crushed into a trash ball, the white paper with its laser-printed words unsalvageable. He'd had to read the damn thing three times, and not just because he was severely dyslexic and written English was a largely insurmountable obstacle course for his brain.

Talk about lighting him up. He was not a hillbilly. He'd been raised in an educated family, and he'd gone to Auburn University, and he knew everything about making bourbon from the chemical processes involved to that intangible artistry stuff.

In fact, he was the highly respected Master Distiller of the most prestigious bourbon brand on the market, and the son of the most respected Master Distiller in the history of the commercial alcohol industry.

But at the moment? He wanted to get in his half-ton and ram the grill of that F-150 right into the lobby of William Baldwine's office at Easterly. Then he wanted to take his hundred-year-old hunting rifle and put some holes in the desks of all those corporate idiots.

Coming to a halt, he leaned back and looked at the racks that stretched up to the warehouse's exposed beam ceiling. The branded number codes and dates that had been burned into the fronts of the barrels had been put there on orders first by his father, and then by himself, and there was a progression of both, the precious containers resting in peace for four years, ten years, twenty years, longer. He regularly inspected them, even though he had plenty of people who worked for him who could do that. The way he saw it, though, these were the only children he was ever going to have and he wasn't going to let them get raised by the equivalent of a nanny.

At thirty-eight, he was a loner, thanks to both choice and necessity: This job, this twenty-five-hour-a-day, eight-day-a-week job was his wife and his mistress, his family and his legacy.

So getting this memo, which he'd found on his desk when he'd come in, was like a drunk driver ramming into the minivan that his entire life was riding in.

The recipe for bourbon was really simple: grain mash, which by Kentucky law had to be made up of a minimum of fifty-one percent corn, and which was, here at the Bradford Bourbon Company, a further combination of rye, malted barley, and about ten percent wheat for smoother taste; water, drawn from an underground limestone aquifer; and yeast. Then, after the magic happened, the nascent bourbon was put into white oak barrels that were charred on the inside and left to grow up to be big and strong and beautiful in storage houses like this one.

That was it. Every single bourbon maker had those five elements of grain, water, yeast, barrel and time to work with, period. But as the good Lord turned out an endless variation of people from the core elements of what made a human, so, too, did each family or company produce different shades of the same thing.

Reaching out, he put his hand on the rounded flanks of one of the barrels he had first filled when he'd taken over as master. That had been almost ten years ago, although he had worked for the company since he was fourteen. It had always been the plan to step into his father's shoes, but Pop had died too soon, and there you had it. Mack had been left behind in classic sink or swim territory, and he sure as hell had had no intention of drowning.

So yeah, here he was, at the top of his game and young enough still to create a dynasty of his own — supposedly working for the aristocracy of bourbon makers, the company who created The Perfect Bourbon.

It was the tagline on everything BBC did, the tip of the spear of the company's brewing, business and marketing philosophy.

So why in God's green earth was management expecting him to accept these proposed delays in grain delivery? It was like those idiots with the MBAs didn't understand that while they had enough product that was four years old today, if he didn't keep the sills going, they were going to run out of that kind of bourbon to sell forty-eight months from now — and that applied to every level, running out ten years from now, twenty years from now.

He knew exactly where all this was headed. A nationwide shortage in corn, the result of global warming coming home to roost and screwing up the weather patterns last summer, meant that the bushel price was sky high right now — but it wasn't likely to stay that way. Clearly, the bean counters in the home office, a.k.a. Mr. Baldwine's estate, had decided to save a couple of bucks by halting production for the next couple of months and expecting to catch up when the corn prices self-regulated.

Assuming that the drought that had rocked the nation the year before wasn't repeated.

Which was not a bet he, personally, was willing to take.

There were many faults to this "business" logic, but the core issue was that those suits and ties didn't understand that bourbon was not a widget produced on an assembly line that had an easy on/off switch. It was a process, a unique and special culmination and expression of trial-and-error choices that had been made and refined over a period of over two hundred and fifty years: You had to cultivate the bourbon's taste, coax out the flavors and the balance, guide the elements to their apex of existence —

and then send it out to your customers under a label of distinction. Hell, he took as much pride in safeguarding the No. 15 brand, the company's most successful but less-expensive line, as he did the higher-cost, longer-aged products, such as Black Mountain, Bradford I, and the ultra-exclusive Family Reserve.

If he interrupted production now? He knew damn well they were going to come back to him in six months and tell him to mislabel the barrels.

Six months to the suits was just half a year, twenty-six weeks, two seasons.

But to his palate, he could distinguish a nine-and-a-half-year bourbon from a ten-year and one-day bourbon. And maybe a lot of their customers couldn't tell the difference, but that wasn't the point, was it. And the fact that many of their competitors mislabeled on a regular basis? Hardly the standard to follow.

If Edward were here, he thought, he wouldn't have to worry about it. Edward Baldwine was that rarity in the Bradford family — a true distiller, a throwback to the early era of the august lineage, a man who valued the product that was produced. But that presumptive heir to the throne was now not involved with the company anymore.

So there was nowhere to go with this.

And the fact that the memo had just been left on his desk to be found? It was typical of the way things had been running ever since Edward's tragedy. The pussies at the business center knew he'd have a fit over this, but they didn't have the balls to come and tell him in person. Nope. Just write a memo and throw it on top of all the other papers, like it wasn't going to fundamentally affect the core of the business.

Mack went back to staring up at the rafters that were made out of old-growth timber felled a century ago. This was the very oldest of the company's storage facilities, and it was used to house the very special barrels. Located by the original still site — which was now both a museum for tourists as well as where his office was housed — this place was a damn shrine.

The soul of his father walked these corridors.

Mack was convinced he could feel his old man at his heel right now.

Convinced, too, that on a quiet day like today, when the only things in the warehouse with him were the sunlight that drifted in from the cloudy windows, the sound of his boots on the concrete, and the mist of the angels' share drifting in and out of those shafts of illumination . . . he was one of the very few champions of tradition left in the company.

The new kids that were coming in — even the ones who wanted to get where he was — professed love for the rituals and the fundamentals and claimed to be committed to the process, but were really just corporate minions in khakis rather than suits. They were from a generation of special snowflakes who expected trophies for showing up, and everything to be easy, and for everybody to care about them and safeguard them as their parents would.

They had no more depth than their Facebook posts. Than their relentless egoism. Than their soulless frivolities.

In comparison to the forebearers of this company, who had shepherded this product through famines and wartime, disease and the Depression . . . through Prohibition, for godsakes . . . they were boys trying to do a man's job.

They just didn't know it, and with a corporate culture like this? They never would.

"Mack?"

He looked over his shoulder. His secretary, Georgie O'Malley, who had run his father's office before Pops had died, had come in behind him without making a sound. At the ripe age of sixty-four, she was forty-one years with the company and showing no signs of slowing down. A self-professed farmer's wife who was without a husband or a farm, she was a kindred spirit in the war against the current climate of everything being disposable.

"You okay, Mack?"

Mack looked back up at the angels' share wafting in and out of the shafts of light so high above.

The angels' share was sacred: Each white oak barrel was charred on its inside before being filled with fifty-three gallons of bourbon. Stored in a place like this, in an environment that was purposely not climate controlled, the wood of the barrels expanded and contracted seasonally, the bourbon inside becoming colored and flavored by the caramelized sugars from that burned hardwood.

A not-insignificant portion of those gallons evaporated and was absorbed into the barrels over time.

That was the angels' share.

It was what his father had considered the sacrifice to the past, the serving that went to the forebearers to drink up in Heaven. It was also the pay-it-forward to your own passing . . . the hope that the next shepherd of the tradition would do the same for you when you were dead and gone.

"There's going to be nothing left of us, Georgie," he heard himself say.

"Whatchya'll talkin' about?"

He just shook his head. "I want you to tell the boys to shut down the sills."

"What."

"You heard me." Mack lifted his fist over his shoulder so she could see what he'd wadded up. "Corporate's putting a freeze on corn orders for the next three months. Minimum. They'll let us know when we can make more mash. Any rye, barley, and wheat we got right now is to be repurposed."

"Repurposed? What does that mean?"

"They can't sell it to a competitor. This gets out to people like the Suttons? Or the general press? It's going to make the ten cents they save look like the most expensive fuck-up in company history."

"We've never shut production down."

"Nope. Not since Prohibition — and that was only for show, anyway."

There was a long pause. "Mack . . . what are they doing?"

"They're going to ruin this company — that's what they're doing." He walked over to the woman. "They're going to take us under on the guise of maximizing profit. Or hell, maybe they're going to do an IPO finally — every other bourbon maker except Sutton's is publicly owned now. Maybe they're trying to artificially inflate profit right before a private sale. I don't know, and I don't care. But I'm pretty damn sure Elijah Bradford is rolling in his grave."

As he headed for the exit, she called after him, "Where are you going?"

"To get drunk. On a whole lot of beer."

Six

As Lane stood outside of his bedroom and stared down at his "wife," he thought, just like Easterly, she was the same, too.

Chantal Blair Stowe Baldwine was, in fact, *exactly* the same: the whole haircut, spray tan, makeup, and expensive pink clothing routine identical to what he'd left behind. And her voice — still right out of central casting under the heading of Genteel Southern Lady of Leisure.

She still babbled, too, words leaving her mouth in a stream with no consideration of rationing for the listener's benefit. Then again, for her, conversation was performance art, her hands moving like the wings of doves, arching up and down, that big diamond she'd wanted so badly flashing like a strobe light.

"— Derby weekend! Of course, Samuel Theodore Lodge is coming tonight. Gin's *all* excited about seeing him . . ."

Unbelievable. They had literally not seen each other or said a word to one another for nearly two years, and she was talking about who was on the guest list for dinner.

What in the hell had he ever seen in her —

"Oh, Lisa! Excuse me, could you please ask Newark if this Mr. Baldwine could have his car brought around? We're going to the club for lunch."

Lisa? he thought. *Then again, there had been staff turnover since he'd —*

Lane glanced over his shoulder. Lizzie was standing by his father's bedroom door, two vases of perfectly good, but no doubt freshly replaced, bouquets in her grip.

"Mr. Harris is just over there," Lizzie said stiffly.

"I don't like to shout. It's not appropriate." Chantal leaned in the direction of the other woman, like they were two girlfriends sharing a secret. "Thank you so much, you're such a help —"

"Are you out of your mind?" Lane demanded.

Chantal recoiled, her head rearing back, her eyes going from ingenue to hired killer in the blink of her false, but tasteful, eyelashes.

"I beg your pardon," Chantal whispered to him.

Lane tried to catch Lizzie's stare while he muttered, "Go tell him yourself."

Lizzie refused to acknowledge him. With a professionally impassive expression, she walked forward, her lithe strides taking her past him and down the long hall to the staff staircase. Meanwhile, Chantal was talking again.

"— address me in front of the help like that," she hissed.

"Her name's Lizzie, not Lisa." Now he was the one leaning in. "And you know that, don't you."

"Her name is irrelevant."

"She's been here longer than you." He smiled coldly. "And I'm willing to bet she'll be here way after you're gone."

"What is that supposed to mean?"

"You don't have to be under this roof and you know it."

"I'm your *wife*."

Lane stared down at her — and wondered why in the hell she was still anywhere near his life. The easy answer was that he'd been pretending that Charlemont didn't exist. The harder reasoning was tied to what she had done.

I'm your wife.

"Not for long," he said in a low voice.

Those penciled brows of hers lifted, and

instantly, that Persian-cat-dragged-through-a-toilet-bowl expression disappeared: She became as calm and smooth as a mirror. "Let's not fight, darling. Our reservation at the club is in twenty minutes —"

"Let me make myself perfectly clear. I'm not going anywhere with you. Except to a lawyer's office."

In his peripheral vision, he noted that Mr. Newark or Mr. Harris — whatever the butler's name was — was pulling a discreet turnaround, whisking Mrs. Mollie, the housekeeper, off in the opposite direction.

"Be serious, Tulane."

God, he hated the sound of his full name on Chantal's lips: Toooooooouulayne. For godsakes, it had two syllables, not three hundred.

"I am," he said. "It's time to end this between us."

Chantal took a slow, deep breath. "I know you're upset about poor old Miss Aurora and you're saying things you don't mean. I get it. She's a very good cook — and they are very, very hard to find."

His molars ground together. "You think she's just a cook."

"Are you saying she's your accountant?"

God, why had he ever . . . "That woman

means more to me than the one who bore me."

"Don't be ridiculous. Besides, she's black —"

Lane grabbed Chantal's arm and yanked her up close. "Don't you *ever* talk about her with that kind of attitude. I've never hit a woman before, but I guarantee I will *beat* the shit out of you if you disrespect her."

"Lane, you're hurting me!"

At that moment, he realized that a maid was frozen in the doorway of one of the guest rooms, her arms full of stacked, folded towels. As she ducked her head and hustled off, he shoved Chantal away. Jacked up his slacks. Glared at the hallway's runner.

"It's over, Chantal. In case you haven't noticed."

She clasped her hands together as if in prayer — and he didn't buy it for a second. The fake torture in her voice didn't sway him, either, as she whispered: "I think we should work on our relationship."

"I agree. This marriage of ours needs to be put out of its misery. That is the work."

"You don't mean it."

"The hell I don't. Get yourself a good lawyer or don't — either way, you're out of here."

Cue the tears. Big fat ones that made her

blue eyes shimmer like pool water. "You can be so cruel."

Not like she could be, he thought, not even close. And for godsake, he really should have followed through with that prenup, but too bad, so sad, whatever. The good news was that there was always going to be more money — even if she sued him for millions, he could make that up in a year or two.

"I'm going to go speak with Mother," he said. "And then call Samuel T. Maybe he can serve you papers over dinner tonight."

Annnnnnd just like that, the iron core came out again, those eyes growing cold. "I will ruin you and your family if you go through with this."

What she didn't know was that she'd already ruined his life. She'd cost him Lizzie . . . and so much more. But the losses were going to stop there, goddamn it.

"Be careful, Chantal." He didn't break the eye contact. "I will do anything, in- and outside of the law, to protect what's mine."

"Is that a threat?"

"Just a reminder that I'm a Bradford, my darling. We take care of things."

Striding away from the woman, Lane knocked on his mother's door. Even though there was no answer, he stepped into the fragrant inner reaches of the suite and shut things behind him.

Closing his eyes, he needed a second to dose the fury before he faced off this dubious reunion. Just a second to pull it together. Just . . .

When he reopened his lids, he found yet another stage set that was utterly unchanged.

His mother's white and cream room was just as it had always been, huge windows overlooking the gardens adorned with ball-gown drapes of blush-colored silk, Maxfield Parrish paintings glowing like jewels worn by the walls, fine French antiques too precious to sit on or use properly in the corners. But none of that was the focal point, as impressive as it all was.

The canopied bed across the way was the true showpiece. As resplendent and awesome as Bernini's *Baldacchino di San Pietro,* the massive steamboat-sized platform had carved columns that rose heavenward and a top that was festooned with waterfalls of that pale pink silk. And there she was, Virginia Elizabeth Bradford Baldwine, laying as still and well preserved as a saint, her long, thin body buried under the profusion of satin comforters and down pillows, her pale blond hair perfectly coiffed, her face made up even though she wasn't going anywhere and wasn't even conscious.

Beside her, on a marble-topped bombé chest, a dozen orange medicine vials with white tops and white labels were arranged in neat rows, like a platoon of soldiers. He had no clue what was in them and, likely, neither did she.

She was the Southern Sunny von Bülow — except his father had never tried to kill her. At least not physically.

The bastard had done other kinds of damage, though.

"Mother, dear," he said, striding over to her. When he got in range, he took her cool, dry hand with its paper-thin skin and blue veins into his palm. "Mother?"

"She's resting," came a voice.

A woman of about fifty, with red hair and a white and gray nurse's uniform, came in from the walk-in closet. She was a perfect fit for the decor, and he wouldn't have put it past his mother to have hired her on that basis alone.

"I'm Patty Sweringin," she said, offering her hand. "You must be young Mr. Baldwine."

"Lane." He shook what she put out. "How is Mother doing?"

"She's resting." The smile was as pressed

and professional as her uniform. "She's had a busy morning. The hair colorist and stylist were here."

Ah, yes, HIPAA, he thought. Which meant she wasn't allowed to tell him about his own mother's condition. But that wasn't the nurse's fault. And if his mother was exhausted by getting a couple of foils crimped on her head and a blow-dry? How the hell did he think she was doing.

"When she wakes up, tell her I . . ." He glanced back over at his mother.

"Tell her what, Mr. Baldwine?"

He thought of Chantal.

"I'm going to be here for a few days," he said grimly. "I'll tell her myself."

"Very good, sir."

Back out in the hall, he closed the door and leaned against it. Staring across at an oil painting of some Bradford or another, he found that the past came back again like a bee sting.

Fast and painful.

"What are you doing here?"

Lizzie had spoken the words to him out in the garden, out in the darkness, out in a hot, humid summer night. Overhead, thunderclouds had shut out the moonlight, leaving the blooming flowers and specimen trees in the shadows.

He could remember everything about the way she had stood in front of him on the brick walkway, her hands on her hips, her stare meeting his with a directness he wasn't used to, her Easterly uniform as sexually alluring as any set of lingerie he had ever seen.

Lizzie King had caught his eye the first time he'd seen her on his family's estate. And with each return during semester breaks from his masters programs, he'd found himself looking for her on the grounds, seeking her out, trying to get in her path.

God, he loved the chase.

And the capture wasn't half bad, either.

Of course, he didn't have much experience past that — nor did he want it.

"Well?" she demanded. Like if he didn't get on topic quick, she was going to start tapping her foot — and her next move was going to be knocking his block off for wasting her time.

"I've come for you."

Wait, that came out wrong. He'd meant to say that he'd come to *see* her. Talk to her. Look at her up close.

But those four words were also the truth. He wanted to know what she tasted like, what she felt like underneath him, what —

She crossed her arms over her chest. "Look, I'm going to be honest with you."

Lane smiled a little. "I like honesty."

"I don't think you're going to feel that way when I'm done with you."

Okaaaaay, now he was getting hard — and funny, that wouldn't have bothered him with the kinds of women he usually toyed with. Standing in front of this particular female with an urge to rearrange himself in his pants, however, seemed kind of . . . tacky.

"I'm going to spare you a lot of wasted time here." She kept her voice low, like she didn't want to be overheard, but that didn't detract from the power of her message. "I am not, and never will be, interested in someone like you. You are nothing but an entitled bad boy who gets off causing chaos with the opposite sex. That stuff was boring when I was a fifteen-year-old, and considering that I'm clos-ing in on thirty this year, I'm even less at-tracted to it. So do us both a favor — go to the country club, find one of those interchangeable blond women by the pool, and turn them into your twenty-minute Stair-Master. You are *not* going to get that from me."

He blinked like an idiot.

And he supposed the fact that he was so shocked that anyone would call him on his behavior proved her point.

"Now, if you'll excuse me, I'm going home.

I've been here working since seven a.m. —"

Snapping out his hand, he took hold of her arm as she turned away. "Wait."

"Excuse me?" She glanced down at the contact and back up into his eyes. "Unless you have something related to the flowers in this garden, you have nothing to say to me."

"You're not going to give me a chance to defend myself? You're just going to play judge and jury —"

"You are not serious —"

"Have you always been so prejudicial?"

She stepped out of his grip. "Better that than naive. Especially with a man like you."

"Don't believe everything you've seen in the papers —"

"Oh, please. I don't need to read about it — I've seen it firsthand. Two of them left yesterday morning out the back of the house. The night you came here, you brought a redhead home from a bar. And then they say when you went for your annual physical on Wednesday, you came back with a hickey on your neck — presumably from when the woman asked you to turn your head and cough?" She cut him off again, putting her palm out to his face. "And before you think I'm keeping this happy catalog of conquests because of some latent attraction to you, it's because the women on staff keep track of these things and won't stop talking about them."

"You want to give me a word in edgewise?" he countered. "Or are you good just keeping this conversation going on your own. Jesus, and you think I'm stuck-up."

"What?"

"You think I'm entitled? Well, you're putting me in the shade on that one, sweetheart."

"Excuse me?"

"You've decided you know everything about me just because a bunch of other people, who also don't know me, are talking about things they know nothing about. That's pretty damn arrogant."

"Which is not the same as entitled."

"You really want to argue Webster's dictionary with me?"

Right, the fact that they were bickering should not have been a total flippin' turn-on, but holy hell it was. For every lob she tossed at him, he found himself looking at her body less and focusing on her eyes more — and that made her even sexier.

"Listen, can we just be done here?" she said. "I have to be back at the crack of dawn, and this conversation is not as important as the sleep I need to get."

This time when she turned away, he stopped her with his voice. "I saw you out by the pool yesterday."

She glared at him over her shoulder. "Yes, and I was pulling weeds. You got a problem with that?"

"You were staring at me. I saw you."

Touché, he thought as she blinked.

"I was in the pool," he whispered as he took a step closer to her. "And you liked what you saw, didn't you. Even though you hate who you think I am, you like what you saw."

"You're delusional —"

"Honesty. You were the one to bring it up first." He leaned in, turning his head to the side as if he were going to kiss her. "So do you have the guts to be honest?"

Her hands fiddled with the collar of her Easterly polo. "I don't know what you're talking about."

"Liar." He smiled a little. "Why do you think I stayed out there so long? It was because of you. I liked that you were watching my body."

"You're crazy."

God, her false denial was better than the last full blown orgasm he'd had.

"Am I?" He focused on her lips, and in his mind, he started kissing them, licking his way into her, pulling her up against him. "I don't think so. And I'd rather be a philandering snob than a coward."

That was how he left her.

100

He'd turned away on that brick path, and walked toward the house, leaving her behind.

But he'd known, with every step he took away from her, that she wasn't going to be able to let things rest like that.

Next time, she would come to him . . .

And sure enough, she did.

Seven

"I'm sorry, what was that?"

As Lizzie spoke, she stared at the flowers in the vase she was holding, and couldn't remember what she'd meant to do with them — oh, right, put them in a bucket until she got off work; after which she would wrap them in a damp paper towel and a Kroger's plastic bag, and take them home.

"I'm sorry, come again?" she said, glancing across the conservatory at Greta.

"I was speaking in English that time, too, you know."

"I'm just all up in my head."

"The tent people are demanding to be paid up front? Or they're going to take down everything they're putting up."

"What?" Lizzie put the bouquet down next to the empty silver bowls. "Is this a new policy for them?"

"Guess so."

"I'll go talk to Rosalinda — do you have

the total?"

"Tvelve sousand, four hundred, fifty-nine, zeventy-two."

"Hold on, let me write that down." Lizzie grabbed a pen. "One more time?"

After she got the total scribbled into her palm, she glanced out to the garden. The tent people had just stretched the fabric panels out flat and were beginning to lay the poles down as some of them got to stitching the huge sections together with ropes.

Two hours more work for them. Maybe three.

"They're still going strong out there," she murmured.

"Not for long." Greta resumed cleaning the pink garden roses. "The rental office called me, and they're prepared to order them back into the truck."

"There's no reason to get hysterical about this," Lizzie muttered as she headed outside.

Rosalinda Freeland's office was in the kitchen wing, and she took the longer, outdoor route because she was pretty damned sick and tired of running into Lane.

She was about halfway across the terrace, passing by the French doors that led out of the dining room, when she looked over toward the business center.

The facility was located where the original stables used to be, and like the conservatory, it opened out to the gardens and the river. The architecture that had been added had been precisely matched to that of Easterly, and the total square footage was nearly the same as the mansion's. With over a dozen offices, a conference room the size of a college lecture hall, and its own catering kitchen and dining room, William Baldwine ran his wife's family's multi-national bourbon company out of the state-of-the-art compound.

You almost never saw anyone loitering around over there, but apparently something was going on because a group of people in suits was standing on the terrace outside of the main conference room, smoking and talking in a tight enclave.

Strange, she thought. Mr. Baldwine was a smoker, so it was unlikely those folks had been banished to the terrace just to get their nicotine fix.

And what do you know, she actually recognized the single nonsmoking woman in the mix. It was Sutton Smythe, heir to the Sutton Distillery Corporation fortune. Lizzie had never met her personally, but there had been a lot of press about the fact that a female might, just might, in the next decade, head one of the largest liquor companies in the world.

Frankly, it looked like she was already the boss, with her dark hair coiffed and her no-nonsense, super-expensive, black pant suit. She was actually quite a striking woman, with bold features and a curvy body that could have taken her into bimbo territory if she'd been so inclined to play that card — which she obviously wasn't.

What was she doing here, though?

Talk about sleeping with the enemy.

Lizzie shook her head and went in through the rear kitchen door. Whatever was happening over there was not her problem. She was far, far, far down the totem pole, just looking to get a tent erected for her flower arrangements —

Wow.

Talk about a lotta chefs, she thought as she scooted in and out and around all the white-coated, toque-hatted men and women who were giving themselves scoliosis making filo-dough and stuffed-mushroom'y thingies.

On the far side of all of the Gordon Ramsay, there was a heavy, swinging door that opened into a plain corridor full of cleaning closets, laundries, and the maids' break room — as well as the butler's living quarters, the controller's office and the back staff stairwell.

Lizzie went to the door on the right that was marked Private and knocked once. Twice. Three times.

Given that Rosalinda was as efficient and punctual as an alarm clock, the controller clearly wasn't in. Maybe she'd gone to the bank —

"— shall check again in an hour," Mr. Harris said as he entered the hall at the far end with the head housekeeper. "Thank you, Mrs. Mollie."

"My pleasure, Mr. Harris," the older woman muttered.

Lizzie locked eyes with the butler as Mrs. Mollie pared off. "We have a problem."

He stopped in front of her. "Yes?"

"I need just over twelve grand for the tent company and Mrs. Freeland is not here. Can you cut checks?"

"They require twelve thousand dollars?" he said in his clipped accent. "Whyever for?"

"The tent rental. It's a new company policy I'm guessing. They've never done this before."

"This is Easterly. We have had an account with them since the turn of the century and they will defer. Allow me."

Pivoting on his spit-polish shoeshine, he

headed for his quarters — no doubt to call the rental company's owner personally.

If he could pull this off and Lizzie could keep her tents and tables? His PITA attitude might well be worth the trouble.

Besides, if worst came to worst, Greta could write the check.

One thing was certain, Lizzie was *not* going to ask Lane for it and they needed that tent: In less than forty-eight hours, the world was descending on the property, and nothing pissed off the Bradfords more than something, anything out of place.

As she waited for the butler to reemerge, all triumphant in his penguin suit, she leaned back against the smooth, cool plaster wall and found herself thinking about the dumbest decision she had ever made . . .

She should have let the whole thing rest.

After the dreaded Lane Baldwine had sought her out in the dark in the garden, she should have let the argument between them go. Why on earth did she care how wrong he was about her? How insane, egocentric, and ridiculous that silver-spooned fool was? She didn't owe him any kind of world-view realignment — besides, that wasn't going to happen without a sledgehammer.

Not that she wouldn't enjoy an attempt on

those terms.

The problem was, however, that among her own deficiencies was the paralytic need not to be misinterpreted by Channing Tatum's doppelgänger.

So she had to set him straight. And in fact, she talked to him all the way home that night. As well as all the way back to Easterly the following morning. And then throughout the next week.

Eventually, she became convinced he was avoiding her: For the first time since he'd come home on his break from graduate school, she didn't see him for seven days straight. The good news, if you could look at it that way, was that at least there weren't any females coming around the house and leaving at odd hours in porn combinations. The bad news was that she was now overprepared with all her speeches, and in danger of revealing exactly how much time she'd wasted yelling at him in her head.

And Lane was definitely still at Easterly. His Porsche — like he would drive anything else — was still around by the garages, and whenever she was forced to take a bouquet up to his room, she could smell his cologne in the air and see his wallet on the bureau with his gold cuff links.

He was playing her — and as much as she

hated to admit it, the act was working. She was getting more frustrated and more determined to find him, instead of less so.

He was a master at women, all right.

The bastard.

With yet another fresh bouquet in hand, she headed up the back stairs for his room. She didn't expect him to be in there, but somehow, the idea of walking into his space and throwing out a couple of choice sound bites was going to offer her a release. When she knocked on his door, it was a hard demand, and after a moment, she pushed her way in —

Lane *was* there.

Sitting on the edge of his bed. Head in his hands, body bowed.

He did not look to the door.

Didn't seem to know anyone had come in at all.

Lizzie cleared her throat once. Twice. "Excuse me, I'm here to switch out your flowers."

He jumped and twisted around toward her. Red-rimmed eyes seemed to struggle to focus, and when he spoke up, his voice was rough. "Sorry? What?"

"Flowers." She lifted the bouquet a little higher. "I'm here to replace your flowers."

"Oh. Thank you. That's awfully good of you."

Clearly, he had no clue what he was saying

to her. The politeness seemed like just a reflex, the conversational equivalent of a lower leg kicking when its knee was hit with a rubber hammer.

This is not your business, she told herself as she went across to the bureau.

The swap took a split second, and then she had the barely wilted, old one in her hands, and was walking back over to the half-open door. She told herself not to look over at him as she left. For all she knew, his favorite hunting dog had ringworm . . . or maybe that girlfriend of his in Virginia had found out about all his extracurricular exercise here in Charlemont.

That biggest mistake thing happened just as she got to the jambs.

Later, when things had blown up in her face, after she'd overridden her walls of self-protection and gotten burned, she would become convinced that if she'd only kept going, she would have been fine. Their lives wouldn't have slammed into each other's and left such shrapnel all over her.

But she did look back at him.

And she just had to open her mouth again: "What's wrong?"

Lane's eyes swung up to her. "I'm sorry?"

"What's your problem?"

He braced his hands against his knees. "I'm sorry."

She waited for something else. "About what?"

His eyes closed, his head ducking down again.

Even though he made no sound, she knew he was weeping.

And that was so completely not what she expected from someone like him.

Closing the door, she wanted to protect his privacy for him. "What happened? Is everyone all right?"

Lane shook his head, took a deep breath, and recomposed himself. "No. Not everyone."

"Is it your sister? I've heard she's had some issues —"

"Edward. They took him."

Edward . . . ? God, she had seen the man around the estate from time to time — and he appeared to be the last person anyone could "take" anywhere. Unlike his father whose office was at Easterly, Edward worked down at BBC headquarters in the heart of the city, and from what little she knew, he was the anti-Lane, a very serious, extremely aggressive businessman.

"I'm sorry, I'm not quite following?" she said.

"He was kidnapped in South America, and the ransom is being negotiated." He rubbed his face hard. "I can't imagine what they're doing to him — it's been five days since the demand. Jesus Christ, how did this happen? He was supposed to be protected down there. How did they let this happen?"

Then he shook himself, and pegged her with hard eyes. "You can't say anything. Gin doesn't even know yet. We're keeping everything quiet so it doesn't get out in the press yet."

"I won't. I mean, I won't say a word. Are the authorities involved?"

"My father's been working with them. This is a nightmare — I *told* him not to go down there."

"I am so sorry." What a pathetic statement. "Is there anything I can do?"

Which was just another pathetic bunch of syllables.

"It should have been me," Lane muttered. "Or Max. Why couldn't it have been one of us? We're worthless. It should have been one of us."

The next thing she knew, she'd put the vase down somewhere and was over by the bed. "Is there someone I can get for you?"

"It should have been me."

She sat down next to him and lifted a hand to touch his shoulder, but then she thought better of that —

112

A cell phone went off on the bedside table, and when he made no move to answer it, she asked, "Do you want to pick that up?"

When he didn't reply, she leaned to the side and looked at the screen. Chantal Blair Stowe.

"I think it's your girlfriend."

He glanced over. "Who?" Lizzie reached around and picked up the phone, showing the screen to him. "No, I don't want to talk to her. And she's not my girlfriend."

Is she aware of that, Lizzie wondered as she put the thing back.

Lane shook his head. "Edward's the only one of us who's worth a dime."

"That's not true."

He laughed in a hard burst. "The hell it's not. And that was your point last week, wasn't it."

Abruptly, Lane focused on her, and there was a strange silence, as if it were only then that he realized who was in the room with him.

Lizzie's heart began to pound. There was something in those eyes of his that she hadn't seen before — and God help her, she knew what it was.

Sex with a playboy was nothing she was interested in. Raw lust with a real man? That . . . was so much harder to walk away from.

"You need to go now," he said in a tight voice.

Yes, she told herself. *I do.*

And yet for some crazy reason, she whispered, "Why?"

"Because if I wanted you when it was just a game" — that stare of his locked on her mouth — "in my current mood, I'm desperate for you."

Lizzie recoiled, and this time when he laughed, it was deeper, lower. "Don't you know that stress is like alcohol? It makes you reckless, stupid, and hungry. I should know . . . my family deals so well in —"

"It is taken care of, Miss King."

Lizzie jumped out of her skin with a gasp. "What!"

Mr. Harris frowned. "The tent rental. It has been taken care of."

"Oh, yes, great. Thanks."

She stumbled as she turned away from the butler. Then she went the wrong way down the hall, heading toward the public rooms of the house. Before Mr. Harris called that to her attention, she doubled back, found a door to the outside, and broke out —

Right into the garden.

Right below Lane's bedroom window.

Putting her hands to her face, she remembered how he had kissed her two nights after she had sat with him in his bedroom.

She had been the one to seek him out — and there hadn't been any flower excuse that time: She had waited for as long as she'd been able to stand it, and then she'd deliberately gone to his room at the end of her work day to see how he was doing, what was going on, whether there had been any resolution.

Nothing had made it into the press at that point. All that coverage had come later, after Edward had finally come home.

That second time she'd gone to his bedrom, she had knocked more softly — and after a moment, he had opened the way in . . . and she could still picture how much he had aged. He'd been gaunt, unshaven, with black circles under his eyes. He had changed his clothes, although they were just different versions of what he had always worn: A monogrammed button-down — except it was untucked on one side. Expensive slacks — except they were creased at the bend of the pelvis and unpressed at the heads of the knees. Gucci loafers — no, he'd only had dark socks on.

And all that pretty much told her what she needed to know.

"Come with me," she'd said to him. "You

need to get out of this room."

In a hoarse voice, he'd asked her what time it was, and she'd told him it was after eight. When he'd looked confused, she'd had to clarify that it was at night.

She had led him down the back stairs as if he were a child, taking him by the hand, talking about nonsense. The only thing he said was that he didn't want anyone to see him — and she had made sure that happened, directing him away from the talk in the dining room, keeping him safe from prying eyes.

As she had drawn him out into the warm night, she had heard laughter from where dinner was being eaten in that grand formal room.

How could they do that? she'd wondered. Chatter on as if there were nothing wrong . . . as if one of them weren't far, far away, in danergous hands.

At the time, she had had no idea what she was doing with Lane or why she cared so much that he was suffering. She only knew that the one-dimensional playboy she'd written off as a waste of privilege had become human, and his pain mattered to her.

They hadn't gone far. Just down the brick walkway, in between the flowering shrubs and beds and over to the gazebo in the garden's far corner.

They had sat together and not said much. But when she had reached for his hand, he had taken what she offered and held on tight.

And when he had turned to her, she had known what he wanted — and it wasn't talking. There had been a moment of traffic jam in her head, all kinds of *whoa, wait, stop, too far . . .*

But then she had leaned in and their lips had touched.

The thoughts had been so complicated. The connection had been so simple.

But it hadn't stayed that way. He had grabbed her, and she had let him. He had put his hands into her clothes, and she had let him.

Somewhere in the middle of it all, she had realized that she'd hated him because she was attracted to him. Crazy attracted. And she had watched him in the pool that afternoon, although there had been so much more than that: Every time he had come to the house or left, she had tried to get a look at him — even though she would have denied it to anyone and everybody. News that he was imminently arriving at Easterly had had the ability to electrify her, and his departures had subdued her. And the pathetic reality was that she had envied those women, those dumb blondes with their perfect bodies and their Southern drawls who had put the proverbial revolving door to his bedroom to good use.

The truth that she had not wanted to admit to herself was that she would have found something to dislike in him no matter what his demographics had been.

It hadn't been about his money, his old family, the multiple women, his too-good looks or too-slick smile.

What she had hated about him was how he made her feel. The vulnerability had been a vicious intruder into her life, an unwelcome houseguest that had moved in, and traveled with her to work, and dogged her even in her dreams.

In retrospect, she should have listened to that fear. Chosen that instinct over the incredible attraction.

Life wasn't always that proactively wise, however.

Sometimes you didn't heed the warning signs, and you put the pedal to the metal, and you went screaming around the blind turn.

She still had pain from the crash, that was for sure.

EIGHT

Red & Black Stables, Ogden County, KY

As the sun began to set, its golden rays penetrated Stable B's open bay, spilling onto the broad concrete aisle and leaving a trail of pure magic through which hay and dust particles ambled. The rhythmic sound of a box broom whisking down the way brought out the mares' heads, their intelligent eyes and graceful muzzles popping forward in inquiry.

Edward Westfork Bradford Baldwine went slow on the sweeping, his body not what it once had been. And the effort wasn't all that bad, the constant pain he was in ceding to the gentle exercise. The chronic discomfort would return, however, as soon as he stopped or fell into a different series of movements.

He had become used to that.

The combination of muscles and bones and organs that supported his brain on its journey through this current mortal incarnation was a machine that no longer made transitions well. It much preferred entrenched activity, repeated effort in a prescribed fashion or sustained rest in any position. His physical therapists, a.k.a. the Sadists, told him to stay active with varied pursuits, rather like, as they had explained, someone who was having to rewire their brain through occupational therapy.

The more he kept changing things up, the better for his "recovery."

He always put that word in quotation marks. True recovery to him was a return to what he had been — and that was never going to happen even if he were able to walk right, eat right, sleep through the night.

There was no going back to that other person, who had been a younger, better-natured, better-looking version of himself.

He hated the Sadists, but they were just part of a long list of things for which he held enmity. And this broken body they seemed so intent on rehabbing was simply not getting with the program. He'd been at it for how long? And still the pain, all the time the pain, to the point where it was hard to gather the energy to break through that wall of fire and get to where he was in this moment, where things were working in some semblance of order.

It was as if he were meeting the same mugger in every alley he tried to go down.

He sometimes wondered if he would feel less worn out if it were a different criminal from time to time, a different foe making off with his quality of life.

The robberies had been from a consistent thief, however.

"What are you doing, girl?" He paused to stroke a black muzzle. "You good?"

After a chuffing reply from the thoroughbred, Edward kept going. The breeding season had gone very well, and he had ninety percent of his twenty-three mares in foal. If all went as planned, their babies would be born the following January, critical for ensuring start-of-the-year birth dates: For racing, the clock began ticking by the calendar, not the actual drop date — so if you wanted the future three-year-old you'd run in the Derby to be as mature and strong as possible? You better get those mares foaling no later than March for their nearly year-long pregnancies.

Most racing people operated in a stratified system where the breeders were separate from the yearling breakers, who were different from the track trainers. But he had enough money and time on his hands so that he not only bred, but ushered his horses through elementary school here on his farm, to middle school at a center he'd bought last year, to the booking blocks of stalls at Steeplehill Downs in Charlemont and Garland Downs in neighboring Arlington, Kentucky.

The money required for his breeding and racing operation was astronomical, and any return on investment was a hypothetical — which was why syndicates of investors were typically formed to spread the financial exposure and risk. He, on the other hand, didn't do syndicates. Co-investors. Partners.

He hadn't lost anything yet. In fact, he was almost making money. His operation, in the last year and a half, had produced remarkable results — all thanks to Nebekanzer, his stallion, who happened to be the biggest, meanest sonofabitch anyone had ever come across. That nasty bastard bred fast sons and daughters, though — something he had discovered when he'd moved here to the Red & Black's caretaker's cottage and bought the four-hooved spawn of the devil and three of Neb's two-year progeny at auction. The following year? All three descendants had won more than two hundred grand apiece by April, and one of them had been second in the Derby, third in the Preakness, and first in the Belmont.

And that had been his farm off to the races, as they say. This year, he was slated to do even better. He had two horses in the Derby.

Both from Neb's loins.

He couldn't say that his heart was in the business, but it certainly was better than sitting around and ruminating on everything he had lost.

Just like all those racehorses, he had been bred, born, and trained for a given future: to take over the Bradford Bourbon Company. But like a thoroughbred who had broken his leg, that was no longer his future.

"Buenas noches, jefe."

Edward nodded at one of his eleven stable hands. *"Hasta mañana."*

He resumed his sweeping, ducking his head —

"Jefe, hay algo aquí."

"Who?"

"No sé."

Edward frowned and used the broom as a cane, limping down to the open bay. Outside, on the circular drive, a two-acre-long black limousine was rolling to a halt over in front of Barn A.

Moe Brown, the stable manager, walked out to the monstrosity, the man's long strides eating up the distance. Moe was sixty, lanky as a fence rail, and smart as a mathematician. He also had "the eye": That guy could pretty much tell a horse's future from the moment the animal stood up on its hooves for the first time. It was spooky — and invaluable in the business.

And he was slowly but surely teaching his secrets to Edward.

Edward's innate knack, on the other hand, was the breeding. He just seemed to know which bloodlines to cross.

As Moe stopped at the limo, a uniformed chauffeur got out and went around to the rear doors — and Edward shook his head when he saw what emerged.

The Pendergasts were sending in the heavy guns.

The forty-ish woman emerging from the vehicle's backseat was thinner by three times than even Moe, dressed in pink Chanel, and had more hair than what was in Neb's entire tail. Beauty-queen pretty, pampered as a Pomeranian, and with a will to give those Steel Magnolias a run for their money, Buggy Pendergast was used to getting her way.

For example, about five years ago she'd played her hand and gotten one of the scions of an old oil family to throw out his perfectly good first wife in favor of her. And ever since then she'd been dumping his money into thoroughbreds.

Edward had already told her no three times over the phone.

No syndicates. No co-investors. No partners.

He bred for himself and no one else.

The man who got out after Buggy was not her husband, and given the briefcase he was holding, one had to assume he was an accountant of some kind. Certainly wasn't a security guard. Too short, and those glasses were a testosterone drain if Edward had ever seen one.

Moe started jawing with them, and Edward could tell it was not going well. Then things went from bad to worse when that briefcase got summarily laid on the hood of the limousine and Buggy opened it with a flourish — like she was lifting up her skirt and expecting everyone to moan with approval.

Edward came out into the late sunshine with his broom-cane and his bad mood. As he approached, Buggy didn't look over. And when he stopped behind Moe, she gave him nothing but a glare — as if she didn't appreciate a stable hand playing witness to all this.

"— quarter of a million dollars," she said, "and I'm leaving with my colt."

Moe moved the piece of straw he was chewing on to the other side of his mouth. "Don't think so."

"I have the money."

"Y'all need to leave the property —"

"Where is Edward Baldwine! I demand to speak with —"

"I'm right here," Edward said in a low voice. "Moe, I'll handle this."

"And the Lord grants us small miracles," the man muttered as he walked off.

As Buggy's colored contacts went up and down Edward's body, even her Botoxed face strained with the shock she clearly felt. "Edward . . . you look . . ."

"Smashing, I know." He nodded at the money. "Close that ridiculous show up, get back in your vehicle and go on about your business. I told you over the phone, I do not sell my stock."

Buggy cleared her throat. "I, ah, I heard what happened to you. I didn't realize, however —"

"The plastic surgeons did a fine job with my face, don't you think."

"Ah . . . yes. Yes, they did."

"But enough of catching up. You are leaving."

Buggy pinned a smile on her face. "Now, Edward, how long have our families gone back?"

"Your husband's family and mine have known each other for over two hundred years. I don't know your kin and have no intention of making their acquaintance. What I am very sure of, however, is that you are not leaving here with rights to any foal. Now, g'on. Get going."

As he turned away, she said, "There is two hundred and fifty thousand dollars in that briefcase."

"Is that supposed to impress me? My dear woman, I can find a quarter of a million in the cushions of my couch so I assure you, I am wholly unswayed by your show of liquidity. More to the point, I can't be bought. Not for one dollar. Not for a billion." He glanced over at the chauffeur. "Am I getting my shotgun. Or are you squeezing yourself back into that limo and having your driver hit the gas?"

"I am going to tell your father about this! This is disgraceful —"

"My father is dead to me. You're more than welcome to discuss my business with him, but it will get you no further than this wasted trip out into the country. Enjoy your Derby weekend — elsewhere."

Pushing into the broom handle, he started to shamble his way back to the barn. In his wake, the chorus of multiple car doors opening and closing and the limo's tires squealing out on the asphalt suggested that the woman was on her cell phone, bitching to her twenty-years-older husband about the shameful way she'd just been treated.

Although considering gossip had her having been an exotic dancer in her twenties, he could guess she'd been exposed to rather a lot worse in her previous life.

Before he went back inside and resumed his sweeping, he looked over the vista of his farm: The hundreds of acres of rolling grassland that was cut into paddocks with dark brown five-rail fences. The three stables with their red and gray slate roofs and their black siding with red trim. The outbuildings for the equipment, and the state-of-the-art trailers, and the white farmhouse where he stayed, and the clinic and the exercise ring.

His mother owned all of it. Her great-grandfather had bought the land and started the equine enterprise, and then her grandfather and father had continued to invest in the business. Things had coasted after her father died some twenty years ago — and Edward had certainly never considered getting involved.

As the eldest son, he'd been destined to step into the leadership role at the Bradford Bourbon Company — and actually, more than what legacy or primogeniture dictated, that had been where his heart was. He had been a distiller in his blood, as scrupulous with his products as a priest.

But then everything had changed.

Red & Black Stables had been the best, post-everything solution, a diversion that occupied his days until he could drink himself to sleep. And even better, it was something his father wasn't involved in.

What little future he had was here with the bluegrass and the horses.

It was all he had.

"You enjoyed that, didn't you," Moe said from behind him.

"Not really." He shifted his weight and began to sweep the aisle again. "But no one is getting a part of this farm, not even God Himself."

"You shouldn't talk like that."

Edward glanced over his shoulder to remind the man what his face looked like. "You really think there's anything I'm afraid of now?"

As Moe made the sign of the cross, Edward rolled his eyes . . . and went back to his work.

NINE

"— Laying in bed and playing with my breasts." Virginia Elizabeth Baldwine, "Gin" to her family, leaned back in her padded chair. "And then I'm putting my hand between my legs. What do you want me to do with it now that it's there? Yes, I'm naked . . . what else would I be? Now, tell me what to do."

She tapped her cigarette over the Baccarat crystal wineglass she'd emptied about ten minutes ago and crossed her legs under her silk robe. The tugging on her hair was beyond annoying, and she glared at her hairstylist in the mirror of her bathroom.

"Oh, yes," she moaned into her cell phone. "I'm wet . . . so wet, only for you . . ."

She had to roll her eyes at the good girl reference, but that was what Conrad Stetson liked because he was an old-fashioned kind of man — he needed the illusion that the woman he was being unfaithful to his wife with was monogamous to him.

So silly.

But Gin did rather miss the early days of their relationship. It had been heady stuff to draw him slowly, inexorably away from his marriage. She had reveled in how hard he'd fought the attraction to her, the shame he'd felt when they'd first kissed, the way he'd tried so valiantly not to call her, see her, seek her out. And for a week or two, she'd actually been interested in him, his attention a drug well worth bingeing on.

Once she'd fucked him a few times, though? Well, it was too much missionary, for one thing.

"Oh, yes, yes, yes . . . I'm coming, I'm coming . . ."

As she "orgasmed," her stylist flushed from embarrassment but kept pinning her dark hair in place while a maid came in from the walk-in closet with a velvet tray in her hands. On it were two parures, one made of Burmese rubies by Cartier in the forties and the other a sapphire creation done in the late fifties by Van Cleef & Arpels. Both were her grandmother's, one having been given to Big Virginia Elizabeth by her husband on the birth of Gin's mother, and the other presented on her grandparents' twentieth wedding anniversary.

She made a moaning noise; then hit mute and shook her head at the maid. "I want the Winston diamonds."

"I believe Mrs. Baldwine is wearing them."

As Gin pictured her sister-in-law, Chantal, with the hundred-plus carats of D flawless on, she smiled and spoke slowly, as if addressing a dolt. "Then take the diamonds my father bought my mother off that bitch's neck and ears and bring them here to me."

The maid blanched. "My . . . pleasure."

Just before the woman stepped out of the bedroom, Gin called over, "Make sure you clean them first. I can't stand that drugstore perfume she insists on wearing."

"My pleasure."

It was a bit of a stretch to refer to Flowerbomb by Viktor & Rolf as "drugstore," but it certainly wasn't Chanel. Honestly, though, what could you expect from a woman who hadn't even made it through Sweet Briar?

Gin unmuted the phone. "Baby, I've got to go. I need to get ready. I'm so sorry you can't be here, but you understand."

Cue that Peanuts' routine, where the adult's voice turned muffled.

God, had he always had that thick of a Southern accent? Bradfords didn't have any kind of dreadful garbled twang — only enough of a drawl to prove what side of the Mason-Dixon Line they were born and lived on and that they knew the difference between bourbon and whiskey.

The latter being beneath contempt.

"Bye, now," she said, and hung up.

As she ended the call, she decided to end the relationship. Conrad had started talking about leaving his wife, and she didn't want that. He had two children, for godsakes — what was he thinking. It was one thing to have some fun on the side, but children needed the illusion of two parents.

Plus, she'd already proven she had no business being a mother to anything. Not even a goldfish.

A half hour later, she was dressed in a Christian Dior gown made of U of C red and had that Harry Winston necklace laying heavy and cool on her collarbones. Her perfume was Coco by Chanel, a classic that she had decided she could carry off when she hit thirty. Her shoes were Loubou's.

She was not wearing panties.

Samuel Theodore Lodge was coming to the dinner.

As she stepped out into the hall, she looked to the door opposite hers. Sixteen years ago to the day, she had given birth to the young girl who lived in there. And that had been about it for her involvement with Amelia. A baby nurse, followed by two full-time nannies, coupled with a sufficient passage of time, and they were now in prep-school territory.

So she didn't even catch a glimpse of her daughter anymore.

Indeed, Amelia had not come home for spring break, and that had been good. But the summer was looming, and the girl's return from Hotchkiss was not something anyone, even Amelia most likely, looked forward to.

Could you even send a sixteen-year-old off to summer camp?

Maybe they could just ship her over to Europe for a two-month tour. Victorians had done that a hundred years ago, before even airplanes and cars with air bags.

They could pay someone to be her chaperone.

And actually, the urge to keep the girl away from Easterly wasn't because Gin didn't love her daughter. It was just that the girl's presence was too stark a condemnation of choices and actions and lies that were Gin's own and no one else's — and sometimes it was best not to look too closely at those things.

Besides, Europe was grand. Especially if

one did it right.

Gin walked on, heading for the straight-out-of-Tara staircase that bifurcated on a middle landing before bottoming out on both sides of Easterly's tremendous marble foyer. The dress spoke up with each of her strides, the fall of silk rustling against the tulle underskirting in a way that made her imagine the hushed conversation of the Frenchwomen who had put the stitches in the gown.

As she came to the landing and chose the right side, as it was closer to the parlor cocktails were always served in, she could hear the patter of voices. There would be thirty-two for dinner tonight, and she would be seated in the chair her mother should be in, opposite and down the long table from her father at the head.

She had done this a million times and would do it a million times hence, this acting as the lady of the house — and usually it was a duty she carried out with pride.

Tonight, however, there was a mourning behind her heart for some reason.

Probably because it was Amelia's birthday.

Best to get drinking.

Especially given that when she had called her daughter, Amelia had refused to come down and get on her dorm's house phone.

It was the kind of thing Gin would have done.

See? She was a good parent. She understood her child.

Lane refused to dress in black tie for dinner. He just kept his slacks on, and traded his shirt for a button-down that he'd left behind when he'd gone to live with Jeff up north.

He was willing to be on time and that was it.

As soon as he hit the first floor, he started avoiding people's stares and looking for a drink — and he ran into an old friend before he got to the Family Reserve.

"Well, well, well, the New Yorker has returned to his roots finally," Samuel Theodore Lodge III said as he came over.

Lane had to smile. "How's my favorite southern-fried attorney?"

While they embraced and clapped each other's backs, the blond woman who was with Samuel T. hung off to the side, her eyes missing nothing — which was more than you could say about her dress. Anything shorter up top or on the bottom and she'd be in her underwear.

So she was right down Samuel T.'s alley.

"Allow me to introduce Miss Savannah

Locke." Samuel T. nodded to the woman as if giving her permission to come forward, and she was right on it, leaning in and offering her pale, slender hand. "Go get us a drink, darling, would you? He'll have the Family Reserve."

As the woman hightailed it for the bar, Lane shook his head. "I can serve myself."

"She's a stewardess. She likes to wait on people."

"Aren't they called flight attendants now?"

"So what made you decide to come back? It can't be the Derby. That's Edward's thing."

Lane shrugged off the question, not about to go into the situation with Miss Aurora. Too raw. "I need your help with something. In a professional capacity, that is."

Samuel T.'s eyes narrowed and then moved down to Lane's wedding ring-free hand. "Cleaning house, are you."

"How fast can you make it happen? I want things kept quiet and over with quick."

The man nodded once. "Call me tomorrow morning. I'll take care of everything."

"Thank you —"

Up on the grand staircase, his sister, Gin, made the corner at the landing and paused, as if she knew people were going to want to examine what she was wearing — and the

137

red gown and all those jewels were in fact worth the check-out. With acres of crimson silk falling to the floor and that set of Princess Di diamonds, she was the Oscars, *Town & Country,* and the Court of St. James all at once.

The hush that quieted through the foyer was both from awe and condemnation.

Gin's reputation preceded her.

Didn't that run in the family.

When she caught sight of him and Samuel T., her eyebrows arched, and for a split second, she smiled honestly, that old light returning to her eyes, the years peeling away until the three of them were who they had been before so much had happened.

"If you'll excuse me," Samuel T. said. "I'll go see about our drinks. I think my date got lost on the trip back."

"The house isn't that big."

"Maybe to you and me."

As Samuel T. turned away, Gin lifted the skirting of her red gown and finished her descent. When she hit the black and white marble, she came right across to Lane, her stilettos clipping over the floor that had been laid a hundred years before. He expected to do a gentleman's hold on her as they embraced, in deference to her pinned-up hair and her jewels — but she was the one who squeezed until he felt her tremble.

"I am so glad you're here," she said in a rough voice. "You should have let me know."

And that was when he did the math and realized it was Amelia's birthday.

He was about to say something when she pulled back and put her mask in place, her Katharine Hepburn features falling into a perfectly vacant arrangement that made his chest ache.

"I need a drink," she announced. "And where did Samuel T. go?"

"He's not alone tonight, Gin."

"As if that matters?"

When she walked off with her head high and her shoulders back, he felt sorry for that poor blond stewardess. Lane didn't know who Samuel T's escort was, but she had certainly gotten the right read on her date: Over at the bar, she'd set herself at his hip like a holstered revolver — as if she were fully aware that she was going to have to protect her turf.

At least he'd have something to watch over dinner.

"Your Family Reserve, sir? Mr. Lodge sends it with his highest regard."

Lane turned and smiled. Reginald Tressel had been the bartender at Easterly forever, and the African-American gentleman in his black dress coat and shined shoes was more distinguished than many of the guests, as usual.

"Thank you, Reg." Lane took a squat cut-crystal glass from the silver tray. "Hey, thanks for calling me about Miss Aurora. Did you get my voice mail?"

"I did. And I knew you'd want to come down."

"She looks better than I thought she would."

"She puts up a front. You're not leaving anytime soon, are you?"

"Hey, how's Hazel doing?" Lane deflected.

"She's much better, thank you. And I know that you won't go back up north until things are finished here."

Reginald gave him a smile that didn't change the grim light in those dark eyes, and then the man returned to his duties, walking through the crowd like a statesman, people greeting him as an equal.

Lane could remember when he was young people saying that Mr. Tressel was the unofficial mayor of Charlemont, and that certainly hadn't changed.

God, he wasn't ready to lose Miss Aurora. That would be like having to sell Easterly

— something he couldn't fathom in a universe that was functioning properly —

The scent of cigarette smoke made him stiffen.

There was only one person allowed to smoke in the house.

On that note, Lane went in the opposite direction.

His father had always been a smoker in the Southern tradition, which was to say that even though the man had asthma, he viewed it as a patriotic right to give yourself lung cancer — not that he was sick, or would get sick. He believed that a real man never let a lady pull in her own chair at a table, never mistreated his hunting dogs, and never, ever got sick.

Good code of conduct. The problem was, that was it. Nothing about your kids. The people who worked for you. Your role as a husband. And the Ten Commandments? Just an old list used to govern the lives of other people so that you weren't inconvenienced by them shooting one another up.

It was funny. Courtesy of his father, Lane had never smoked — and not as some kind of rebellion. Growing up, he and his brothers and sister had known whenever the man was coming by the smell of tobacco, and it had never been good news. Consequently, he pulled a tensed-up Pavlov whenever anybody lit up.

Probably the only thing his father had contributed to his life in a positive way. And even so, it was a backhanded benefit.

The ice in his glass sounded like chimes as he walked through the house, and he didn't know where he was going . . . until he came up to the double doors that opened into the conservatory. Even though they were shut, he caught the scent of the flowers, and he stood for a time staring through the panes of glass into the verdant, now-colorful enclave on the other side.

Lizzie was no doubt in there, arranging the bouquets as she did every year the Thursday before Derby.

Moth to a flame and all that, he thought as he watched his hand reach out and turn the brass handle.

The sound of Greta von Schlieber speaking in that German-tinted voice almost made him turn back around. Courtesy of everything that had gone down, the woman hated him — and she was not one to hide her opinions. She was also likely to have a set of garden shears in her hands.

But the pull to Lizzie was stronger than any urge for self-preservation.

And there she was.

Even though it was past eight at night, she was sitting on a rolling stool in front of a table set with twenty-five silver bowls the size of basketballs. Half of them were filled with pale pink and white and cream flowers, and the others were ready to get their due, wet floral sponges waiting to anchor countless blooms.

She glanced over her shoulder, took one look at him . . . and kept on speaking without missing a beat. "— tables and chairs under the tent. Also, can you get some more preservative spray?"

Greta was not so phlegmatic. Even though she was obviously on her way out, with a big, bright green Prada bag up on her shoulder, a smaller orange one in her hand, and her car keys dangling from her grip, that glare, coupled with her abrupt silence, suggested she wasn't heading off anywhere until he went back to his family's party.

"It's all right," Lizzie said quietly. "You can go."

Greta muttered something in German. Then went out the door into the garden, speaking under her breath.

"What was she saying?" he asked when they were alone.

"I don't know. Probably something about

a piano falling on your head."

He took a draw off the rim of his glass, sucking the cold bourbon in through his teeth. "That it? I would have expected something more bloody."

"I think a Steinway dropped from even a short height could do some damage."

There were half a dozen five-gallon plastic buckets around her, each stuffed with a different kind of flower, and she chose from them as if she were playing notes on a musical instrument: this one, then that one, back to the first, then the third, fourth, fifth. The result, in a short order of time, was a glorious head of petals sprouting above the highly polished silver container.

"Can I help?" he said.

"Yes, by leaving."

"You're almost out of those." He looked around. "Here, I'll bring you another bucketful —"

"Will you just go back to your dinner," she snapped. "You're not helping —"

"And you're nearly done with these, too."

He put his glass down on a table full of empty bowls and started hauling the heavy loads over.

"Thank you," she muttered as he removed the empties, taking them over to the ceramic sink. "You can head off now —"

"I'm getting a divorce."

Her face showed no reaction, but her hands, those sure, strong hands, nearly dropped the rose she was drawing out of the bucket he'd brought her.

"Not on my account I hope," she said.

He tipped over one of the empties and sat down on its bottom, holding his bourbon between his knees. "Lizzie —"

"What do you want me to say — congratulations?" She glanced at him. "Or are you in the mood for more of a two-hankie, throw-myself-at-you-in-tearful-relief reaction? Because I'll tell you right now, that's the last thing you're going to get from me —"

"I never loved Chantal."

"As if that matters?" Lizzie rolled her eyes. "The woman was having your child. So maybe you didn't love her, but you were clearly doing something *with* her."

"Lizzie —"

"You know, that exasperated, be-reasonable tone of yours is really flipping annoying. It's like you think I'm doing something wrong by not giving you a platform to talk about alllllll the ways you were a victim. Here's what I know to be true: You came after me long and hard, and I gave in because I felt sorry about what was going on with your brother. At the same time, you were lining up the perfect, socially acceptable beard to hide the fact that you were banging the help. Your problem came when I refused to be your shameful little secret."

"Goddamn it, Lizzie — it wasn't like that —"

"Maybe on your side —"

"I have never treated you as an inferior!"

"You've got to be kidding. How did you think I was going to feel when you told me you were in love with me and then I read about your engagement in the society pages the next morning?" She threw up her hands. "Do you have any idea what that was like for me? I am a smart woman. I have my own farm that I'm paying for with my own money. I've got a master's from Cornell." She pounded on her chest. "I take care of myself. And still . . ." Her eyes shot away from his. "You still got me."

"I didn't put that announcement out."

"Well, it was a great picture of the two of you."

"It was not my fault."

"Bullshit! Are you trying to tell me there was a gun to your head when you married Chantal?"

"You wouldn't speak to me! And she was

pregnant — I didn't want my kid to be born a bastard. I figured it was the only way to be a man in the situation."

"Oh, you were a man, all right. That was how she ended up carrying your baby."

Lane cursed and dropped his head. God, he'd wasted so much time wishing he could do things over with Lizzie — starting way before they'd gotten together, when he'd been having casual sex with Chantal and had believed her when she'd told him she was on the pill.

But everyone knew how that had turned out.

And the pregnancy hadn't been the only surprise Chantal had had in store for him. The second one had been even more devastating.

"So can we be done here?" Lizzie asked as she moved on to the next bowl. "This is really none of my business."

"Why didn't I stay here with her?" He leaned forward. "You've got this all figured out, so why didn't I stay here with her — why've I been gone for almost two years? And if I wanted a child with her, why didn't she get pregnant again after she lost the first one?"

Lizzie shook her head and stared at him. "What part of 'not my business' are you failing to comprehend?"

And that was when he went for her.

As with their first kiss in the garden, in the darkness, in the summer heat, he rode an out-of-control emotion as he took her mouth, the instinct nothing that he was going to fight: One moment they were arguing, the next he'd lunged across the distance, grabbed her by the nape and was kissing her hard.

And just as before, she kissed him back.

It wasn't passion on her side, though. He was pretty damn sure that for her, the meeting of mouths was nothing but an extension of their conflict, the verbal argument going nonverbal.

Lane didn't care. He'd take her any way he could get her.

TEN

It was, of course, a perfectly stupid idea.

But as Lizzie kissed Lane back, it was as if she were funneling two years of anger, frustration, and pain directly into him. And damn him to hell, he tasted of bourbon and desperation and raw sex — and she liked it.

She missed it.

And didn't that just make her more mad. She wanted to say that this was horrible. Against her will. A violation.

None of that was true. She was the one who thrust her tongue into his mouth, and she was the one whose fingers bit into his shoulders, and she was the one, God help her, who brought their bodies up close together.

So that she felt his erection.

His body hadn't changed in the time they'd been apart, all hard muscle and long limbs. And he kissed the same as he had before, rough and hungry in spite of the fact that he'd been raised a gentleman. And the heat was just as hot.

And then, to make things even worse? Memories of them being together, skin to skin, straining, rocking, egged her on, burying all the hurt and sense of betrayal under an avalanche of erotic recollections.

For a split second, she realized that she was going to have sex with him then and there.

Yeah. 'Cuz that would show him she meant business.

Real Gloria Steinem moment.

Instead, something got knocked over on the table and a clatter broke the silence; then a splash draped her hip and upper thigh in a shock of cold water. Jumping up, she shoved him away with such force, he tripped and fell back, landing on the tile floor.

With a slash of her forearm, she wiped her mouth off. "What the hell are you doing!"

Dumb question. More like what was *she* doing.

He was up on his feet a heartbeat later. "I've wanted to kiss you since I came back."

"The feeling is not mutual —"

"Bullshit." He reached for his glass and took a swig. "You still want me —"

"Get out!"

"You're kicking me out of my own conservatory?"

"Either you leave or I do," she snapped, "and these flowers are not going to get into those bowls themselves. Unless you want half your tables empty at your Derby party?"

"I don't care what they look like. Or about the damn party. Or any of this —" As he waved his hand around, it might have been more convincing if he hadn't had a ration of his family's bourbon in that glass of his. "I've left this behind, Lizzie. I'm really done with it."

Motrin. That's what she needed.

Less being around him, more pain relief in a bottle.

"I give up," she muttered. "You win. I'll go."

As she turned away, he caught her and spun her around, dragging her against that body of his. It was then that she noticed how much older he'd gotten since she'd seen him last. His face was leaner, his stare more cynical, and the crow's-feet were deeper at the corners of his eyes.

Unfortunately, it only made him look more handsome.

"None of the crap with Chantal is what you think," he said darkly.

"Even if only half of it was —"

"You don't understand —"

"I was *in love* with you." As her voice cracked, she pushed away from him. "I didn't think we were going to get married necessarily, but not because you were heading to the altar with someone else. Who was pregnant — and got that way while you were with me."

"I'd ended it with her, Lizzie. Before I came back here that April, I told her it was over."

"That didn't stick, though, did it —"

"She was three months along when I found out, Lizzie. Do the math with me. The night before I came home for Mother's birthday at the end of March was the last time I was with Chantal. You and I . . . we got together that May, and it was at the end of June that I found out about the pregnancy. If you remember, I didn't leave Easterly that entire time. You knew where I was every night and day because I was with you." He stared down at her. "Three months along. Not two months, not one month. Three, Lizzie."

She put her hands to her face, fighting the logic. "Please stop doing that."

"Doing what?"

"Saying my name. It gives you the illusion

152

of credibility."

"I'm not lying. And I've wanted to tell you this for nearly two years." He cursed again. "There's more, but I don't want to get into it. It doesn't affect what's between you and me."

Before she was aware of making a conscious decision to sit down, she discovered she was in the rolling seat she'd been using. Staring at her hands, she flexed her fingers, feeling the stiffness in the joints — and for some reason, she thought of Chantal's perfectly manicured tips and smooth, unmarked palms. Talk about your opposites. The hands she was looking at were a workman's, with scratches on the backs from errant rose thorns and dirt under the nails that she would get out only when she was home tonight. There were freckles, too, from digging in the sun without gloves on — and absolutely, positively no million-dollar diamonds.

"I married Chantal at the courthouse after you left me," he said starkly. "It wasn't the baby's fault, and having grown up without parents, I wasn't going to do the same to any kid I had — regardless of how I felt about its mother. But then I just had to get out of town. Chantal didn't get that the marriage was in name only so I went up north to New York and stayed with a buddy of mine from U.Va. It was shortly after that that Chantal called to tell me she'd lost the pregnancy."

The bitterness in his voice made the words so low that she could barely understand them.

"She doesn't love me, either," he muttered. "Didn't then, doesn't now."

"How can you be so sure," Lizzie heard herself say.

"Trust me on that one."

"She seemed pretty excited to have you back."

"I didn't come here for her and I made that clear. And that woman is capable of getting attached only to a meal ticket."

"I thought she had her own money."

"Nothing compared to mine."

Yes, she imagined that was true. There were European countries with lesser annual revenue than the Bradfords had.

"You're the love of my life, whether you're with me or not." When she looked up in shock, he just shrugged. "I can't change what happened and I know there's no going back . . . all I ask is that you don't fall for appearances, okay? You've had ten years around this family, but I've been with them and the people who surround them all my life. That's why you're the one I want. You're real. You're not capable of being what they are and that's a very, very good thing."

She waited for him to say something else, and when he didn't, she looked back down at her hands.

For some reason, her heart was pounding, sure as if she were too close to the edge of a cliff. Then again, she supposed that was the truth — because his words were getting into her brain and shuffling her mental decks.

In ways that didn't really help her.

"I am so terrified of you," she whispered.

"Why?"

Because she wanted to believe what he was saying with the desperation of an addict.

"Don't be," he said when she didn't reply. "I never meant for any of this to happen. And I've wanted to make it right for so long."

It seemed appropriate that they were surrounded by all the flower bowls that she had been filling. The evidence of her work, of her sole purpose in being on the estate, was a reminder of the divide that would always put distance between them.

And then she took pains to recall that photograph and article in the *Charlemont Herald* about the marriage, two grand

Southern legacies joining in a feudal arrangement. And she remembered the days and nights right after she'd found out about Chantal, all those hours of suffering until she'd felt like she were dying.

Although he was right about one thing. Pride had mandated that she continue working at Easterly, and so she had been on the estate every day but Sunday for essentially the last twenty-four months. Lane had not come back. For two years . . . he had not come back to see Chantal.

Not much of a marriage.

"Let my actions speak for me," he said. "Let me prove to you that what I'm telling you is the truth."

In her mind, she heard her cell phone ringing, over and over again. Right after the break-up, he had called her a hundred times, easy — sometimes leaving messages she never listened to, sometimes not. She had taken two weeks of vacation right after she'd found out, escaping even her farm in Indiana, and going back northeast to Plattsburgh and the apple orchards of her youth. Her parents had been so glad to see her, and she had passed those days tending to McIntosh trees with the other manual laborers.

By the time she had returned, he'd been gone.

The phone calls had dried up after a while. And eventually she had stopped flinching every time a car pulled up to the front court.

"Please, Lizzie . . . say something. Even if it's not what I want to hear —"

The sound of a woman laughing softly cut him off and brought both of their heads around to the doors that opened into the garden. When Greta had left, one of panels hadn't shut all the way, and through the opening, Lizzie could see two people walking down a brick path toward the pool in the far corner.

Even in the subtle glow from the landscaping lights, it was clear that the gown the woman had on was a brilliant red, its voluminous folds trailing behind. Beside her, a tall man in a suit had gallantly offered her his arm and was staring down at her with the kind of attention one might reserve for a meal.

"My sister," Lane said unnecessarily.

"Is that Samuel T.?" Lizzie asked.

"Who cares."

She looked back at Lane. "You broke my heart."

"I'm so sorry. It wasn't what I wanted,

157

Lizzie, not in any way. I swear to God."

"I thought you were an atheist."

He was quiet for a time, his eyes roaming around her face. "I'll baptize myself a hundred times if that's what it takes. I'll memorize the Bible, I'll kiss a ring, I'll do whatever you want — just please —"

"I can't go back, Lane. I'm sorry. I just can't."

He fell silent. And then after a long while, he nodded. "All right, but can I ask you for one thing?"

No. "Yes."

"Just don't hate me anymore. I'm doing plenty of that on my own time."

The garden was as fragrant as a woman fresh out of a bath, as precisely arranged as a parlor, and as private as a college library.

Which was to say, it was semi-private. Easterly's many windows overlooked the carefully tended beds of white and cream flowers, all of which were discreetly lit.

Fortunately, Gin had no problem having sex in public.

As she hung on to the powerful arm of Samuel Theodore Lodge III, she didn't bother to hide her smile. "So how long have you been with her?"

"When did we arrive here? An hour ago?"

She laughed. "Why, oh, why, dear Samuel, do you bother with women like that?"

"What other kind is there?"

It was hard to tell who was steering whom into the darker recesses of the farthest corner, where the brick walls met on the back side of the pool house. But that was where they were both headed.

"I didn't know you were coming," she said, reaching up to touch the diamonds at her throat . . . and then allow her fingertips to drift downward over her bodice. "I would have bothered to put panties on."

"Trying to turn over a new leaf, are you."

"I like it when you take them off of me. Particularly when you get frustrated and rip things."

"I'm not in an exclusive club, though, am I."

"Don't be coarse."

"You're the one who brought up underwear. You're also the one who wanted me to come out here with you. Unless you actually needed fresh air for once?"

Gin narrowed her eyes at him. "You are a bastard."

"Not according to the dictionary. My parents were well and truly married when I was conceived." He cocked a brow. "Which I don't believe you can say about your own daughter, can you."

She stopped, the tide turning in a direction she had not intended. "That is over the line, Samuel. And you know it."

"It's a bit odd, you talking about propriety. Aren't you fucking that married partner in my law firm? I believe I heard that somewhere recently."

Ah, so that was why he was acting this way.

"Jealous?" she drawled, her smile returning.

"He can't satisfy you. Not for long, and not the way I can."

When he went to grab her, she let him — and enjoyed the way his hands bit into her waist and his mouth ground against hers. It didn't take him long to lift her skirting up her thighs, and keep it there in spite of all the crinolines.

Then again, he'd been getting under yards of fine material since he was fourteen and going to cotillions.

Samuel T. groaned as he discovered for himself that she hadn't lied about having nothing on underneath her dress, and his fingers were rough as he pushed his way inside of her. The heat and the need that came next were such a blissful relief from everything she didn't want to think about,

160

the sex washing away her regrets and her sadness, giving her nothing but pleasure.

There was no reason to fake the orgasm she actually had, her nails sinking into the smooth shoulders of his tuxedo jacket as she gasped, his old-fashioned Bay Rum cologne such a throwback, it made him way ahead of his time.

As she gave herself up to him, he was the only man she had ever loved — and the only one she would never truly have. Samuel T. was like her, just worse — a soul who could never settle down even as he strolled down the brick pathways of social expectation.

"Fuck me," she demanded against his lips.

He was breathing hard, his body rigid under that expensive suit, ready for her . . . but instead of giving her what she wanted, he stepped back, dropped her skirt, and stared at her remotely.

"Samuel?" she demanded.

With deliberate slowness, he raised his fingers to his mouth and sucked them in. Then he ran his tongue up and down and between them, licking her essence from his skin.

"No," he said. "I don't think so."

"What."

Samuel leaned in. "I'm going to go back to your father's party and sit down at his table. I went ahead and switched the seating arrangement so Veronica is next to me. You'll know when I put my hand between her legs — you're going to see her stiffen and try to keep her composure as I do to her what I just did to you. Watch her face, Gin. And know that as soon as we leave, I'm going to fuck her in the front seat of my Jaguar."

"You wouldn't dare."

"Like I said, watch me, Gin."

As he turned away from her, she wanted to throw something at the back of his head. Instead, she gritted out, "Isn't it Savannah?"

He glanced over his shoulder. "Like I care about her name? The only thing that matters is . . . she's not you."

On that note, he strode off, his fine patent leather shoes clapping out over the bricks, his shoulders set, his head up.

Wrapping her arms around herself, she noticed for the first time that the night was cold. Even though it was eighty degrees.

She should have told him about the lawyer, she decided. Then again, she had picked the doughy little man precisely because she knew that sooner or later Samuel T. would find out.

At least one thing was for sure. Samuel T. would be back. Somehow the two of them couldn't stay away from each other for long.

And eventually, she was going to have to tell him about Amelia, she thought. But not tonight. Not . . . anytime soon.

If that man found out she had hid his daughter from him all these years?

He might just kill her.

ELEVEN

After Lane left the conservatory, the idea of going back to his father's party was utterly unappealing — especially as he heard the quiet gonging that announced dinner was being served. But considering his other option was to go see Edward, he —

"Lane?"

Refocusing, he looked through the archway into the dining room. A tall brunette woman in a pale gray gown was standing in front of one of the antique Venetian mirrors, the view of her bare shoulders as lovely from the back as it was from the front.

Speak of the devil, he thought. But he smiled as he went over to her and kissed her smooth cheek. "Sutton, how are you?"

More like, *what are you doing here?* She and her kin were the "enemy," the owners of the Sutton Distillery, makers of the famous Sutton brand of bourbons and liquors — which was not to say he, personally, had anything against the woman. Traditionally, however, people from that bloodline were *persona non grata* at Easterly . . . in conversation . . . in nightly prayers.

And they were KU fans. So they wore blue, not red, at games.

Now that was something he could actually get worked up about.

As they embraced, she smelled like the rich woman she was, her delicate fragrance lingering in his nose as he stepped back, just the way her perfect body and couture gown flashed again when he blinked.

But that wasn't because he was attracted to her. It was more in the way he'd remember a museum-quality painting or a Duesenberg.

"I didn't know you were coming down this weekend." She smiled. "It's good to see you after all this time. You're looking well."

That was funny, he felt like shit. "And you, beautiful as always."

"Are you staying through the Derby?"

Over Sutton's shoulder, he caught sight of Chantal entering the dining room, her floor-length, brilliant yellow dress sweeping in along with her butter-wouldn't-melt-in-my-mouth attitude.

Only long enough to get papers filed, he thought.

"Lane?" Sutton prompted.

"Sorry. Actually, I have to go back up to New York soon." After all, those poker games weren't going to play themselves. "I'm glad to see you — surprised it's at Father's dinner, but glad."

Sutton nodded. "It's a bit of a surprise for me as well."

"Here on business?"

She took a sip from her glass of wine. "Mmm."

"That was supposed to be a joke."

"Tell me, have you seen . . ."

As she trailed off without throwing in a proper noun, there was, once again, no reason for her to finish the sentence with "Edward." For a number of reasons.

"Not yet. But I'm going to go out to the farm."

"You know, Edward never comes into town." Sutton took another delicate draw off the razor-sharp lip of her glass. "I used to see him a lot back before he was . . . well, we were on the University of Charlemont board together even though I'm a KU fan, and . . ."

As the woman continued on, he had the sense she was not so much informing him of things he already knew, but reliving a period of her life the loss of which she mourned. Not for the first time, he had to wonder what had really happened between his family's golden boy and their competitor's lovely daughter.

"If it isn't the prodigal son returned."

The sound of his father's voice was like a warning shot across his bow, and Lane covered his distaste by taking a drink of his bourbon. "Father."

William Baldwine was almost as tall as he was, with the same dark hair and blue eyes, the same jaw, the same shoulders. The differences were in the aging details, the gray at the temples, the tortoiseshell bifocals, the furrow at the brow from decades of frowning. Somehow, though, those AARP-isms didn't lessen his father's stature. If anything, they just backed up the aura of power.

"Do I need to have a place set for you." Behind those glasses, his father's eyes regarded Lane's clothes with the kind of disdain more appropriate to dog feces in the parlor. "Or are you leaving?"

"Let me think." Lane narrowed his stare. "As much as I would enjoy degrading your table in this button-down, I'd have to be in your presence for at least three courses. So I think I'll take my leave."

Lane put his Family Reserve down on the nearest sideboard and bowed to Sutton, who was looking like she'd prefer to go with him rather than stay.

"Sutton, as always, a pleasure." He glanced at his sire. "Father, fuck you."

With that grenade having been lobbed, he strode through the gathering crowd, nodding at the politicians and the socialites, those two actors from that HBO series he was addicted to, and Samuel T. and his girlfriend of the nanosecond.

Lane made it out to the front foyer, and was almost at the grand door, when a set of stilettoes came after him.

"Where are you going?" Chantal hissed as she grabbed his arm. "And why aren't you dressed."

"None of your business." He shook off her hold. "On both accounts."

"Lane, this is unacceptable —"

"Those words should *never* pass your lips, woman."

Chantal shut her perfectly lined mouth. Then she took a deep breath like she was having a problem tucking her anger into bed for the night. "I would like to spend some time with you this evening to talk things over, and discuss . . . our future."

"The only future you need to think about

is how many Vuitton suitcases you're going to have to pack to move out of here."

Chantal kicked up her chin. "You have no idea what you're saying."

He leaned in and dropped his voice to a whisper. "I know what you did. I know that you didn't 'lose' the baby. If you'd wanted to keep that abortion of yours quiet, you shouldn't have taken one of my family's chauffeurs up to Cincinnati to that clinic."

As she blanched, he remembered exactly where he'd been when the man who'd taken her there had tenderfooted around the reveal.

"No response? No denial?" Lane chided. "Or will those come after the shock of having been found out passes."

There was a stretch of silence, and he knew she was weighing her options, trying to figure out which approach would work in her best interests.

"What was I supposed to do?" she finally said in a hushed voice. "You left me here with no explanation, no support, no money, no way to contact you."

He motioned around at the oil paintings and the Oriental rugs. "Yes, because this is such a damned depraved wilderness."

"You abandoned me!"

"So the solution was to get your figure

169

back and try to seduce someone else, right? I'm assuming that was why you did it — you needed to fit into your size fours again, didn't you, my darling *wife*."

"Lane, you are saying things you don't mean —"

"You killed an innocent —"

Reginald came out of the parlor with a silver tray of used glasses, took one look at the pair of them, and backtracked, disappearing once again into the now-vacant room.

Ah, yes, life at Easterly. Where privacy was less common than diamonds and doled out only in relative terms. But at least he knew he could trust that man even more than he could his own family.

Not that that was saying much.

"I'm not doing this with you here," Lane rasped. "And you are leaving this house. As soon as the Derby's run, your free ride is over."

Chantal arched one of her perfect eyebrows. "Divorce me if you want, but I am going nowhere."

"You have no right to be under this roof after that ring is off your finger."

The smile she gave him was chilling. "We'll just see about that." She nodded to the front door. "Go wherever you like, run away — that's your thing, isn't it. You can rest assured, however, that I will be here when you get back."

Lane narrowed his eyes. Chantal was a lot of things, but delusional had never been one. She was too much of a self-promoter for that.

And she was staring back at him as if she knew something he didn't.

What the hell else had been going on while he'd been gone?

Out at the Red & Black, Edward sat in an old leather armchair in front of a television that was so ancient it still had bunny ears poking out on either side of its cereal-box-sized screen. The room he was in was dim, but gleaming — the result of the countless racing trophies that were crammed into the floor-to-ceiling bookshelves across the way.

The stables' cottage had one bedroom, a bath with a claw-foot tub, a galley kitchen, and this area here, which was a library, study, living room, and parlor all rolled into one. There was no second floor, only an attic full of old horse-racing memorabilia, and no garage. Total square footage was less than the dining room of Easterly — and ever since he'd moved in, he'd learned the value of having a place small enough so you could hear and see almost everything. Back at the mansion, you never had a clue who else was in the sprawling house, where they were, what they were doing.

For someone like him, whose only mistress was night terrors and whose primary job was attempting to keep his brain from cannibalizing itself, the tight quarters were much easier to handle — especially around this time of the year. Such a shame he'd been down in South America right before the Derby when he'd been kidnapped. The anniversary of him getting held for corporate ransom ruined what had always been a most enjoyable weekend.

He checked his watch and cursed. Now that the sun was down, the evening hours presented themselves in a hazy twist, minutes lasting a century and a second at the same time. His night job? To somehow make it to sunrise without screaming.

At his elbow, the bottle of vodka was nearly finished. He'd started off with five cubes of ice in his tall glass, but they were long gone and he was drinking things neat at this point. Last night it had been gin. Two evenings ago he'd had three bottles of wine: a pair of reds and a white of some variety.

During the initial, acute stage of his

"recovery," he'd had to learn the ins and outs of pain management, how you timed your pills and your food so that riding the nerve impulses of a ruined body was not worse than the torture he'd endured to earn his wounds. And that Master's in Medication Management had translated nicely over to this second, chronic part of his "recovery." Thanks to the early trial and error he'd had with the bottles of pills, he was able to arrange things for optimal sedative effect: Every afternoon, he would have a meal of some sort around four p.m., and by six o'clock, when the stables flushed out of employees, he could start drinking on an essentially empty stomach.

Nothing set his quick temper off faster than someone getting in the way of his buzz —

When the knock sounded out, he reached for the handgun beside the Grey Goose and tried to remember what day it was. The Derby was the day after tomorrow . . . so Thursday. It was Thursday night at some hour past sunset.

So this was not one of the prostitutes he paid to come service him. They were Friday. Unless he'd scheduled a twofer this week — and he hadn't done that.

Right . . . ? Or had he.

Reaching for his cane, he pushed himself off the chair and shuffled over to the front window. As he parted the drapes, the gun in his hand was steady, but his heart was pounding. Even though logically he knew there were no mercenaries here in Ogden County looking for him, even though he was aware that he was safe behind all of the locks and the security system he'd installed, and in spite of the forty millimeter against his palm . . . his brain had been permanently rewired.

When he saw who it was, he frowned and lowered the weapon. Going over to the door, he undid the chain, three dead bolts, and the latch and opened up, the hinges squeaking like mice — another warning mechanism for him.

"Wrong client," he muttered dryly at the small blond woman wearing old jeans and a clean muscle shirt. "I order brunettes. In ball gowns."

For a reason he preferred to keep to himself.

She frowned. " 'Scuse me?"

"I only take brunettes. And they are supposed to be dressed properly."

He wanted long dark hair that curled at the end, a gown that reached the floorboards, and they had to wear Must de

Cartier. Oh, and keep their mouths shut. They weren't allowed to speak to him as he fucked them: Although the whores could get the outside almost right, the fragile illusion would be broken the instant their voices didn't sound like the woman he wanted but could not have.

He had enough trouble keeping an erection going as it was — in fact, the only way he could get it up at all was if he believed the lie for the duration it took him to pump his way to an orgasm.

The woman standing on his doorstep put her hands on her hips. "I don't believe I know what you're talkin' 'bout. But I know I'm in the right place 'chere. You're Edward Baldwine, and this is the Red and Black."

"Who are you?"

"Jeb Landis's daughter. Shelby. Shelby Landis."

Edward closed his eyes. "Goddamn it."

"I'll appreciate you not takin' the Lord's name in vain in my presence. Thank you."

He cracked his lids. "What do you want?"

"My father's dead."

Edward focused over her head, at the moon that was rising above Barn C. "You want to come in?"

"If you put that weapon away, yes."

He tucked the gun into the waistband of

175

his jeans and stepped back. "You want a drink?"

As she came in, he realized how truly short she was. And she probably weighed ninety pounds tops — soaking wet while holding a bale of hay.

"No, thank you. I do not abide by alcohol. But I would care to avail m'self of your facilities. I've had a long trip."

"They're over there."

"Thank you kindly."

He leaned out his door. The pickup truck she'd evidently driven here from God only knew where was parked on the left, the engine still ticking after she'd turned it off.

As he shut the heavy weight and went through the procedure of relocking things, a toilet flushed in the back of the house and the water ran. A moment later, the girl emerged and went over to look at the trophies.

Edward returned to his chair, grimacing as he arranged himself. "When?" he asked as he poured the rest of the vodka into his glass.

"A week ago," she replied without looking over at him.

"How."

"Trampled. Well, the doctors say his heart gave out, but it was caused by a trample.

That how you got maimed?"

"No." He took a long drink. "So what are you doing here."

Now she turned around. "My father always said I was to come and find you if anything ever happened to him. He said you owed him. I never asked for what."

Edward regarded her for a long time. "How old are you? Twelve?"

"Twenty-two."

"Jesus, you're young —"

"Watch your mouth around me."

He had to smile. "You're just like your old man, you know that?"

"So people say." She put her hands back on her hips. "I'm not lookin' for no handouts. I need a place to stay and work to do. I'm good with horses, just like my father, and bad with people — so you're warned up front on that one. I got no money, but my back is strong and I'm not afraid of nothing. When can I start."

"Who says I'm looking for any help?"

She frowned. "My dad said you'd need it. He said you'd have to have more help."

The Red & Black was a big operation, and there were always vacancies. But Jeb Landis was a complicated blast from the past — and his kin was contaminated by association.

And yet . . . "What can you do?"

"It's not rocket science to muck stalls, keep the horses in shape, watch the pregnancies —"

He waved away her words. "Fine, fine, you're hired. And I'm just being a prick because, like you, I can't get along with people anymore. There's a vacant apartment next to Moe's over in Barn B. You can move in there."

"Point the way."

Edward grunted as he got back to his feet and he purposely brought his glass with him as he led the way to the door. "Don't you want to know how much I'll pay you."

"You'll be fair. My father said that dishonesty was not in your character."

"He was being generous on that one."

"Hardly. And he knew men and horses."

As Edward went through the unlocking procedure again, he could feel her looking at him and hated it. His injuries were the result of a hell he would have prefered to keep private from the world.

Before he let her out of the cottage, he stared down at her. "There's only one rule."

"What's that?"

For some reason, he took stock of her features. She was nothing like her father physically — well, other than that small frame. Shelby — or whatever her name was — had eyes that were pale, not dark. And her skin wasn't the consistency of leather. Yet. She also didn't smell like horse sweat — although that would change.

Her voice, however, was all Jeb: That twang of hers was backed up by a solid core of strength.

"You don't go near my stallion," Edward said. "He's mean to the core."

"Nebekanzer."

"You know him."

"My father used to say that that horse had gasoline in his veins and acid in his eyes."

"Yeah, you know my horse. Don't go near him. You don't muck his stall, you don't approach him if he's out to pasture, and you never, ever put anything over that stall door if you want to keep it. That includes your head."

"Who takes care of him?"

"I do." Edward limped out into the night, the heavy, humid air making him feel like he couldn't breathe. "And no one else."

As he tried and failed to take a deep inhale, he wondered if all those doctors had missed an internal injury. Then again, maybe the sense of suffocation was the image of this small woman anywhere near that hateful black stallion. He could just imagine what Neb could do to her.

She went ahead of him and grabbed a backpack out of the passenger side of the truck. "So you're in charge here."

"No, Moe Brown is. You'll meet him tomorrow. He'll be your boss." Edward started off toward the barns. "Like I said, the apartment next to his is furnished, but I don't know when the last person lived in it."

"I've slept in stalls and on park benches. Having a roof over me is enough."

He glanced down at her. "Your father . . . was a good man."

"He was no better or worse than anyone else."

It was impossible not to wonder who the woman's mother was — or how anyone could have put up with Jeb long enough to have a child with him: Jeb Landis was a legend in the industry, the trainer of more stakes winners than any other man, alive or dead. He'd also been an alcoholic sonofabitch with a gambling problem as big as his misogynistic streak.

One thing Edward was not worried about was whether this Shelby could handle herself. If she could survive living with Jeb? Working an eighteen-hour shift on a breeding farm would be a piece of cake.

As they came up to Barn B, the motion-activated exterior lights came on and horses stirred inside, clomping their hooves and whinnying. Entering through the side door, he bypassed Moe's office and the supply rooms, and took her to the staircase that rose up to what had once been a hayloft stretching the full length of the massive roof beams. Sometime in the seventies, the space had been converted to a pair of apartments, and Moe had the front one that looked out over the drive.

"You go first and wait for me at the top," he gritted. "It takes me a while."

Shelby Landis hit the stairs at the kind of clip he had once enjoyed but had failed to appreciate, and it felt like it took a hundred thousand years to join her on the upper floor.

And by then, he was out of breath to such a degree he was wheezing like a stuck tire.

Turning away from her, he found that there was no light shining under Moe's door, but he wouldn't have bothered the man with any kind of introduction anyway. With the Derby running in less than forty-eight hours, the man, assuming he was home, would be passed out.

Especially considering one of their two

horses might have to be scratched from the race.

As Edward went across and tried the doorknob to the other flat, he didn't know what he was going to do if it was locked. He had no clue where keys might be —

The door opened wide, reminding him that he was in the minority of paranoids out here on the farm. The light switch was to the left on the wall, and as he clicked it on, he was relieved that the place didn't smell too musty and that there was, in fact, a couch, a chair, a table, and a tiny kitchen that made the galley one he had look industrial by comparison.

"Did your father ever tell you why I owe him?" he said as he limped over to a darkened doorway.

"No, but Jeb wasn't a talker."

Flipping a second switch, he found that, yup, there was a bedroom and bath, too.

"This is what you've got," he said, pivoting around and becoming exhausted as he measured the distance back to the door.

Fifteen feet.

It might as well have been miles.

She walked over to him. "Thank you for the opportunity."

She put out her hand and met his eye — and for a moment, he felt an emotion other than the worm of anger that had been churning and burning in his gut for the last two years. He wasn't sure how to define it — the sad thing was, though, he wasn't sure he welcomed the shift.

There was a certain clarity to having such a unilaterally hostile operating principle.

He left that palm hanging in the breeze as he dragged his body over to the exit. "We'll see if you thank me later."

Abruptly, he thought of the whole don't-cuss, no-alcohol thing. "Oh, one more rule. If my drapes are drawn, don't bother me."

The last thing he needed was for her to find out he cavorted with loose women. And paid them for the privilege. He could just imagine that conversation.

"Yes, sir."

He nodded and shut the door. Then slowly, carefully, executed his descent.

The truth was, Jeb Landis had been the one to turn him around, such as he was. Without that man's swift kick in the ass, heaven only knew whether Edward would still be on the planet. God, he could remember with such clarity the trainer coming to see him in that rehab hospital. In spite of Edward's no-visitors, no-exceptions rule, Jeb had gotten past the nursing station and marched into his room.

They had known each other for well over a decade before that intrusion, Edward's interest in, and ownership of, racing horses, coupled with his previous commitment to being the best at everything, meaning that there was only one man he wanted training his stock.

He would never have predicted the guy to be some kind of savior for him, however.

Jeb's come to Jesus had been short and to the point, but it had gotten through, to the extent it had, better than all the cajoling and handholding had. And then a year after Edward had moved in here, thrown out his business suits, and decided this would be his life, Jeb had told him he was leaving the Red & Black and going to California.

Probably because the bookies up in Chicago wanted a piece of the guy.

In all those years, before and after the kidnapping, the subject of Jeb having any offspring had never come up. But, yes, of course, he would take the man's daughter in.

And fortunately, she looked like she could take care of herself.

So the repayment of the debt was going to come cheap.

At least, that was what he told himself that first night.

Turned out that wasn't true, however . . . not by a long, long shot.

TWELVE

"It cost me a hundred thousand dollars to sit next to you."

As Gin used an antique Tiffany fork in the Chrysanthemum pattern to toy with her food, she barely heard the words spoken into her right ear. She was too busy focusing through the crystal stemware on the bouquet in front her. Samuel T. was off to the left, and with this rose-centric focal point, her peripheral vision could keep tragic track of him and his little girlfriend, Veronica/Savannah.

"So you can at least speak to me."

Shaking herself, she glanced over at the dreaded Richard Pford IV. The man was as his boyhood self had been: tall and thin, with eyes that could cut glass and a suspicious nature that was in contrast to his enviable position in the Charlemont social hierarchy. The son of Richard Pford III, he was the sole heir to Pford Liquor and Spirits

Distributors, a nationwide network that funneled wine, beer, bourbon, gin, vodka, champagne, whiskey, etc., onto the shelves of bars and stores across America.

Which was to say, he could well afford to pay six figures for a specific seating assignment every night of the week and twice on Sunday.

He was swimming in millions — and people hadn't even started to die in his family yet.

"My father's deals are not my own," she countered. "So it looks like you've wasted that money."

He took a sip from his wineglass. "And to think it went to the U of C basketball program."

"I didn't know you're a fan."

"I'm not."

"No wonder we don't get along." KU. She should have known. "Besides, didn't I hear that you got married?"

"Rumors of my engagement were greatly exaggerated."

"Hard to imagine with all your redeeming qualities."

Over on the left, Veronica/Savannah jerked in her chair, her fake eyelashes flaring, her fork clattering down to her plate. As her colored contacts flashed over to Samuel T., the bastard casually wiped his mouth with his damask napkin.

Samuel T. didn't look at his girlfriend, however. No, he was staring over that bouquet of roses directly at Gin.

The sonofabitch.

Deliberately, Gin turned to Richard and smiled. "Well, I'm delighted with your company."

Richard nodded and resumed cutting up his filet mignon. "That's more like it. Please do not stop."

Gin spoke smoothly, although she didn't have a clue what was coming out of her mouth. But Richard was nodding some more and answering her back, so she must have been doing a good job of the social stroking — then again, whether it was conversations she had no interest in or orgasms with men she didn't care about, she'd had a lot of practice faking it.

And yet she was exquisitely aware of what Samuel T. was doing. Achingly so.

His eyes burned as they remained on her. And all the while, just as he'd promised, the tart next to him struggled to retain her composure.

"— saving myself for you," Richard stated.

Gin frowned, that particular combination of syllables registering in spite of her preoccupation. "What did you say?"

"I was set to get married, but then I came to terms with your father. That is why I ended the engagement."

"Came to terms with my f— what are you talking about?"

Richard smiled coldly. "Your father and I have come to an agreement about the future. In exchange for marrying you, I am prepared to grant certain favorable terms to the Bradford Bourbon Company."

Gin blinked. Then shook her head. "I am not hearing this correctly."

"Yes, you are. I have even purchased the diamond."

"No, no, no — wait a minute." She threw down her napkin even though she was not done eating, and neither were the other thirty-one people at the table. "I am not marrying you or anybody."

"Really."

"I am quite sure that you 'bought' a seat at this table. But no one makes me do a damn thing, and that includes my father."

She supposed it was a sad commentary that she didn't question whether her dear old dad could sell her to benefit the family's share price.

Richard shrugged beneath his fine suit. "So you say."

Gin looked down the table at William Baldwine, who sat at the head with total command, as if there were a throne keeping him off the floor and the assembled were his subjects.

The man didn't sense her glaring regard and was thus unaware that this bomb had been dropped — or maybe he'd planned things this way, knowing that Richard would not be able to keep quiet and she might be diverted from making a scene because there were witnesses.

And damn it, her father was right on that one. As much as she wanted to jump up and start yelling, she would not demean the Bradford name in that fashion — certainly not with Sutton Smythe and her father, Reynolds, in the room.

Over to the left, a moan was covered with a delicate cough.

Gin shifted her glare from her father to Samuel T. — whereupon the lawyer promptly cocked a brow . . . and sent an air kiss her way.

"Yes, you can take her plate away," she heard Richard say to the uniformed waiter. "She's finished —"

"Excuse me?" Gin pivoted toward Richard. "But you have no right to —"

"I approve of your lack of appetite, but

let's not chance fate, shall we?" Richard nodded to the waiter. "And she won't have dessert, either."

Gin leaned in to the man and smiled at him. In a whisper, she said, "Don't get ahead of yourself. I remember the days you stuffed your jockstrap with socks. Two pairs because one didn't go far enough."

Richard mirrored her. In an equally quiet voice, he retorted, "Don't pretend you have any say in this."

"Watch me."

"More like wait for you." He eased back and shot her the self-satisfied expression of a man with a royal flush in his hand. "Don't take too long, though. The carat weight of your ring goes down hourly."

I am going to kill you, she thought to herself as she looked at her father. *So help me God, I'm going to fucking kill you.*

As Lizzie took a turn off a country road, the dirt lane she headed onto cut through wide-open corn fields and was barely big enough for her Yaris. Trees stood guard on either side, not in an orderly row, but with a more casual planting pattern, one driven by nature more than a landscaper's hoe. Overhead, great limbs linked up to form a canopy that was bright green in the spring, emerald colored in the summer, yellow and orange in the fall, and skeletal in the winter.

Usually, this processional was the beginning of her relaxation, the quarter of a mile to her farmhouse a decompression chamber that she'd often thought was the only reason she was able to sleep after a day of Easterly's issues.

Not tonight.

In fact, she wanted to look over her shoulder to make sure there was no one behind her in the rear seat of the car. Not that you could fit somebody larger than a twelve-year-old back there — but still. She felt pursued. Chased. Mugged . . . even though her wallet remained in her purse and she was, in fact, alone in her POS.

Her farmhouse was classic Americana, exactly what you'd see on a poster for a Lifetime movie that took place over the Fourth of July weekend: white with a wraparound porch that had on it pots of pansies, rocking chairs, and a bench swing off to one side. Both the requisite red brick chimney, and the gray slate, peaked roof were originals that dated back to its construction in 1833. And the coup de grâce? A huge maple tree that provided shelter from the summer heat and a buffer to the cold wind in the winter.

She parked underneath the tree, which was the closest thing she had to a garage, and got out. Even though Charlemont was hardly Manhattan, the difference in ambient noise was stark. Out here, there were tree frogs, fireflies that had nothing to say, and a great horned owl that had started guarding the old barn out back about two years ago. No highway murmuring. No ambulance sirens. No drifting strains of Bluegrass music from the park down by the river.

Shutting her door, the sound was magnified by the darkness, and she was relieved when she walked forward and triggered motion-activated lights that were mounted on either side of the glossy red front door. Her boots scuffed the way up the five creaky steps, and the screen door welcomed her with a spring of its hinges. The dead bolt lock was brass, and relatively new — it had been installed in 1942.

Inside, everything was pitch-black, and as she confronted the emptiness, she wished she had a dog. A cat. A goldfish.

Hitting the light switch, she blinked as her comfy/cozy was illuminated by soft yellow light. The furnishings were nothing like the Bradfords'. In her house, if something was antique, it was because it was useful and

193

had been made by a Kentucky craftsman: an old wicker basket, a pair of faded, tissue-soft quilts that she'd mounted on the walls, a rocking chair, a pine bench under the windows, the heads of old hoes and spades that she'd found in her planting fields, framed herself, and hung up. She also had a collection of musical instruments, including several fiddles, many jugs, some washboards, and her treasure of treasures, her Price & Teeple upright piano from 1907. Made of quarter-sawn oakwood, and with incredible copper hinges, pedals, and hardware, she'd found the old girl in a barn rotting in the western part of the state and had her lovingly restored.

Her mother called the house a museum to folklore, and Lizzie supposed that was true. To her, there was great comfort in connecting with the generations of men and women who had worked the soil, carved out lives, and passed their survival knowledge on to next generations.

Now? Everything was about 3G, 4G, LTE, and smaller, faster computers, and smarter smartphones.

Yup, because that was a legacy of honor and perseverance to give to your kids: how you struggled to wait in line for the new iPhone for twenty-six minutes with only a

Starbucks in your hand and an online blog about something pointless to pass the time.

Back in her forties-era kitchen — which was that style not because she'd gone to Ikea and Williams-Sonoma and bought lookalikes, but because that was what had been in the farmhouse when she'd bought the hundred-acre parcel seven years ago — she cracked the icebox and stared at the leftover chicken pot pie she'd made Monday night.

It was about as inspirational as the idea of eating paint chips heated in a sauce pan.

When her cell phone started to ring, she looked over her shoulder at where she'd put her bag down in the hall.

Let it go, she told herself. Just . . .

She waited until the ringer silenced and then waited longer to see if there was a call back — on the theory that if it were an emergency with her mother, there would be an immediate re-ringing. Or at least a chirp that she had a new voice mail.

When neither came, she walked over and fished through her purse. No message. The number was one she didn't recognize, but she knew the area code: 917.

New York City. Cell phone.

She had friends up there who called her from that exchange.

Her hand shook as she went into the call log and hit dial.

The answer came before the first ring had even finished. "Lizzie?"

Her eyes closed as Lane's voice went into her ear and through her whole body.

"Hello?" he said. "Lizzie?"

There were a lot of places to sit down in her living room or her kitchen — chairs, benches, sofas, even the sturdy coffee table. Instead of putting any of them to use, she leaned against the wall and let her butt slide down to the floor.

"Lizzie? You there?"

"Yes." She put her forehead in her hand. "I'm here. Why are you calling?"

"I wanted to make sure you got home all right."

For no good reason, tears came to her eyes. He'd always done this. Back when they'd been together, no matter when she'd left, he'd called her just as she was coming in the door. Like he'd put a timer on his phone.

"I don't hear the party," she said. "In the background."

"I'm not at home."

"Where are you?"

"At the Old Site. In the barrel room." There was some rustling, as if he, too, were sitting down. "I haven't been out here for a long time. It smells the same. Looks the same."

"I've never gone there."

"You'd like it. It's your kind of place — everything simple and functional and handmade."

She glanced over at her living room and then focused on the first spade she'd found out in those fields that she planted with corn every year. The thing was old and rusty, and to her, beautiful.

The period of silence that followed made her feel like he was in the room with her.

"I'm glad you haven't hung up," Lane said finally.

"I wish I could."

"I know."

She cleared her throat. "I thought about what you told me all the way home. I thought about the way you looked when you were talking to me. I thought . . . about the way things were."

"And?"

"Lane, even if I could get past everything — and I'm not saying I can — what exactly do you want from me?"

"Anything you'll give me."

She laughed in a tense burst. "That's honest."

"Do I have a shot with you again? Because I'll tell you this right now — if there's any chance you'll have me, I —"

"Stop," she breathed. "Just . . . stop."

When he did, she pulled at her hair, tugging, tugging, so hard it made her eyes water even harder. Or maybe that was happening for other reasons.

"I wish you hadn't come home," she heard herself say. "I wish . . . I was almost over you, Lane. I was getting my breath back, my life back. I was . . . and now here you are, saying things that I want to hear, and looking at me like you mean them. But I don't want to go back. I can't."

"Then let's go forward."

"Like that's so easy."

"It's not. But it's better than nothing."

As the quiet stretched out again, she felt the need to speak, to explain things further, to go into greater detail. But as words jammed in her head, she gave up the fight.

"There hasn't been a night, a day, that I haven't thought of you, Lizzie."

The same was true for her, but she didn't want to give him that kind of ammunition against her. "What have you been doing all this time up there?"

"Nothing. And I mean that. I've been staying with my friend Jeff . . . drinking, playing poker. Waiting, hoping to get a chance to speak with you."

"For two years."

"I would have waited a dozen."

Lizzie stopped with the hair pulling. "Please don't do this —"

"I want you, Lizzie."

As what he said sank in, her heart pounded so hard her she could feel the increase in blood pressure all across her chest and face.

"I've never stopped wanting you, Lizzie. Thinking about you. Wishing you were with me. Hell, I feel like I've been in a relationship with a ghost. I see you on the streets of New York constantly, some blond woman passing me by on the sidewalk — maybe it was the way she had her hair, or the sunglasses, or it was the color of her blue jeans. I see you in my dreams every night — you're so real that I can touch you, feel you, be with you."

"You've got to stop."

"I can't. Lizzie . . . I can't."

Closing her eyes, she started to weep in the solitude of her oh-so-modest farmhouse, the one she had bought and was almost finished paying for, the very best symbol of why she didn't need a man in her life now or ever.

"Are you crying?" he whispered.

"No," she choked out after a moment. "I'm not."

"Are you lying?"

"Yes. I am."

THIRTEEN

As Lane stared across at the old still that had been made by one of his ancestors, he knew he was under the legal alcohol limit to drive a car, but that wasn't going to last. At his hip was a bottle of No. 15 that he'd snagged from a shipping carton, and although he hadn't cracked the seal on it, he had every intention of drinking the thing dry.

All around him, the Old Site was dark, and he'd been surprised that the lock pad and the security alarm had had the same codes as before. Then again, he would have broken in if he'd had to. He felt some compelling drive to be here . . . as if connecting to his family's beginnings would somehow improve where he was at.

He knew he should leave Lizzie alone.

"I'm sorry," he muttered. "I want to say all the right things, do the right things, and I know I'm not. I know I didn't. Goddamn it, Lizzie."

He cocked his head to the side and held the phone between his shoulder and his ear. Picking up the bourbon, he opened the bottle and put it to his mouth.

The idea he'd made her cry again ate him alive.

"Are you drinking?" she asked.

"It's either that or bang my head into a wall until it bleeds."

As she exhaled, he took another pull. And a third.

When he was finished swallowing and the burn down his throat had eased, he asked the question he'd been dreading the answer to. "Are you with someone else?"

She took a long time to answer. "No."

Now he was the one exhaling. "I don't believe in God, but at this moment? I'm willing to call m'self a Christian."

"What if I don't want you anymore? What are you going to do then?"

"Are you saying that's true?"

"Maybe."

He closed his eyes. "Then I'll back off. It'll ruin me . . . but I'll go away."

More quiet. Which he passed by working on his bottle.

"Friends," she said eventually. "That's as far as I'm going. That's all I can do."

"Okay. I respect that."

He could hear the relief in her voice: "Thank you —"

"But," he interjected, "what exactly does that mean?"

"Excuse me?"

"Well, friends . . . like, what is that? I can call you, right? And friends can share a meal now and then so they keep each other up on the news — you know, divorces, moving plans, new directions, this kind of thing."

"Lane."

He smiled. "I love when you say my name like that."

"When I'm annoyed?"

"It's sexy."

Lizzie cleared her throat. "That is not a friendship word, okay?"

"I was merely making a statement of fact."

"Opinion."

"Fact —"

"Lane, I'm telling you right now, you need to . . ."

As she went off on him, talking in her typical straightforward, no-nonsense way, he closed his eyes and listened to the orders, letting the tone of her voice wash over him. Deep in his gut, that old familiar lust stirred, a dragon woken up — and the urge was so strong, he wanted to get in his car and head out over the bridges to Indiana.

"Are you still there?" she demanded.

"Oh, yeah." Rearranging his erection in his pants, he held back a groan. "Yes, I am."

"What are you doing?"

He moved his hand way, waaaaay away from ground zero. "Nothing."

"Well?" she said. "Are you?"

"Am I what?"

"Falling asleep on me?"

"Hardly," he muttered.

There was a heartbeat of a pause. Then a tight, "Oh . . ."

Like she'd caught his drift.

"I better go," he said roughly. "You take care and I'll talk to you tomorrow."

Except now she didn't seem to want him to get off the phone — and his cock was very truly happy about that: "So you're really staying?" she said.

Can we talk about something else, his erection thought.

Down, boy.

"Yes, I am." As he shifted on the hard floor, he tried to ignore the way that zipper stroked at him. "I have to meet with Samuel T. about my divorce."

"So you're really going to . . ."

"Yes," he said. "Immediately. And, no, it's not just about you. I made a mistake, and

I'm fixing it for everybody."

"Okay." She cleared her throat. "Yes."

"I'm only looking forward, Lizzie."

"So you say. Well . . . good-bye —"

"No," he cut in. "Not that. We say good night, all right? Not good-bye, not unless you want me showing up to sleep on your doorstep like a stray dog."

"All right."

Before she ended the call on her side, he mouthed, *I love you.* "Good night, Lizzie."

"Good . . . night, Lane."

Ending the connection, he let his arm fall down, and the phone hit the concrete floor with a crack. "I love you, Lizzie," he muttered out loud.

Taking another draw off the bottle, he thought how convenient it was that his family's fortunes were based on something that could get him drunk — as opposed to the countless other consumer products which wouldn't have helped him in his current situation: pencils, car batteries, Band-Aids, chewing gum.

When his phone went off again, he snapped to and picked the thing up. But it wasn't Lizzie calling him back.

"Jeff," he said, even thought he didn't really want to talk to anybody.

His Manhattan host's voice was dry.

"You're still alive."

"Pretty much." He put the bottle to his mouth again. "How's you?"

"Are you drinking?"

"Yup. Number Fifteen. I'd share it with you if you were here."

"Such a Southern gentleman." His buddy cursed. "Lane, where are you?"

"Home."

Cue the crickets over the connection. "As in . . ."

"Yup."

"Charlemont?"

"Born and bred I was and back to the fold I have returned." Huh. Guess he was getting drunk; he sounded really Southern. "Like you and the Upper East Side, only we have chitterlings and fried chicken —"

"What the hell are you doing there?"

"My . . ." He cleared his throat. "A very important person got sick. And I had to come."

"Who?"

"The woman who raised me. My . . . well, mother — even though she's not my biological mother. She was sick a couple of years ago, but, you know these things. They can return. She says she's going to be fine, though, and I'm hanging on to that."

"When're you coming back?"

Lane took another drink. "Did I ever tell you I got married?"

"What?"

"It was right before I came up north and started crashing with you. I'm going to stay down here until I know Miss Aurora's okay and that dumb idea is taken care of. Plus . . . anyway . . . there's this other woman."

"Hold on. Just, fucking hell, hold on."

There was some rustling, then the *chk-chk-chk* of someone trying to get a lighter to spit out a flame . . . followed by some puffing. "I'm going to need a Cuban to get through this. So . . . there's a *wife*?"

"I told you I wasn't gay."

"And is that the reason you haven't been with anyone up here?"

"No, that's because of the other female. The one I didn't marry. The one who is naturally beautiful and way too good for me."

"I'm going to need a Venn diagram," the guy muttered. "Goddamn it, why didn't you talk about all this?"

Lane shook his head even though his old friend couldn't see him. "I was in running mode." Man, he hated that Chantal had called it right. "It was all too loud in my head. The whole thing. So how's you?"

"You drop all that and cap it with a how'm I?"

"I got drinking to do. Talking is only slowing me down, but I'm free to listen." He swallowed a long draft. "So . . . what's up?"

"I'm good, you know, work is the same. Ten thousand screamers calling, a boss who's up my ass, and sixteen Motrin a day to keep my head from exploding. Same ol', same ol'. At least the money's there — especially now that you're not taking me for a quarter of a million dollars every week across the felt."

They spoke for a while more about nothing in particular. Poker games, Wall Street, the woman Jeff was banging. And even though Lane wasn't much for phone convos, he realized he missed the guy. He'd gotten used to the quick talk, the fast wit, and especially that hint of a Jersey accent where words that ended in "a" were pronounced with "er" and people waited on line instead of in line. And it was "birfday," instead of "birthday."

"So I guess this is good-bye," his old college roommate said.

Lane frowned and pictured Lizzie. Heard her voice. Remembered her caution.

Then he rearranged his persistent arousal. Was there a possibility he might not go back to New York, he wondered.

Then again, he shouldn't get ahead of himself. When it came to getting Lizzie back, it took two to tango. Just because he was ready to resume the relationship didn't mean she was ever going to jump back into things. And then there was his family. As if he could imagine living at Easterly again? Even if Miss Aurora got back on her feet fully and he and Lizzie worked things out, the idea of coexisting with his father was enough to make him think fondly of the Canadian border. And even that wouldn't be far enough away.

"I don't know if I'm staying permanently."

"You can always come back here. My couch misses you already — and nobody plays Texas Hold'em like you do."

The two of them hung up after a set of good-byes, and as Lane did another round with the lax-arm, phone-flopping-down-on-the-concrete-floor thing, he refocused on the ancient still across the way. The thing had been used for decades around the turn of the century and was now an artifact to be viewed by the tens of thousands of visitors a year that came to the Old Site.

For some reason, it dawned on him that he'd never had a job. The extent of his "professional endeavors" was avoiding the paparazzi — which was more about survival than anything you should make a career out of. And courtesy of all his trust fund junkie stuff, he didn't know about bosses, or annoying cube mates, or bad commutes. He didn't think about needing to be somewhere at a certain time, or performance reviews, or headaches caused from too many hours at a computer screen.

Funny, he'd never once considered the fact that he had so much in common with Chantal. The only difference between them? Her family money wasn't enough to keep her in the lifestyle she'd been accustomed to — which was why she'd had to marry him.

And then there was Lizzie, working so hard, paying off that farm of hers. Knowing her, she'd probably hit her goal already.

It just made him respect her even more.

Also made him wonder exactly what he had to offer a woman of substance. Two years ago, he'd been all raging hard-ons and family drama, so hungry for her physically, so captivated by her mentally that he'd never looked at himself from her point of view. All his money and social position were only valuable to people like Chantal. Lizzie wanted more, deserved more.

She wanted real.

Maybe he wasn't so above that wife of his, after all.

Ex-wife, he corrected himself as he kept drinking.

FOURTEEN

"To what do I owe this honor."

As Gin's father spoke, it was a statement, not a question, and the tone suggested that her standing in the doorway to his bedroom was an intrusion.

Too bad, she thought.

"I want to know what the hell you've done with Richard Pford."

Her father didn't miss a beat over at his bureau, continuing to take the gold studs out of his French cuffs. His black tuxedo jacket had been folded once and laid on the foot of the chaise lounge, and his black and red suspenders had been shucked from his shoulders and dangled from his waist like ribbons.

"Father," she barked. "What have you done."

He left her hanging until he'd undone his bow tie and pulled the thing free from his collar. "It's time you settled down —"

"You are hardly in a position to advocate for marriage."

"— and Richard is a perfect husband."

"Not for me."

"That remains to be seen." He turned and faced her, his eyes cool, his handsome face impassive. "And make no mistake, you *will* marry him."

"How dare you! This isn't the turn of the century. Women are not chattel — we can hold property, have our own bank accounts — we can even vote. And we sure as hell can decide whether or not we want to walk down the aisle — and I will not, ever, go on a date with that man, much less marry him. Especially if it benefits you in some way."

"Yes, you will." For a split second, his stare flicked up over her shoulder and he seemed to shake his head as if he were dismissing someone who was out in the hall. "And you will do so as soon as possible."

Gin twisted around, expecting somebody to be standing behind her on the threshold. No one was there.

She refocused on him. "You'll have to put a gun to my head."

"No, I won't. You're going to do it on your own, voluntarily."

"I will not —"

"Yes, you will."

In the quiet that followed, her heart skipped a number of beats. Over the course of her life, she had learned to both hate and fear her father — and in this tense, air-less silence between them, she wondered not for the first time what he was truly capable of.

"You can choose to fight," he said smoothly. "Or you can be efficient about this. You are only going to hurt yourself if you don't do this for the family. Now, if you'll excuse me, I'm going to retire for the evening —"

"You can't treat me like this." She forced some strength into her voice. "I'm not some corporate executive you can hire and fire, and you can't order me around, not when it's going to ruin my life."

"Your life is already ruined. You had a child at seventeen, here in this house, for godsakes, and have followed that up with the kind of promiscuous behavior typically reserved for Las Vegas strippers. You barely graduated from Sweet Briar due to an affair with your married English professor, and as soon as you moved back here, you slept with my chauffeur. You are a disgrace to this household, and what is worse, I get the distinct impression that part of your enjoyment in these exploits is the embarrassment it causes your mother and me."

"Maybe if I'd had a good male role model to look up to, I wouldn't find men so universally unappealing."

"Would that you found *any* of them unappealing. That is not your problem, however. For some reason, Richard is undaunted by your reputation, an error in judgment he will no doubt come to regret. Thankfully, that is not my concern."

"I hate you," she hissed.

"The sad thing is, my dear, you lack sufficient depth for that level of enmity. If you had any intelligence at all, you'd realize that Richard Pford will be able to keep you in the lifestyle that you require as much as air itself for the rest of your days. And you will be ensuring the further success and financial health of the family who gave you those high cheekbones and lovely peaches and cream complexion. It will be, when all is said and done, the only contribution you will ever make to the name 'Bradford.' "

Gin was dimly aware of breathing hard. "Someday you're going to pay for your sins."

"Are you getting religious now? I would think any kind of conversion for you might be difficult even for the likes of Jesus."

"How can you be so hateful? I've never met anyone as cold as you —"

"I am taking care of you the only way I

know how. I'm giving you a fortune at your disposal, a worthy name, and you can even take Amelia with you if you want. Or she can stay here —"

"As if she's a piece of luggage?" She shook her head. "You are depraved. You are absolutely, clinically depraved —"

He bolted forward and grabbed her arm, for once allowing some emotion to escape that aristocratic mask of self-assurance. "You have *no* idea what is required to keep this family afloat. None. Your most difficult task day to day is prioritizing whether to get your hair or your nails done first. So do *not* talk to me about depravity when I am solving a problem for all of the leeches under this roof. Richard Pford's favorable terms will help us continue to afford this." He shook the skirt of her gown. "And this —" He jabbed his forefinger at the necklace around her throat. "And all the other things that you take advantage of every day without pausing to reflect, for even an instant, how they are provided to you or at what cost. Marrying that man is the one and only thing that has ever been required of you in exchange for the blind luck of your birth and the freedom of your avarice. You are a Bradford through and through, capable only of consumption, but sometimes payment must be made, so *yes,*" he spat, "I can assure you that you will become the very happy, very beautiful, and very married Mrs. Richard Pford. You will give him children and be faithful to him, or so help me God, I will spank you like the five-year-old you are. Do we understand each other? Or perhaps you would like a crash course in trying to be like the people who wash your cars, make your food, clean your room, and press your clothes. Perhaps you'd like to know how hard it is to work for a living."

"I despise you," she said, shaking from head to foot.

Her father was likewise breathing hard, and he coughed into his fist. "As if I care. Go have your temper tantrum and kick and scream — it will only prove me right. If you are any kind of a woman, instead of a spoiled little brat, you will wake up in the morning and do your duty for once in your life."

"I could kill you right now!"

"But that would require getting and loading a gun, wouldn't it. Not exactly something you can ask your maid to do, assuming you don't want to get caught."

"Don't under estimate me —"

"Given the low standard you've set for

yourself, that would certainly be difficult to do."

Spinning around, she tripped out of the room, and ran down the hall to her suite. Throwing herself over her threshold, she locked herself in and panted.

Oh, hell no, she vowed. *You are not going to do this to me.*

If he thought she'd been trouble before, wait'll he got a load of what she was going to do now.

As she marched between her bath and her bedroom, plans twisted in her head, many of which involved felonies and her father. Eventually, she had to get out of her dress, and she left the thing where it fell on the floor, stepping free of the pool of silk before continuing to pace in her bustier and her stilettoes and those diamonds that her brother's slut wife had tried to get first tonight.

As she seethed, all she could think about was the very first time she had hated her father . . .

She'd been six, maybe seven, when it had happened. New Year's Eve. She'd woken up because of the fireworks, which had crackled and bloomed over the distant downtown area. Scared, she'd gone looking for Lane, the one

218

she had always taken solace from . . . only to find him down in the parlor with Max.

Gin had insisted on staying with her brothers and doing whatever they did. It had been the story of her life back then, her always running to keep up, get some attention, be on anybody's radar. The household had revolved around her parents and catered to her brothers. She was the footnote, the afterthought, the rug that was tripped over on the way out the door to something better, more interesting, more important.

She hadn't wanted to drink that stuff in the bottle. The bourbon had smelled bad, and she knew it was a no-no, but if Max and Lane were going to have some, she was going to as well.

And then they'd been caught.

Not once, but twice.

As soon as Edward had come into the parlor, he'd ordered her to go back to bed, and she had left via the back way as he'd told her to. When she'd gone down the staff hall, however, she'd heard voices and had had to hide in the shadows or be discovered . . . when her father had come out of Rosalinda Freeland's office.

He'd been in his dressing robe and in the process of tying the two halves together as he'd emerged, and he'd been glaring, as if he were angry — but there was no way he could have heard any of their voices down in the parlor. Gin's first instinct was to run for the front of the house to warn her brothers. Fear had stopped her, though — and then Ms. Freeland had stepped out and grabbed her father's arm.

Her young mind had wondered why the office lady's blouse had been untucked, and her hair, which had always been so orderly and stiff, was at bad angles.

The two of them had argued in hushed tones, saying things that she couldn't hear over the pounding of her heart. And then her father had marched off and Ms. Freeland had disappeared back into her office and shut her door.

Gin had remained there for what had felt like a year, afraid to leave in case Ms. Freeland came back out. Except then she had gotten scared that her father would come back down that way and find her.

He shouldn't have been there with that woman.

He would not be pleased that she had seen him.

In her bare feet, she had whispered to the staff stairs and stuck close to the cold plaster wall as she ascended. Up on the second floor, she had become frozen as another round of fireworks went off, and as soon as they finished, she had taken shelter in the open door of a guest suite, wishing she had somewhere safe to go.

Going back to her room alone had seemed terrifying. Plus what if her father was looking for her?

Curling into a sit, she had tucked her legs up against her chest and hugged her knees. Their father must have found her brothers. There was no way the man would have missed them if he'd used the front stairs.

And that frightened her more than any noise outside.

Moments later, Edward came up the grand staircase, and her father was behind him, looming like a monster. For some reason, her brother's gait was sloppy, and the skin of his face was gray. Her father had been as straight-backed and disapproving as a church pew.

Where were the other two?

No words were spoken as the pair of them proceeded to their father's door. And when they arrived at their destination, Edward stepped off to one side and then stumbled into the dark room as the way was opened for him.

"You know where the belts are."

That was all their father had said.

No, no, she thought. *This was not fair —*

Edward wasn't involved! Why was he —

The door shut with a clap, and she trembled at what was going to come next.

Sure enough, a sharp, slapping sound was followed by a swallowed grunt.

And again.

And again . . .

Edward never cried. He never cursed.

She had listened to this enough times to know.

Gin put her head down on her thin forearms and squeezed her eyes shut. She didn't know why their father hated Edward so much. The man disliked the rest of them, but her brother made him furious.

Edward never cried.

So she cried for him . . . and decided, then and there, that if her father could hate Edward? Two could play that game.

And she was going to pick the one who was at this very minute wielding that belt.

She was going to hate her father from now on.

Refocusing, Gin found that she had sat down on her bed, put her knees to her chest, and linked her arms around herself — as if she were once again sitting just inside that guest room with nothing but a Lanz nightgown to keep her warm, and what was happening in her father's room terrifying her to the core.

Yes, that was when it had started for her — and William Baldwine had never given her cause to reconsider her hatred. This business with Richard Pford was just another entry on a very long list.

But it wasn't the worst.

No, the worst that man had done was something that only she seemed to suspect, something that no one else had brought up, whether it was under Easterly's roof or in the newspapers.

She was convinced that her father was the one who had had Edward kidnapped.

Her brother had been to South America rather often, and as with American executives of his position and stature, he had always traveled with bodyguards and security hired by the BBC. With that kind of coverage, no one should have gotten within twenty yards of the man, and yet somehow her brother had been taken — not on the road traveling, or even at some remote destination.

But from his very hotel suite.

How the hell did that happen?

The first thing she had thought of, when she'd finally been told about the ordeal, was that her father had had a hand in it.

Did she have any evidence? No, she did not. But she had spent her childhood watching that man stare at Edward as if he had despised the very air the child breathed. And then later, when Edward had gone to work at the company, she had had the impression that the relationship between the pair had chilled even further, especially as the Board of Trustees had given Edward more and more responsibility.

What better way to get rid of a rival than have him killed overseas? In a way that would make William Baldwine look like a victim because he was a "mourning" father.

God, Edward had nearly been buried there — and when he'd finally come back? He'd been in terrible shape. Meanwhile, her father had been front and center with the media, the Trustees, and the family, but he had not, even once, gone to see his ruined son.

Disgraceful. And confirmation in her mind that William Baldwine had tried to get rid of a corporate threat he couldn't fire.

No wonder she didn't trust men.

No wonder she was never getting married.

Especially not to make her father happy.

FIFTEEN

When Lizzie arrived at Easterly the next morning, it took her two tries to get the Yaris into a proper parking space — which was a sad commentary on her mental state, considering the car was the size of a bicycle. Getting out, she fumbled with her bag and dropped the thing — and as she leaned down to pick her sunscreen off the already hot asphalt, she realized she'd forgotten to bring her lunch.

She closed her lids. "Damn it —"

"You okay there, girl?"

Lizzie straightened up and turned to Gary McAdams. The head groundsman was walking over the grass verge, his gimp foot barely slowing him down, his weathered face wrinkled with concern — like he was assessing a tractor that was about to lose its wheelbase.

Did she look that bad? she wondered.

Then again, she hadn't slept at all.

"Oh, yeah, I'm fine." She forced a smile. "Fine and dandy."

"You sure about that?"

No. "Yes. How's your team doing?"

"I got the mowin' done, the ivy's trimmed, and I'ma have 'em blow the terrace after ten." Because that was when they were allowed to make that kind of noise around the house. "Tents are up, catering area is ready with the grills in place, but there's a problem."

Lizzie jogged her bag up higher on her shoulder and thought she was so ready to deal with an issue she could solve. "What?"

"That Mr. Harry is wanting to talk at you. There's a problem with those there champagne glasses."

"The placement of them on the tables?" She shut her car door. "Because they're going to be passed, I thought."

"No, they done got only half the order. He thinks you changed the number."

"Wha— why would I do that?"

"He said you was the only person with access to the rental people."

"I ordered the tents, that's it. He's supposed to handle the cutlery and the glassware and the plates — I'm sorry. Am I yelling? I feel like I'm yelling."

He put his paw on her shoulder. "Don't

you worry 'bout it, girl. Mr. Harry drives me stupid, too."

"It's Mr. Harris."

"I know."

She had to laugh. "I'll go deal with him."

"Anytime you get bored of him, I got a shovel and a backhoe. Plenty of open country at my place."

"You are a gentleman."

"Hardly. Gimme your bag, girl. I'll walk you up."

"It weighs nothing. I can handle it." She started toward the pathway that led up to Easterly's servant wing. "Besides, I can use it to hit him over the head if I have to."

"Remember my backhoe," he called out.

"Always."

With every step on the cobblestones, her chest tightened, and the choking sensation got worse as the vast back of the white mansion came into view in the distance.

After having passed the wee hours staring up at her ceiling, she had come to no conclusions about her and Lane. What had stuck with her? The sound of him at the end of that call. She remembered that sexy tone in his voice: It had usually meant he was going to find a way to get her alone and undressed ASAP.

It seemed like a complete and total

betrayal that her body was nothing but *oh, yeah* — as if her libido had been waiting for the return of its master. But come on, she was so much more, so much better, than a stolen orgasm or two with a man she should be handling with barbeque tongs and a fire extinguisher.

Craziness.

When she finally got up to the house, she went through the side entrance of the garden and cut across to the rear kitchen door just so she could check that everything for the party was where she'd left it the night before.

Which was silly. Like a bunch of elves had come in and f'ed everything up under the moonlight?

Putting the staff entrance to use, she walked into the vast kitchen that was, for the moment, clean and cold and empty, just waiting for the arrivals of the chefs who were slated to work from eight to eight. The place wasn't completely deserted, however. Miss Aurora was in front of the industrial stove, an iron pan full of bacon crackling to her left, a second one to the right full of bright yellow scrambled eggs. Four plates were set out on the main island's stainless-steel countertop, along with bowls of fresh raspberries and blueberries, a silver service of sugar, cream, and coffee on a tray, and a basket of some manner of homemade pastries.

"Miss Aurora?"

The woman looked over her shoulder. "Oh, there she is. How you doing? You eat?"

"Yes, ma'am."

"Not enough. You and Lane, too skinny." The cook turned back to her eggs and flipped them around with a red spatula. "You should let me feed you."

"I don't want to be any trouble." There was a grunt of disapproval, and before their usual argument started up, Lizzie cut in, "You're looking so well."

"I told that butler I didn't need no ambulance."

"Clearly, you were right." And Lane must be so relieved. "Have you seen Mr. Harris?"

"In his office. You want me to go with you?"

"So you heard about champagne-gate?"

"I was the one who gave Gary the heads-up 'cuz I knew he'd see you first. Didn't want you to walk in here without being forewarned."

"I didn't switch any order."

"Of course you didn't." Miss Aurora lifted up the fifteen-pound frying pan like it weighed no more than a paper plate. As she

229

portioned out the eggs, she shook her head. "And there's a perfectly good explanation."

"What is it?"

"Not my business."

"Okaaaaay." Lizzie took a moment to give the cook an opportunity to elaborate, but she didn't. "Well, anyway, I'm going to go take care of this. I'm really glad you're up and around, Miss Aurora."

"You're a good girl, Lizzie. But you'd be better if you'd let me make you some breakfast."

"Maybe in my next life."

"You only get one. Then you go to Heaven."

"That's what my father always told me."

"Mine, too."

Walking over the tiled floor, Lizzie pushed open the double flap doors and went down the staff hall. Mr. Harris's office was right across from Rosalinda's, and she knocked on the butler's door. Knocked again. Tried a third time even though it was a waste of knuckles.

Sniffing at the air, she grimaced and thought that the corridor needed some serious airing out. Then again, the Bradfords refused to put central AC or heat in this part of the house. Staff, after all, could suck it up.

Going over to Rosalinda's varnished door, she gave that one a try, too, even though the family's controller was a strict nine-to-five'er, with a thirty-minute lunch at twelve noon precisely and two fifteen-minute breaks at ten-thirty and three. The regimented schedule had seemed bizarre at first, but however many years later, it was just another of the rules and regs at Easterly. And it made sense — a woman who did nothing but pay bills and add and subtract money out of accounts probably had slide rules in her veins and serious control issues.

Thus, her title.

Putting her hands on her hips, Lizzie knew that the butler was probably waiting on the family in the small dining room. Including Lane.

She checked her watch. She was not going to wait for Mr. Harris to come back here, and there was no way she was having this confrontation out in the open. Plus, there was real work to do — she hadn't finished the bouquet bowls the night before.

Heading for the conservatory through back channels, she tossed out the tangle in her brain and focused on what she had to do. After the flowers were finally finished, she could put the tablecloths out because there was no chance of rain or wind before the brunch tomorrow. And she was usually in charge of getting all the glassware and plates where they needed to be at the bars and food service stations around the garden. Greta was due in —

"Good morning."

Lizzie froze with her hand on the conservatory's door.

Glancing over her shoulder, she met Lane's eyes. He was sitting off to the side in an armchair, legs crossed at the knee, elbows on the rests, long fingers steepled in front of his chest. He was dressed in the same clothes he'd been wearing the night before and his hair was a mess, as if he'd slept somewhere other than his bed.

"Waiting for me?" she heard herself say as her heart pounded.

Up in her bedroom, Gin fisted a Prada blouse and crammed the thing into the corner of her Louis Vuitton rolling suitcase. "Tissue paper . . . you're supposed to put tissue paper in here. Where is . . ."

Going on the hunt, she found the pastel pink sheets with her initials stamped on them in a large, flat drawer in her wardrobe room. Back at where she was packing, she licked her forefinger, peeled one free and a waft of Coco tickled her nose — because her maid had sprayed each one individually when they'd arrived. Stuffing the delicate paper around the wad of silk, she backed that up with a McQueen skirt.

Repeating the process until she had four outfits in there, she leaned back and checked out her work. Horrible. Nothing like what Blanche did for her, but she was not waiting until that woman came in for her shift at noon.

Gin was in the process of closing things up when she realized she had no underwear, no shoes, no bra, no toiletries.

She took out a second LV roller, and screwed the tissue paper.

What did she care, anyway. She was just going to buy whatever else she wanted.

When she was finished, she picked up the house phone over by her bed, dialed Rosalinda's office, and couldn't believe it as voice mail kicked in. "Where the hell is that woman —"

A quick glance at the Cartier clock on her desk and she discovered it was just eight-thirty. God, she hadn't been up this early in how long?

Arrangements for the jets could also be made through her father's executive assistant — and that robot was always at her desk. But Gin didn't want him to know she was leaving until she was halfway to California, and undoubtedly his bulldog in a skirt would hop right on the phone to him if she called.

God, that expression on his face last night had made her blood run cold. She'd never seen him so furious.

But, again, she was nothing if not her father's daughter: As with hatred, two were going to play at this game of chicken.

Ten minutes later, Gin pulled out the handles on her luggage and tripped over the damn things as she rolled herself out into the corridor. With her matching monogrammed bag slapping against her side and one of her heels popping out of the back of her Louboutins as she shut her door, she cursed the lack of a bellman.

But she didn't trust that butler, either.

As a matter of fact, she trusted no one in the house.

Before she took the elevator down to the basement level, she went to Amelia's room and opened the door up.

For the first time, the decor truly registered on her.

The pink and white canopied bed was a queen size even though her daughter barely weighed more than a pillow, and there were no Taylor Swift or One Direction posters on the walls. The vanity was French and antique, the en suite bathroom was marble and brass that was sixty years old, and the chandelier in the center was Baccarat and suspended on a silk-sheathed chain below a handmade, gold-leafed medallion.

It was more the suite of a fifty-year-old than someone who was fifteen.

Sixteen, as of last night, Gin reminded herself.

Tiptoeing across the needlepoint rug, she took her favorite picture of her dark-haired little girl, who was now not so dark haired as she was getting blond highlights every six weeks and hardly so little given that she was a sophomore at Hotchkiss.

The mere thought of her daughter made leaving Easterly feel even more right. She had two friends waiting for her in Montecito, and she'd stay out there until the point had been made that her father might run a billion-dollar-a-year corporation but he was not in charge of her. After that? She would come back here just so he could see her on a regular basis and realize his mistake.

Out in the hallway again, she kept the cursing to a minimum as she hobbled down to the elevator and loaded herself in. She broke a nail punching repeatedly at the door-closing button, and nearly snapped one of her stiletto heels off when she got off on the cellar level and had to pull the suitcases out.

She had no idea which way to go. Where the garages were. How to orientate herself underground.

It took her nearly twenty minutes to find the tunnel that ran out to where the fleet of cars was, and when she surfaced in the ten-bay facility, she felt like she'd not just run a marathon, but won it.

Except no car keys. Not in the Bentley. Not in the Drophead. And she wasn't taking the Porsche GTS or the Ferrari thingy or that ancient Jaguar that was like Samuel T.'s — because they were all stick shifts that she couldn't drive. Same with the 911s and the Spyker.

And the Mercedes sedans weren't good enough for her.

"Damn it!" As she stamped her foot, one of her rolling cases fell over like it had fainted. "Where are the keys?"

Abandoning the luggage, she marched down toward the office space. Which was locked. As were the garage doors.

This was totally unacceptable.

Taking out her cell phone, she was about to dial — well, she didn't know who, but someone — when the lockbox over against the wall caught her eye. Going across to the three-foot-by-one-foot metal door, she pulled at the toggle, and was unsurprised when it didn't budge.

The good news? She really felt like hitting something.

Looking around, she saw nothing out of place. From car covers, to spare tires, to cleaning supplies, everything was arranged down the wall with military precision in shelving, on hooks, under container lids.

Except for the crowbar she found leaning against a neat stack of chamois cloths that were monogrammed with the family crest.

Gin smiled as she *clip-clip-clipped* her way over and hefted the hunk of metal up. Back at the lockbox, she swung the thing above her head and had at the key storage like it was her father's head, hitting, hitting, hitting, the sharp ringing sounds stinging her ears.

Even though she had almost no nail tips left by the time she was finished, that cover was hanging open from its one remaining hinge.

The Bentley, she decided.

No, the Rolls. It cost more.

Taking her luggage to the Phantom Drop-head, she opened the suicide door, shoved the suitcases into the back seat and got behind the wheel. Then she punched her high-heeled shoe into the brake, hit the start/stop button, and the engine flared to life with a latent growl.

Reaching up to the rearview mirror, she pushed every button there was until the door in front of her rose up.

And she was off.

The bitch in her made her want to take the front road down so that she passed by the house's family rooms, but it was more important for her to get off the property without anyone knowing — so she settled for flipping her middle finger off at Easterly in that rearview mirror as she used the staff lane.

When she got to River Road, she hung a left, checked the clock and got out her phone. Rosalinda had to be in by now, and she could finally make the arrangements for a jet — which wouldn't be a problem. Gin called for a plane once a week or more.

Voice mail. Again.

The damn brunch. She forgot. All the staff were distracted.

But *she* had needs.

Gin dialed another number, one that was just a single digit different from Rosalinda's. On the third ring, she was about to give up when the unmistakable British accent of that butler came over the connection.

"Mr. Harris speaking, how may I help you?"

"I need a plane and I can't reach Rosalinda. You're going to have to arrange it now — leaving ASAP going to LAX."

The butler cleared his throat. "Miss Baldwine, forgive me —"

"Do *not* tell me you're too busy. You can make the phone call to the pilots directly, you've done it before, and then you can go back to whatever brunch-related stupidity —"

"I'm sorry, Miss Baldwine, but there will not be a plane available for you."

"Are you kidding me." No doubt because of all the corporate guests coming in for the Derby. But she was *family,* for godsakes. "Fine, just delay someone else and I'll —"

"That will not be possible."

"I am first priority!" The Phantom picked up speed as she stomped on the accelerator — at least until she nearly rammed the car in front of her. "This is unacceptable. You call that control tower, or that list of pilots or . . . whatever you need to do and get me a fucking plane to the West Coast!"

There was a long pause. "I'm sorry, Miss Baldwine, but I will not be able to provide that service to you."

A cold warning tightened the back of her neck. "What about later this morning."

"That will not be possible."

"This afternoon."

"I'm sorry, Miss Baldwine."

"What did my father tell you?"

"It is not my place to comment on —"

"What the fuck did he tell you!" she screamed into her phone.

The exhale the man released was as close as he was going to come to cursing out loud. "This morning, I received a memo addressed to the controller and myself, indicating that the resources of the family would no longer be made available to you."

"Resources . . . ?"

"And that includes petty cash, bank accounts, travel and hotel accommodations, and access to the other Bradford properties around the world."

Now her foot slipped off the accelerator, and when the car behind her began to sound its horn, she eased off onto the side of the road.

"I wish there were something I could do to be of aid," he said in a flat tone that suggested that was, in fact, not the case. "But as I stated, I am unable to assist you."

"What am I supposed to do?"

"Perhaps coming home would be best. I just saw you leave in the Rolls-Royce."

"I'm not marrying Richard Pford," she said, and then ended the call.

As she stared out through the windshield, the jagged skyscrapers of downtown seemed daunting for the first time in her life. She had never been impressed with the city of Charlemont before, having been around the world several times. But all that travel had occurred when she had had unlimited resources at her disposal.

With a shaking hand, she took out her wallet and popped the flap. She had five one-hundred-dollar bills and a couple of twenties . . . and seven credit cards, including an Amex Centurion. No driver's license because she always took a chauffeur. No health insurance card because she used concierge physicians affiliated with the Bradford Bourbon Company. No passport, but she hadn't planned on leaving the country.

Two hundred yards up on the left, there was a gas station, and she put the Phantom in drive and jerked out into the rush-hour traffic. When she got to the Shell sign, she cut in front of an oncoming truck and stopped next to one of the sets of gas pumps.

When she got out, it was not to pump fuel. The tank was full.

She took out a random Visa card, put it into the reader and pulled the plastic free. Punched in her zip code. Waited to see if the hypothetical transaction was accepted.

Not Approved.

She tried her Amex and got the same response from the computer. When two more Visas didn't work, she stopped.

He'd killed her cards.

Back behind the wheel, everything went blurry. There were trust funds all over the place, money that was hers . . . but only in two years, when she turned thirty-five, and not one moment before then — something she'd learned when she'd tried to buy a house in London last year on a whim and been turned down by her father: No matter how much she had yelled at her trust company, they'd refused to disperse any funds, stating that she was not allowed access to them until she met the age criteria.

There was only one place she could think of to go.

She hated begging, but it was better than that marriage — or admitting defeat to her father.

Once again in drive, she barged back into traffic and headed in the direction she'd come in. She was not returning to Easterly, however. She was going to —

All at once, the car went dead. Everything stopped — the engine, the air-conditioning, the dashboard lights. The only things that worked were the steering and the brakes.

As she jabbed at the start/stop button, she watched her frantic, impotent action from a distance, noticing absently how ragged her fingernails were, the ends snapped off, the perfect cherry-red lacquer chipped. Forced to admit the engine wasn't coming back on, she jerked over to the side of the road so she wasn't rear-ended and —

Sirens sounded out in the distance and she looked up into the rearview mirror.

The Charlemont Metro Police car that pulled in behind her kept its lights on as it skidded to a halt. And then a second unit settled onto the shoulder in front and backed up until the Phantom was blocked in.

Both officers approached her with their hands on their holstered guns, as if they were unsure whether they were going to need to use the weapons.

"Get out of the vehicle, ma'am," the taller one said in a commanding voice.

"This is my car!" she hollered through all

the closed windows. "You have no right to
—"

"This vehicle is Mr. William Baldwine's,
and you are not authorized to use it."

"Oh, my God . . ." she whispered.

"Get out of the car, ma'am —"

Shit, she didn't have her license. "I'm his
daughter!"

"Ma'am, I'm ordering you to unlock your
doors and vacate the vehicle. Otherwise I'm
going to charge you with resisting arrest. As
well as operating a stolen vehicle."

SIXTEEN

"Of course I've been waiting for you." As soon as Lane spoke, he put out his palms to Lizzie, all hold-up, wait-a-minute. "But only as a friend. Who wanted to make sure you got into work okay."

Damn, she looked good. She was once again in her black Easterly polo and pair of khaki shorts, and her hair was pulled back in a ponytail . . . but somehow, she seemed exotically beautiful.

Then again, it had been over twelve hours since he'd seen her.

A lifetime, really.

As she rolled her eyes, he caught her trying to hide a smile. "I've done the drive a few times, you know," she said.

"And how was it this morning?"

There was a pause . . . and then something magical happened. Lizzie burst out laughing.

Covering her mouth, she shook her head.

"I'm sorry, but you look like hell. Your hair is all —" She waved a hand around his head. "— a mess, your eyes are barely open, and are you aware that you're weaving back and forth even though you're sitting down?"

He grinned. "You should see the other guy."

"Tough, was he?"

"His hood ornament is now his earring." Lane lifted up an arm and flexed his biceps. "Real man over here —"

As a set of sharp footfalls came toward them, Lizzie glanced over her shoulder and muttered something under her breath.

Turned out it was that English butler making a beeline for her — except the guy pulled up short as he saw Lane.

"Will you excuse us, Lane," Lizzie said quietly. "I've got to work something out here."

"Work out what?" he asked the butler.

The Englishman smiled in a way reminiscent of a mannequin at a men's store. "Nothing that you need to be concerned with, Mr. Baldwine. Miss King, if you would be so kind as to come to my office when you are finished with —"

"What's happened?" Lane demanded.

"Just a misunderstanding," Lizzie muttered.

"About. What."

Lizzie focused on Mr. British Holier Than Thou. "The champagne flute order was cut, and he thinks I called Mackenzie's and changed it, but I didn't. I'm happy to help with setup when the stemware and plates arrive, but I'm not responsible for coordinating any of that part of the order. The tents and tables are my job, and they're exactly what and where they need to be."

Mr. Harris's eyes narrowed. "This is a conversation best conducted in my —"

"So it has nothing to do with her." Lane smiled coldly at the butler. "And you're done here."

Lizzie put a hand on his arm, and the contact was such a surprise, it actually shut him up. "It's okay. Again, I'm happy to do whatever I can to help. Mr. Harris, do you want me to go speak with Mackenzie's and try to figure out how to fix this snafu?"

The butler glanced back and forth between them. "I know what I ordered. What I cannot explain is why only half the count arrived here."

"Look, I don't want to tell you your business," Lizzie said. "But mistakes on their end have happened before. What we need to do is find out what else is missing and give them a call. It shouldn't be a problem

— did you put the order in personally or go through Rosalinda?"

"I utilized Ms. Freeland, and I gave her the proper counts."

Lizzie frowned. "She knows how much we order. She's done this for years."

"She assured me all would be taken care of. I assumed that the only explanation was someone else on the account reduced the number."

"You go find her, and I'll get Greta and start counting through everything. We'll get this sorted — at least we found out today and not tomorrow morning."

There was an awkward moment during which the butler said nothing — and Lane wondered how much of the very reasonable plan he was going to have to cram down the little dictator's throat.

"Very well," the butler said. "Your assistance is much appreciated."

As Mr. Harris walked away, Lizzie took a deep breath. "And so we enter the T-minus twenty-four hours stage of things."

"Can't some of the other staff do the counting? It's not your problem."

"It's all right. At least if Greta and I do it, I know it's right. Besides, everyone else on Easterly's staff is swamped, and it's not like the adjunct chefs can spare —"

Lane's phone started ringing, and he took it out of his pocket to silence the noise. "Who the hell is this?" he asked when he saw the local area code.

She laughed again. "You can find out by — brace yourself — answering the call."

"Are you giving me a hard time?"

"Someone's got to."

Lane smiled so wide, his cheeks stretched. "Okay, let's roll the dice and see who it is." He hit the green means go and said in his best Lurch voice, "Yooooou raaaaaaa-aannnng —"

"Lane — oh, God, Lane, I need help."

"Gin?" He sat up in the chair. "Gin, are you okay?"

"I'm downtown at the Washington County Jail. You have to come bail me out — I —"

"What the hell? What are you —"

"I need a lawyer —"

"Okay, okay, slow down." He got to his feet. "You're talking so fast I can't understand you."

His sister took a pause and then said four complete sentences that bottomed him out.

"All right," he said grimly. "I'm coming right now. Yes. Right. Okay. I will."

When he hung up, all he could do was trace Lizzie's face with his eyes.

"What's wrong?" she asked.

"My father had Gin arrested. I've literally got to go and bail her out at the county jail."

Lizzie put her hand over her mouth with shock. "Is there anything I can do?"

"No, I'm going to take care of her. But thank you."

It took all his self-control not to lean in and kiss her like he used to. Instead, he settled for reaching up and brushing her cheek — and leaving before she could marshal a "friends don't do that."

Holy hell, what was his father up to now.

Back when Edward had been a smoker, he had frequently woken up in the morning in mid-reach, his arm and hand going for his Dunhill Reds before he was conscious of having so much as rolled onto his side.

Now he did the same, only he was going for the bottle of Advil.

Shaking four gelcaps into the palm of his trembling hand, he put the pills in his mouth and swallowed them down with the dregs of the vodka he'd taken to bed with him. Grimacing as his version of breakfast headed to his stomach, he lay back on his pillow.

He'd given up smoking during his recovery. Actually, the abduction had been the first step in breaking him of the habit.

Ironic, that nearly getting killed was probably responsible for helping him to live a longer life.

He toasted the bottle into the air. *"Gracias, muchachos."*

Before his brain could get locked into that endless loop of hideous, Day It Happened sequences, he shifted his legs to the floor and sat up. He didn't look at his right thigh or calf. For one, the ragged seams of his Frankenstein flesh were burned into his mind. For another, he didn't sleep naked anymore, so there was nothing showing.

The cane was necessary to get him upright, and his balance was off not just because of the injuries, but the lack of sleep and the fact that he was still drunk. Limping to the bathroom, he left the lights off so the mirror wasn't an issue, and he used the toilet, washed his face and hands, and brushed his teeth.

The confirmation that God still hated him came when he stepped outside the cottage ten minutes later and was blinded by the bright sunlight — and his hangover headache.

What time was it? he wondered.

He was halfway to Barn B when he realized he'd taken the bottle of hooch with him. Kind of like a safety blanket.

Rolling his eyes, he kept going. Miss No-Cussing-Ever might as well get used to him and the booze now — no reason to present her with an illusion of daylight teetotaling that would only get shattered later. If she couldn't deal with his habit, she might as well leave on her first day.

The sound of a squeaky wheel turned his head to the right, and a split second later, Shelby came out of the far end of the barn, her body cocked at the waist behind a tremendous load of horse manure in an old rusty wheelbarrow.

Guess Moe had put her to work already.

"Hey," he called out.

Without losing a beat, she waved over her shoulder and kept going to the compost area behind the nearest outbuilding.

As he watched her, he envied her strong body — and maybe noticed, absently, that the sun on her hair turned the many blond streaks nearly white. She was wearing a navy blue T-shirt, a pair of dark blue jeans, and the same high-quality boots she'd been in the night before. And after disappearing around the lip of the walling, she reappeared twice as fast as she should have, considering the amount of manure she'd had to dump.

So she was efficient, too.

As she approached, her eyes were bright

and alert, her cheeks flushed with the effort. "Almost done. I'll start on 'C' next."

"Jesus, Moe has you — sorry," he said before she corrected him. "Damn, Moe has you working already? And don't tell me I can't use 'damn.' I'll drop the God and the JC references, but that is as far as I'm going."

She let the feet of the wheelbarrow settle on the cropped grass. "Orange juice."

"Excuse me?"

Jeb Landis's daughter nodded down at his bottle. "Y'all can keep the 'damn,' but I'd like to see you with something other than —"

"Have you always been so judgmental?"

"— vodka in your hand this early in the day. And I'm not judging you."

"Then why do you want to change a stranger's behavior?"

"You're not a stranger." She wiped her brow with her forearm. "It's not even nine a.m. I gotta wonder why you think you should have a drink so early."

"I was feeling dehydrated."

"No running water in your house? There was last night."

He sloshed the liquid around. "This does the job just fine. Think of it as my version of vitamin C."

She muttered something under her breath as she leaned back down to the handles.

"What did you say?" he demanded.

"You heard me."

"No, I didn't." Which was not exactly true.

Shelby just shrugged and kept going, that body of hers moving underneath her simple clothes, performing its duty without any apparent discomfort.

And then it dawned on him. "Shelby."

She paused and glanced over her shoulder. "Yes?"

"You said you'd gotten all the horses."

"Yup."

"In A and B."

"Yup."

He hustled over and grabbed her arm. "I told you. One rule. You don't go in my stallion's stall."

"Ain't going to muck itself —"

His hand squeezed down hard of its own volition. "He killed a stable hand a year ago. Trampled him to death in there. Don't ever do that again."

Those sky-blue eyes of hers got wide. "He was fine with me."

"I'm the only one who goes in there. Do we understand each other? You do that one more time, I'll pack your shit up," he said deliberately, "and send you back where you came from."

"Yessir."

He stepped away and tried not to stumble. "Okay, then."

"All right."

She blew a stray hair out of her face and resumed her trek, her shoulders as tense as her walk.

Uncapping the vodka, Edward took a long pull off the bottle, and probably should have stopped to notice how the liquor didn't sting at all.

But that was yet another thing he didn't want to think about.

Just like anything happening to Jeb Landis's daughter on his watch.

Damn it.

SEVENTEEN

The Washington County Courthouse and Jail was a complex of modern buildings that took up two entire city blocks downtown, the facility's halves linked by a pedi-way that stretched over the traffic below. There were a number of entrances, and as Lane pulled up in his Porsche, countless people were streaming in and out of them, men and women in suits striding up and down the marble steps, officers in patrol cars and sheriff's SUVs parking and unparking in specially marked spots, people with ratty clothes smoking on the fringes.

His 911 Turbo let out a low cough as he decelerated and stared up at the looming buildings. No logical layout that he could see. No street addresses, either.

Like if you had to ask where to go, you didn't belong there —

From out of nowhere, a uniformed African-American man stepped directly in front of his car.

"Shit!" Lane nailed the brakes hard. "What the hell are you — Mitch?"

Deputy Sheriff Mitchell Ramsey didn't answer. He just pointed to a marked spot directly behind him that was vacant.

As Lane shot forward and parallel parked on the first try, he was aware of the deputy standing right along his bumpers, arms thick as cruise-ship ropes crossed over the chest of a professional football player. Those dark eyes were hidden behind a pair of Ray Bans, and his shaved head made his neck and shoulders look even bigger than they were.

Lane uncurled his body from the sports car. "Hey, do you know where my sister —"

"I gotchu."

The two of them clapped palms and went in for a hard embrace. As they stood chest to chest, Lane was transported back to nearly two years prior, to the private airstrip west of town, to the night when Edward had finally come home from his captivity.

Mitch had brought him back to the States. Back to the family.

God only knew how. No one had ever asked the details, and Lane had always had the sense that the former Army Ranger wouldn't have shared the how's and who's anyway.

"She's not doing well in there," Mitch said.

"Not surprised."

Lane followed the sheriff, the pair of them taking the fifty steps up to one of the many revolving entrances two at a time. When they got in range, Mitch routed them over to something marked LAW ENFORCEMENT ONLY and then the man barged them through security, the other officers waving them past with nods of respect.

"I worked fast as soon as I saw the name," Mitch said as their footsteps joined all the others echoing into the high ceiling of the main concourse. "She's up for stolen vehicle, no license, no proof of insurance —"

"How the hell did this happen?"

"— and resisting arrest. I've already quarantined the incident, but I can't keep it off the police blotter indefinitely."

"Wait." Lane pulled the man to a halt. "My sister stole a car?"

"Rolls-Royce. Registered in the Bradford Bourbon Company name."

"You mean . . . our Rolls. The Phantom Drophead?"

"Your father called the Metro Police

personally and told them to pick her up, stating that she did not have permission to operate the vehicle."

"You can't be serious." Lane dragged a hand through his hair. "What am I saying — of course he can do that. He's done worse."

"You got a lawyer?"

"Samuel T. should be here —"

"Lane," came a shout.

Samuel T. strode through the teeming crowd, standing out for so many reasons. For one, his blue and white seersucker suit made him look like he should have been on the grand porch of his gentleman's farm, sipping a mint julep with a pair of hunting dogs asleep at his feet. For another, he was too good-looking to be among mortals.

"Thanks for coming quick," Lane said as they shook hands. "You know Mitch —"

"Certainly do. Deputy."

"Mr. Lodge."

With the greetings over, the three of them made fast time to escalators that went up to the open second floor.

"She's in general." Mitch led the way to the pedi-way. "But I've cleared the delays for her bail hearing. As soon as you're ready, Mr. Lodge —"

"Call me Samuel or Sam."

"Samuel." Mitch nodded. "Soon as you're ready, I'll slide her in with Judge McQuaid. I've spoken with the prosecutor. His hands are tied, especially with Mr. Baldwine pushing as hard as he is. The only thing I can really do is expedite, expedite, expedite."

Lane gritted his molars. Gin was a lot to handle, and clearly, their father had had it with her — but this was so damned public. "I'm going to owe you for this one, Mitch."

"Not the way I see it."

The deputy got them through the various security points, and then they were in the jail portion of the facility. Although Lane had pulled a number of less-than-legal stunts as a kid, all of his transgressions had been discreetly "taken care of." So this was his first trip into the county clink, and he couldn't say he was in a big hurry to ever come back.

The waiting area had cream concrete walls. Cream floor. Plastic chairs in orange and yellow and red. The smell in the air was old sweat, dirty clothes, and Lysol.

Thanks to Mitch, they steamed right over to the registration counter with its bulletproof glass windows and lineups of officers with their various catches of the day. Talk about a wake-up call on the other half. Oily men and stringy young boys . . . barely clothed working girls . . . seedy, worn-out older women . . . all of them stood or weaved in place next to their arresting officers, their faces showing the grind of hard lives lived badly.

"Over here, Deputy Ramsey," someone called out by a reinforced door.

After going through the checkpoint, they headed by a number of conference rooms that had red lights above the entrances and bars over little chicken-wired windows.

"If you'll wait in here," the officer said by one of the rooms, "I'll bring her down."

"Thanks, Stu." Mitch opened the door and stood to the side. "I'll be out here."

"Much appreciated." Lane clapped the guy on the shoulder. "And we're probably going to need more of your help."

"Anything you want, I'm here."

Samuel T. paused by the deputy. "Has anyone talked to the press yet?"

"Not on our side," Mitch replied. "And I'll try to keep it that way."

"My sister doesn't have the best reputation." Lane shook his head. "The fewer people who know about this, the better."

Mitch closed them in together, and although there were four chairs bolted to the floor around a steel table that was likewise secured, Lane couldn't sit down.

Samuel T. did, though, putting his ancient briefcase to the side and steepling his hands.

The attorney shook his head. "She's going to be pissed to high heaven you brought me here."

"Like I'd call anyone else?" Lane rubbed his aching eyes. "And after this, you're still helping me with my divorce, right?"

"Just another busy morning with the Bradfords."

At least they let her keep her own clothes on, Gin thought as she was led down yet another concrete corridor painted the color of month-old vichyssoise.

She'd had a terror of undressing in front of some hairy-chested female officer and then getting violated by a gloved hand before being thrown into an orange jumpsuit the size of a circus tent. When that had not happened, she'd then become obsessed about being put in some kind of filthy holding cell with a bunch of drug-addled prostitutes coughing AIDS all over her.

Instead, she'd been put in a cell by herself. A cold cell, with just a bench and a stainless-steel toilet with no seat or toilet paper.

Not that she would ever use something like that.

Her diamond stud earrings and her

Chanel watch had been confiscated, along with her LV bag, her phone, and those hundred-dollar bills and useless credit cards she had in her wallet.

One call. That was all she'd been allowed — just like in the movies.

"In here," the guard said, stopping by an African-American man in uniform and opening a thick door.

"Lane — !" Except she stopped rushing toward her brother when she saw who was sitting at the table. "Oh, God. Not him."

Lane came in for a tight embrace as the door was shut. "You need a lawyer."

"And I'm free," Samuel T. drawled. "Relatively speaking."

"I am not talking in front of him." She crossed her arms over her chest. "Not one word."

"Gin —"

Samuel T. cut her brother off. "Told you. Guess I'll just take my things and go."

"Sit. Down," Lane barked. "Both of you."

There was a heartbeat of silence — which Gin took as a sign that Samuel T. was as surprised by that tone of command as she was. Lane had always been, out of the four Baldwine children, the go-with-the-flow type. Now, he sounded like Edward.

Or the way Edward had used to be.

After she settled uneasily in a chair as hard and chilly as an ice block, Lane jabbed a finger in her direction. "What did you do?"

"Excuse me?" she said on a recoil. "Why is this my fault? Why do you think it was me —"

"Because it usually is, Gin." He slashed his hand through the air when she started to argue. "Cut the shit, I've known you too long. What did you do this time to piss him off? I will get you out of this, but I gotta know what I'm dealing with."

As Gin glared up at her brother, she wanted nothing more than to tell him to fuck off. But all she could think of was that image of her credit cards going into the slot of that gas pump and the words *Not Approved* flashing on the digital screen. Who else was going to help her?

She glanced over at Samuel T. He wasn't looking at her, and his face was impassive, but the haughty disapproval he was enjoying was as obvious as the scent of his cologne in the air.

"Well?" Lane demanded.

Weighing her options, she realized she was wholly unfamiliar with situations involving rocks and hard places. With enough money and amnesia, there was nothing she'd been unable to opt out of, whether it was through paying someone off, refusing to stay, or refusing to go.

Unfortunately, those endless arrays of options had been funded by a lifestyle that had only looked like something that was hers. In fact, it had been owned by someone else. She simply hadn't known that until this morning.

She cleared her throat. "Samuel T., will you . . . give me a moment alone with my brother." She put her hand out. "I'm not — I'm not saying you can't be my lawyer, I just need to be in private with him. Please."

Samuel T. cocked a brow. "First time I've heard you say that word. At least with your clothes on."

"Watch it, Lodge," Lane growled. "That's my sister."

The man shook himself, as if he'd forgotten he wasn't alone with her. "My apologies. That was inappropriate."

"Don't go far." Lane started pacing around, his hand yanking at his short, dark hair. "For the love of God, we need good representation."

As Gin's attorney, lover, and baby daddy — though he didn't know that last part — left, she stared down at the pointed toes of her silk stilettos. The left one had a smudge running across the top of the toe box, something she'd gotten while sliding herself into the back of the cop car.

There was a *click* as the door shut behind Samuel T., and she didn't wait for another prompting. "He wants me to marry Richard Pford."

"Richard . . . I'm sorry, what?"

"You heard me. Father is cutting me off unless I marry the man. He says it's because that goddamn distributing company will give us better rates or something."

"Is he insane?" Lane breathed.

"You wanted to know why I took the car — that's why I took the car, and that's why Father called the police." She looked up at her brother. "I'm not marrying Richard. No matter what our father does to me — and that is what you're dealing with."

Getting up, she went over to the door and opened it herself. "You can come back in."

"Such an honor," Samuel T. murmured.

As her lawyer resettled in the chair by his briefcase, she said, "So how do I get out of here."

"You make bail," Samuel T. replied. "And then we try to get the charges dropped, either because we plea you out or your father gets over whatever you've done."

"What kind of bail are we talking about?" Lane asked.

"First-time offender works in her favor, the flight risk does not. Only about fifty grand, tops. McQuaid is a friendly judge to people like us, so it's not going to be high."

Fifty thousand dollars, she thought. Indeed, that had never seemed like much before. Nothing but a trip to Chanel in Chicago.

She thought of what little was in her purse. "I don't have that kind of money."

Samuel T. laughed. "Of course you do —"

"I'll make sure it's paid," Lane cut in.

Samuel T. opened his briefcase and took out some papers. "Do you authorize me to represent you in this matter, Virginia?"

Since when did he call her by her proper name? Then again, maybe he didn't want her brother to pound him into the concrete floor by any further familiarity. "Yes."

His eyes, those piercing gray eyes, held her stare. "Sign this." After she did, he muttered, "Don't worry, I'll get you out of here."

Her breath rattled in her chest as she exhaled. "But then what."

What exactly was going to be different on the other side of all this? It wasn't like her father was suddenly going to turn over a new leaf. Edward had barely survived William Baldwine's willingness to choose business over his children.

"We get you out first," Lane said. "Then we'll deal with the rest of it."

Glancing at her brother, she realized she had never seen him so serious before: As he leaned against the bare wall of the ugly little square room, he was so much older than when he'd left two years ago, so much more in command.

She had grown to expect such authority from Edward; never Lane, the Playboy.

"He's going to win," she heard herself say. "Father always wins."

"Not this time," Lane gritted out.

"What the hell is going on here?" Samuel T. asked.

Lane just shook his head. "You take care of this, Samuel. You just get my sister out of here. I'll handle the rest."

God, she hoped that was true. Because clearly her attempt at crossing their father hadn't gone so well.

EIGHTEEN

As Lane came to a halt in front of Easterly's front entrance, he hit the brakes on the Porsche so hard that he dragged half of the drive's cobblestones with him into a park. He didn't kill the engine; just got out and flew up the stone steps, passing through the double doors like a draft.

Nothing registered as he entered the mansion, not the maid cleaning the parlor. Or the butler who spoke to him. Not even his Lizzie, who stepped into his path as if she had been waiting for his appearance.

Instead, he left the house through the door at the base of the dining room and strode for the business center, crossing through the orderly arrangement of round tables under the tent and then dodging the groundskeepers who were stringing lights in the blooming trees.

His father's place of business had a terrace onto which a series of French doors opened out, and he headed for the pair that was all the way down on the left. When he got to them, he didn't bother trying the handle, because it would be locked.

He banged on the glass. Hard.

And he didn't stop. Not even as he felt a wetness on the outside of his hand, which seemed to indicate he'd broken something —

Oh . . . he'd smashed the glass out of the first pane of his father's office and moved on to another.

The good news, he thought, was there were plenty more where that came from.

"Lane! What are you doing?"

He stopped and turned his head toward Lizzie. In a voice he didn't recognize, he said, "I need to find my father."

William Baldwine's exceedingly professional executive assistant raced into the office and her gasp came through loud and clear through the shattered glass.

"You're bleeding!" the woman exclaimed.

"Where is my father."

Ms. Petersberg unlatched the door and opened things up. "He's not here, Mr. Baldwine, he's gone to Cleveland for the day. He just left, and I'm not sure when he'll be back. Was there something you needed?"

As her eyes went to the blood dripping off

his knuckles, he knew she was heading in a may-I-bring-you-a-hand-towel direction, but he didn't care if his veins emptied all over the place.

"Who told my father Gin left?" he demanded. "Who called him? Was it you? Or a spy in that house —"

"What are you talking about?"

"Or did you call the police on my sister? I know for a fact my father wouldn't know how to dial nine-one-one himself even though they said he did."

The woman's eyes flared, and then she whispered, "He told me she was going to hurt herself. That she was going to try to leave this morning, and that I had to do what I could to stop her. He said that she needs help —"

"Lane!"

He whipped his head around to Lizzie just as things went off-balance, his body listing to one side.

With a strong hold, she caught him, and kept his weight off the ground. "Come on. Back to the house."

As he let himself get rerouted, blood fell to the flagstone terrace, speckling the gray with dark red spots. Glancing back at the assistant, he said, "You tell my father I'm waiting for him."

"I don't know when he's returning."

Bullshit, he thought. The woman scheduled William down to his bathroom breaks. "And I'll be here until Hell freezes over."

There was so much rage in him, he was blind to his surroundings as Lizzie guided him off. The fury was about Edward. And Gin. His mother.

Max —

"When was the last time you ate anything?" Lizzie said as she muscled him through a doorway into Easterly.

For a moment, he felt like he was hallucinating. And then he realized all the men and women in white were chefs, and that he and Lizzie were in the kitchen.

"I'm sorry, what?" he mumbled.

"Food. When."

He opened up his mouth. Closed it. Frowned. "Noontime yesterday?"

Miss Aurora entered his field of vision. "Lands, what is wrong with you, boy."

There was some conversation at that point, none of which he tracked. Followed by a bandaging of his hand which he didn't pay attention to. Then more talk.

He didn't come back online properly until he was sitting in the staff break room, at the table, with a plate of scrambled eggs, six slices of bacon, and four pieces of toast in front of him.

Lane blinked as his stomach roared: Even as his brain remained a mess, his hand picked up the fork and started shoveling.

Lizzie sat down across from him, her chair squeaking on the bald wooden floor. "Are you okay?"

He glanced past her to Miss Aurora, who was standing by the door as if she were about to leave. "My father is an evil man."

"He's got his own set of values."

Which was the closest she would get to ever condemning anyone.

"He's trying to sell my sister." Cue the gasps. "It's like . . . out of a bad novel."

He was in the middle of sharing the details when his phone went off — and the second he saw who it was, he answered. "Samuel, where are we?"

Samuel T. had to raise his voice over the chatter in the background. "Seventy-five thousand for the bail, it's the best we could do. As soon as you bring a certified check, you can pick her up."

"I'm on it. Are you leaving?"

"Not until she gets out of here. She has the right to consult with her attorney, so as long as I'm around, she won't have to be in some cell alone — or God forbid, with someone else."

"Thanks."

As he cut the connection, Miss Aurora ducked out to keep an eye on her chefs, and he turned to Lizzie. "I'm going to go get the bail money now. After that . . . I don't know what."

She reached out and put her hand on his forearm. "As I said before, is there anything I can do?"

It was like a strike of lightning. One minute, he was as normal as any male could be in the situation . . . the next? Lust pumped through his veins, hardening him, rechanneling the crazy in his head into something truly insane.

Lowering his lids, he muttered, "You sure you want me to answer that."

Lizzie swallowed hard and looked down at where she was touching him. When she didn't say anything, but she also didn't pull away, he leaned in and lifted her chin with his forefinger. Locking eyes on her lips, he kissed her in his mind, picturing himself dipping down and putting his mouth on hers. Pushing her back into that hard chair. Getting under her clothes as he knelt down between her legs with —

"Oh . . . God," she whispered, her eyes avoiding his.

But still, she didn't turn away.

Lane licked his lips. Then he dropped his hand and eased out of range. "You need to go. Now. Or I'm going to do something you'll regret."

"What about you?" she whispered. "Would you regret it?"

"Kissing you? Never." He shook his head, recognizing that his emotions were all over the place . . . as well as completely out of control. "But I won't touch until you ask me to. That much I can promise."

After a moment, she got up with none of her usual grace, the chair she'd been in skipping over the floor, her feet tripping. He gave her enough time to get out of the break room and go some distance down the hall before he went to leave himself.

Any closer and he was liable to grab her, put her up on the table and give them both the release they needed.

Because she did want him. He had seen it for himself just now.

Not that he could dwell on that.

He had to go get his father to pay the bail — it wasn't that Lane didn't have the money. He had plenty of poker winnings, and unlike his sister, he was thirty-six, so he had that first level of access to his trusts. But William Baldwine had created this mess, and the fact that the man was out of town on business was going to make cutting the check and having it certified at the bank all the easier.

A minute later, Lane was at the controller's office and he didn't bother knocking, just went for the doorknob.

Locked.

Just as he'd done on his father's glass, he pounded on the stout oak — with his uninjured hand.

"Is she not in?" Mr. Harris inquired from the doorway of his own suite.

"Where's the key to this door?"

"I'm not permitted to open —"

Lane wheeled around. "You get the fucking key or I'm going to break the goddamn thing down."

What do you know. A split second later, the butler came over with a heavy hunk of old brass. "Allow me, Mr. Baldwine."

Except the key didn't get them anywhere. It went into the mechanism just fine, but there was no turning it.

"I'm terribly sorry," the butler said as he jimmied things around. "It appears to have jammed."

"Are you sure that's the right key?"

"It is marked here." The man flashed the little tag that hung off the ornate end. "Perhaps she will be in shortly."

"Let me try."

Lane moved the penguin suit out of the way, but got nowhere with the key, either. Losing his patience, he put his shoulder to the panels, and —

The crack of splintering wood drowned out his shout of rage, and he had to catch the panels as they bounced back at him —

"What the hell!" he barked as he pulled a Dracula and recoiled from the stench.

As Mr. Harris started to cough and had to tuck his face into the lapel of his jacket, someone else said, "Oh, dear Lord, what is that —"

"Get everyone out of the hall," Lane ordered the butler. "And make sure they stay away."

"Yes, yes, of course, Mr. Baldwine."

Lane put his forearm back up and breathed into his shirt sleeve as he leaned inside. The office was impossibly dark, the heavy curtains having been pulled shut against the bright sunlight, the air-conditioning unit in one of the windows likewise turned off. Patting around the doorjamb with his free hand, he had a feeling about what he was going to find and couldn't believe it.

Click.

Rosalinda Freeland was sitting in the

stuffed chair in the farthest corner, her face frozen in a gruesome smile, her gray fingers dug into the padded, chintz-covered cushions, her unblinking eyes staring straight ahead at whatever version of the afterlife had come upon her.

"Jesus . . ." Lane breathed.

Her professional suit and skirt were perfectly arranged, her reading glasses hanging from a gold chain on her silk blouse, her sensible salt-and-pepper bob mostly arranged well. The shoes didn't make sense. No somber black leather flats, as she had always worn, but a pair of Nikes, as if she were about to go on a power walk.

Shit, he thought.

Jamming his hand into his pocket, he took out his phone and dialed the only person he could think to call. And as the sound of electronic ringing purred in his ear, he looked around the office. There was no clutter anywhere, which was what he could recall of the woman who had been working at Easterly for thirty years: The desk with its computer and its green-shaded lamp had nothing else on it, and the bookshelves that discreetly hid the other office equipment and files were tidy as a library's.

"—llo?" came the voice on his cell phone.

"Mitch," Lane said.

"You coming down with a check for her bail?"

"I got a problem."

"What can I do?"

Lane closed his eyes and wondered how in the hell he'd lucked out to have the guy on his side. "I'm staring at the dead body of my family's controller."

Instantly, the deputy's voice dropped an octave. "Where."

"In her office at Easterly. I think she may have killed herself — I just busted through the door."

"Have you called nine-one-one?"

"Not yet."

"I want you to call it in now while I head your way — so it's in the log properly and Metro Police can come. They'll have jurisdiction."

"Thanks, man."

"Do *not* touch anything."

"Only the light switch as I came in."

"And do not let anyone enter the room. I'll be there in five."

As Lane ended the connection and dialed emergency services, his eyes traced those shelves and he thought of all the work that had been done by the woman in this little office.

"Yes, my name is Lane Baldwine. I'm calling from Easterly." The mansion didn't have a street number. "There's been a death in the house . . . yes, I'm very sure she is no longer living."

He paced around as he answered a couple of questions, confirmed his phone number, and then hung up again.

Glancing over at the desk, he respected Mitch's orders, but he had to get the household checkbook. Dead body or no dead body, he still needed to free Gin from jail.

Taking out his handkerchief, he walked across the Oriental carpet. He was about to pull open the flat drawer in the center when he frowned. Sitting in the middle of the leather blotter, perfectly aligned as if set there with a ruler . . . was a USB drive.

"Mr. Baldwine? Shall I do aught?" Mr. Harris called to him.

Lane glanced over at the corpse. "The police are on their way. They don't want anything disturbed in here so I'm coming out now."

He picked up what Rosalinda had so obviously left for whoever found her. Then he opened that drawer and snagged the eight-and-a-half-by-eleven leather-bound checkbook, tucking it into the small of his back and covering the thing with his shirt.

He turned back to the controller. That expression on her face was like the Joker's, a horrible grimace that was going to show up in his nightmares for a long time.

"What has my father done now," he whispered into the death-stained air.

Nineteen

Lizzie was in the glass-walled conservatory, on the phone with the rental company, when she caught sight of a Washington County Sheriff's SUV coming up Easterly's front drive.

Were they serving Chantal divorce papers already? Jeez —

"I'm sorry," she said, shaking herself back to attention. "What was that?"

"The account is past due," the sales rep repeated. "So no, we can't fill any more of the order."

"Past due?" That was as inconceivable as the White House not covering its light bill. "No, no, we paid for the tent in full yesterday. So we can't be —"

"Listen, y'all are one of our best customers, we want to work with y'all. I didn't know the account was still past due until the owner told me. I shipped as much as I could, but he's shut it off until the balance is paid."

"How much is owed?"

"Five thousand, seven hundred and eighty-five, fifty-two."

"That won't be a problem. If I bring a check over now, can you —"

"Everything's been cleaned out. We got nothing left to rent, what with all the parties across the city this weekend. I called Rosalinda last week and left her three messages about the balance. She never called me back. I held the rest of the order as long as I was able 'cuz I was wanting y'all to be taken care of. But I didn't hear anything and other orders had to be filled."

Lizzie took a deep breath. "Listen, thank you. I don't know what's going on, but we'll make it work — and I'll make sure you get paid."

"I'm really sorry."

As she ended the call, she leaned in to the glass and tried to see the sheriff's vehicle.

"— rental company say?"

She turned back to Greta, who was spraying the finished bouquets with floral preservative. "I'm sorry, what — oh, it's a billing issue."

"So we're going to get the extra five hundred champagne flutes?"

"No." She headed over to the door into

the house. "I'm going to go talk to Rosalinda and then break the bad news to Mr. Harris. He's going to be pissed — but at least we got the tents and the tables and chairs. Glasses we can wash as they come in, and the family's got to have a hundred or so of their own."

Greta looked up through those tortoiseshell glasses of hers. "There are close to seven hundred people coming. You really think we can keep up with that demand? With only five hundred flutes?"

"You are not helping."

Stepping out of the conservatory, she cut through the dining room and headed for the staff hallway. As she pushed her way inside, she stopped dead. Three maids in their gray and white uniforms were clustered together, talking with a great deal of animation but little volume — as if they were a TV show that had had its sound turned down. Miss Aurora was beside them, arms crossed over her chest, and Beatrix Mollie, the head of housekeeping, was next to her. Mr. Harris was standing in the center of the corridor, his diminutive body blocking the way to the kitchen.

Lizzie frowned and approached the butler — and that was when she got a whiff of a smell that, as a farm owner, she had some familiarity with.

An African-American man in a sheriff's uniform came out of Rosalinda's office, along with Lane.

"What's going on?" Lizzie asked, a cold chill shooting through her chest.

Dear Lord, was Rosalinda . . .

Was that why the hall had smelled so badly this morning? she thought with a pounding heart.

"There's been a difficulty," Mr. Harris said. "And it is being handled appropriately."

Lane met her eyes as he spoke with the deputy and he nodded to her. When she motioned over her shoulder toward the conservatory, he nodded again.

Ms. Mollie made the sign of the cross over her heart. "It comes in threes. Death always comes in threes."

"Nonsense," Miss Aurora muttered as if the woman had been wearing her out with that line of reasoning. "God's plans determine it for us all. Not counting on your fingertips."

"Threes. Always threes."

Heading back to the conservatory, Lizzie closed the door behind her and looked at the hundred or so bouquets of pink and white flowers.

"What's wrong?" Greta asked. "Did something else get left off the order —"

"I think Rosalinda is dead."

There was a clatter as the spray bottle slipped out of Greta's hands and bounced on the slate floor, spraying the woman's work shoes. *"What."*

"I don't know."

As a stream of German boiled up and out of her partner, Lizzie muttered, "I know, right? I just can't believe it."

"When? How?"

"I don't know, but the sheriff's here. And they didn't call for an ambulance."

"Oh, mein Gott . . . das ist ja schrecklich!"

With a curse, Lizzie walked over to the view of the garden and stared out at the resplendent green of the cropped grass and the elegant setup for the party. They were seventy-five percent there, and already things were beautiful — especially the glowing heads of the hundreds of late-blooming paper-whites that she and Greta had planted in the beds under the flowering fruit trees.

"I've got a really bad feeling about all this," she heard herself say.

About an hour after Metro Police arrived at Easterly, Lane was allowed to leave the scene for a short period of time. He wanted to talk to Lizzie to let her know what was going on, but he had to take care of Gin first.

The Bradford Family Trusts were all administered and managed out of the Prospect Trust Company, a privately held firm with billions of dollars of assets under their control and a speciality in handling the super-wealthy in Charlemont. As they were not a traditional bank, however, the household checking accounts were run out of the local branch of PNC — and that was where he went with the checkbook he'd taken out of Rosalinda's desk.

Parking in the lot by the one story boutique building, he wrote the check out as payable to Cash in the amount of seventy-five thousand dollars, forged his father's name on the signatory line, and endorsed the back as payable to the Washington County Jail.

As soon as he pushed into the beige and white lobby, he was intersected by a young woman in a navy blue suit and discreet jewelry. "Mr. Baldwine, how are you?"

I just found a dead body. Thanks for asking. "Fine, I need to get this check certified?"

"Of course. Come into my office." Leading him over to a glass enclosure, she shut the door and took a seat behind a tidy desk.

"We're always pleased to help your family."

He slid the check across the blotter and sat down. "I appreciate it."

The sound of fingernails tippity-tapping on the computer's keyboard was mildly annoying, but he had so much bigger fish to fry.

"Ah . . ." The bank manager cleared her throat. "Mr. Baldwine, I'm sorry, there are not sufficient funds in the account."

He took out his phone. "No problem, I'll just call Prospect Trust and initiate a transfer. How much do we need?"

"Well, sir, the account is overdrawn by twenty-seven thousand, four hundred, eighty-nine dollars and twenty-two cents. The overdraft protection is covering that, however."

"Give me a moment." He went into his contacts and called up the PTC administrator in charge of the family's funds. "I'll just wire it in."

Obvious relief bloomed in her face. "Here, let me give you some privacy. I'll be out in the lobby when you're ready. Take your time."

"Thanks."

While he waited for the connection to ring through, Lane tapped his loafer on the marble floor. "Oh, hey, Connie, how are you. It's Lane Baldwine. Good. Yes, I'm in town for Derby." *Among other things.* "Listen, I need you to wire some money into the general household account at PNC."

There was a pause. And then the woman's smooth, professional voice became strained. "I'd be happy to, Mr. Baldwine, but I don't have access to your accounts anymore. You removed them from Prospect Trust last year."

"I meant out of my father's accounts. Or my mother's."

There was another pause. "I'm afraid you're not authorized to effect transfers of that nature. I'd need to speak to your father. Is there a way you could get him to call in?"

Not if he wanted the money. Given that dear ol' daddy was trying to squeeze Gin, there was no way the grand and glorious William Baldwine was going to help facilitate her release.

"My father's out of town and unreachable. How about I put my mother on the phone?" Surely he could go to her and keep her conscious long enough to order a hundred and twenty-five grand into the household account.

Connie cleared her throat just as the bank manager had. "I'm so sorry, but that . . .

that will not be sufficient."

"If it's her account? How can it not be?"

"Mr. Baldwine . . . I don't want to speak out of turn."

"Sounds like you'd better."

"Will you please hold for a moment?"

As piped-in music drawled into his ear, he burst up out of the stiff chair and paced in between the potted plant in the corner, which he discovered was plastic when he tested a leaf, and the floor-to-ceiling, double-hung windows that looked out onto the four-lane road beyond.

There was a beeping tone and then a male voice came over the connection. "Mr. Baldwine? It's Ricardo Monteverdi, how are you, sir?"

Great, the CEO of the company. Which meant whatever the answer was had tripped the "delicate situation" wire. "Look, I just need a hundred and twenty-five thousand in cash, okay? No big deal —"

"Mr. Baldwine, as you know, at Prospect Trust, we take our fiduciary responsibility to our clients very seriously —"

"Stop right there with the disclaimers. Either tell me why my mother's word isn't good enough for her own money or get off my phone."

There was a period of silence. "You are

leaving me no choice."

"What. For God's sake, what?"

The next stretch of quiet was so long and dense, he took his phone from his ear to check he hadn't lost the call. "Hello?"

Cue the throat clearing. "Your father declared your mother mentally incompetent per the rules of her trusts earlier this year. It was the opinion of two qualified neurologists that she was, and is, incapable of making decisions at this time. So if you require funds from either of their accounts, we will be more than happy to accommodate you — provided the request comes from your father in person. I hope you understand that I am walking a fine line here —"

"I'll call him right now and get him to phone in."

Lane ended the call and stared out at the traffic. Then he went over to the door and opened it. Smiling at the manager, he said, "My father's going to have to call Prospect to initiate the transfer. I'll have to come back."

"We're open until five o'clock, sir."

"Thanks."

Back out in the bright sun, he kept his phone in his hand as he strode across the hot pavement, but he didn't use the thing. He also didn't remember the drive home.

What the hell was he going to do now?

When he got back to Easterly, there were two more police units in the courtyard by the garages and a couple of uniforms standing at the front door. He parked the Porsche in its usual waiting spot to the left of the mansion's main entrance and got out.

"Mr. Baldwine," one of the officers said as Lane approached.

"Gentlemen."

The sensation of their eyes following him made him want to send the group far away from his family's house. He had a tweaking paranoia that there were things happening behind the scenes he knew nothing about, and he'd just as soon eyeball those skeletons privately first — without the benefit of Metro Police's prying stares.

Taking the stairs up to the second floor, he went to his room and shut the door — then locked it. Over by his bed, he picked up the receiver on the house phone, dialed nine for an outside line, and then entered *67 so that the number of the extension he was calling from would not register on any caller ID. When a dial tone came over the line, he entered a familiar exchange and four-digit series.

He cleared his throat as it rang once. Twice —

"Good morning, this is Mr. William Baldwine's office. How may I assist you —"

Assuming his father's clipped business tones, he said, "Get me Monteverdi at Prospect on the line right now."

"Of course, Mr. Baldwine! Right away."

Lane cleared his throat again as classical music came across the connection. The good news was that his father was anti-social unless human interaction benefited him business-wise, so it was unlikely there were any recent personal conversations between the two men that would give the lie away.

"Mr. Baldwine, I have Mr. Monteverdi on the line."

After the click, Monteverdi jumped right in. "Thank you for finally returning my call."

Lane dropped his tone and added a boatload of Southern: "I need one hundred and twenty-five thousand into the general household —"

"William, I told you. I can't make any more advances, I just can't. I appreciate your family's business, and I am committed to helping you sort all of this out before the Bradford name runs into difficulty, but my hands are tied. I have a responsibility to my board, and you told me the money you borrowed would be repaid by the annual meeting — which is in two short weeks. The fact that you require additional funds — of such a small amount? My confidence is now *not* high."

What. The. Hell.

"What is the total owed?" he asked in his father's heavy Virginian accent.

"I told you in my last voice mail," Monteverdi bit out. "Fifty-three million. You have two weeks, William. Your choice is to either repay it, or go to JPMorgan Chase and get them to do asset lending against your wife's primary trust. She has over a hundred million in that account alone, so their lending profile is met. I sent you the paperwork on your private e-mail — all you have to do is put her signature on them and this goes away for the both of us. But let me make myself perfectly clear — I am very exposed in this situation, and I will not permit that to continue. There are remedies I could bring to bear that would be very uncomfortable for you, and I shall use them before anything affects me personally."

Holy.

Shit.

"I'll get back to you," Lane drawled, and hung up.

For a moment, all he could do was stare

at his phone. He literally couldn't string two thoughts together.

Then came the vomiting.

With a sudden heave, he jerked in half, barely getting the wastepaper basket over in time.

Everything that he'd eaten in the staff room came up.

After the gagging subsided, his blood ran cold, the sense that nothing was as it should be making him wonder — then pray — that this was some kind of nightmare.

But he didn't have the luxury of fading into neutral — or worse, falling apart. He had to deal with the police. His sister. And whatever was going on here . . .

God, he wished Edward were still around.

TWENTY

An hour later, as Gin slid into the passenger seat of her brother's dark gray Porsche, she closed her eyes and shook her head. "This has been the worst six hours of my life."

Lane made some kind of grunt, which could have meant a lot of things — but most certainly didn't come close to the "Oh, God, I can't believe you lived through that" she was looking for.

"Excuse me," she snapped. "But I was just in jail —"

"We're in trouble, Gin."

She shrugged. "We made bail, and Samuel T. is going to make sure that it stays out of the press —"

"Gin." Her brother looked over at her while shooting them into traffic. "We're in real trouble."

Later, oh, so much later, she would remember this moment of their eyes meeting across the car's interior as the start of the downfall, the tip of the first domino that made all the other ones fall so fast it was not possible to stop the sequence.

"What are you talking about?" she asked softly. "You're scaring me."

"The family is in debt. Serious debt."

She rolled her eyes and slashed a hand through the air. "Seriously, Lane, I've got bigger problems —"

"And Rosalinda killed herself in the house. Some time in the last two days."

Gin put a hand to her mouth. And remembered calling the woman and getting no answer just hours ago. "Dead?"

"Dead. In her office."

It was impossible not to have a case of the skin crawls as she pictured the phone ringing next to the corpse of their controller. "Dear God . . ."

Lane cursed as he glanced in the rearview mirror and changed lanes with a jerk of the wheel. "The household's checking account is overdrawn, and our father has somehow managed to borrow fifty-three million dollars from the Prospect Trust Company for God only knows what. And the worst part? I don't know how much farther this goes and I'm not sure how to find out."

"What are you . . . I'm sorry, I don't understand?"

His reiteration didn't help her at all.

As her brother fell silent, she stared out the front windshield, watching the road ahead curve to the contour of the Ohio River.

"Father can just repay the money," she said dully. "He'll repay it and it'll all go away —"

"Gin, if you need to borrow that kind of cash, it's because you're in deep, deep trouble. And if you haven't paid it back? You can't."

"But Mummy has money. She has plenty of —"

"I don't think we can take anything for granted."

"So where did you find the bail? To get me out?"

"I have some cash and also my trust, which I broke away from the family funds. The two aren't nearly enough to take care of Easterly, however — and forget about paying back that kind of loan or keeping Bradford Bourbon afloat if it comes to that."

She looked down at her fucked-up manicure, focusing on the decimation of that which had been perfect when she'd woken up that morning. "Thank you. For getting me out."

"No problem."

"I'll pay you back."

Except with what? Her father had cut her off . . . but worse, what if there was no money to give her her allowance anyway?

"It's just not possible," she said. "This has to be a misunderstanding. Some kind of . . . a miscommunication."

"I don't think so —"

"You've got to think positively, Lane —"

"I walked in on a dead woman in her office about two hours ago, and that was before I found out about the debt. I can assure you that lack of optimism is not the problem here."

"Do you think . . ." Gin gasped. "Do you think she stole from us?"

"Fifty-three million dollars? Or even a part of that? No, because why commit suicide — if she embezzled funds, the smart thing would be to take off and change her identity. You don't kill yourself in your employer's house if you've successfully taken cash."

"But what if she was murdered?"

Lane opened his mouth like he was going to "no way" her. But then he closed it back up — as if he were trying that idea on for size. "Well, she was in love with him."

Gin felt her jaw drop. "Rosalinda? With Father?"

"Oh, come on, Gin. Everyone knows that."

"*Rosalinda?* Her idea of letting her hair down was to tie that bun of hers lower on her head."

"Repressed or not, she was with him."

"In our mother's house."

"Don't be naive."

Right, it was the first time she had ever been accused of that. And suddenly, that memory from all those years ago, from New Year's Eve, came back . . . when she had seen her father leaving that woman's office.

But that had been decades ago, from another era.

Or maybe not.

Lane hit the brakes as they came up to a red light next to the gas station she'd visited that morning. "Think about where she lived," he said. "Her four-bedroom Colonial in Rolling Meadows is more than she could afford on a bookkeeper's salary — who do you think paid for that?"

"She has no children."

"That we know of."

Gin squeezed her eyes shut as her brother hit the gas again. "I think I'm going to be ill."

"Do you want me to pull over?"

"I want you to stop telling me these things."

There was a long silence . . . and in the tense void, she kept going back to that vision of her father coming out of that office and doing up his robe.

Eventually, her brother shook his head. "Ignorance isn't going to change anything. We need to find out what's happening. I need to get to the truth somehow."

"How did you . . . how did you find all this out?"

"Does it matter?"

As they rounded the final curve on River Road before Easterly, she looked off to the right, up to the top of the hill. Her family's mansion sat in the same place it always had, its incredible size and elegance dominating the horizon, the famous white expanse making her think of all the bourbon bottles that bore an etching of it on their labels.

Until this moment, she had assumed her family's position was set in stone.

Now, she feared it might be sand.

"Okay, so we're all set here." Lizzie strode down the rows of round tables under the big tent. "The chairs look good."

"*Ja,*" Greta said as she made a slight adjustment to a tablecloth.

The pair of them continued on, inspecting the positioning of all seven hundred seats, double-checking the crystal chandeliers that were hanging from the tent's three points, making further tweaks to the draped lengths of pale pink and white.

When they were finished, they stepped out from underneath and followed the lengths of dark green extension cords that snaked around the exterior and supplied electricity to the eight cyclone fans that would ensure circulation.

They had a good five hours of work time left before dark, and, for once, Lizzie thought they'd actually run out of punch-list priorities. Bouquets were done. Flower beds were in perfect condition. Pots at the entrances and exits of the tent were done up fit to kill with combinations of plant material and supplemental blooms. Even the food-prep stations in the adjunct tents had been arranged per Miss Aurora's instructions.

As far as Lizzie was aware, the food was ready. Liquor delivered. Waitstaff and additional bartenders had been coordinated through Reginald, and he was not the type to drop any balls. Security to make sure the press stayed away were off-duty Metro Police officers and all ready to go.

She really wished there were something to occupy her time. Nervous energy had made her even more productive than usual — and now she was left with nothing but the knowledge that there was a criminal investigation going on about fifty yards away from her.

God, Rosalinda.

Her phone went off against her hip, the vibration making her jump. As she took the cell out, she exhaled. "Thank God — hello? Lane? Are you okay — yes." She frowned as Greta looked over. "Actually, I left it in my car, but I can go get it now. Yes. Sure, of course. Where are you? All right. I'll get it and bring it right to you."

When she ended the call, Greta said, "What's going on?"

"I don't know. He says he needs a computer."

"There must be a dozen of them in the house."

"After what happened this morning, you think I'm going to argue with the guy?"

"Fair enough." Although the woman's expression screamed disapproval. "I'm going to check the front of the house beds and pots, and confirm the parkers are going to arrive on time."

"Eight a.m.?"

"Eight a.m. And then I don't know, I'm thinking of heading home. I'm getting a migraine, and it's a long day tomorrow."

"That's terrible! I say go now and come back ready to roar."

Before Lizzie turned away, her old friend gave her a stern look through those heavy glasses. "Are you all right?"

"Oh, yeah. Absolutely."

"There's a lot of Lane around here. That's why I'm asking."

Lizzie glanced over at the house. "He's getting a divorce."

"Really."

"That's what he says."

Greta crossed her arms over her chest and her German accent became more apparent. "About two years too late for that —"

"He's not all bad, you know."

"Excuse me? Is this — *nein,* you can't be serious."

"He didn't know Chantal was pregnant, okay?"

Greta threw up her hands. "Oh, well, that makes all the difference, then, *ja*? So he voluntarily married her while he was with you. Perfect."

"Please, don't." Lizzie rubbed her aching eyes. "He —"

"He got to you, didn't he. He called you, he came to you, something."

"And if he did? That's my business —"

"I spent an entire year calling you, getting you out of that farmhouse, making sure you went to work. I was there for you, worrying about you — cleaning up the mess he made. So do not tell me I don't get to have a re-action when he whispers in your ear —"

Lizzie put her hand up to the woman's face. "Done. We're done here. I'll see you in the morning."

Marching off, she cursed under her breath the entire way down to her car, and after she got her laptop, she f-bombed the long way back to the house. Deliberately avoiding the kitchen and the conservatory — because she didn't want to run into Greta as the woman packed up — she entered through the library, and without thinking, headed for the hallway that led to the staff stairs and the kitchen. She didn't get far. Just as she rounded the corner, she was stopped by two police officers — and that was when she saw the body on a rolling stretcher.

Rosalinda Freeland's remains had been placed in a white bag with a five-foot zipper that had mercifully been pulled closed.

"Ma'am," one of the officers said, "I'm going to have to ask you to step aside."

"Yes, yes, sorry." Ducking her eyes and swallowing her nausea, she wheeled around.

Tried not to think about what had happened.

Failed.

She'd given her name to the police, just
like the rest of the staff had, and provided a
brief statement of where she'd been all
morning as well as over the past few days.
When asked about the controller, she hadn't
had much to offer. She hadn't known
Rosalinda any better than anyone had; the
woman had kept to herself and her bill
processing and that was that.

Lizzie wasn't even sure if there were any
family to notify.

Using the main staircase was a violation
of that Easterly etiquette, but considering
there was a coroner's van parked out front
and a crime scene down that staff hall, she
was confident in letting go of business as
usual. Up on the second floor, she made
her way over the pale runner, passing by the
oil paintings and the occasionals that
gleamed with age and superior craftsman-
ship.

As she came up to Lane's door, she
couldn't remember the last time she and
Greta had fought about anything. God, she
wanted to call the woman and . . . but what
could she say?

Drop the laptop off and leave, she told

herself. *That's it.*

Lizzie knocked on the door. "Lane?"

"Come in."

Pushing her way into the bedroom, she found him standing at the windows, one foot planted on the sill, his forearm braced on his raised knee. He didn't turn and acknowledge her. Didn't say anything else.

"Lane?" She glanced around. No one was with him. "Listen, I'll just leave it —"

"I need your help."

Taking a deep breath, she said, "Okay."

But he stayed silent as he stared out at the garden. And God help her, it was impossible not to run her eyes over him. She told herself she was looking for signs of strain — that she wasn't measuring his muscular shoulders. The short hair at the base of his neck. The biceps that had curled up and were straining the short sleeves of his polo shirt.

He'd changed clothes since she'd seen him last. Had taken a shower, too — she could smell the shampoo, the aftershave.

"I'm sorry about Rosalinda," she whispered. "What a shock."

"Hmm."

"Who found her?"

"I did."

Lizzie closed her eyes and hugged the

307

laptop to her chest. "Oh, God."

Abruptly, he put his hand into the front pocket of his slacks and took something out. "Will you stay with me while I open this?"

"What is it?"

"Something she left behind." He showed her a black USB drive. "I found it on her desk."

"Is it a . . . suicide note?"

"I don't think so." He sat down on the bed and nodded at her laptop. "Do you mind if I . . . ?"

"Oh, yes." She joined him, flipping open the Lenovo and hitting the power button. "I have Microsoft Office so . . . yeah. Word documents are no problem."

"I don't think that's what it is."

Signing in, she passed the computer over to him. "Here."

He pushed the drive in and waited. When the screen flashed a variety of options, he hit "open files."

There was only one on the drive, and it was marked "William-Baldwine."

Lizzie rubbed her eyebrow with her thumb. "Are you sure you want me to see this?"

"I'm sure I can't look at it without you here."

Lizzie found herself reaching up and resting her hand on his shoulder. "I'm not going to leave you."

For some reason, she thought of that peach lingerie she'd found behind his father's bed. Hardly something that Rosalinda would wear — a lighter tone of gray was the closest the controller had ever come to whoopin' it up on the wardrobe front. Then again, who knew what the woman had underneath all those proper skirts and jackets?

Lane clicked on the file and Lizzie was aware of her heart pounding like she'd run a full-tilt mile.

And he was right. It wasn't some kind of love letter or a suicide note. It was a spreadsheet full of columns of numbers and dates and short descriptions that Lizzie was too far away from the screen to read.

"What is all that?" she asked.

"Fifty-three million dollars," he muttered, scrolling down. "I'll bet it's fifty-three million dollars."

"What do you mean? Wait . . . are you saying she stole that?"

"No, but I think she helped my father to."

"What."

He glanced over at her. "I think my father finally has blood on his hands. Or at least . . . blood we can see."

TWENTY-ONE

Refocusing on the computer in his lap, Lane scrolled down the Excel spreadsheet, tracing the entries, trying to add up a rough total. But he needn't have bothered. Rosalinda provided the sum to him at the very end, in a bolded box offset at the far right of all the columns.

It was not, in fact, fifty-three million dollars.

Nope, it was sixty-eight million, four hundred eighty-nine thousand, two hundred forty-two dollars and sixty-five cents.

$68,489,242.65.

The explanations on the withdrawals ranged from Cartier and Tiffany to Bradford Aviation, LLC, which was the corporation that ran all the company's planes and pilots, and Bradford Human Resources Payroll — which most likely took care of the household staff's paychecks. But there was a repeating entry that he didn't recognize: WWB Holdings.

William Wyatt Baldwine Holdings.

Had to be.

But what was that?

The lion's share had gone into it.

"I think my father . . ." He glanced over at Lizzie. "I don't know, the trust company says he's put himself — or the family, I guess — into huge debt. For what, though? Even with all this spending, there should be plenty of cash coming in through Bradford Bourbon Company distributions to shareholders, of which we are the largest group."

"The rental company . . ." Lizzie murmured.

"What?"

"The rental company didn't get paid — their accounts payable called Rosalinda last week and she never got back to them."

"Who else do we owe, I wonder?"

"How can I help?"

He stared over at her, his brain churning, churning. "Letting me get into this file is a good start."

"What else?"

God, her eyes were blue, he thought. And her lips, those naturally red lips of hers were so perfectly shaped.

She was talking to him, but he couldn't hear her. It was as if a muffling had come down around him, making him unaware of any sounds around him. And then the computer in his lap and all of its secrets revealed disappeared, too, so that neither the glow of the screen nor the pattern of the columns nor the numbers and letters registered, either.

"Lizzie," he said, cutting her off.

"Yes?"

"I need you," he heard himself say hoarsely.

"Of course, what can I —"

He leaned in and put his lips to hers, brushing quick —

She gasped and pulled away.

Lane waited for her to get up. Tell him off. Maybe go eighties romance and slap him with an open palm.

Instead, she brought her fingertips up and touched her mouth. Then she closed her eyes. "I wish you hadn't done that."

Fuck. "I'm sorry." He dragged a hand through his hair. "I'm not in my right head."

She nodded. "Yes."

Perfect, he thought. His life was on fire on too many fronts to count, so why shouldn't he drop another load of flames somewhere else. You know, just to help the inferno along.

"I'm sorry," he said. "I should have just —"

She launched herself at him with such a quick shift, he nearly jerked away himself. What saved him was the wanting . . . the vicious craving he'd always had for her that was all pent up from the time they'd been apart.

Lizzie spoke against his mouth. "I'm not in my right head, either."

With a curse, he wrapped his arms around her and dragged her into his lap, the computer sliding off onto the thick carpet — which was fine. He wanted to forget about the money, his father, Rosalinda . . . even if just for a moment.

"I'm sorry," he said as he pushed her down on the mattress with a twist. "I need you. I just . . . I need to be in you —"

Knock, knock, knock.

They both froze, their eyes meeting.

"What," he barked out.

As a muted female voice said something about towels, all Lane thought about was the fact that that door was not locked.

"No, thank you."

Lizzie pushed her way out from under him, and he moved so she could get to her feet. Meanwhile, the maid in the hall kept talking.

"I'm good. Thanks," he said roughly.

His eyes tracked Lizzie's hands as they yanked her shirt back down and finger brushed her hair.

"Lizzie," he whispered.

She just shook her head as she paced around, looking as if she were considering a leap-out-the-window strategy for escape.

More talk from the maid, and he just lost it. Exploding up to his feet, he stalked over and ripped open the door, blocking the way into his room. The blond twenty-five-year-old on the other side was the same one who'd been in the hallway when he and Chantal had been arguing.

"Oh, hi." She smiled up at him. "How are you?"

"I don't need anything. Thanks," he said roughly.

As he turned away, she reached out and took his arm. "I'm Tiphanii — that's with a 'ph' and a double 'i' at the end."

"Nice to meet you. If you'll excuse —"

"I was just going to come in and check your bathroom."

That smile of hers gave her away. That and the little change in position where her pelvis tilted toward him and one of her legs got extended like she was wearing stilettos instead of Crocs.

Lane rolled his eyes — he couldn't help it. The woman he really wanted had just gotten out from under him, and this piece of taffy was thinking she had anything to offer?

Make that *taphii.*

"Thanks, but no. I'm not interested."

He closed the door on her because he didn't have the energy to be pleasant, and he didn't want to say something he was going to regret.

Pivoting around, he found Lizzie across the room by the window. She was deliberately standing off to the side, as if she didn't want to be seen from down below, and her arms were crossed over her chest.

"You sounded so sincere," she said roughly.

"When I'm with you, I am —"

"With that maid just now."

"Why wouldn't I be?"

"You know what I really hate?"

"I can only imagine," he muttered.

"How she just propositioned you . . . and still, all I can think of is taking your clothes off. Like you're some kind of toy I'm fighting with her over."

His erection twitched in his pants. "There is no fight — I'm yours. If you want, here and now. Or later. A week, a month, years from now."

Shut up, his arousal said. *Just shut up, buddy, with that timeline stuff.*

"I'm not falling back into you, Lane. I'm just not."

"You said that over the phone."

Lizzie nodded and unplugged from the view of the garden. As the light began to fade from the sky, she marched across the room, clearly heading for the door.

Damn it —

Not the door.

She did not, in fact, go to the door.

Lizzie stopped at him and let her fingers do the walking, taking his face, bringing his mouth back to hers.

"Lizzie," he groaned, licking into her mouth.

The kiss got out of control fast, and he was not going to lose the chance with her. Spinning her around, he pushed her against the wall, the oil painting next to them bouncing so hard, the thing threw itself off its hook and splintered to the floor. He didn't care. His hands shot under her clothes, finding skin, riding upward to feel her breasts.

He never thought he'd get this again, and though he would have liked to do a slow-and-sweet, he couldn't. Too desperate.

He was rough with the waistband of her shorts, tearing at the button, the zipper, ripping them down her legs. And then he slid his hand between her thighs, pushing her cotton panties out of the —

Lizzie called out his name in a hoarse voice that nearly made him come right then and there. And as her fingers bit into his shoulders, he stroked her harder.

"Hurt me," he growled as she dug into him. "Make me bleed . . ."

He wanted the pain along with the pleasure, everything that was going on with his father and his family making him raw and dark on the inside — to the point where he wondered dimly if maybe this was what drove his brother Max. He'd heard about those things Maxwell did — or rumors about them.

Maybe this was why. He felt like he had to get the darkness out or it was going to consume him.

Lifting Lizzie up off the floor, he relished the way she locked on to him with her powerful arms. One tearing jerk of the zipper on his slacks and his arousal was ready to go. He split her underwear in two, and then —

The roar he let out into her neck was like that of an animal, but he paid no attention to the sound. The slick hold of her sex was a sensation he felt over his entire body, and he orgasmed immediately. So long . . . so long, that he had dreamed of her, and regretted what had happened, and wanted to do things differently. And now he was where he had prayed to be: With every pumping release into her, he was rewinding time, putting things back to rights, repairing the wrongs.

He'd wanted to get with her to briefly take himself out of the present, but it turned out that the experience was more than that. So much more.

But that had always been true about Lizzie. He'd had sex many times in his life.

None of it had ever mattered, though . . . until he'd been with her.

Lizzie hadn't meant to take things this far.

As Lane orgasmed inside of her, she was swept up along with him, her release echoing his. Fast, so fast, it was all so fast and furious, the deed done and over within moments, the pair of them remaining locked together as the initial wave passed.

Had they just done this? she wondered.

Well . . . yeah, she thought as he twitched inside of her.

And then she noticed . . . oh, God, he smelled the same. And his hair was still impossibly soft.

And his body was every bit as powerful as she remembered.

Tears speared into her eyes, and she hid her face in his shoulder. She didn't want him to know about the emotions — she was having a hard enough time acknowledging the confusing jumble to herself.

Just sex, she told herself. This had been only about a physical craving on both sides. And God knew, the lust thing had never been a problem for them — from the instant she'd seen him yesterday, that connection of theirs had simmered under the surface of her skin.

Under his, too.

Okay. Fine. She hadn't been able to say no in this single, discrete instance — even though she should have.

Whether or not it was a mistake was going to depend on how she handled things from here.

Pulling herself together, she eased back in his hold, acutely aware that they were still linked where it mattered most.

The expression on his face made her catch her breath. As did the way he reached up and brushed her cheek.

He seemed so vulnerable.

But before she could make some calm, reasonable, comment, he started moving deep inside of her once more. Slowly, oh, so slowly, up and out, up and out. In response, she closed her eyes and went limp, his arms supporting her, the hard wall against her back buttressing her against him. Part of her was utterly present, every movement registering with the vividness of a lightning strike, all the panting tightness of her chest and the sizzle in her blood taking over everything.

The other half of her was on the run.

Oh, God, the feel of his hand in her hair, his mouth kissing hers so deep, his hips curling up and retreating. It was coming home in all the ways that her body had wanted for so long.

And it was also bad news.

"Lizzie," he said in a voice that cracked. "I missed you, Lizzie. So bad it hurts."

Don't think about it, she told herself. *Don't listen —*

His name broke out of her once again, the snap of pleasure making her sex contract around his erection as he jerked into her, pumping her against that wall, banging her until her head hit.

When they fell still but for the breathing, she collapsed against him.

"This can't be the last time," he groaned, as if he knew what she was thinking. "It just can't."

"How did you know . . ."

"I don't blame you." He eased back and his heavy-lidded eyes burned. "I just don't want this to be —"

"Lane —"

The knock on the door made her jump. And him curse.

"Fucking hell!" he spat.

And considering he wasn't a big curse man, she had to smile a little.

"What!" he bit out.

"Mr. Baldwine," the butler's voice cut in. "Mr. Lodge is here for you."

Lane frowned. "Tell him I'm busy —"

"He says it's urgent."

Lizzie shook her head and pushed herself out of his arms for a second time. As her feet hit the floor in silence, she got a visceral reminder that they hadn't used a condom.

And yup, everything got very, very real as she yanked up her shorts and hustled to the bathroom. She took care of everything the best she could as Lane talked to the Englishman through the door — and when she came back out, he'd pulled his pants back up and was pacing around.

She put her palm out before he could say anything. "Go see him."

"Lizzie —"

"If even a quarter of what you're worried about is true? You're going to need him."

"Where are you going?"

"I don't know. I think we're basically done until first thing tomorrow."

In so many more ways than one.

"Can you stay?" he blurted.

Her brows lifted. "Stay as . . . you don't mean in here for the night. That's insane."

In a household where staff couldn't technically use half the doors, her waking up in the youngest son's bed and still working at Easterly was a total non-starter.

Ah, yes, she thought. The good ol' days of dating him, when she'd exhausted herself trying to keep everything a secret.

"Anywhere," he said. "One of the cottages. I don't care."

"Lane. Listen, this is not — we're not going back to the way it was before, remember? I don't know why I did what I just did, but it doesn't mean —"

He came at her, pulling her in for a kiss, his tongue penetrating her mouth. God help her, after a moment, she kissed him back.

Even as her head was telling her no, her body had its own ideas.

"It matters," he said against her lips. "This matters to me even more than my family. Do you hear me, Lizzie? You have always, and will always, matter most to me."

On that, he left and went to the door, pausing to level a stare at her over his shoulder — the kind that was a vow if she'd ever seen one.

Sitting down on the foot of his bed, she looked over at the wall they'd had sex against. The oil painting on the floor was utterly ruined, the canvas scratched and torn, but she didn't go over to try to assess the damage. She just sat there and tried to convince herself it wasn't a sign from God.

It was a while before she left his room, and she was careful over by the door, listening for voices or the sounds of footsteps before cracking the panels and peeking out. When there was nothing except silence, she all but leaped into the middle of the corridor and started walking fast.

Chantal's room was across the hall and down a little, and as she passed it by, she could smell the woman's expensive perfume.

Such a good reminder — not that she needed it — of why she should have left after that first interruption.

Instead of taking it to the next level at a dead run.

She had only herself to blame.

Twenty-Two

As Lane jogged downstairs, all he could think of was how much he wanted a drink in his hand. The good news — probably the only he was getting — was that when he arrived in the parlor, Samuel T. was helping himself to some Family Reserve, the sound of bourbon hitting ice needling Lane's own craving into a full-blown addict's claw.

"Care to share the wealth?" he muttered as he slid the wood-paneled pocket doors into place on both sides of the room.

There was so much he didn't want anyone else to hear.

"My pleasure." Samuel T. presented him with a healthy share in a squat crystal glass. "Long day, huh."

"You have no idea." Lane clinked his rim with the other man's. "What can I do you for?"

Samuel T. drank his bourbon down and went back to the bar. "I heard about your controller. My condolences."

"Thank you."

"You found her?"

"That's right."

"Been there, done that." The attorney turned back around and shook his head. "Rough stuff."

You don't know the half of it. "Listen, I don't want to rush you, but —"

"Are you serious about that divorce?"

"Absolutely."

"Do you have a prenup?" When Lane shook his head, Samuel cursed. "Any chance she cheated on you?"

Lane rubbed his temple and tried to pull out of what had just happened with Lizzie . . . and what he had seen on that laptop. He wanted to tell Samuel T. to get with him tomorrow, but the problems with Chantal were going to be waiting in the wings, whether or not his family was going down in flames financially.

In fact, it was probably better to get that ball rolling rather than sit on it in light of the stuff with his father. The quicker he got her out of the house? The less insider information she could sell to the tabloids.

Not that he couldn't see her becoming a talking head to the lowest common denominator if things went badly for the

Bradfords.

"I'm sorry," he said between sips. "What was the question?"

"Has she cheated on you?"

"Not that I know of. She's just been in this house for two years, living off my family and getting manicures."

"That's too bad."

Lane cocked a brow. "Didn't know you had such a jaundiced view of marriage."

"If she cheated on you, that can be used to reduce alimony. Kentucky's a no-fault state for divorce, but misdeeds like affairs or abuse can be used to mediate spousal support."

"I haven't been with anyone else." Well, except for Lizzie just now, upstairs — and about a hundred thousand times before that in his mind.

"That doesn't matter unless you're seeking support from Chantal."

"Not a chance. A clean break is all I want from that woman."

"Does she know this is coming?"

"I've told her."

"But does she *know*?"

"Have you got papers for me to sign now?" When the attorney nodded, Lane shrugged. "Well, then, she'll be aware of how serious I am as soon as she gets served."

"Once I get your John Hancock, I'll go directly downtown and file this petition. The court is going to have to conclude that the marriage is irretrievably broken, but I think, given that the pair of you have been living apart for about two years, that will not be a problem. I will warn you — there is no way she's not going to hit you for support. And there's a potential that this is going to cost you, especially because her standard of living has been so high here in this house. I'm guessing some of your trusts have kicked in?"

"I'm on the first tier. Second tier is triggered when I'm forty."

"What's your annual income?"

"Does that include poker winnings?"

"Does she know about them? Do you file income taxes on those funds?"

"No and no."

"Then we'll leave that off the table. So what's your number?"

"I don't know. Nothing ridiculous, just a million or so? It's like a fifth of the income generated off the corpus."

"She'll go after that."

"But not the corpus, right? I think there's a spendthrift clause."

"If it's the Bradford Family Irrevocable of

1968, which I believe it is, my father drafted the terms, so you can bet your best flask no soon-to-be ex-wife is invading anything. I'll need to see a copy of the documents, of course."

"Prospect Trust has everything."

Samuel T. ran through various *file this, counter that, disclose whatever,* but Lane checked out. In his mind, he was upstairs in his bedroom with the door shut and Lizzie fully naked in his bed. He was all over her with his hands and his mouth, closing the distance of the years and going back to where they had been before Chantal had showed up in designer maternity clothes.

Whatever he was facing with his father and the debt . . . it would be so much easier if he had Lizzie with him, and not in just a sexual way.

Friends helped each other, right?

"Sound good?"

Lane replugged into his lawyer. "Yes. How long?"

"Like I said, I'll file everything today with another 'friendly' judge who owes me a favor or two. And Mitch Ramsey has agreed to serve her the summons immediately. Next comes hashing out the marital settlement — and my guess is, she'll get one hell of an attorney on her side for you to pay for. You've been living apart for more than sixty days, but she's going to need to leave this house ASAP if you're going to stay here. I don't want to trip that wire and delay this two months, thanks to a cohabitating argument from the other side. My guess is she's going to contest everything, because she's going to want as much money from you as possible. My goal, however, is to get her out of your life with the clothes on her back and that quarter-of-a-million-dollar engagement ring you gave her — and that's it."

"Sounds good to me." Especially as he didn't know if there was a pot to piss in anywhere else but his own accounts. "Where do I sign?"

Samuel T. made short work with various pieces of paper, presenting them for a scrawl in blue ink on the corner of the bar cart. It was all over quicker than Lane could finish his first bourbon.

"You want me to give you a retainer?" he asked as he gave the Montblanc back to his attorney.

Samuel T. finished his own drink; then put more ice and more Family Reserve in his glass. "This is free of charge."

Lane recoiled. "Come on, man, I can't let you do that. Let me —"

"No. Frankly, I don't like her, and she doesn't belong in this house. I'm looking at this divorce case as housekeeping. A broom sweep to get the trash out."

"I didn't know you disliked her so much."

Samuel T. put his hands on his hips and stared at the Oriental. "I'm going to be completely honest here."

Lane knew where things were going just by the way the attorney was gritting his jaw. "G'on."

"About six months after you left here, Chantal called me up. Asked me to come over — when I said no, she showed up at my house. She was looking for 'a friend,' as she put it — then she shoved her hand down my pants and offered to get on her knees. I told her she was out of her mind. Even if I were attracted to her, which I have never been, your family and mine have been linked for generations. I would never, ever be with a wife of yours, divorced or separated or together. Besides, Virginia is a fine state to go to college in, but I wouldn't marry a girl from there — and that was what she was actually after."

Man, he hated being right about that bitch sometimes, he truly did.

"I'm not surprised, but I'm glad you told me." Lane put out his palm. "I'll repay you the favor. Someday."

"I am certain you will. Now, if you'll excuse me, I'll run these down to the courthouse."

The attorney shook what was offered to him, bowed ever so slightly, and then left with the glass still in his hand.

"They can arrest you for open container," Lane called out. "Just FYI."

"Not if they can't catch me," Samuel T. hollered back.

"Crazy," Lane muttered as he finished his own drink.

As he went to pour another, his eyes drifted over to the oil painting over the mantelpiece. It was of Elijah Bradford, the first member of the family to make enough money to distinguish himself from his peers by sitting for a major American artist.

Was he, at this very moment, rolling in his grave?

Or would that come later . . . because where they had all sunk to got even worse.

Gin rode a wave of panic down Easterly's grand staircase.

As soon as she'd seen the vintage maroon Jaguar pull up to the house, she had changed out of the clothes she'd worn to *jail,* for godsakes, and put on a silk dress that ended well north of her knees. She'd also taken a moment to brush her hair. Mist more perfume on. Slide her feet into a pair of pumps that made her ankles look thinner than ever.

Going by the closed parlor doors, she knew her brother was talking to Samuel T. about The Situation. Or . . . Situations.

She left them be.

Instead of barging in, she went out the front door and waited by that old-fashioned convertible. The temperature was still eighty degrees in spite of the fact that the sun had started to go down, and there was a mugginess in the air — or maybe that was her nerves. To get some shade, she kept herself in the lee of one of the big magnolias that grew up close to the house.

As she stared at the car, she remembered the times she had been in the thing with Samuel T., the night wind in her hair, his hand between her legs as he drove them along the winding roads to his farm.

The convertible had been purchased by Samuel T., Sr., on the day of the birth of what had turned out to be the man's one and only living offspring. And it had been given to young Samuel T. on his eighteenth birthday with strict instructions that he was not to kill himself in the damn thing.

And funny, the instruction had found home: It was only when he was behind the wheel of a car that Samuel T. was careful. Gin had long suspected it was because he knew that if anything happened to him, his family tree was over.

He was the only member of his generation who had survived.

Lot of tragedy.

For which, until this very moment, she had had little appreciation.

While she waited, her heart beat fast, but not hard, the fluttering in her chest making her light-headed. Or perhaps it was the heat —

Samuel T. pulled open the front door and strode out of Easterly, crystal glass of bourbon in his hand. He cut quite the dashing figure with that perfectly beautiful seersucker suit, and his astonishing face, and his monogrammed briefcase. He had put on a pair of gold-rimmed sunglasses, and his thick, dark hair was brushed back off his high forehead, that cowlick in the front making it seemed styled when in fact that had never been necessary.

He stopped as he saw her. Then drawled, "Come to thank me for saving you?"

"I need to talk to you."

"Oh? Trying to negotiate a retainer using

something other than cash?" He tossed back the liquor and put the glass on the front step — as only someone who had lived with help all his life could. "I am amenable to all suggestions."

She measured every step he made toward her and his car. She knew so well that body of his, that hard, muscular body that belied him for the farmer he was in his soul under all his fancy, barrister trappings.

Amelia was going to be tall like he was. And she was smart like he was.

Unfortunately, the girl was also stupid like her mother, although maybe she would grow out of that.

"Well?" he said as he put his briefcase in the jump seat. "Do I get to pick the way you pay your bill?"

Even through his sunglasses, she could feel his eyes on her. He wanted her, he always wanted her, and at times, he hated her for that: He was not a man who appreciated constraints, even of his own making.

She was the same way.

Samuel T. shook his head. "Do not tell me the cat has that luscious tongue of yours. It would be such a pity to lose that particular piece of your anatomy —"

"Samuel."

The instant he heard the tone in her voice,

he frowned and took his sunglasses off. "What's wrong?"

"I . . ."

"Did anyone mistreat you in that jail? Because I will go down there personally and —"

"Marry me."

He froze, everything stopping — his expression, his breathing, maybe even his heart. Then he punched out a laugh. "Right, right, right. Sure you do —"

"I'm serious."

The car door opened silently, a testament to the meticulous care that was paid to the vehicle. "The day you settle down with any man is the eve of the Second Coming."

"Samuel, I love you."

He shot her a sardonic look. "Oh, *please* —"

"I need you."

"Jail really bothered you, didn't it." He lowered himself into the bucket seat and stared out over the hood of the car for a moment. "Look, Gin, don't feel bad about having gone in there, okay? I've managed to scrub everything down at HQ so that it won't even get on the blotter. No one's going to know."

"That's not why. I just . . . let's get married. Please."

Looking across at her, he frowned so deeply, his eyebrows came all the way together. "You actually sound serious."

"I am." And she was no fool. She'd tell him about Amelia afterward, when it was harder for him to run, when there was paperwork in place to hold them together until he got over what she'd done. "You and I were meant to be together. You know it. I know it. We've been skirting around this relationship for a lifetime, maybe longer. You date waitresses and hairdressers and masseuses because they're not me. You hold every woman up to my standard and they all fail. You're obsessed with me just like I am with you. Let's stop the lie and do it right."

He shifted his eyes back out to the hood and ran his beautiful hands around that wooden steering wheel. "Let me ask you something."

"Anything."

"How many men have you said that to?" He glanced back at her. "Huh? How many, Gin? How many times have you used those lines?"

"It's the truth," she said in a voice that cracked.

"Did you try out the pleading tone with them, too, Gin? Give them those eyes?"

"Don't be cruel."

After a long silence, he shook his head. "Do you remember my thirtieth birthday party? The one we had out at my farm?"

"That has nothing to do with —"

"It was a good surprise. I had no idea that y'all were waiting for me. I walked into my house — surprise! All those people cheering, and I looked for you —"

She threw her hands up. "That was five years ago, Samuel! It was —"

"Actually, it's been the whole story of our relationship, Gin. I looked for you — I went through the crowd, searching for —"

"It didn't matter! They don't matter —"

"— you because, like you said, I'm a sap, and you were the only person I truly wanted there. And I found you, all right. Fucking that Argentinean polo player who was a guest of Edward's on my bed."

"Samuel —"

"On my bed!" he thundered, slamming his fist into the dashboard. "My fucking bed, Gin!"

"Fine, and what did you do?" She jerked forward on her hips and jabbed her finger at him. "What did you do then? You took my college roommate and her sister and had sex with them in the pool —"

He cursed out loud. "What was I supposed to do? Let you walk all over me? I'm a man, not one of your pathetic little fuck buddies! I'm not going to —"

"I was with the polo player because the week before you went out of your way to sleep with Catherine! I've been friends with her since I was *two,* Samuel. I had to sit through her going on and on about how you'd given her the orgasms of her life in the back of this very car. After you'd been with me the night before! So don't talk about how you were the one who was —"

"Stop." Abruptly, he pushed a hand through his hair. "Stop it, stop all of — we're not going to do this anymore, Gin. We're fighting over the same dynamic we had when we were teenagers —"

"We fight because we care and we're too proud to admit it." As he fell silent again, she had a bourgeoning hope that he was thinking things over. "Samuel, you're the only man I've ever loved. And I'm the same for you. That's just the way it is. If we need to stop anything, it's the fighting and the hurting. We're both too proud and stubborn for our own good."

There was a long silence. "Why now, Gin."

"It's just . . . it's time."

"All because you were strip searched at ten a.m. this morning?"

"Must you."

Samuel T. shook his head. "I don't know if you're serious or not, but that is not my problem. Allow me to be perfectly clear —"

"Samuel," she broke in. *"I love you."*

And she meant it. Meant it down to her soul: The terrifying conviction that things were going to go badly for her family had taken root and spread, bringing with it a kind of clarity that she had never had before.

Or maybe that was more . . . a courage she had been lacking. For all their years together, she had never told him how she truly felt. It had been all about posturing and one-upping. Well, and his daughter's birth — not that he knew about that yet.

"I love you," she whispered.

"No." He dropped his head and squeezed that wheel as if looking for some kind of strength inside of himself. "No . . . you can't do this, Gin. Not with me. Don't try to take the pretend down this deep. It's not healthy for you . . . and I don't think I'll survive it, okay? I need to function — my family needs me. I won't let you fuck with my head this much —"

"Samuel —"

"No!" he shouted.

Then he looked over at her, and his pale eyes were cold and narrow, as if he were staring down an enemy. "First of all, I don't believe you, okay? I think you're lying to manipulate me. And secondly? I will not *ever* allow a wife of mine to disrespect me the way you will your husband. You are constitutionally incapable of monogamy, and more to the point, you're too bored to value a sustainable relationship. You and I can have a roll or two from time to time, but I will *never* honor a whore like you with my last name. You disparage waitresses? That's fine. But I would so much rather someone like that have my ring on her finger than a spoiled, disloyal brat like you."

He started the engine, the sweet smell of oil and gasoline briefly flaring on the hot breeze. "I'll see you the next time I have an itch I can't scratch myself. Until then, have fun with the rest of the population."

Gin had to put both hands over her mouth as he backed up and took off, the old-fashioned car disappearing along the long drive down the hill.

In his wake, tears fell from her eyes, melting her mascara off — and for once she didn't care.

She had taken her one shot with him.

And failed.

It was her worst nightmare come true.

TWENTY-THREE

"Oh, Lisa?"

As soon as Lizzie heard the Southern drawl percolate through the conservatory, she froze — which was awkward because she was breaking down the bouquet-making tables, and had one balanced on its side.

"Lisa?"

Looking over, she found Lane's wife standing in the doorway like she was posing for a camera, one hand on her hip, the other pushing her hair back. She was wearing pink silk Mary Tyler Moore pants from the Laura Petrie era and a low-cut loose blouse that was sunset orange. The shoes were pointed hard in front and had little tiny heels, and topping it off? A dramatic, filmy scarf in acid yellow and green that was wrapped around her shoulders and tied over her perfect breasts.

All in all, the whole thing created an impression of Fresh, Lovely, and Tempting

— and made someone who was Tired, Anxious, and Stressed feel deficient not just on a hair and wardrobe level, but down to molecular genetics.

"Yes?" Lizzie said as she went back to pounding on one of the legs to collapse it.

"Could you please stop that? It's very loud."

"My pleasure," Lizzie gritted out.

For some reason, as that woman played with her goldilocks, the flashing of the big diamond on her left hand was like somebody dropping the F-bomb repeatedly.

Chantal smiled. "I need your help for a party."

Can we just get through tomorrow first?

"My pleasure."

"It's a party for two." Chantal smiled as she loosened that scarf and came in further. "Oh, my, it's hot in here. Can you do anything about that?"

"The plants do better in the warmth."

"Oh." She swept her wrap off and put it down beside some of the bouquets that were going to be placed in the public rooms of the house. "Well."

"You were saying?"

That smile came back. "It's Lane's and my anniversary soon, and I'd like to do something special."

Lizzie swallowed hard — and wondered if this was some kind of sick game. Had the woman heard something through the door upstairs? The walls? "I thought you were married in July?"

"How kind of you to remember. You're so thoughtful." Chantal tilted her head to the side and locked eyes as if they were having a moment. "We *were* married in July, but I have some special news to share with him, and I thought we could celebrate a little early."

"What were you thinking?"

Lizzie didn't track much as all kinds of ideas were thrown out. The only thing that stuck was "romantic" and "private." Like Chantal was looking forward to giving her husband a lap dance.

"Lisa? Are you writing this down?"

Well, no, because I don't have a pen and paper in my hand, do I? And PS, I think I'm going to vomit. "I'm happy to do whatever you want."

"You are *so* helpful." The woman nodded toward the garden and the tent outside. "I know everything is going to be beautiful tomorrow."

"Thank you."

"And we can talk more later. But again, I'm thinking a romantic dinner in a suite downtown at the Cambridge Hotel. You can provide the flowers and special decorations — I want to drape everything in fabric so that it's as if we're in an exotic place, just the two of us."

"All right."

Had Lane lied to her? And if he had . . . well, she could have Greta take care of everything at The Derby Brunch while she stayed at her farm with a gallon of chocolate ice cream.

Except she and her partner weren't speaking.

Fantastic.

"You're the best." Chantal checked her diamond watch. "It's about time for you to go home, isn't it? Big day tomorrow — you're going to need your beauty rest. Bye for now."

When Lizzie was alone again, she sat down on one of the overturned buckets and put her hands on her thighs, rubbing up and down.

Breathe, she told herself. *Just breathe.*

Greta was right, she thought. She wasn't on the level of these people, and not because she was just a lowly gardener. They played a game she could only lose.

Time to head out, she decided. Beauty sleep wasn't going to happen, but at least she could try and get her head on straight before the bomb went off in the morning.

Getting up, she was about to leave when she saw that scarf. The last thing she wanted to do was deliver the piece of silk back to Chantal like she was a Labrador returning a tennis ball to its owner. But the thing was right next to all those bouquets, and knowing her luck, something would leak or drop on it and she'd have to save up three months of paychecks to buy a new one.

Chantal's wardrobe was more expensive than whole neighborhoods in Charlemont.

Picking the thing up, she thought the woman couldn't have gone far in those stupid kitten-heeled shoes.

It was not going to be difficult to track her down.

Gin was still standing underneath the magnolia tree where Samuel T. had left her when a vehicle came up the winding front drive. It wasn't until the SUV stopped in front of her that she realized it was from the Washington County Sheriff's department.

Good God, what was her father trying to get her arrested for now: Courtesy of this morning's awful field trip downtown, her first instinct was to run, but she was in high heels, and if she really wanted to get away from the officer, she was going to have to bolt through a flower bed.

Breaking her leg was not going to help her in jail.

Deputy Mitchell Ramsey got out with a sheaf of papers in his hand. "Ma'am," he said, nodding at her. "How are you?"

He didn't take out any handcuffs. Didn't seem more than politely interested in her.

"Are you here for me?" she blurted.

"No." His dark eyes narrowed. "Are you okay?"

No, not at all, Deputy. "Yes, thank you."

"If you'll excuse me, ma'am."

"So you've not come for me?"

"No, ma'am." He walked up to the front door and started to ring the bell. "I have not."

Maybe it had to do with Rosalinda?

"Here," she said, going over to him. "Do come in. Are you looking for my brother?"

"No, is Chantal Baldwine at home?"

"Most likely." She opened the grand door, and the deputy took his hat off again as he entered. "Let me find — oh, Mr. Harris. Will you please take this gentleman to my sister-in-law?"

"My pleasure," the butler said with a bow. "This way, sir. I believe she's in the conservatory."

"Ma'am," the deputy murmured to her, before striding away after the Englishman.

"Well, this should be interesting," came a dry voice from the parlor.

She pivoted around. "Lane?"

Her brother was standing in front of the painting of Elijah Bradford, and he lifted his squat glass. "Cheers to my divorce."

"Really." Gin walked in and got busy at the bar because she didn't want Lane to focus on her red-rimmed eyes and swollen face. "Well, at least I won't have to take Mother's jewelry off her neck anymore. Good riddance, and I'm surprised you don't want to enjoy the show."

"I've got bigger problems."

Gin took her bourbon and soda over to the sofa and kicked her stilettos off. Tucking her legs under her seat, she stared up at her brother.

"You look terrible," she said. As bad as she felt, actually.

He sat down across from her. "This is going to be rough, Gin. The money thing. I think this is really serious."

"Maybe we can sell stock. I mean, you can do that, right? I have no idea how all this works."

And for the first time in her life, she wished she did.

"It's complicated because of the trust situation."

"Well . . . we'll be all right." When her brother didn't say anything, she frowned. "Right? Lane?"

"I don't know, Gin. I really don't know."

"We've always had money."

"Yes, that has been true."

"You make it sound past tense."

"Don't kid yourself, Gin."

Leaning her head back, she stared up at the high ceiling, imagining her mother laying in that bed of hers. Was that going to be her own future, too? she wondered. Was she some day going to retire and pull the curtains so that she could live in a drug haze?

Certainly sounded appealing at the moment.

God, had Samuel T. really turned her down?

"Gin, have you been crying?"

"No," she said smoothly. "Just allergies, dear brother. Just spring allergies . . ."

TWENTY-FOUR

Lizzie hustled out of the conservatory with Chantal's fragrant wrap, all the perfume on the floaty fabric thick in her nose, making her want to sneeze. Funny, she could be surrounded by a thousand real blooms, but this fancy, falsely curated stuff was enough to send her over the Claritin edge.

Off in the distance, she heard Chantal's unmistakable Virginian drawl and headed in the direction of the dining room to —

"What is this?" Chantal demanded.

Lizzie stopped short and leaned around the heavy molding of the archway.

At the head of the long, glossy table, Chantal was standing next to a uniformed sheriff's deputy who'd apparently just given her a thick envelope.

"You have been served, ma'am." The deputy nodded. "Have a good day —"

"What do you mean 'served.' What does that — no, you're not leaving until I open

350

this." She ripped the envelope apart. "You can stay right there while I . . ."

The papers came out in a bundle that had been folded three times, and as the woman unfurled them, Lizzie's heart pounded.

"Divorce?" Chantal said. *"Divorce?"*

Lizzie rolled out of sight and went flush against the wall. Closing her eyes, she hated how relieved she felt, she really did. But it wasn't like she could pretend that not being a fool for a second time wasn't a good thing.

"This is a divorce petition!" Chantal's voice grew sharp. "Why are you doing this!"

"Ma'am, my job is to serve the papers. Now that you've accepted them —"

"I do not accept them!" There was a fluttering sound as if she might have actually thrown them at the man. "You take them back —"

"Ma'am," the deputy barked. "I'm going to advise you to pick those papers off the floor — or don't. But any more of that and I'll drag you down to the courthouse strapped to the hood of my patrol vehicle just for getting aggressive with an officer of the peace. Are we clear. Ma'am."

Cue the waterworks.

Between sniffles and what had to be a heaving bosom, Chantal back-pedaled at a dead run. "My husband loves me. He

351

doesn't mean this. He's —"

"Ma'am, that is none of my business and none of my concern. Good day."

Heavy footsteps sounded out and drifted away.

"Goddamn it, Lane," the woman hissed with perfect diction.

Guess the acting happened only when there was an audience.

Without warning, the *clip-clip-clip* of those kitten heels across the floor headed in Lizzie's direction. Crap, there was no time to get out of the —

Chantal rounded the corner and jumped back when she saw Lizzie.

Even though the woman had turned on the waterworks for that deputy, her eyes were clear and free of tears, her makeup not marred in the slightest.

Instant. Rage.

"What are you doing!" Chantal hollered, her body quivering. "Eavesdropping!"

Lizzie held out the scarf. "I was bringing this to you —"

Chantal snatched the wrap. "Get out of here. Get out! *Get out!*"

And you do not have to ask twice, Lizzie thought as she wheeled away and gunned for the great outdoors.

As she cut through the tent and weeded

around the tables and chairs, she took out her phone and texted Lane a cheerful, No-big-deal, I'm-heading-home-after-a-long-day message.

God knew that man was going to have a lot on his hands as soon as Chantal found him.

The good news, at least for Lizzie?

No anniversary party to plan.

And Lane had been true to his word.

It was hard to stop a small smile from surfacing on her face. And when it refused to go away, she let the thing stay where it was.

Lane's phone let out an electronic *bing!* just as Chantal marched by the parlor, screaming his name as she headed for the grand staircase. He did nothing to tip off his whereabouts, just let her go upstairs to cause whatever scene was going to roll out in front of the closed door of his empty bedroom.

Funny, just a few hours before, the fact that she was on the warpath would have been an issue he'd have dealt with. Now? It was down oh, so low on his list of priorities.

"I need to go see Edward," Lane said without bothering to check who had texted him.

Gin shook her head. "I wouldn't. He's not well, and the news you will share can only make things worse."

She had a point. Edward hated their father already. The idea the man had stolen funds?

Gin got to her feet and went over to the bar for a refresh. "Is tomorrow still going forward?"

"The brunch?" He shrugged. "I don't know how to stop it. Besides, it's mostly been paid for already. The food, the liquor, the rentals."

He was ashamed of the other reason to keep the event on track: The idea that the world might know even a hint of the problems his family was potentially facing was unacceptable to him.

The sound of someone coming down the carpeted stairs at an absolute tear made his sister cock an eyebrow. "Looks like you're about to have a marital moment."

"Only if she finds me —"

Chantal appeared in the parlor's doorway, her normally pale and placid face ruddy as a tar layer's at a BBQ.

"How *dare* you," his wife demanded.

"Guess you're packing your bags, darling," Gin said with a Christmas-morning smile. "Shall I call for the butler? I think we can grant you that last courtesy. Consider it your going-away gift."

"I am *not* leaving this house." Chantal ignored Gin. "Do you understand me, Lane."

He circled the ice in his glass with his forefinger. "Gin, will you give us a little privacy?"

With an obliging nod, his sister headed for the archway, and as she went by Chantal, she paused and glanced back at him. "Make sure the butler checks her suitcases for jewelry."

"You are such a *bitch,*" Chantal hissed.

"Yes, I am." Gin shrugged as if the woman was barely worth the breath to speak. "And I also have a right to the Bradford name and legacy. You do not. Bye, now."

As Gin threw out a toodle-oo wave, Lane stepped up and moved his body between the two of them so they could avoid an Alexis/Krystle lily pond moment. Then he went over and slid the panels shut, even though he didn't want to be alone with his wife.

"I'm not leaving." Chantal wheeled around on him. "And this is *not* happening."

As she tossed the divorce petition to the floor at his feet, all he could think of was that he didn't have time for this. "Listen,

Chantal, we can do this the easy way or the hard way — it's your choice. But know if you choose the latter, I will go after not only you, but your family. How do you suppose your Baptist parents would feel if they received a copy of your medical records on their front doorstep? I don't think they're pro-choice, are they?"

"You can't do that!"

"Don't be stupid, Chantal. There are all kinds of people I can call on, people who owe my family debts that they are eager to pay off." He walked back to the bar and poured more Family Reserve into his glass. "Or how about this one. How about those medical records fall into the hands of the press, or maybe an online site? People would understand why I'm divorcing you — and you'd have a hell of a time finding another husband. Unlike up north, we Southern men have standards for our wives, and they do not include abortion."

There was a long stretch of silence. And then the smile that came back at him was inexplicable, so confident and calm, he wondered if she'd gone daft in the last two years.

"You have more to keep quiet than I do," she said softly.

"Do I." He took a deep draw from the

edge of his glass. "How do you figure that. All I did was the right thing by a woman I supposedly got pregnant. Who knows if it was mine, anyway."

She pointed to the paperwork. "You are going to make that go away. You are going to allow me to stay here for however long I want. And you are going to escort me to the Derby festivities tomorrow."

"In what parallel universe?"

Her hand went to her lower belly. "I'm pregnant."

Lane barked out a laugh. "You tried that once before, sweetheart. And we all know how it ended."

"Your sister was wrong."

"About you stealing jewelry? Maybe. We'll see about that."

"No, about the fact that I don't have every right to be here. And so does my child. As a matter of fact, my child has as much right to the Bradford legacy as you and Gin do."

Lane opened his mouth to say something — and then slowly closed it. "What are you talking about."

"I'm afraid your father is no better a husband than you are."

A tinkling rose up from his glass, and he looked down, noting from a vast distance that his hand was shaking and causing the ice to agitate.

"That's right," Chantal said in a slow, even voice. "And I think we're all aware of the delicate condition of your mother. How would she feel if she knew that her husband had not only been unfaithful, but that a child was going to be born? Do you think she'd take more of those pills she's already so reliant on? She probably would. Yes, I'm sure she would."

"You *bitch,*" he breathed.

In his mind, he saw himself locking his hands around the woman's throat and squeezing, squeezing so hard that she started to struggle as her face turned purple and her mouth gaped.

"On the other hand," Chantal murmured, "wouldn't your mother enjoy knowing that she was going to be a grandmother for the second time? Wouldn't that be cause for celebration."

"No one would believe it's mine," he heard himself say.

"Oh, but they will. He's going to look just like you — and I've been going up to Manhattan on a regular basis to work on our relationship. Everyone here knows it."

"You lie. I've never seen you."

"New York City is a big place. And I've made sure that all are aware in this family are aware that I've seen you and enjoyed your company. I've also talked about it to the girls at the club, their husbands at parties, my family — everybody has been so supportive of you and me."

As he remained silent, she smiled sweetly. "So you can see how those divorce papers aren't going to be required. And how you aren't going to say a thing about what happened between us with our first baby. If you do, I'm going to blow the lid wide open on your family and embarrass you in front of this community, your city, your state. Then we'll see how long it takes you to have to put on your funeral suit. Your mother's out of it, but she's not totally isolated — and her nurse reads her the paper every morning right beside her bed."

With a self-satisfied expression, Chantal turned away and shoved the panels open, clipping her way out into the marble foyer, once again the lady of leisure with the *Mona Lisa* smile.

Lane's entire body shook, his muscles screaming for action, for vengeance, for blood — but the rage was not aimed at his wife any longer.

It was all directed toward his father.

Cuckold. He believed that was the old-fashioned word that was used to describe this kind of thing.

He'd been cuckolded by his own god-damn father.

When in the hell was this day going to be over, he thought.

TWENTY-FIVE

Lizzie told herself she was not checking her phone. Not when she took the thing out of her purse and transferred it into her back pocket as soon as she walked through the front door of her farmhouse. Not as, a mere fifteen minutes later, she made sure that the ringer was on. And not even when, ten minutes after that, she unlocked the screen and made sure she hadn't missed any texts or calls.

Nothing.

Lane hadn't pinged her to make sure she'd gotten home. Hadn't responded to her text. But come on, like he didn't have a wet cat on his hands?

Jeez.

And yet she was antsy as she paced around. Her kitchen was spotless, which was a shame because she could have used something to clean up. The same was true with her bedroom upstairs — heck, even her bed was made — and she'd done her laundry the night before. The only thing that she found out of place was the towel she'd used that morning to dry off with after her shower. She'd hung it loosely over the shower curtain, and since it was still inside the two-day rule for going into the hamper, all she could do was fold the thing the long way and thread it back through the rod that was on the wall.

Thanks to a mostly cloudless day, her house was warm up on the second floor and she went around and opened all the windows. A breeze that smelled like the meadow around the property blew in and cleaned out the stuffiness.

Would that it could pull the same trick with her head. Images from the day bombarded her: her and Lane laughing when she'd just come in to work; her and Lane staring at her laptop; the two of them . . .

All up in her head, Lizzie returned to the kitchen and opened the door to the refrigerator. Nothing much there. Certainly nothing she had any interest in eating.

As the urge to check her phone again hit, she told herself to cut it out. Chantal could be a problem on a good day. Slapped with divorce papers with the scene witnessed by one of the help —

The sound of footsteps out on the front porch brought her head up.

Frowning, she shut the fridge and walked ahead to her living room. She didn't bother to check to see who it was. There were two choices: her next-door neighbor on the left, who lived five miles down the road and had cows who frequently broke through his fence and wandered into Lizzie's fields; or the next-door neighbor on the right, who was a mere mile and a quarter away, and whose dogs frequently wandered over to check out the free-range cows.

She started her greeting as she opened things up. "Hi, there —"

It was not her neighbors with apologies for bovines or canines.

Lane was standing on her porch, and his hair looked worse than it had in the morning, the dark waves sticking straight up off his head like he'd been trying to pull the stuff out.

He was too tired to smile. "I thought I'd see if you made it home all right firsthand."

"Oh, God, come here."

They met in the middle, body to body, and she held him hard. He smelled like fresh air, and over his shoulder, she saw that his Porsche had its top down.

"Are you all right?" she said.

"Better now. By the way, I'm kind of drunk."

"And you drove here? That's stupid and dangerous."

"I know. That's why I'm confessing."

She stepped back to let him come in. "I was about to eat?"

"You have enough for two?"

"Especially if it will sober you up." She shook her head. "No more drinking and driving. You think you have problems now? Try adding a DUI to your list."

"You're right." He looked around, and then went over to her piano and rested his hand on the smooth key guard. "God, nothing's changed."

She cleared her throat. "Well, I've been busy at work —"

"That's a good thing. A great thing."

The nostalgia on his face as he continued to stare at her antique tools and her hanging quilt and her simple sofa was better than any words he could have spoken.

"Food?" she prompted.

"Yes. Please."

Down in the kitchen, he went right over and sat at her little table. And abruptly, it was as if he had never been gone.

Be careful with that, she told herself.

"So how would you like . . ." She rifled through the contents of her cupboards and her refrigerator. ". . . well, how'd you like some lasagna that I froze about six months ago, with a side order of nacho chips from a bag I opened last night, capped off with some old Graeter's Peppermint Stick ice cream."

Lane's eyes focused on her and darkened.

Okaaaaaaaaaaaaay. Clearly, he was planning on having something else for dessert — and as her body warmed from the inside out, that was more than all right with her.

Shoot, she so wasn't listening to common sense here. Getting rid of his wife was only the tip of the iceberg for them, and she needed to keep that in mind.

"I think that sounds like the best meal in the world."

Lizzie crossed her arms and leaned back against the refrigerator. "Can I be honest?"

"Always."

"I know that Chantal got served with divorce papers. It was something I walked in on. I didn't mean to see the deputy do the deed."

"I told you that I was ending things."

She rubbed her forehead. "About two minutes before that, she came to me to plan an anniversary dinner for the pair of you."

There was a quiet curse. "I'm sorry. But I'm telling you right now, there is no future in the cards for her and me."

Lizzie stared at him long and hard — and in response, he didn't move, he didn't blink, he didn't say another word. He just sat there . . . and let his actions speak for him.

Damn it, she thought. She really, really didn't need to fall for him again.

As night settled over the stables, Edward found himself falling into his normal evening routine. Glass of ice? Check. Booze? Check — gin, tonight. Chair? Check.

Except when he sat down and faced all of those necessaries, he drummed his fingers on the armrest instead of putting them to use to crack the seal on the bottle.

"Come on," he said to himself. "Get with the program."

Alas . . . no. For some reason, the door out of the cottage was talking to him more than the Beefeater when it came to things he needed to open.

The day had been a long one, what with a trip to Steeplehill Downs to check on his two horses and make the call, with his vet and his trainer, that Bouncin' Baby Boy had to be scratched because of that tendon problem. Then he'd been back here, getting an assessment on five of his broodmares and their pregnancies, and reviewing the books and accounts with Moe. At least there had been good news on that front. For the second month in a row, the operation was not just self-sustaining, but pulling a profit. If this kept up, he was going to end those transfers from his mother's trust, the ones that had been providing a regular injection of cash into the business since back in the eighties.

He wanted to be totally independent of his family.

In fact, one of the first things he'd done when he'd gotten out of the rehab hospital was refuse his trust distributions. He didn't want to have anything to do with funds even remotely associated with the Bradford Bourbon Company — and the entire stock position of his first- and second-tier trusts was straight-up BBC. In fact, he hadn't found out about the transfers from his mother to the Red & Black until about six months in, and at that time, he'd been barely waking up to life at the stables. If he'd stopped them at that point? The operation would have gone under.

It had been a long time since someone with any kind of business acumen had been at the horse enterprise, and whatever his weaknesses were now, his knack for making money had remained unscathed.

One more month. Then he'd be free.

God, he was more exhausted than usual. More achy, too. Or maybe the two were inextricably intertwined?

And yet he still couldn't pick up the bottle.

Instead, he got to his feet with his cane and gimped his way to the drapes, which had been closed since the day he'd moved in. It was pitch-black outside now, only the big sodium lights at the heads of the barns throwing a peach glow against the darkness.

Cursing under his breath, he went to the front door and opened it. Paused for a moment. Limped out into the night.

Edward crossed the grass on a ragged gait and told himself he was going to look in on that mare who was having problems. Yes. That's what he was doing.

He was not checking in with Shelby Landis. Nope. He was not, for example, concerned that he hadn't seen her leave the farm all day and that meant that she probably had no food in that apartment of hers. He was also not, say, making certain that she had hot running water because, after the twelve hours she'd put in hauling wheelbarrows, sacks of grain that were the size of her truck, and itchy hay bales, she probably was going to be sore and in need of a good shower.

He was absolutely, positively —

"Damn it."

Without even being aware of it, he'd gone to the side door to Barn B . . . the one that opened up to the office, as well as the set of stairs that would take him to her place.

Well, considering he was here already . . . he might as well see how she was doing. Out of loyalty to her father, of course.

He did not run a hand through his hair before he turned the knob —

All right, maybe just a little, but only because he needed a haircut and the stuff was in his eyes.

Motion-activated lights came on as he stepped into the office area, and all those steps to the old hayloft area loomed over his head like a mountain he was going to have to struggle to climb. And what do you know, his pessimism was well founded: He had to take a breather halfway up. And another as soon as he reached the top.

Which was how he heard the laughter.

A man's. A woman's. Coming from Moe's apartment.

Frowning, Edward glanced toward Shelby's door. Shuffling over, he put his ear to the panels. Nothing.

When he did the same to Moe's? He could hear them both, the strong Southern drawls going back and forth like the fiddle and the banjo of a Bluegrass Band.

Edward closed his eyes for a moment and sagged against the closed door.

Then he picked himself up and caned his way down those stairs, out onto that grass, and back to his cottage.

This time he had no problem opening his booze. Or pouring it into his glass.

It was during his second serving that he realized it was Friday. Friday night.

Wasn't that a lucky draw.

He had a date, too.

TWENTY-SIX

Sutton Smythe looked over the crowd that had filled the Charlemont Museum of Art's main gallery space to capacity. So many faces she recognized, both those she knew personally and those she had seen on newscasts, on television, and on the big screen. Many people waved at her as they caught her eye, and she was cordial enough, lifting her palm in return.

She hoped that none of them came up to her.

She wasn't interested in connecting over a kiss on the cheek and an inquiry about their spouse or an introduction to their escort of the night. She didn't want to be thanked, yet again, for her generous donation last month of ten million dollars to kick-start the capital campaign for the museum's expansion. She also didn't want to have to acknowledge her father's permanent loan of that Rembrandt or the Fabergé egg that had been gifted outright in honor of her dearly departed mother.

Sutton wanted to be left alone to search the crowd for that one face she was looking for.

The one face she wanted . . . needed . . . to see.

But Edward Baldwine was, once again, not coming. And she knew this not because she'd been standing here in the shadows for the past hour and a half as the guests arrived to the party she was throwing on behalf of her family, but because she'd insisted on seeing a copy of the RSVP list once a week, and then daily, leading up to the event.

He hadn't responded at all. No, "Yes, I shall attend with pleasure," nor any "No, I am sending my regrets."

Could she really be surprised?

And yet it hurt. In fact, the only reason she'd gone to William Baldwine's party the night before was in hopes of seeing Edward in his own home. After he had not returned her calls for days, months, and now years, she had thought that maybe he would make an appearance at his father's table and they could organically reconnect.

But no. Edward had not been there, either —

"Miss Smythe, we're ready to seat the guests, if that's all right with you? The salads are down on the tables."

Sutton smiled at the woman with the clipboard and the earpiece. "Yes, let's dim the lights. I'll make my remarks as soon as they're in their chairs."

"Very well, Miss Smythe."

Sutton took a deep breath and watched the herd of expensive cattle do what they were told and find their places at all those round tables with their elaborate centerpieces, and their golden plates, and their engraved menus on top of linen napkins.

Back before the tragedy, Edward had always been at these things: Shooting her sardonic smiles as yet another person glommed on to him to ask him for money for their causes. Asking her to dance as a rescue maneuver when she got cornered by a close talker. Looking at her and winking . . . just because he could.

They had been friends since Charlemont Country Day. Business competitors since he'd graduated from Wharton and she'd gotten her MBA from the University of Chicago. Social cohorts since they'd entered the charity-dinner circuit when her mother had passed and his had started to go to her room with greater and greater frequency.

They had never been lovers.

She had wanted to them to be. For as long as she had known him, it seemed. But Edward had stayed away, sticking to the sidelines, even setting her up with other people

Her heart had always been his for the taking, but she'd never had the guts to walk over that line that he'd seemed so very determined to draw between them.

And then . . . two years ago had happened. Dear Lord, when she'd heard about him heading off for another of those South American business trips of his, she'd had a premonition, a warning, a bad feeling. But she hadn't called him. Reached out. Tried to get him to take more security or something.

So in some way, she had always felt partially responsible. Maybe if she'd . . .

But who was she kidding. He wouldn't have stopped going down there for any reason other than bad weather. Edward had been a true competitor in the liquor industry, the heir apparent to the Bradford Bourbon Company not just by birthright, but by his incredible work ethic and savvy.

After the kidnapping and the ransom demand, his father, William, had tried so hard to get him free, negotiating with the kidnappers, working with the US Embassy. Everything had failed until, eventually, a special team had been sent in and had rescued Edward.

She couldn't imagine what had been done to him.

And this was the anniversary of when he'd gotten ambushed while traveling.

Such a shame, the whole thing. South America was one of the most beautiful places in the world with delicious food, fantastic landscapes, and an amazing history — she and Edward had always joked that they would retire down there on side-by-side estates. The kidnapping and ransoming of business executives was one of the travel advisories for certain areas, but that was no different than someone being told not to go through Central Park at three in the morning: Bad elements could be found wherever you were, and there was no reason to condemn an entire continent because of a minority of bad actors.

Unfortunately, Edward had become one of the victims.

After all this time, she just wanted to see him with her own eyes. There had been a couple of blurry photos that had been in the press, and they had certainly not set her mind at ease. He had appeared so much thinner, his body hunched over, his face always turned down and away from the cameras.

To her, he would still be beautiful, however.

"Miss Smythe, we're ready if you are?"

Shaking herself into focus, Sutton saw that the one thousand person crowd was seated, picking at their salads, and ready to hear her speak —

Without warning, a sudden roar of dreadful energy pounded through her, bringing sweat out across her chest, over her forehead, under her arms. As her heart leaped into a snare-drum rhythm, waves of lightheadedness caused her to reach out and steady herself on the wall.

What was wrong with her —

"Miss Smythe?"

"I can't," she heard herself say.

"I'm sorry?"

She pressed the index cards she'd so carefully written out into the hands of the assistant. "Someone else needs to —"

"What? Wait, where are you —"

She put her palms up and backed away. "— give the speech."

"Miss Smythe, you're the only one who —"

"I'll call you on Monday, I'm sorry, I can't

do this —"

Sutton had no idea where she was going as her high heels clipped a retreat over the marble floor. In fact, it wasn't until a wave of heat hit her that she realized she'd left the building via a fire exit and had emerged on the west side of the complex, out in the humid night air.

Far from the parking lot where her chauffeur was waiting.

Collapsing against the museum's stuccoed wall, she took deep breaths that did nothing to relieve a crushing sense of suffocation.

She couldn't stay out here all night. More to the point, she wanted to run fast and far away, run until this feeling of ambient terror worked its way out of her system. But that was crazy . . . right?

God, she was losing her mind. Finally, the pressure of everything was getting to her.

Or maybe it was, once again and always, Edward Baldwine.

Time to get moving. This was ridiculous.

Shucking her stilettos and holding them by the ankle straps, she started out over the grass, staying close to the pools of illumination thrown by the security lights. After what seemed like forever, the parking lot she was in search of appeared when she turned yet another corner — except then she was confounded by the number of cars and limousines parked in the open-air space.

Where was her —

By some stroke of luck, the black Mercedes C63 found her, the large sedan drawing up in front of her, its passenger-side window going down soundlessly.

"Ma'am?" her chauffeur said in alarm. "Ma'am, are you all right?"

"I need the car." Sutton walked around to him, the headlights flaring brilliant white against her silver gown and her diamonds. "I need the car, I need . . ."

"Ma'am?" The uniformed man got out from behind the wheel. "I'll drive you wherever you have to go —"

She took a hundred-dollar bill out of her tiny evening bag. "Here. Please get a cab, or call someone, I'm sorry. I'm so sorry, I need to . . . go —"

He shook his head at the cash. "Ma'am, I can take you anywhere —"

"Please. I need the car."

There was a short pause. "All right. Do you know how to drive this —"

"I'll figure it out." She put the money against his palm and curled his hand into a fist. "Keep this. I'll be fine."

"I'd rather drive you myself."

"I appreciate the kindness, I truly do." She

shut herself in, put the window up, and looked around for the gear shift or the —

At the knock on the tinted glass, she put the thing back down.

"It's there — to the side of the wheel," the chauffeur said. "That's where your drive and reverse are. There you go. And the directional signal is — yup, that's right. You shouldn't need the windshield wipers, and the headlights are already on as you can see. Good luck."

He stepped back, kind of like you'd do if someone were about to put a match to fireworks. Or a bomb.

Sutton hit the gas, and the powerful sedan lurched forward as if there were a jet engine under the hood. In the back of her mind, she did a quick calculation on how many years it had been since she'd actually driven herself anywhere — and the answer was not encouraging.

But just like everything else in her life, she was going to figure it out — or die trying.

"Mind if I have some more?"

As Lizzie gave him an *Oh, please, do,* Lane got up and headed back for the fridge. The food was helping clear his head — or maybe it was her company.

Probably more just being in her presence.

"This is really good," he said as he broke open the ice box and took out another serving.

Her soft laugh made him pause and close his eyes, so the sound could sink into him even more deeply.

"You're just being nice," she murmured.

"God's honest."

Putting his plate into the microwave, he hit six minutes and watched as the frozen block went around and around.

"So I'm going to have to talk to Edward," he heard himself say.

"When was the last time you saw him?"

He cleared his throat. Felt that itch for a little drink. "It was . . ."

For a moment, he got lost in wondering how he could ask her if she had any booze in the house. "Wow."

"That long?"

"Actually, I was thinking about something else." Namely, that it was entirely possible that he had a drinking problem. "But come on, after a day like today, who wouldn't be an alcoholic?"

"What?"

Oh, shit, had he spoken out loud? "Sorry, my brain's a mess."

"I wish there was something I could do to help."

"You are."

"So when did you see Edward last?"

Lane closed his eyes again. But instead of doing some mental calculation that would reveal the sum of how much he sucked as a brother, he went back in time to that New Year's night when Edward had gotten beaten for the rest of them.

He and Maxwell had stayed in the ballroom, silent and trembling, as their father had forced Edward upstairs. As the two sets of footfalls had ascended the grand staircase, Lane had screamed at the top of his lungs — but only internally.

He was too much of a coward to jump out and stop the lie that had saved him and his brother.

"I should go up there," he said as time passed.

"But what can you do?" Max whispered. "Nothing will stop Father."

"I could . . ."

Except Max was right. Edward had lied, and their father was making him pay for a transgression that was not his own. If Lane told the truth now . . . their father would simply beat them all. At least if he and Maxwell stayed put here, they could avoid . . .

No, this was wrong. This was dishonorable.

"I'm going up there." Before Maxwell could say anything, Lane grabbed his brother's arm. "And you're coming with me."

Max's conscience must have been bothering him as well, because instead of arguing like he always did with everything, he followed mutely up the front stairs. When they got to the top, the grand hallway was empty save for the fancy moldings, the oil paintings, and the bouquets sitting on antique tables or bureaus.

"We've got to stop this," Lane hissed.

One after the other, they moved quickly over the carpeted runner . . . to their father's door.

On the other side of the panels, the sounds of the whipping were sharp and loud, from the slaps of leather hitting bare skin to the grunts as their father put strength into it.

Edward was silent.

And meanwhile, the two of them just stood there, silent and stupid. All Lane could think about was how neither he nor Max would be even half as strong. They would both have ended up crying.

The drive to be righteous and honest grew weaker with each of those hits . . . until Lane's nerve was totally lost.

"Let's go," he choked out with shame.

Once again, Max did not put up a fight. He was obviously too much of a coward as well.

The room they shared was down farther,

and Lane was the one who opened the door. There were plenty of bedrooms to spare for them to sleep separately, but when Maxwell had started getting night terrors a couple of years before, they had become roommates by default: Max had started sneaking into Lane's room and waking up there in the morning. Eventually, Miss Aurora had moved another bed in, and that was that.

Their bathroom was a Jack and Jill — and the room on the far side of the long, thin space was Edward's.

Max got in his bed and stared straight ahead. "We shouldn't have gone down there. It's my fault."

"It's both our fault." He glanced down at Max. "You stay there. I'm going to go wait for him to come back in."

As he went into the loo, he closed the door behind himself and prayed Max followed orders. He had a bad feeling about what kind of condition Edward was going to be in when their father was done with him.

Oh, how Lane wanted to go back to earlier and redo the decision to go to the parlor.

Putting the toilet seat down, he sat and listened to the pounding of his heart. Even though he couldn't hear the whipping anymore, it didn't matter. He knew what was happening across the hall.

For some reason, he kept looking over at their three toothbrushes, which were standing up in a silver cup by the folded hand towels on the counter. The red one was Edward's because he was the eldest and always got to pick first. Max went for green because it was the manliest of what was left. Lane got stuck with yellow and hated it.

No one ever wanted KU blue —

A soft click and the rasp of a door being opened broke the quiet. Lane waited until there was a second click and then he got to his feet and peered into Edward's room.

In the dimness, Edward was walking toward the bathroom all bent over, with one arm around his belly, and the other thrown out to steady himself on the bureau, the wall, the desk.

Lane rushed forward and took ahold of his brother's waist.

"Sick," Edward groaned. "Gonna be sick."

Oh, God, he was bleeding down his face, their father's signet ring having cut into his skin when he'd been cuffed.

"I've got you," Lane mumbled. "I'll take care of you."

The going was slow, Edward's legs struggling to hold his torso up. Part of his pj's top had gotten stuck in the waistband of the pants when they'd been pulled back into place after the whipping, and all Lane could think about was what was underneath. The welts, the blood, the swelling.

Edward barely made it to the toilet in time, and Lane stayed throughout the vomiting. When it was done, he took that red toothbrush out of the silver cup and got the Crest. After a brushing, he helped his brother back out and over to the bed.

"Why don't you cry," Lane said roughly as his brother settled on the mattress like his entire body hurt. "Just cry. He'll stop as soon as you do."

That was the way it was whenever he and Max got beaten.

"Go to bed, Lane."

Edward's voice was exhausted.

"I'm sorry," Lane whispered.

"It's okay. Go to bed."

It had been hard to leave, but he'd already screwed up badly once that night and look what had happened with that.

Back in his own room, he'd gotten in between his sheets and stared up at the ceiling.

"Is he okay?" Max asked.

For some reason, the shadows in their room were completely threatening, seeming to have been thrown by monsters moving and lurking on the periphery.

"Lane?"

"Yes," he lied. "He's fine —"

"Lane?"

Lane shook himself, and glanced over his shoulder. "What?" Lizzie pointed at the microwave. "It's done?"

Beep . . .

Beep . . .

He just stood there and blinked, trying to return from the past. "Right, sorry."

Back at the table, he put the steaming food down and sat in his seat . . . only to discover that he'd lost his appetite. When Lizzie reached across and put her hand on his, he took what she offered and brought it to his mouth for a kiss.

"What are you thinking about?" Lizzie asked.

"You really want to know?"

"Yes."

Well, didn't he have so many things to pick from.

As she waited for an answer, he stared at her face for the longest time. And then he smiled a little. "Right now . . . this very moment . . . I'm thinking that if I have a chance with you, Lizzie King, I'm going to take it."

The blush that hit her face was covered when she put her palms up. "Oh, God . . ."

He laughed softly. "You want me to change the subject?"

"Yes," she said from hiding.

He didn't blame her. "Fine, I'm really glad I came out here. Easterly is like a rope around my throat right now."

Lizzie rubbed her eyes, and then dropped those hands. "You know, I can't believe about Rosalinda."

"That is just plain horrific." He sat back in his chair, respecting her need for another topic. "And get this. Mitch Ramsey, the sheriff's deputy? He called me on the way here. The medical examiner's initial thought is hemlock."

"Hemlock?"

"Her face . . ." He circled his own with his hand. "That gruesome smile? It was caused by some kind of facial paralysis — which happens to be well documented with that variety of poison, apparently. Man, I'll tell you what, I'm not likely to forget what that looked like for a very long time."

"Is it possible she was killed?"

"They don't think so. You need a good dose of hemlock to get the job done, so it's more likely she did it herself. Plus her Nikes were brand new and had grass on the bottoms."

"Nikes? She doesn't wear anything except flats."

"Exactly, but she was found with this pair of running shoes on, which she'd evidently just bought and walked around in outside. From what Mitch said, back in Roman times, people used to take the poison and then ambulate to make it work faster. So again, that points to her doing it herself."

"How . . . horrific."

"The question is why . . . and unfortunately, I think we know the answer to that one."

"What are you going to do now?"

He stayed silent for a while. And then his eyes lifted to hers. "For starters, I was thinking of taking you upstairs."

Lizzie blushed again. "And what are you going to do with me on the second floor?"

"Help you fold your laundry."

She barked out a laugh. "I hate to disappoint you, but that's already been done."

"Make your bed?"

"Sorry. Done."

"Curse your work ethic. Darn your socks? Any buttons that need replacing?"

"Are you saying you're good with a needle and thread?"

"I'm a fast learner. So . . . care to sew with me?"

"I'm afraid I've got nothing like that to attend to."

"Is there something else I can help you with then," he said in a low voice. "Some kind of ache I could soothe. Some fire I could put out — with my mouth, maybe?"

Lizzie closed her eyes, and swayed in her chair. "Oh . . . God . . ."

"Wait, I've got it. How 'bout I take you to the second floor and we mess up your bed — then we can remake it."

When she finally looked over at him, her lids were low and her eyes were hot. "You know . . . that sounds like a perfect plan."

"I love it when we're both on the same page."

They stood up together, and before she could stop him, he went over and picked her up.

"What are you doing?" She pushed at his hold as she started to laugh. "Lane —"

"What does it look like." He headed out of the kitchen. "I'm carrying you upstairs."

"Wait. Wait, I weigh too much —"

"Oh, *please*."

"No, I really — I'm not one of those tiny little females —"

"Exactly. You're a real woman." He hit the stairs and kept going. "And that's what real men are attracted to. Trust me."

She let her head fall on his shoulder, and as he felt her eyes search his face, he thought of what Chantal had done with his father. Or at least, what she had said she'd done.

Lizzie had never betrayed him. Not in thought Not in deed.

She simply wasn't hardwired like that.

Which made her a real woman, and not just because she was no hundred-pound, social X-ray.

"No, you don't have to say it," he murmured as the old steps creaked under his feet.

"Say what?"

"That this doesn't mean anything in the larger scheme of things. I know you want me as a friend only, and I accept that. You should be aware of one caveat, though."

"What's that," she breathed.

He let his voice deepen. "I'm prepared to be a very patient man when it comes to you. I will seduce you for however long it takes — give you space if you need it or follow you tight as sunshine on your shoulder if you'll let me." His eyes locked on hers. "I lost my chance with you once, Lizzie King — that is not going to happen again."

TWENTY-SEVEN

As Edward sat in his chair, he was floating on a cloud of Beefeater gin, his body numb to the point where he was actually able to entertain a fantasy of potential strength and flexibility. In fact, he could imagine that getting to his feet would be an impulse easily followed, an uncomplicated, unconscious change of location requiring nothing more than a passing thought and a pair of thigh muscles that were happy enough — and capable enough — to do the job.

He was not drunk enough to actually give it a try, however —

The sound of a knocking on his door brought his head up.

Well, well, well. Given that he wasn't prepared to try the whole verticality thing, at least this arrival represented another alternative reality he could partake in.

And this one he would not deny.

With a grunt, he tried to sit a little

straighter in his chair. There would be no going and opening the way for the woman, and he felt badly about that. A gentleman should always perform such a service for a member of the fairer sex, and he didn't care that his guest was a prostitute — the female deserved to be treated with respect.

"Come in," he called out, slurring his words. "Come on in . . ."

The door opened slowly . . . and what was on the other side, standing directly under the porch light was —

Edward's heart stopped beating. And then began to hammer.

"They got it right," he breathed. "Finally, Beau got it right."

The woman blinked. "I'm sorry?" she said roughly. "What did you say?"

The voice, too. How had they matched the voice?

"Come in," he rasped, motioning with his free hand, the one that didn't have the glass in it. "Please."

And do not be afraid, he thought to himself.

After all, in his current position, he was sitting in darkness, the illumination on the countless trophies in those shelves not quite reaching his face or his body. Which was deliberate, of course. He didn't like looking at his own self — there was no reason to make the whore's job harder by forcing her to have a clear picture of him.

"Edward?" she said.

In his drunken haze, all he could do was close his eyes as he went both limp . . . and hard in a very critical place. "You sound . . . as beautiful as I remember."

He hadn't heard Sutton Smythe's voice in person since before his trip down way south, and after he'd returned, he'd been unable to listen to any of her voice mails.

To the point where he'd ended up throwing that particular phone and number away.

"Oh, Edward . . ."

Dear Lord, there was pain in that voice. As if the woman were looking into his soul and responding to the tangle of anguish he'd carried around with him since he'd been told he was, in fact, going to live.

And indeed, it was so close to what Sutton actually sounded like. Funny, during his captivity, he'd lost consciousness three times over the course of the eight days he'd been held. Each time he had been in the process of fainting, Sutton had been the last thing he'd thought of, envisioned, heard, mourned. It hadn't been his family. Not his beloved business. Not the house he'd grown up in, nor the wealth, nor all the things he was going to leave undone.

It had been Sutton Smythe.

And that third time? When he'd been unable to see anymore, when he'd been unable to tell what was his sweat and what was his blood, when the torture had taken him to a place where the survival switch had been flipped off and he no longer prayed to get free, but for death . . .

Sutton Smythe had, once again, been the only thing on his mind.

"Edward —"

"No." He held up his hand. "Don't speak anymore."

She was doing so well already. He didn't want the woman to get ahead of herself and screw it all up.

"Come here," he whispered. "I want to touch you."

Opening his eyes, he drank in her approach. Oh, what a perfect silver dress that was, the hem of the gown down to the floor, her surprisingly tasteful jewels sparkling even when the light was behind her. And she also had the kind of clutch Sutton had always taken with her to formal events, the small, silk-covered square perfectly dyed to the hue of the dress even though, as she herself had always said, "matchy-matchy" was "so fifties."

"Edward?"

There was both confusion and yearning in his name.

"Please," he found himself begging. "Just . . . no talking. I only want to touch you. Please."

As her body trembled before him, he felt reality shift and he allowed himself to go with the ruse, falling into a fantasy that it actually was Sutton, that she had come to him, that they were, finally, going to be together.

Even though he was ruined.

God, it was enough to make him teary. But that didn't last long . . . because she stumbled and her eyes grew impossibly wide.

Which meant she had seen his face.

"Don't look too hard," he said. "I know I'm not as I used to be. That's why the lights are low."

Edward reached out and showed her his hands. "But these . . . these are unmarred. And unlike many parts of me, they still work just fine. Let me . . . touch you. I'll be careful — but you have to kneel down. I'm not too well on my feet anymore, and I must confess to having imbibed."

The prostitute was shaking from head to toe as she started to lower herself, and he sat forward, offering her his arm as if she were a lady disembarking from a car — as opposed to a working girl who was prepared to let a cripple have sex with her body in exchange for a thousand dollars.

When he eased back again, a sudden wave of dizziness came over him, testament that more of the alcohol was pumping into his system. Like all drunks, however, he knew that that was a temporary glitch that would self-regulate.

Especially given all that he had to focus on: Even with his fuzzy vision, even with the dimness, even being drunk off his ass . . . he was in awe.

This one was so beautiful, almost too beautiful to touch.

"Oh, look at you," he whispered, reaching out to brush her cheek.

Her eyes flared again, or at least he thought they did — maybe he was just imagining things because of the way she drew in a quick breath. It was so hard to know, hard to track what was happening . . . reality was going all wonky on him now, twisting around on itself until he wasn't sure how much the prostitute actually looked like Sutton and how much he was projecting onto her just because she had long dark hair, and arching brows, and a mouth that was Grace Kelly perfect.

The woman's hair was down, just as he'd asked it to be, and he brushed his hand over the waves until he felt the curve of her shoulder. "You smell so good. Just like I remembered."

And then he was touching more of her, his fingertips traveling across her collarbone, over her diamond necklace, down to the curves of her décolleté. In response, she began to breathe harder, the pump of her lungs bringing her breasts close to his palms.

"I love this dress," he murmured.

The gown was just Sutton's style: beautifully put together, tailored to the body that filled it out, made from chiffon that was the gray of a dove.

Sitting forward, he brought his meager chest to her spectacular one and reached around to find the carefully hidden zipper. As he drew the thing downward, the sound of the unfastening seemed so very loud.

He could have sworn she gasped as if he had shocked her. And that was oh, so perfect. Exactly what Sutton would have done.

And then yes, oh, yes, the whore returned his exploration, her shaking hands going up his thin arms. God, he hated all that trembling on her part, but then he was no doubt hard to have sex with.

At least with the way he was now.

"I wish I had done this before," he said in a voice that cracked. "My body was once something worth seeing. I should have . . . I should have tried to have you before, but I was too much of a coward. I was an arrogant coward — but the truth was, I could have withstood anything except you turning me down."

"Edward —"

He cut her off by putting his mouth against hers.

Oh, she was good. As good as he'd always imagined she would be, the slick feel of his tongue slipping into her and the way she moaned like she'd been waiting a lifetime for this making him forget what he had become.

That gown melted away, falling from her body as if it were in on the gig — as if it were perhaps getting a kickback for making the session happen faster. And he took advantage of the skin that now showed, kissing his way down to her perfect breasts, suckling on her nipples, getting greedy fast. Bless the poor woman's heart, she managed to fake things so well, her hands threading into his hair just as he wanted them to, her grip bringing him closer to her, even though that couldn't possibly be what the prostitute actually wanted.

He tried not to be rough with her, but God, he was so hungry all of a sudden.

"Get into my lap," he groaned. "You're going to have to get into my lap."

It was the only way he could have sex. Especially as he didn't want to subject either one of them to the embarrassment of her having to help him off the floor after it was over.

"Are you sure?" she said roughly. "Edward —"

"I have to have you. I've waited too long. I almost died. I need this."

There was a heartbeat's worth of pause. Then she moved with admirable quickness, rising from the floor, kicking the gown free, revealing — sweet Jesus, she had a thong on and nothing else, no stockings, no garters. And rather than wasting time to take the thing off, she pushed it to the side as he fumbled with the belt that kept his pants from falling off his jutting hip bones.

In spite of how the rest of him had faded away, his cock was still as hard and long and thick as ever — and he was oddly grateful to that organ for being the only thing that wasn't completely humiliating about this for him.

Shoving his arms into the chair, he pushed himself even farther forward, and she pretzeled herself, mounting him with enviable coordination —

His arousal penetrated her deeply, and the tight, hot hold she brought to him made him orgasm immediately — but that was not the amazing thing. Apparently the feel of him, by some miracle, did the same for her.

As she called out his name, she seemed to find her own release as well.

Either that or she'd missed her calling and should have been an Oscar-caliber actress.

Before Edward knew what he was doing, he began to move. It was weak, and rather pathetic, but she followed the lead, that first release soon getting eclipsed by an even greater orgasm for them both. Shuddering, rocking, straining, she held on to him for dear life, her hair getting into his face, her breasts pressing in to him, her body taking him on a ride like nothing he'd ever had.

The sex seemed to go on forever.

When it was finally finished, after a third orgasm for him, he collapsed back into the chair and panted. "I'm going to need you again."

"Oh, Edward —"

"Tell Beau . . . next week. Same time,

same day."

"What?"

He let his head loll to the side. "Money's over there. Only you. I only want you again."

Abruptly, probably because he'd exerted himself more in the last twenty minutes than he had over the previous twelve months, he began to feel faint — and indeed, it seemed appropriate to pass out and let the prostitute leave on her own.

He could keep the fantasy going more easily that way.

"Thousand . . . by the door," he mumbled. "Take it. Tip will come . . ."

Edward meant to say "Tip will come later. I'll have someone drop it off at Beau's" or something to that effect. But consciousness became a luxury he could no longer afford . . . and he gave himself up to the oblivion.

Once again, thinking only of Sutton Smythe.

Sutton stumbled out of Edward's cottage. Her shoes were off and dangling from their straps, but unlike her earlier trip through the grass around the museum building, the porch boards and then the cobblestone path hurt.

It wasn't as though she cared.

401

As she bolted for the Mercedes, she was a mass of contradictions, her brain a jammed-up mess, her body all loosey-goosey.

He'd thought she was a *prostitute*?

But why else had he been talking about money and some guy named Beau? Next week?

Oh, God, they'd had sex . . .

How had they done that? How had she let . . .

Dear Lord, his poor face, his body.

Around and around the thoughts spun in her head, until, as if by centrifugal force, everything weeded out except for the fact that Edward was not at all as he had once been. His handsome looks were gone, the scars on his cheeks and across the bridge of his nose and forehead making it virtually impossible to reconstruct by memory the perfection that had once been there.

She'd been aware that he'd been treated badly. Newspaper and television reports, her only source of information because he had refused to see anyone, had detailed the lengths of his hospital and rehabilitation stays — and that kind of extensive treatment did not happen without tragically good reason. But seeing him in person had been a total shock.

He'd been a polo player before the abduction. An event jumper. A runner. A basketball, tennis, and squash player. A swimmer. And because Edward had been a golden boy not just in business, but in every other aspect of his life, he had excelled at all of them.

I wish I had done this before. My body was once something worth seeing.

Sutton struggled to open her car's driver's-side door, her hand slipping off over and over again like she'd had some kind of a stroke and could no longer grip things properly. And when she finally was able to get herself into the car, she ran out of energy and just collapsed into the seat.

I should have tried to have you before, but I was too much of a coward. I was an arrogant coward — but I could have withstood anything except you turning me down.

What had he been saying — and who had he thought he'd been saying it to? Her heart broke with the idea that he was in love with someone like that.

He'd been so drunk. To the point where right before she bolted, she'd checked to make sure his heart was still beating and he was breathing — because, yes, the idea that she might have killed him because they'd . . .

"Dear Lord."

How was it possible that, after years of thinking about it, they'd actually had sex. But only because he'd thought she was a whore he'd ordered from somewhere?

And no, they hadn't used protection.

Fabulous. This veering off the beaten path thing tonight was just all-around wonderful . . . especially because, even though he'd been drunk . . . even though she'd been a head case . . . and in spite of the physical condition he'd been in . . . the sex had been incredible. Maybe it was all that pent-up wondering, maybe it was compatibility, maybe it was because it had been a one-time-only, stars-aligned kind of event.

But whatever the reasons, he had just blown away the few men she had been with.

And, she feared, scorched the earth for anybody else.

Reaching forward, she pushed the start/stop button — and as the car's engine let out a purr, the headlights flared and made her panic. There were other people on the grounds — had to be — and the last thing she wanted was to get caught. She was going to need to figure out how to deal with this, and having the gossip mill get to churning was not going to be part of her coping strategy, thank you very much —

At that very moment, another car came

down the alley of trees and, instead of heading for one of the barns or outbuildings, it pulled up right next to her.

The woman who got out was . . . tall, brunette, and dressed in a full-length evening gown.

She frowned as she looked at the Mercedes.

And came over.

Sutton put her window down, because what else was she supposed to do? At the same time, she also started searching for the right lever, button, whatever, to get the sedan into reverse.

"I thought I was on the schedule for this tonight?" the woman asked pleasantly enough.

"I . . . ah . . ." As Sutton stammered, a flush ran through her. "Ah . . ."

"Are you one of the new girls Beau was talkin' about? I'm Delilah."

Sutton shook the hand that was offered. "How do you do."

"Oh, you sound so posh!" The woman smiled. "So did you take care of him?"

"Ah . . ."

"It's okay if you did. Sometimes these things happen, and I've got two other calls tonight." She reached up and yanked what turned out to be a wig off her head. "At least I can be free of this. Is he okay?"

"I'm sorry?"

The woman rubbed at her cropped blond hair as she nodded in the direction of the cottage. "Him? We all look after him, the poor guy. Beau won't tell us who he is, but he must be someone important. He's always so generous, and he treats us all real good. Such a sad case, really."

"Yes. It is very sad."

"Well, I'll head out. You want me to let Beau know we're all set?"

"Ah . . ."

"I'll take care of next week, then."

"No," Sutton heard herself say. "He told me . . . the man said he wanted me again?"

"Oh, okay, no problem. I'll pass that word along."

"Thank you. Thank you very much."

Maybe this was some kind of a bizarre fever dream?

As Sutton resumed her search for the right lever, the prostitute leaned back down. "Are you looking for reverse?"

"Ah, yes, yes, I am."

"It's that one right there. Move it up for reverse. All the way down is drive, and you push in the end for park."

"Thank you. It's hard."

"One of my regulars has this exact car.

It's a real beauty! Drive safe."

Making a noncommittal noise, Sutton backed her way around carefully, very aware that the other woman was standing oh, so close with that brunette wig in her hand.

Heading off to the main road, she decided this had to be the result of her having contracted the flu and taken to her bed. Any moment she was going to wake up . . .

Really.

She was.

Holy shit, how did all that just happen?

Twenty-Eight

The day of the Derby dawned bright and clear, although, as Lizzie drove in to work, there could have been thunder and lightning, torrential flooding, and hurricane winds, and she would still have smiled the entire ride to Charlemont.

Lane and she had played rock, paper, scissors to decide who went in first, and in spite of the fact that he had won three times in a row, they'd decided she should leave before him. One, she had a lot to do, and two, he had been in no hurry to go anywhere.

Every time she blinked, she saw him laying back in her sheets, his naked chest on display, his very naked lower body hidden underneath.

She had never felt so rested after having had little to no sleep all night long.

Passing by the main entrance to Easterly, she had to shake her head. You never knew where you were going to end up, did you.

So much for the whole "friends" only thing.

Coming around to the staff road, she promptly had to hit her brakes and join a long line of delivery trucks and cars. She was relieved to see so many of the former in light of the problem they'd had with the rental company, but nervous about how Lane and his family would pay for all the additional help considering the latter.

When she finally got to the parking lot, she had to squeeze the Yaris into a spot in the back. There were about a hundred waiters and waitresses coming to staff the party, and their vehicles all had to go somewhere. In another hour? The lower road was going to be lined with pickup trucks and motorcycles and twelve kinds of sedans.

Getting out, she hooked up with the parade of people trooping to the house on the back path. Nobody was saying anything, and that was fine with her. In her head, she was working her punch list and prioritizing the things she wanted to do before the floodgates opened and over six hundred of the most important people in town for the races came through Easterly's front door.

Number one on her list?

Greta.

She had to somehow fix things with Greta

because they were going to have to work as a team in order to survive the next four hours.

As she saw the conservatory looming on the far side of the garden, she braced herself. Her partner had to be in there already, was no doubt picking over all of the bouquets, making sure that not a single wilted petal or leaf marred the perfect presentations before they were taken out to the tables.

She'd probably been here since 6:45.

Just as Lizzie should have been.

And would have been, except for that whole Lane-in-her-bed thing.

"I'm a grown woman," she told herself. "I say who, I say when, I say . . ."

Great. She was quoting *Pretty Woman.*

The problem was, if her business partner asked her why she was late, things were going to go from really bad to totally worse. She was a horrible liar, and all the tomato red that was going to hit her face before she could stutter out a non-answer was going to give her away like a billboard.

I SPENT ALL NIGHT BONING LANE BALDWINE.

Or whatever German phrase came close to that.

Squaring her shoulders, Lizzie hiked her

bag up a little higher on her shoulder and marched over to the double doors.

As she opened them and stepped into the fragrant, thick air of the conservatory, she decided to lead with —

"You're a grown woman," Greta blurted as she looked up from a bouquet. "And I'm sorry. I had no right to . . . you're a grown woman and you're entitled to make your own decisions. I'm really sorry."

Lizzie released her breath on a oner. "I'm sorry, too."

Greta pushed her tortoiseshell glasses higher on her nose. "What for? You didn't do anything wrong. I just — look, I'm ten years older than you. So it's not just that I have more wrinkles on my face or more wear and tear on my body. I feel like I have to take care of you. You haven't asked me to, and you probably don't need it, but that's how it is —"

"Greta, really. You don't have to apologize. We're both under a lot of stress —"

"And besides, I heard he served her with divorce papers yesterday."

"Word travels fast." She put her bag down. "How did you find out?"

"One of the maids saw her throw the papers at the deputy." Greta shook her head. "So classy."

"I told him not to do it because of me."

"Well, whatever his reasoning, he followed through on it." Greta resumed working her way down the tables. "Just promise me something. Watch out for him. This family, they've got a history of treating people as disposable, and that never goes well for the toy of the moment."

Lizzie put her hands on her hips and stared down at her work boots. Which she'd put on in front of Lane — giving him a show that he'd been very vocal about enjoying.

Ouch, she thought. Her chest really hurt at the very salient reminder that with them resuming their physical relationship, things had changed totally . . . and not at all.

"I just don't want to see you hurt like that again." Greta cleared the emotion out of her voice. "Now, let's get to work —"

"He's not like his family. He isn't."

Greta paused and stared out at the garden. After a moment, she shook her head. "Lizzie, it's in his blood. He's not going to be able to help it."

When Lane got back to Easterly, he parked his Porsche off to the side, in the shadows of the paved lane that led around back to the garages.

"I'm home now," he said into his phone. "You want me to come up and re-explain the plan?"

His sister took a while to answer him, and he could just picture Gin shaking her head as she pushed her hair over her shoulder.

"No, I think you've covered everything," she intoned.

He repositioned his U of C baseball cap on his head and stared up at the sky so high above. He'd put the top down as he'd left Lizzie's, and the roar of the wind as he'd sped home had given him the illusion of freedom he'd been looking for.

God . . . Lizzie. The only reason he was going to get through today in even halfway decent shape was because of the night he'd spent with her. He'd made love to her for hours . . . and then, as she'd slept, he had stared up at that ceiling of hers and figured out, step by step, how he needed to proceed.

"Are you going to talk to him today?" Gin asked him roughly.

For once, the "him" was not Edward.

"I want to." Lane ground his molars. "But not yet. I'm not saying one thing to Father until I know the scope of it all. If I have that conversation before I can prove anything? He's just going to slash and burn whatever he hasn't shredded already."

"So when will you get with him?"

He frowned. "Gin, you say nothing. Are we clear? Do not say one goddamn word — especially to Father."

"I hate him."

"Then take the long view. If you want him to get what's coming? You need to let him hang himself. Do you understand what I'm saying? You confront him, you're actually helping him. I'm going to take care of this, but there's a process. Gin? Do you hear me?"

After a moment, there was a soft chuckle. "You sound like Edward used to."

For a split second, he felt a bolt of high-octane pride. Then again, every one of them had always looked up to Edward.

"That's about the nicest thing you've ever said to me," he muttered gruffly.

"I mean it."

"So radio silence today, Gin. And I'll let you know how we're progressing."

"Okay . . . all right."

"Good girl. I love you. I'm going to take care of us. All of us."

"I love you, too, Lane."

Lane ended the connection and kept watching the clouds. Off in the distance, he could hear the patter of talk, and as he leveled his head, he saw down by the garage a vast group of uniformed waiters clustered around Reginald, the lot of them getting their marching orders.

Gin better keep her mouth shut, he thought.

William Baldwine was already going to be twitchy from Rosalinda's death. If Lane — or God forbid Gin, with the likes of her mouth — came at him? He would hide things, disappear records, destroy details.

Assuming anything like that was left.

Lane lolled his head to the side so that he stared at Easterly. How much of this would be left, he wondered.

God. He never would have imagined that thought ever going through his mind.

Well, one thing was clear: William Baldwine's reign was about to come to an end. Whether it was payback for what the man had done to Edward for all those years . . . or the fact that his mother had been disrespected . . . or the reality that it was likely Rosalinda had killed herself because of him . . .

Funny, that stuff with his own *wife* was the least of what was getting him vindictive.

Had Chantal really gone for his father? And gotten herself pregnant?

Unbelievable.

Made him think he should give his lawyer a little heads-up. A woman capable of that could pull anything out of her derby hat —

Wait, hadn't Samuel T. said that adultery could be used to reduce alimony?

"Sir? Would you like me to park this car?"

Lane glanced at the uniformed parker who'd walked over. As opposed to the crew of fifty down at the bottom of the hill, there was only one guy stationed up here — and his sole purpose was to handle the University of Charlemont men's basketball coach's car. Oh, and route the Presidents' and the various Governors' teams of cars and SUVs around.

But Coach's sedan was the primary and most important priority.

"No, thanks." He took off the baseball cap and rubbed his hair. "I'm gonna leave —"

"Oh, Mr. Baldwine. I didn't know it was you."

"Why would you." Lane got out and offered his palm. "Thanks for helping us today."

The young kid stared at the hand he'd been offered for a moment, and then he moved in slowly, like he didn't want to mess things up or look like an idiot. "Sir. Thank you, sir."

Lane clapped the parker on the shoulder. "I'm just going to leave her here, okay? I'm not sure whether I'm going to the track or not."

"Yes, sir. She sure is pretty!"

"Yeah, she is."

As soon as Lane stepped through the front door, that English butler came forward with a stern expression on his face — as if he'd had to turn a number of people away already. That act was dropped immediately when he saw who it was.

"Sir, how are you?"

"Well enough. I have a request."

"How may I serve you?"

"I need a suit —"

"I took the liberty of ordering you up a seersucker, blue, with a white shirt — French collar and cuffs — and a pink bow tie with pocket square. It was sent over late yesterday afternoon and pre-tailored to the specifications that Richardson's had on file. If you require further adjustment to jacket or slacks, I shall send up a maid. And there are also silk socks in pink and a pair of loafers."

What do you know — that efficiency act might be more than an illusion.

"Thank you so much." Although he didn't need it for the Derby and that was clearly what the butler was thinking. "I'll —"

The sound of the knocker pounding on

that massive door made them both turn around.

"I shall take care of that, sir."

Lane shrugged and headed for the stairs. It was time for him to go through those dressers of his and throw on another change of clothes —

"Brunch workers are to go to the rear entrance," the butler said in a haughty tone. "You shall have to —"

"I'm here to see William Baldwine."

Lane froze as he recognized the voice.

"That is absolutely not possible. Mr. Baldwine is not receiving privately —"

Lane wheeled around and recoiled at the sight of the lean, dark-haired man in the disheveled clothes and the expensive leather boots. "Mack?"

"— remove yourself immediately from the —"

Cutting the butler off, Lane went over to a guy he'd grown up with. "Mack? Are you all right?"

Okay, the answer to that was clearly "no." Bradford's Master Distiller was looking worse for wear, his normally sharp eyes hung with dark circles, a shading of stubble on his handsome-as-sin face.

"Your father is ruining this company," Mack blurted out in a series of slurs.

"I've got this," Lane said, dismissing the butler and taking the distiller under the arm. "Come with me."

He dragged the drunken man up the grand staircase and then frog-marched him down the hall to his bedroom. Inside, he led Mack over to the bed, sat him down, and turned away to shut the door —

The *thump!* of deadweight hitting the floor resounded all around the room.

With a curse, Lane doubled back and lifted the guy off the carpet and back up onto the mattress. Mack was babbling about the integrity of the bourbon-making process, the importance of tradition, the lack of reverence that management was showing the product, how much of a cocksucker someone was . . .

They were going to get nowhere like this.

"Time to wake up," Lane said as he got his old buddy up on his feet again. "Come on, big guy."

Mack had been to the house countless times, but never pickled like this — well, not since they'd transitioned into adulthood. You coupled that with Rosalinda's information and the fact that the distiller thought William was ruining the company?

Another piece of the pie, Lane thought. Had to be.

In the marble bathroom, he cranked on the shower and shoved Mack under the cold spray fully clothed.

The howl was loud enough to shatter glass, but at least the shock got the guy to stand up on his own.

Leaving him under the water, Lane went over to the *petit déjeuner* closet in the corner and got to work on the coffee pot, firing up the Keurig.

"You awake now, Mack?" he asked as he brought a mug with the Bradford crest on it into the bath. "Or should I add some ice to the mix?"

Mack glared through his wet hair and the spray. "I should punch you."

Lane opened the shower's glass door. "How many of me are there?"

"Two." The man accepted the mug with his wet hands. "But that's down from four and a half."

"So it's working."

Mack took a draw of the java at the same time he reached around and juiced the "H" handle. "Coffee's not bad."

"Would you know if it were paint thinner?"

"Probably not."

Lane pointed over his own shoulder. "I'll be in there, waiting. Robe's on the back of the door. Do me a favor and don't come out naked."

"You couldn't handle me."

"Too right."

Closing things up, Lane went into his closet, put on a set of fresh clothes and then took a load off where Mack had failed to retain verticality. A little later, the Master Distiller made his grand, robed appearance.

The two of them had played basketball together for Charlemont Country Day before they'd gone to college, and the guy was as athletic as he'd always been, with no fat on him and the lanky build of a man who could play golf like a pro, run a marathon better than idiots ten years younger than he was, and still plow the lane on a b-ball court.

Oh, and there was still nothing stupid in those unusual, pale brown eyes. In a romance novel, Mack's peepers would have been called whiskey or something — but it wasn't the uncommon color that had gotten all those women into the guy's bed.

No, there had been so much more to all of that.

And people called him a lady's man? Lane thought to himself. Edwin MacAllan was worse.

"You got any more of this?" Mack held

the mug up. "I think another gallon should do it."

"Help yourself. It's single-serve, in there."

The guy glanced over at the open door to the little kitchen. "Right, I make bourbon. I should be able to handle caffeine."

"On that note, let me do the duty again. I need some myself, and burning down the house this morning would be a buzzkill."

The two of them ended up in the chaise lounges over by the windows like a pair of little old ladies. Little old ladies who both needed a shave.

"Talk to me." Lane plugged his elbows into his knees. "What's going on at the company."

Mack shook his head. "It's bad. I've been drunk for two days."

"Like the latter's ever stopped you before. We went on spring break together, remember? Six times. Of which only two were actually on the school calendar."

Mack smiled, but the expression didn't last. "Look, I've kept my thoughts about your father to myself —"

"And you can stop that right now. Do you think I don't know what he's like?"

There was a long pause. "I didn't know how high up the memo went. I thought maybe the stop-buy came from the suits, but I was wrong. I asked around — it was at your father's specific direction. I mean, the man runs a billion-dollar business. Why does he care about —"

"You need to back up. I have no clue what you're talking about?"

"He's cutting me off. He's stopping production."

Lane jerked forward. *"What?"*

"I got a memo the day before yesterday on my desk. I'm not allowed to buy any more corn. No corn, no mash. No mash, no more bourbon." He shrugged and took another hit of the coffee. "I shut the stills down. For the first time since the move to Canada during Prohibition . . . I stopped it all. Sure, I've got some silos that are full, but I'm not doing a goddamn thing. Not until I speak with your father and find out what the hell he's thinking. I mean, is the board up to something? Are they selling us to China and want things to look better on paper by cutting expenses? But even that doesn't make any sense — they want us to delay for six months in the middle of this bourbon boom the country is experiencing?"

Lane stayed silent, all kinds of bad math happening in his brain.

"I wish Edward were around." Mack

shook his head. "Edward would never let this happen."

Lane rubbed his aching head. Funny, he thought the same thing. "Well . . . he's not."

"So, if you don't mind lending me a set of dry clothes, I'm going to go find that father of yours. To hell with your English bulldog downstairs — William Baldwine is going to see me —"

"Mack."

"— and explain why —"

"Mack." Lane looked the man straight in the eye. "Can I trust you?"

The distiller frowned. "Of course you can."

"I need to get into the company's computer system. I need access to financials, account details, annual reports. And I need you to not say a word about it to anyone."

"What are you — why?"

"Can you help me?"

Mack set the mug down. "As much as I'm able, yeah. Sure."

"I'll meet you down by your car." Lane got to his feet. "I'm driving. Help yourself to anything but the seersucker suit in the closet —"

"Lane. What the hell's going on here?"

"There's a possibility that the cut-off isn't

a business strategy."

Mack frowned as if something had been spoken to him in a foreign language. "I'm sorry, what?"

Lane looked out the window, down to the garden, to the tent. He pictured the people who would be under there in about two hours, all of them basking in the extended glory and wealth of the great Bradford family.

"If you ever say a word about this to anyone —"

"Really. You're warning me about that."

Lane glanced back at his friend. "We may be out of money."

Mack blinked. "That's not possible."

Heading for the door, Lane said over his shoulder, "We'll see. Remember, anything but the seersucker."

Twenty-Nine

The first thing Edward did when he woke up was curse. Head was pounding. Body was a patchwork of pain, nausea, and stiffness. Brain was . . .

Surprisingly crystal clear.

And for once, that wasn't a bad thing.

As he gathered up the strength to get to his feet, he let images of that woman from the night before filter through his mind. He was still drunk — or pickled, was more like it — so he was able to immerse himself totally in memories of the feel, the smell, the taste of her. The context might have been fake all around, something that had been scheduled and paid for, but the experience had been . . .

Beautiful, he supposed the word was.

Rearranging himself in his pants, he grabbed his cane, heaved himself up, and wobbled. The bathroom was about seventeen miles away in that corner, and he —

When he went to step forward, he kicked something across the floor.

"What the . . . ?" Frowning, he leaned down, balancing on his cane so that he did not become yet another rug upon the floor.

It was an evening bag.

One of those boxy little silk-wrapped numbers with a rhinestone clasp on it.

The woman had had it with her. He could vaguely recall thinking that it had been exactly the kind of thing Sutton would have used.

Edward was careful as he made his way over and bent to pick the thing up. God only knew what was in it.

Shuffling back to his armchair, he grabbed his phone off the side table. Calling Beau's number, he glanced at the clock across the way. Seven thirty. The pimp would be still up, winding down from his night shift.

"Hello?" a rough voice said. "Edward?"

"The lady left something at my house last night. Her bag."

"Y'all sure about that?"

"I'm sorry?"

"Well, see, I was gonna call you. Your girl, the one what I sent, said someone was done already leaving when she got there?"

Edward frowned, thinking maybe he wasn't quite as with it as he'd thought. "I'm sorry?" he repeated — because that was the only thing that came to him.

"The girl I sent. She come to your place at ten o'clock, but there was another woman leaving, saying she'd taken care of you. Said she was coming back next week. I can't figure out which of my girls it was. Can you open the purse up and tell me who?"

Total, clinical sobriety came over Edward sure as if someone had ice bucketed his head. "But of course."

Holding the phone between his ear and shoulder, he snapped open the bag's flap, a black glossy lipstick tube jumping out and bouncing across the floorboards. There were three thin cards in there, and he bypassed the Centurion Amex and the health-insurance ID . . . and took out the driver's license.

Sutton Smythe.

With the correct address of her family's estate.

"Edward? Hello? Edward, you all right, chere?"

He must have moaned or something. "It wasn't one of your girls."

"No?"

"No. It was . . ." The love of his life. The woman of his dreams. The one person he had vowed not to see again. "An old friend

428

of mine playing a trick on me."

"Oh, that's funny." Beau chuckled. "Well, you still want someone next Friday?"

"I'll get back to you. Thanks."

Edward ended the call and looked over his shoulder toward the sideboard by the door. Sure enough, the thousand dollars was still there, right where he'd put it.

"Oh . . . *fuck*," he whispered, closing his eyes.

After Gin hung up her phone — not with her brother, but with the person she had called after she'd spoken with Lane — she sat in front of her vanity with her head in her hands for the longest time. All she kept thinking of was that she wished she could go back to the night before last, when she'd been on the phone with that idiot from Samuel T.'s law firm, stringing him along as people did her hair and brought her diamonds.

If only she hadn't taken the Phantom. That had been the domino that had started all the others to fall.

Then again, her father would still have been trying to maneuver her into marrying someone she hated, and he would still have been doing whatever he had been with the money, and Rosalinda would still have killed herself.

So actually, no, trying to escape through a reality rewind wouldn't really change anything.

Was fifty-three million dollars a lot of money? On one level, of course it was. It was more than most people saw in a lifetime, several lifetimes, a hundred lifetimes. But was that a blip on the radar for their family? Or a crater?

Or a Grand Canyon?

She couldn't . . . she couldn't imagine a life of nine-to-five. Couldn't fathom budgeting. Saving. Denying.

And that was what had happened to one whole branch of the Bradford clan. Back in the late eighties, before the stock market crash, her mother's aunt's people had bought into a bunch of bad technology and leveraged their Bradford stock to do it. When those "investments" had proven to be nothing but a black hole, they had ended up losing everything.

It was a cautionary tale that had been whispered about by the adults when they'd assumed the children hadn't been listening.

Getting to her feet, she let her silk robe fall to the ground and left the thing where it lay. In her wardrobe room, she walked around and looked at the hundreds of thousands of dollars in fashion, the brilliant swaths and tiny whimsies hanging from crystal holders that had scented tufted pads so that the shoulders of dresses and blouses did not lose shape.

She chose a red dress. Red for blood. For fighting. For the Charlemont Eagles.

And for once, she wore a complete set of underwear.

She also ensured that her hair looked wonderful, making up in buoyancy and bounce what her mood was sorely lacking.

When the knock she had been waiting for finally hit her door, she was out in her bedroom proper, sitting at her dainty French desk.

"Come in," she said.

As Richard Pford entered, his cologne preceded him, and Gin held on to the fact that at least he smelled good. The rest of him left her cold, however. Even though his pale blue suit was cut from the finest cloth and his bow tie was perfectly done, and in spite of the bowler in his hand and the handmade shoes on his feet, he was Ichabod Crane.

Then again, compared to Samuel T., even Joe Manganiello looked like he needed some work.

"Let me make myself perfectly clear," she said as he shut them in together. "I am not doing this for my father. At all. But I expect you to give the favorable terms to the Bradford Bourbon Company as the two of you discussed."

"That is my agreement with him."

"Your agreement is with me now." She smoothed her hair. "We will live here. This is what Amelia is used to, and there is a guest room next door to this suite."

"That is acceptable."

"I am prepared to act as your wife at all social engagements. If you indulge in affairs, and I expect you will, please keep them discreet —"

"I will not be having any extramarital affairs." His voice grew low. "And neither will you."

Gin shrugged. Given the way things were going, she didn't expect herself to find any male of any interest for quite some time.

"Did you hear me, Gin." Richard came across to her and loomed. "You will not like what happens if you disrespect me in that regard."

Gin rolled her eyes. She had been double-crossing boyfriends for years and none of them had found out — unless she'd wanted them to. If the mood struck her, she had no intention of denying herself.

"Gin."

"Yes, yes, fine. Where's the ring?"

Richard reached into his pocket and took out a dark blue velvet box. As he opened it, the emerald-cut diamond inside flashed and sparkled.

At least he hadn't lied about that. It was enormous, on the Elizabeth Taylor scale.

"I have already drafted the announcement," he said. "My representative will get it out to the press as soon as they hear back from me. The wedding will be as soon as possible."

She went to take the ring, but he snapped the lid closed. "There is one other detail to iron out."

"What is that?"

He reached forward and touched her shoulder. "I think you know. And do not tell me to wait until the justice of the peace comes. I do not find that acceptable."

Gin burst out of the chair. "I have no intention of sleeping with —"

Richard grabbed her by the hair and yanked her against him. "And I have no intention of buying a Ferrari just to look at it in my garage."

"Take your hands off me —"

"Intimacy is a sacred part of marriage."

His eyes went to her lips. "And something I am prepared to enjoy —"

"Let go of me!"

He began to drag her over to the bed. "— even if you do not."

"Richard!" She punched at his shoulders, his chest. "Richard, what are you doing — I don't want —"

As he clamped his hand over her mouth and shoved her down, his smile was that of a predator. "How did you know I like it rough? See, we are compatible, after all . . ."

It was unfathomable what happened next. As much as she struggled, as thin as she had assumed he was, he got her skirting up and her panties to the side —

He penetrated her on a hard shove.

A surge of nausea went through her, but she wasn't going to demean herself by showing any weakness in front of him. Focusing on the ceiling, she let him grunt and push into her, the burning sensation deep inside making her think of the color of her dress.

Halfway through it, she fisted up the duvet and winced.

"Tell me you love me," Richard growled in her ear.

"I will not —"

Richard arched up and put his hand

around her throat. As he squeezed, she began to gasp.

"Tell me."

"I will not!"

Black rage narrowed his eyes and he switched grips, raising his right hand . . .

"If you slap me, people will talk," she sneered. "I won't be able to cover the stain up, and I have to go to the brunch. My absence will be noted."

His upper lip peeled back . . . but he dropped his hand. And fucked her so violently, the headboard slammed against the wall.

When he was through, he shoved himself off of her and tucked himself away. "I want you to change. Red is vulgar."

"I will not —"

With a quick move, he grabbed the skirt and ripped it in two, right up the front. Then he jabbed his finger in her face. "You show up in something else red and we shall have words. Test me if you wish."

Richard left, striding out and shutting the door with a declarative clap.

It was only then that Gin started to shake, her body trembling hard, particularly her open thighs. Sitting up, she felt a welling between her legs.

That was when she began to throw up.

She emptied her stomach into the ruined skirt — not that she'd eaten much in the last twenty-four hours, anyway. Wiping her mouth on the back of her hand, she felt her eyes sting, but she pulled herself back from that ledge.

In her mind, she heard her father telling her she was worthless. That marrying Richard Pford was the only thing she would ever do for the family.

She wasn't doing it for the family.

As usual, she had made the decision in her own selfish interest.

After much introspection, she had come to acknowledge a fundamental truth about herself: She couldn't survive in any other world. And Richard could give her this lifestyle she needed — even as her family might no longer be able to.

It was going to cost her, apparently . . . but she had lost her self-respect years ago.

To sacrifice her body at the altar of money?

Fine. She would do what she had to.

THIRTY

In retrospect, it was the very best day to play Hardy Boys with a computer at the Old Site.

As Lane parked Mack's truck behind the two-hundred-year-old cabin and the various storage barns, there was no one around. No administrators. No floor workers. No one accepting deliveries of supplies. No tourists, either.

"That coffee helped," Mack said as they both got out.

"Good."

"You want some of this PowerBar?"

"Not without a gun to my head."

Heading over to the refurbished log cabin, Lane stood to one side as Mack put his pass card through the reader and pushed his way inside. The interior glowed with old wood carefully tended to, the light from outside passing through bubbled glass that had been added in the late 1800s. Rustic armchairs offered those waiting places to sit, and a trestle table with a lot of modern office equipment was clearly where Mack's assistant spent her time.

"How long since you've been here?" the Master Distiller asked as he hit the light switch.

"Actually, about a day or two." When the guy looked over, Lane shrugged. "Needed a place to think, so I went and sat around the barrels. I used the old pass code."

"Ah. Yeah, I do that, too."

"It didn't help."

"Doesn't work for me, either, but maybe one day." Mack nodded to the rear of the reception area. "I'm still here in the back."

The Distiller's office took up most of the cabin's interior, and for a moment, as Lane stepped into the space, he closed his eyes and drew in a deep breath. The M.D. of the Bradford Bourbon Company was nearly a religious figure in not just the organization, but the state of Kentucky as a whole, and that made this place sacred — accordingly, its walls were covered from floor to ceiling with a pastiche of the company's liquor labels dating from the mid-1800s all the way up to the early 2000s.

"God, it's just the same." Lane looked around, tracing the evidence of his family's history. "My grandfather used to take me here when they were putting it all together for the first time as a tourist site. I was five or six and he'd bring only me. I think it was because he wanted an architect in the family, and knew that Edward was company bound, and Max wasn't going to turn into anything."

"What did you end up doing with yourself?" Mack sat down behind his desk and turned on his computer. "Last I heard you were in New York?"

"Poker."

"I'm sorry?"

Lane cleared his throat, and felt inadequate. "I, ah, I play poker. Made more money than I would've if I'd gotten a desk job — considering I majored in psychology and haven't worked my entire adult life."

"So you're good with the cards."

"Very." He changed the subject by nodding at the walls. "Where are your labels?"

The computer let out a *beeeep,* and then Mack signed in at the log-in screen. "Haven't put any up."

"Come on, now."

"My father's thirty-fifth run of Family Reserve, right over there" — he pointed to the far corner, by the floor — "was the last."

Lane grabbed a chair from a conference

table and rolled it across the bare, polished floorboards. "You need to get your batches counted."

"Uh-huh." Mack sat back in the great leather throne. "So what do you need? What can I try to find for you?"

Lane moved in next to the guy and focused on the blue-green glow of the computer screen. "Financials. I need profit and loss statements over time, account balances, transfer records."

Mack whistled under his breath. "That's uphill of my pay grade. Corporate's got all that — wait, the board book."

"What's that?" Jesus, shouldn't he know?

Mack started going through the file system, opening documents, and hitting *Print*. "It's the materials handed out in advance of the Trustees' meetings. Senior management gets them — and so do I. Of course, the real stuff happens behind closed doors with the executive committee an hour before the open session, and there are no notes on that. But this should give you an idea of the company — or at least what they're telling the Board about the company."

As the man started handing over page after page from the printer, Lane frowned. "What exactly goes down at the executive committee?"

"It's where they debate the meat of things, as well as the stuff they don't want anyone else to know about. I don't think there are even minutes taken."

"Who attends?"

"Your father." Over came two more pages. "The company's general counsel. The board chair and vice chair. CFO, COO. And then there are special guests, depending on the issues. I was called in once when they were debating changing the formula for No. Fifteen. I shot that bright idea down and they must have agreed with me because the folly never surfaced again. I was in that boardroom only long enough to be heard, and then I was escorted out."

"Do you know if they have an agenda in advance?"

"I would think so. When I went, there were four other people waiting in the hall with me, so they were working off some kind of plan. It's all run out of your father's offices at your house."

Lane started going through the papers that were still warm from having been through the machine. Minutes of the previous meeting. Attendance. Updates on operations that he didn't understand.

He needed a translator.

Who he could trust.

And greater access.

Mack went on to print out the previous three board meetings' worth of materials. Clipped it all together. Put it in files.

"I need to borrow your truck," Lane said as he stared at the pile.

"Drop me at home and it's yours. I should try to sober up, anyway."

"I owe you."

"Just save this company. And we are more than even."

As Mack put his palm out, Lane shook it. Hard. "Whatever it takes. No matter who it hurts."

The Master Distiller closed his eyes. "Thank you, God."

Like watching exotic animals at the zoo, Lizzie thought.

Standing at the very edge of the tent, she watched the glittering people wind in and out of the tables she and Greta had set up. The talk was loud, the perfume thick, the jewels flashing. All of the women were in hats and flats. The men were in pale suits and a couple even wore cravats and bowlers.

It was the kind of fantasy life that so many thought they wanted to live.

She knew the truth, however. After all these years working at Easterly, she was well aware that the rich were not inoculated against tragedy.

Their cocoon of luxury just made them think they were.

God, those spreadsheets that Rosalinda had left behind —

"Quite a sight, isn't it."

Lizzie looked over. "Miss Aurora — I can't believe you're out here. You never leave the kitchen during the brunch."

The woman's tired eyes surveyed the guests, the setup, the uniformed waiters with the sterling silver mint julep cups on sterling silver trays. "They're moving my food."

"Of course they are. Your menu is exquisite."

"The champagne flutes are holding."

Lizzie nodded and refocused on the crowd. "We've got about a hundred in reserve at the moment. The waiters are doing a great job."

"Where's your partner?"

For a split second, she almost gave the woman a Lane update. Which was crazy — and wouldn't have amounted to much. All she knew was that he'd left with Edwin Mac-Allan, the Master Distiller, about an hour ago. Or had it been two?

"Greta's over there." She pointed to the opposite corner. "She's riding herd on the flutes. Says finding the used ones that have been set aside is an Easter-egg hunt on steroids. Or . . . at least I think that's what she said. Her last report had a lot of German in it — usually not the best sign."

Miss Aurora shook her head. "That wasn't who I was asking about. It was good to see you and Lane in the same room again."

"Ah . . ." Lizzie cleared her throat. "I'm not sure what to say to that."

"He's a good boy, you know."

"Listen, Miss Aurora, there's nothing going on between him and me." Other than eight hours of sex the evening before. "He's married."

"For now. That woman is trash."

Can't disagree there, Lizzie thought. "Well . . ."

"Lizzie, he's going to need you."

Lizzie put up her palms to try to derail the conversation. "Miss Aurora, he and I —"

"You're going to have to be there for him. There's a lot that's going to fall on his shoulders."

"So you know? About . . . everything?"

"He's going to need someone with a level

head to stand by him." Miss Aurora's face became very grim. "He's a good man, but he's going to be tried in ways he never has been. He's going to need you."

"What did Rosalinda tell you?"

Before Miss Aurora could answer, a tall, striking brunette woman came up out of the crowd. And instead of passing by, she stopped and put her hand forward. "Lizzie King, my name's Sutton Smythe."

Lizzie recoiled — but then got with the program and accepted what was offered. "I know who you are."

"I just wanted to tell you how incredibly beautiful these gardens are. Astonishing! You and Mrs. von Schlieber are true artists."

There was nothing lurking behind the woman's open expression, no falsity, no ulterior anything — and the lack of shady made Lizzie think of Chantal's fake lady-like stuff.

"That's very kind of you."

Sutton took a sip from her mint julep cup, and the massive ruby on her right ring finger glowed. "I'd love to have you over to my property, but I know better — and I respect those boundaries. I did have to let you know how much I respect your talent, however."

"Thank you."

"You are so welcome."

Sutton smiled and walked off — or at least tried to. She didn't make it far, people crowding around her, talking at her, the women sizing up her clothes, the men sizing up her non-financial assets.

"You know," Lizzie murmured, "she's a nice person."

When there was no reply, she looked over. Miss Aurora was heading back for the kitchen's door, her gait slow and unsteady as if her feet hurt — and why wouldn't they. Plus come on, she'd been in the ER how many days ago?

Lizzie was glad the cook had come out for once to see the grand finale of all their collective effort. Maybe next year, they could get her to stay for a little while longer.

Across the tent, Chantal was sitting at a table with seven other women who were versions of her, namely brightly colored, expensive birds with their plumage largely paid for by the men in their lives. In twenty years, after whatever children they had had washed out of their households, they were going to look like wax figurines of themselves, everything jacked up, and filled, and enhanced.

And actually, they did work: Their profession was breeding and remaining attractive to their husbands.

A lot like the mares that had given birth to the thoroughbreds who were racing on that track in a couple of hours.

Lizzie thought of her farm, which she had paid for herself. No one could take that away from her — she had earned it.

Far better than being a perpetual suck-up.

As she took out her phone and checked to see if Lane had texted her, she told herself it was different between the two of them because she didn't need his money, she didn't care about his position, and she wasn't going to be told what to do by anybody.

When she saw there was nothing on her phone, a stabbing sensation hit her chest — and she studiously ignored it as she put her cell away.

It *was* different between her and Lane —

Crap. Why was she thinking as if they were back together?

THIRTY-ONE

Samuel T. blew off the line-up of sheep at the base of Easterly's hill, shooting his Jag around the Mercedeses, Audis, Porsches, and limos, and waving at the parkers who tried to flag him down so he'd stop.

Nope. He did not ride in vans with the great unwashed. And he'd be damned if he'd leave his girl in the hands of some sixteen-year-old yahoo who was liable to strip her gears as the little bastard parked her in a marsh at the side of the road.

As he crested the rise, he floated another wave at the solitary attendant up top and didn't spare a glance at the people stepping out of the van that had pulled up in front of the house. Heading for the garages, he parked parallel to the mansion's eastern flank and killed the engine — and immediately, he heard the party on the other side of the garden wall, the patter of talk forming a multi-layered sound rather like a symphony's preamble to some great, dramatic rise of a solo.

It was a long while before he got out of the car.

I love you, Samuel T. This is who we are, who we've been since we were teenagers.

Or something to that effect. He couldn't remember the exact words Gin had used on him because when she'd been talking at him, he'd been too busy trying not to lose his mind.

God, the things he'd been through with that woman. All those years of one-upping each other. And she was right, of course. He did date waitresses and hairdressers because they weren't like her, and he did compare every female he was around against her — and yes, they all came up wanting.

He hadn't slept for more than an hour, maybe two, that conversation running frontward and backward in his mind over and over again.

In the end, the one thing that stuck out most was tied to the passage of time: Over the years, he'd seen Gin in a hundred thousand different moods, but she'd only teared up once before. It had been . . . about fifteen years ago, when he'd been a junior at U.Va. and she'd been a freshman at Sweet Briar. He'd come home for Easter break, mostly because of his parents, only a little because of Gin. Naturally, they had seen each other.

It was a small world. Especially when you wanted to put yourself in the path of someone else in Charlemont, Kentucky.

And strangely, that was what he'd had to do. Gin hadn't been out at any of the parties their group went to. He'd had to use a pickup game of basketball with her brothers as an excuse — not that he'd spent any time at all on the court that had been behind the garages. Ditching Max and Lane as soon as he'd set foot on the property, he'd found her out by the pool, in a sweatshirt and shorts. She'd looked like hell — and she'd told him she was taking a break from Sweet Briar and moving home for a while. That she didn't like college. That she just wanted to rest for a while.

Not a surprise. Wild child that she was, it had been hard to imagine her faithfully adhering to any schedule independently, whether it was as part of an English major, or as a job. She was far better suited to the pursuit for which she had been bred: lady of a grand house.

They'd ended up in argument. They always ended up in an argument.

And he had stormed off.

He'd intended to just leave her, but as usual, he hadn't been able to pull a clean break: Before he'd gone through the gate to get out of the garden, he'd glanced back.

Gin had had her head in her hands and she was weeping.

He'd returned to her, but she had run into the house and gone so far as to lock the French doors behind her.

He hadn't seen her for about a year after that. Mostly because even at the ridiculously young age of twenty, he'd recognized they were no good together. He hadn't been able to make the separation stick, however. He never was able to do that.

Samuel T. thought about what she'd said the day before . . . about those tears of hers.

What if . . . she hadn't been playing him?

For some reason, that terrified him.

And what was just as shocking? He found himself ready to stop the fighting with her. For so long, his pride had demanded responses to what she did, who she did . . . but it wasn't a defeat if the other person put down their sword at the same time you relinquished your own.

The truth? He was kidding himself if he thought there was anyone on the planet for him other than that headstrong, spoiled, pain in the ass.

She'd had his heart in the palm of her hand since the first day he'd laid eyes on her.

Getting out of his car, he brushed his hair back and buttoned the front of his pink, pale blue, and yellow plaid sport coat. Then he bent down, took his straw derby hat from the jump seat and arranged the thing in perfect position on his head.

Using the nearest gate into the garden, he walked into the party.

"Here's the man!"

"Samuel T.!"

"Mint julep for you!"

Buddies of his, gentlemen he'd known since kindergarten, came up to him, clapping hands, talking about handicapping the race, asking about the parties to come later in the day, the night, Sunday morning. He responded with throwaways, his eyes searching the crowd.

"Will you excuse me?" he said.

He didn't wait for any permissions, but strode across the tented space, bypassing waiters with trays and more people who reached out to him and several women anxious to connect with him.

Finally, he found her, standing alone, staring out over the river.

As he approached, he traced the elegant

lines of Gin's body, lingering on the way her shoulders were left exposed by the silk dress she had on. For some reason, she had a long scarf tied around her throat, the ends waving in the wind created by the tent fans, the ends trailing down to her unbelievable legs.

He hated the way his heart beat so hard in his chest. Despised the fact that he had to subtly wipe his palms next to his jacket's double vents. Prayed that his read on her was correct . . . that she had, for once, been speaking from the heart — and that they were ready, finally, to get real about each other.

"Gin?"

When she didn't turn around, but just stayed fixated on the river, he put his hand on her arm —

She wheeled around so fast that her mint julep splashed all over his jacket, leaving a damp line across his midsection.

Not that he cared.

"Jumpy much?" he drawled, trying to recover some of his mojo.

"I'm so sorry." She reached forward with a little monogrammed cocktail napkin. "Oh, I've ruined —"

"Please. I have a backup in the trunk."

Mostly because he always sweated at the

boxes at the track and he'd be damned if he'd spend the rest of the night in that kind of mess.

"So, ready for the big day?" she said as he took off his jacket.

He was folding the thing over his arm when it dawned on him that she wasn't meeting his eyes.

"Well?" she prompted. "My brother has a horse in the running. Maybe two? Sired by that nasty bastard Nebekanzer."

Still no eye contact.

Under his breath, he muttered, "I hate jumping out of airplanes."

That got her to look at him. But only for a moment. "What?"

As those blue eyes of hers went back out to the river, he cursed. "Listen . . . Gin."

"Yes?"

She was so still, he thought. And so much smaller than he was. Funny, he never noticed the height difference when they were going at it — nearly a hundred pounds less and six inches shorter didn't mean a thing when that mouth of hers was going to hell and back.

He took a deep breath. "So I've been thinking about what you said yesterday. And honestly . . . you're right. You're absolutely right. About everything."

He wasn't sure what he was expecting to get in response — but the slump of her shoulders was not it. She seemed . . . utterly defeated.

"I'm not any better at this than you are," he said. "But I want to . . . well . . . goddamn it, Gin, I love —"

"Stop," she blurted. "Don't say it. Please . . . not now. Don't —"

"Good morning, Samuel T. How are you?"

The appearance of a third party registered about as much as a house fly passing through would have.

Except then Richard Pford put his arm around Gin's waist and kept going with, "Have you told him the good news, darling?"

For the first time in his life, Samuel T. felt the cold wash of horror. Which, considering some of the things he'd done in the last two decades, was saying something.

"And what might that be?" he forced himself to drawl. "You two opening a lucrative organ-selling business over the Internet?"

Pford's beady little eyes grew nasty. "You have such an active imagination. It helps your clients, I'm sure."

"With your sense of ethics in business, I wouldn't be casting stones in that glass house, Pford." Samuel T. focused on Gin, his chest turning to stone. "So, you have something to tell me, do you?"

By way of reply, Pford took her left hand and thrust it forward. "We're going to be married. On Monday, actually."

Samuel T. blinked once. But then smiled. "Marvelous news. Truly — and, Richard, let me be the first to congratulate you. She fucks like a wild animal, especially when you do her from behind — but I'm sure you already know that. Half the country does."

As Richard began sputtering things, Samuel T. leaned in and kissed Gin on the cheek. "You win," he whispered in her ear.

Turning away from the happy couple, he went back to his buddies. Grabbed two mint juleps from a passing waiter. Drank them as if they were water.

"What's on your face?" someone asked him.

"I'm sorry?"

"You're leaking."

He passed a hand over the eye that was itching and frowned as he saw the wetness. "I got splashed with a drink over there."

One of his fraternity brothers barked out a laugh. "Some female finally throw one in your face? About time!"

"I got what I deserved, all right," he said

456

numbly as he grabbed his third julep. "But have no fear, gentlemen. I'm getting back on the horse."

The table roared, men backslapping him, somebody pulling over a woman and shoving her forward. As she put her arms around his neck and leaned in to his body, he took what was offered, kissing her deeply, feeling her up even though they were in public.

"Oh, Samuel T.," she whispered against his mouth. "I've waited for you to do this to me forever."

"Me, too, darlin'. Me, too."

She didn't know him well enough to recognize the dead tone in his voice. And he couldn't have cared less about the enthusiasm in hers.

He had to save face somehow . . . or he wasn't going to be able to live in his skin for one goddamn minute longer.

Gin was so much better at this game than he was. If she hadn't just succeeded in shattering his heart into a thousand pieces, he would have given her props.

As Lane pulled Mack's pickup truck through the stone pillars of the Red & Black Stables, the alley of trees before him seemed a hundred miles long, the cluster of stables and buildings so far off in the distance, they might as well have been in a different state.

Proceeding forward, dust kicked up behind him, boiling in the morning light.

He knew this because he kept checking the rearview to make sure he hadn't been followed.

The cobblestone drive circled in front of the biggest of the barns, and he parked off to the side, half on the grass. No reason to lock up as he got out. Hell, he left the keys in the ignition.

One deep breath in and he was back in his childhood, when he'd come out here to muck stalls during his summers off from prep school. His grandparents had believed in instilling a good work ethic. His parents had been less concerned with so much.

Heading over to the caretaker's cottage, it was difficult to believe his brother really lived in such modest quarters. Edward had always been a force of energy in the world, moving, always moving, a conqueror constantly looking for victory, whether it was in sports, in business, with women.

And now . . . this little building? This was it?

When Lane came up to the door, he knocked on the screen's frame. "Edward? You in there, Edward?"

As if he could be anywhere else?

Bang, bang, bang. "Edward? It's me —"

"Lane?" came a muffled voice.

He cleared his throat. "Yes, it's me. I need to talk to you."

"Hold on."

When the door eventually opened, Lane saw his grandfather standing before him, not his brother: Edward was so thin that his jeans hung like old-man pants from his hip bones, and he was slightly hunched, as if the pain he'd suffered had permanently shifted his spine toward the fetal position.

"Edward . . ."

He got a grunt in return and some hand motions indicating it was up to him to open the screen and come inside.

"Pardon me while I sit back down," Edward said as he made his way over to the chair he'd clearly been in. "Standing is not agreeable."

The groan was almost stifled as he lowered himself into position.

Lane shut the door. Put his hands in the pockets of his slacks. Tried not to stare at his brother's ruined face. "So . . ."

"Please don't bother commenting upon how well I look."

"I . . ."

"In fact, let's just nod and you can go. No doubt Miss Aurora made you come here so

459

that you could attest to the fact that I'm still breathing."

"She's not well."

That got his brother's attention. "How so?"

The story came out quickly: ER, looked fine afterward, still working the brunch.

Edward's eyes drifted away. "That's her, all right. She's going to outlive the rest of us."

"I think she'd like to see you."

"I will never go back to that house."

"She could come out here."

After a long moment, that stare swung back. "Do you honestly think that being anywhere near me would do her good?" Before Lane could comment, Edward continued, "Besides, I'm not one for visitors. Speaking of entertaining, why aren't you enjoying The Derby Brunch? I got an invitation, which I found a bit ironic. I didn't bother to RSVP — a horrid breach of manners, but in my new incarnation, social pleasantries are anachronisms from another life."

Lane walked around, looking at the trophies.

"What's on your mind?" Edward asked. "You are never without words."

"I don't know how to say this."

"Try a noun first. A proper noun — provided it is not 'Edward.' I assure you, I'm uninterested in any soapbox preaching about how I should get my life in order."

Lane turned and faced his brother. "It's about Father."

Edward's lids lowered. "What about him."

The image of Rosalinda in that chair was preceded by an auditory replay of Chantal's voice telling him she was pregnant and not leaving the house.

Lane's lip curled up off his teeth. "I hate him. I hate him so fucking much. He's ruined us all."

Before he could start in with all that had happened, Edward put his palm out and released an exhausted sigh. "You don't have to say it. What I want to know is how you found out."

Lane frowned. "Wait, you know?"

"Of course I know. I was there."

No, no, he thought in shock. Edward couldn't have been in on the money losses, the debt . . . the possible embezzlement. The man was not just brilliant with business, but honest as a Boy Scout.

"You couldn't . . . no." Lane shook his head. "Please tell me, you're not —"

"Don't be naive, Lane —"

"Rosalinda is dead, Edward. She killed

461

herself in her office yesterday."

Now it was Edward's turn to look surprised. "What? Why?"

Lane threw up his hands. "Did you think it wouldn't affect her?"

Edward frowned. "What the hell are you talking about?"

"The money, Edward. Jesus Christ, don't be dense —"

"Why would the fact that Father wouldn't pay my ransom affect her?"

Lane stopped breathing. "What did you just say?"

Edward rubbed his eyes like his entire skull hurt. Then he went for the Beefeater bottle next to him and took a deep draw right from the open neck. "Do we have to do this."

"He didn't pay for your release?"

"Of course he didn't. He has always hated me. I wouldn't put it past him to have engineered the entire kidnapping."

All Lane could do was stand there and blink as his head went rush-hour-traffic-jam on him. "But . . . he told the press — he told us — he was negotiating with them —"

"And I was there listening on the other end of the phone. That was not what was occurring. Further, I can assure you, there were . . . repercussions . . . to his failure to comply."

Lane's gut got to churning. "They could have killed you."

After another lift of that bottle, Edward let his head fall back against the chair. "Don't you know, brother . . . they *did* kill me. Now, what the hell are you talking about?"

THIRTY-TWO

She was on a strange type of high, Gin decided as she walked with her new fiancé among her family's guests, nodding to those who made eye contact, speaking when required to.

The cotton-wool sensation that had enveloped her body was something between a saturation-drunk and a Xanax bender, the outside world coming at her through a filter that slowed down time, thickened the air into a custard-like solid, and removed any sense of temperature from her skin.

Richard, on the other hand, seemed very alert as he told everyone about their engagement, the pride in his face akin to a man who had just purchased a new home in Vail or perhaps a yacht. He did not seem to notice the subtle shock that was so very often quickly hid — or maybe he didn't care about that.

You win.

As she heard Samuel T.'s voice in her head, she took a deep breath.

Timing, timing, she thought. Timing was everything.

That and money.

Samuel T. and his people were very wealthy by any standard, but they did not have a spare fifty or sixty million to fill up the debt cavern in her family's balance sheets. Only the likes of Richard Pford IV did — and Gin was prepared to leverage her newfound position as the jackass's wife to help out her kin.

But that was going to have to wait until after she put a ring on him —

A hold on her elbow brought her head around.

Richard leaned in. "I said, come this way."

"I'm going to go inside for a moment."

"No, you're going to stay by my side."

Looking him right in the face, she said, "I'm bleeding between my legs, and you know why. That's hardly something I can ignore."

An expression of both shock and distaste tightened those features she was already learning to hate. "Yes, do take care of that."

As if her body were a car with a dent that required fixing.

Walking off, she found that weeding

around groups of people who spoke too loud and laughed too much caused her a prickling anxiety — and yet the feeling did not dissipate as she stepped into Easterly's cool, quiet interior.

She had bled after Richard had been done with her. But she'd already attended to that need with a panty liner.

No, she'd come inside for a different reason.

And she knew just where to go.

The last time she had had sex in this house — excluding that brief hookup in the garden the other evening and what had just happened in her bedroom earlier — had been well over two years ago: She had ended most of her Easterly romps and excursions as soon as Amelia had gotten old enough to know what a slut was.

No reason for the dear girl to witness in person what others were going to tell her about her mother. At least that way, Gin had always thought, mommy might be able to sport a credible denial.

But . . . two years ago, on a random Thursday evening, after an uneventful sit-down dinner, she had found herself slipping up.

In the wine cellar.

Proceeding down to the staff hallway, she

went past Rosalinda's and Mr. Harris's offices — or rather, where the butler's still was and the controller's had been — and opened a broad door to reveal the stairwell to the basement.

She was entirely unsurprised to find the glow of a light down at the bottom.

There was only one reason for it to be on, especially as all of the bourbon, champagne and chardonnay for the brunch had been delivered to the staging area — and in any event, no part of the family's private collection would ever be used for such an occasion.

Her descent was silent, the pattern of squeaking boards long since memorized from back in her days as a teenager stealing bottles out of the depths of the tremendous basement. As she came to the bottom of the steps, she slipped off her shoes and put them aside. The uneven concrete was a cold relief on the soles of her feet, and her nose threatened a sneeze as the mustiness registered in her sinuses.

Passing by the bomb shelters that had been made in the forties out of lead walling set at right angles, she padded along, wrapping her arms around herself — although that was mainly a reflex, something she did because she should have been chilled down here.

She still felt nothing.

The wine cellar was separated from the larger basement by a fire- and bulletproof glass wall that was outfitted with polished wood supports and a door that had a code to it. Inside, the gleaming, mahogany-paneled room was fitted, floor to ceiling, with handmade bottle shelves, thousands of lots of priceless wine, champagne and liquor protected from both shifts in temperature and thieves of the human variety.

There was also a tasting table in the center surrounded by oxblood club chairs — and she was right, the thing was being put to use.

And there was a tasting of sorts going on.

Samuel T.'s sacrificial lamb was stretched out on the glossy surface, her blond hair spilling all over to hang off the table's far end, her naked body gleaming in the low lighting from the brass fixtures. She was completely naked, her peach dress having been thrown carelessly on the top of one of the chairs, and Samuel T.'s head was between her thighs, his hands gripping her hips as he worked her.

Stepping back into a dark corner, Gin watched him finish what he was doing and then rear up over the woman. With rough hands, he freed his erection and mounted her.

The woman cried out loud enough so that her hoarse voice could be heard on the other side of all that glass.

For once, Gin did not put herself in the female's position.

She had seen him have sex many times before — sometimes when he'd known about it, sometimes when he hadn't — and inevitably, her body had always responded as though she were the one beneath him, on top of him, pushed up against a wall by him.

Not now.

That would have been too painful.

Because she knew she was never going to have him again.

You win.

After all their years of battling, she had put down her armaments first — and he hadn't believed her. And when he finally had taken her seriously, events had conspired against them.

He was not going to play this game with her anymore. She'd seen the hints of resolve when he'd blown off her declaration of love the day before — and the final nail in the coffin had been put in out in the garden.

It was done.

Gin stayed where she was until he orgasmed, and she had to blink away tears as his head jerked back on his spine, and his neck strained, and his body pumped hard four more times. Perhaps unsurprisingly, his face showed no evidence of pleasure, the release having apparently been something generated only by his body.

Throughout the bucking, he remained as grim as she felt, his expression blank, his half-open eyes unfocused.

Meanwhile, however, the female went into spasms that were too ugly to have been faked: No doubt the darling girl would have preferred to impress him with more artful expressions of passion in hopes of this being the start to something, but movie-star sex poses were hard to maintain when Samuel T. was inside of you.

Gin stepped even further back, until the cold, damp wall informed her there was no more retreat permitted.

She knew he was going to leave fast.

And he did.

Moments later, the vapor lock was sprung as the door was opened, and Gin curled in on herself, dropping her eyes and not breathing.

"Sure," Samuel T. said in an even tone. "I'd love to."

"Will you help me do up my dress?"

"You can reach it." He was already striding off. "Come on, we better go."

"Wait! Wait for me!"

Giggles. Jiggles, too, no doubt, as the sound of high heels clipping along the concrete echoed around like the woman was running to catch up to him.

"Hold my hand?" the female asked.

"Sure. I'd love to."

There was a smack of two sets of lips meeting and then the sounds of footfalls on concrete diminished into the distance.

After a while, Gin stepped out of the shadows. The light had been left on inside the wine cellar — which was very unlike Samuel T. What most didn't know about him was that he was a slave to his compulsive need to have things in order. In spite of the fact that he was a hard-living playboy, he couldn't handle things out of place. Everything from the suits he wore to the cars he kept, from his law practice to his stables, from his bedroom to his kitchen to his bathrooms, he was a man with control issues.

She knew the truth, though. She had seen him get stuck in rituals, had had to talk him out of them from time to time.

It was an intimacy she was willing to bet

her only child's life on that he shared with no one else —

Now, she shivered. But not because of the cold air and the damp.

The inescapable sense that she had well and truly ruined something robbed her of breath. Tucking in upon herself, she retreated back against the wine cellar's glass wall, slid down to the concrete floor . . . and wept.

THIRTY-THREE

As Edward listened to Lane's report on the family's finances, and then the further news that their mother had been declared incompetent, and finally the details around the hemlock suicide, he found himself . . . curiously detached from the whole story.

It wasn't that he didn't care.

He had always worried about his siblings, and that kind of regard didn't go away, even after all he had been through.

But the string of bad news seemed like explosions happening far off on the horizon, the flashing and the distant roar something that captured his attention, but didn't affect him enough to get him up out of his chair — literally or figuratively.

"So I need your help," Lane concluded.

Edward brought the gin bottle to his mouth again. This time, however, he didn't drink. He lowered it back down. "With what, precisely?"

"I need access to the BBC's financial files — the real ones that haven't been scrubbed for the Board or the press."

"I don't work for the company anymore, Lane."

"Don't tell me you couldn't get into the servers if you really wanted to."

Lane had a point. Edward had been the one to set up the computer systems.

There was a long silence, and then Edward followed through with another hit of the liquor. "There's still plenty of money around. You have your trust, Maxwell has his, and Gin only has a year or two to go —"

"That fifty-three million dollar loan with Prospect Trust is coming due. Two weeks, Edward."

Edward shrugged. "It has to be unsecured, otherwise Monteverdi wouldn't be so worried. So it's not like they're going to come for the house."

"Monteverdi will go to the press."

"No, he won't. If he did make an unsecured loan of that magnitude using Prospect Trust funds, he'd had to have done it behind his Board's back and in violation of federal trust company laws. If it's not repaid on schedule, the only thing that will happen publicly is an announcement that

Monteverdi is taking early retirement to 'spend time with his family.' " Edward shook his head. "I understand your wanting to know more, but I'm not sure where you think that's going to get you. The debt is not yours to worry about. You live in Manhattan now. Why the sudden interest in those people who live at Easterly?"

"They're our family, Edward."

"So?"

Lane frowned. "I get that you don't feel like William Baldwine's son. After the way he treated you all these years, how could you? But . . . what about the house? The land — the business? Mother?"

"The Bradford Bourbon Company has a billion dollars in yearly revenue. Even if you go net, not gross, on that figure, whether the personal debt is fifty or even a hundred million, that is not a catastrophic event considering how much stock the family owns. Banks will loan between sixty to seventy percent of value against an investment portfolio — you could finance the payback of that amount on your own right now."

"But what if that isn't all that's been borrowed? And shouldn't Father be held accountable? And again, I ask, what about Mother?"

"If I went down the rabbit hole of wanting some kind of justice against that sire of ours, I'd be flat-out insane. And the last time I heard, Mother hasn't been out of her bed except to take a bath in three years. Whether she's at Easterly or in a nursing home, she won't notice the difference." As Lane let out a curse, Edward shook his head again. "My advice to you is to follow my lead and distance yourself. I should go even farther away, actually — at least you have New York."

"But —"

"Make no mistake, Lane — they will eat you alive, especially if you follow this avenging road you're on." As he fell silent, he felt a brief moment of surging fear. "You're not going to win, Lane. There are . . . things . . . that have been done in the past against people who tried to come forward about certain issues. And some of them were done against family members."

He should know.

Lane went over to the bay window, staring out as if its drapes were not closed. "So you're saying you won't help me."

"I'm advising you that the path of least resistance is best for your mental health." Physical, too. "Let it go, Lane. Move past, move on. That which you cannot change must be accepted."

There was another stretch of quiet, and then Lane looked across the stale air between them. "I can't do that, Edward."

"Then it's your funeral —"

"My wife is pregnant."

"Again? Congratulations."

"I'm divorcing her."

Edward cocked an eyebrow. "Not the typical response of an expectant father. Especially given how much child support you're going to owe."

"It's not mine."

"Ah, that explains it —"

"She tells me it's Father's."

As their eyes met, Edward went very still. "I'm sorry, what?"

"You heard me. She says she's going to tell Mother. And that she's not leaving Easterly." There was a pause. "Of course, if it turns out there are money problems, then I won't have to worry about our father's bastard living in our family's house. Chantal will go elsewhere and find another wealthy idiot to glom on to."

As an odd pain shot up Edward's forearm, he glanced at his hand. Interesting. It had somehow locked onto the Beefeater bottle with such a strong grip that his knuckles were nearly breaking through his pale skin.

"Is she lying?" he heard himself ask.

"If she'd named anyone other than Father, I would say maybe. But no, I don't think she is."

As Samuel T. emerged from the wine cellar and strode off, he found that ignoring the woman he'd just screwed was an issue of survival. Her voice was enough of an energy suck; if he actually focused on her words, he would probably slip into a coma.

"— and then we'll go to the club! Everyone's going to be there, and we can . . ."

Then again, the exhaustion he was battling probably wasn't her. It was more likely the result of putting down his weapons after a decades-long battle.

What he was clear on was that he'd had to fuck someone in there, on that table. It was his way of wiping the slate clean, metaphorically burning the last memory he had of being inside Gin here at this house. And the other sites he'd been with her at, whether they were at his farm, or in hotels internationally, or out in Vail, or up in Michigan? He was going to knock them off, too, until he'd covered up every single recollection with another woman.

"— Memorial Day? Because we could go

out to my parents' estate in the Loire Valley, you know, get away . . ."

As the prattling continued, Samuel T. was reminded of why he preferred to sleep with married women. When you had sex with someone who had to worry about a husband? There wasn't this expectation of a relationship.

The stairs back up to ground level couldn't arrive in enough of a hurry. And even though he was ready to take them two at a time just so he could lose the chatterbox behind him, he was enough of a gentleman to stand aside at the bottom and indicate for her to go first.

"Oh, thank you," she said as she hustled up ahead of him.

He was about to follow when he caught a flash of something colorful on the floor.

A pair of stilettoes. Pale, made of satin. Louboutins.

He ripped his head around and searched where he and the woman had come from.

"Samuel T.?" she said from the top. "Are you coming?"

They were Gin's shoes. She was down here. She had come down here . . . to watch?

Well, she certainly hadn't stopped them.

His first impulse was to smile and go on the hunt — but that was a reflex born out of the way they had related for how long?

To remind himself of how things had changed, all he had to do was think of that ring on her finger. That man standing beside her. The news that was soon going to go nationwide.

Funny, he had never cared about all the other men Gin had been with. Whether that came under the eye-for-an-eye exception because he was sleeping with an equal number of other women . . . or whether he had some kind of kink in him that made him want her more knowing she'd fucked and sucked other men . . . or maybe it was something else entirely . . . he didn't know.

One thing that was certain?

Richard Pford was now a source of tremendous jealousy. In fact, it had taken every ounce of Samuel T.'s self-possession not to give that waste of space a glare that left a hole in the back of his skull.

"Samuel T.? Is there something wrong?"

He looked up the stairs. The light coming from behind the woman turned her into nothing but shadow, reducing her to a faceless set of curves with no greater weight than an apparition.

For some reason, he wanted to take Gin's shoes, but he left them behind as he let his ascent answer the lady's question.

Emerging on her level, he cleared his throat. "I'll meet you there."

Her smile drooped. "I thought we would go to the track together."

The track?

Oh, right. It was Derby day.

"I have some business to take care of. I'll see you there."

"Where are you going now?"

The question made him realize that he'd started off toward the kitchen, not the party. "Like I said, business."

"Which box are you in?"

"I'll find you," he called out.

"Promise?"

Walking away, he could feel her staring at him — and he was willing to bet that she was praying to Mary Sue, the Patron Saint of Debutantes, that he turn around, come back over and become the escort that she'd hoped would emerge thanks to that subterranean fucking.

But Samuel T. did not look back nor did he reconsider his exit. And he didn't pay any attention to the host of chefs in Miss Aurora's kitchen.

He wasn't actually aware of anything until he stepped outside.

Closing the mud room's door behind him, he took a breather and leaned back against the hot white-painted panels. Another scorcher of a day, which was not a surprise. Then again, nothing was a shocker in Charlemont when it came to the weather.

If you didn't like the conditions, all you had to do was wait fifteen minutes.

So sleet for Derby would also have been possible.

God, he was tired.

No . . . he felt old —

A throaty growl sounded from over on the left, but it wasn't a sports car. It was an old beater of a truck coming up the service road.

Poor bastard, whoever it was. Staff wasn't allowed to park anywhere near the house on a day like today. Whoever was behind the wheel was volunteering for a proverbial throat punch.

But he had troubles of his own to worry about. Putting his hand in his pocket, he took out his car key; then he stepped off the flat stone and began to head over to where he had tucked his Jag in tight to the house.

He didn't make it far.

Through the windshield of that old truck, he saw a very familiar face. "Lane?"

As the truck stopped by the rear entrance of the business center, he went across. "Lane?" he called out. "You downscaling before Chantal hits us with a response?"

The driver's window went down and the guy made a quick slashing finger across his throat.

Samuel T. glanced around. There was nobody anywhere. Staff were inside or out working the tent and gardens. Guests wouldn't have deigned to come back here where the scrubs might be. And it wasn't like the birds in the trees were going to have an opinion about two humans chatting.

As he came up to the truck, he leaned in. "You really don't need to do this for your divorce —"

He fell silent as he focused on the man sitting beside his newest client.

"Edward?" he croaked.

"How lovely to see you again, Samuel." Except the man didn't look over. His eyes remained fixed on the dashboard ahead of him. "You're looking well, as usual."

As the words were spoken, it was impossible not to take a survey of that face . . . that body.

Dear . . . Lord, the pants were bagging around thighs that were like toothpicks, and the loose jacket hung from shoulders that had all the breadth of a coat hanger.

Edward cleared his throat and reached down to pick a BBC cap off the floorboards. As he put it on his head and drew the bill down low to cover his face, Samuel T. was ashamed of his gawking.

"It's good to see you, Edward," he blurted.

"You didn't," Lane said quietly.

"I'm sorry?"

"You didn't see him." Lane's eyes burned. "Or me. Do you understand, counselor?"

Samuel T. frowned. "What the hell's going on?"

"You don't want to know."

Samuel T. glanced back and forth between the brothers. As a lawyer, he had been involved in a lot of gray areas, both in terms of avoiding them and getting into them with deliberation. He had also learned over time that some information was not worth knowing.

"Understood," he said with an incline of the head.

"Thank you."

Before he stepped away, he forced a smile on his face. "Congratulations on the new addition to your family, by the way."

Lane recoiled. "I beg your pardon?"

"I'm quite sure you wouldn't have chosen Richard Pford as a brother-in-law, but one must adjust when love is in the air."

"What the hell are you talking about?"

Samuel T. rolled his eyes, thinking that was just like Gin. "You mean you don't

484

know? Your sister is engaged to Richard Pford. Have a good Derby, gentlemen. Perhaps I'll see you both —"

But of course, not both of them.

"Ah . . . if either of you need me," he amended, "you know exactly where to find me."

Which would be anywhere their sister was not, he thought as he walked off toward his Jag.

THIRTY-FOUR

Perfect time for a break-in.

As Edward got out of the Master Distiller's truck, he pulled the baseball hat down even lower — although if that brim were any further south, he wouldn't be able to blink.

God . . . was he really back here?

Indeed, he was — and he'd forgotten how enormous Easterly was. Even from the servant entrances in the rear, the mansion was almost incomprehensibly large, all the white clapboards and black shutters rising up from the green grass, a screaming statement of the family's long-held stature.

He wanted to vomit.

But after hearing what their father had done with Lane's wife? There was no way he wasn't going to do this.

In the background, he could hear The Derby Brunch in full swing in the garden and knew that this really was the only time to get in and out of the business center with the information his brother needed. With so many guests on site, there was no way their father would be anywhere but under that tent — he was a reprobate, but his manners had never been assailable. Further, all corporate staff had Derby day off, so not even the "underlings" would be at their desks.

The poor bastards might work Fourth of July, Thanksgiving, Christmas, and Easter, but this was Kentucky. No one worked on Derby day.

As Lane came around to follow him, he put out his palm. "I go alone."

"I can't let you do that."

"I can afford to get caught. You cannot. Stay here."

He didn't wait for a response, but continued onward, knowing that after nearly forty years of his being the eldest, his words would freeze Lane where he stood.

At the rear entrance to his father's facility, Edward punched in an access code that he'd assigned to a third party contractor five years ago as part of the security upgrade. When the red light turned to green and the lock released, he closed his eyes briefly.

And opened things up.

There was a temptation to brace himself before stepping inside, but he didn't have that luxury, either in terms of energy or time. As the door shut behind him, the outdoor light was cut off, and it was a moment before the dim interior registered to his eyes.

Still the same. Everything. From the thick maroon pile rug with its gold edgings, to the framed articles on the company that hung on the silk-covered walls, to the pattern of open glass doorways leading down toward the central waiting area.

Strange . . . that he assumed just because he was different, this place in which he had spent so many hours would have changed as well.

No alarm went off as he proceeded deeper into the facility because of the code he'd used, and he passed by the formal dining room, the conference rooms that looked like Easterly's parlors, and even more offices that were kitted out with the luxury of a top-tier law firm. As always, the drapes on all the windows were pulled to ensure total privacy, and nothing was left out on any desks, everything locked up tight.

The waiting area was a circular space, the center of which was demarcated with the family crest in the carpet. Prominently placed off to the side, and bracketed by an American flag, a Kentucky Commonwealth flag, and a pair of Bradford Bourbon Company banners, the desk of the receiving secretary was as regal as a crown — and yet that wasn't even close to the seat of power. Beyond all that show, there was glassed-in office where the executive assistant occupied space — and finally, behind that bulldog's desk was a door marked yet again with the family crest in shimmering gold.

His father's office.

Edward glanced over to the line of French doors that opened up into the garden. Thanks to the combination of heavy drapes and triple-paned glass, there was not even a peep heard of the six or seven hundred people out there — and there was absolutely no chance of any guests wandering in here.

Edward shuffled forward to the glass office and entered the same code. When the lock released, he pushed his way in and went around to sit at the computer. He turned no lights on and would have not disturbed the chair behind the desk had his legs been capable of supporting his weight for any length of time.

The computer was running, but locked, and he signed on using a set of shadow credentials he'd given himself when he'd had the company's network expanded and reinforced about three years ago.

In like Flynn, as they said.

But now what?

On the trip to Easterly, he had wondered whether his brain would come back online for any of this. He had worried that the painkillers, or the trauma, had damaged his gray matter in a way that was not material when all one did was drink and sweep up stables — but rather dispositive when one attempted to function at a higher level.

That was not the case.

Although his circumnavigation among the file system of secured documents was slow at first, soon enough, he was moving quickly through the information caches, exporting what was relevant to a dummy account that would appear to be a valid BBC e-mail, but was in fact, out of the network.

Yet another shadow.

And what was best about it all? If anyone looked into the activity, they would trace the destination to the name of his father's bulldog executive assistant — in spite of the fact that she herself knew nothing about the account. But that was the point. Anyone in the company who saw that woman's name on something was going to back away and say nothing.

As he sifted through the financials, he focused exclusively on raw data that had yet to be "scrubbed" by accountants, and though there was a temptation to start to analyze, it was more important that he capture as much as he could —

The lights in the reception room flared to life.

Jerking his head up, he froze.

Shit.

Lizzie's phone went off finally just as the first of the guests started to take their leave. And she nearly ignored the vibration, especially as two of the waiters came up to her with a series of demands from a table of twenty-year-olds who were underaged and utterly drunk.

"No," she said as she took the cell out of her back pocket and accepted the call without looking. "They've been cut off for a reason — by their parents. If that bunch of entitled asshats has a problem with the service refusal, tell them to talk to Mommy and Daddy." She put the phone up to her ear. "Yes?"

"It's me."

Lizzie closed her eyes in relief. "Oh, my God, Lane . . . here, let me find somewhere quiet."

"I'm around back. By the garages. Can you come out for a minute?"

"On my way."

Ending the call, she caught Greta's eye across the tent and signaled that she was stepping out for a minute. After the woman nodded, Lizzie hightailed it down the periphery of the party, jogging behind the buffet tables where uniformed servers cut slices off perfectly roasted wedges of locally raised Angus beef.

A couple of waiters raised their hands to try to get her attention, but she held them off, knowing Greta would be on it.

Entering the house through the door that opened into the kitchen, she ducked her head, trying to look as if she were already on a mission. And she supposed she was. In the far corner, by the pantry, there was another door that opened into the mudroom, and after running by all the spring jackets of the help, she emerged outside by the garages.

She looked around for Lane's Porsche —

"Over here," his voice announced.

Turning, she recoiled as she saw him leaning against a truck that was nearly as old as she was. But then she got with the program, jogging across the cobblestones.

"Now, this is my kind of ride," she said as

she came up to him.

Even as he didn't move a muscle, Lane's eyes traveled all over her, as if he were using her presence as a way of grounding himself. "Can I hug you?"

She glanced around, focusing on the windows of the house. "Probably better not to."

"Yeah."

"So . . . what are you doing here? With this F-150?"

"Borrowed it from a friend. I'm trying to keep a low profile. How's the party?"

"Your wife's been giving me the evil eye."

"Ex-wife, remember?"

"Are you . . . are you going to head to the brunch?"

He shook his head. "I'm busy."

Awkward. Pause.

"Are you all right?" she whispered. "How was Edward?"

"Can I stay with you tonight?"

Lizzie shifted her weight back and forth. "Aren't you going to the ball?"

"No."

"Well, then . . . yes, I'd like that." She crossed her arms — and tried not to feel a surging happiness which seemed inappropriate given everything that he was facing. "But I'm worried about you."

"Me, too." He glanced up at his house. "Let me ask you something."

"Anything."

It was a while before he spoke again. "If I decided to leave here . . . would you consider coming with me?"

Lizzie thought about joking it out, referencing Robinson Crusoe, or maybe the Carnival Cruise Lines. But he wasn't laughing in the slightest.

"Is it that bad?" she whispered.

"It's worse."

Lizzie didn't bother checking to see if anyone was looking. She stepped in close to him and put her arms around him — and his response was immediate, his larger body curling around her own, holding on.

"Well?" he said into her hair. "Would you leave with me?"

She thought about her job, her farm, her life — as well as the fact that as of three days ago, they hadn't spoken in almost two years.

"Lane . . ."

"So it's a no?"

She pulled back . . . stepped away. "Lane, even if you never come back here again, you aren't going to be free of this place, these people. It's your family, your core."

"I lived without them perfectly well for

two years."

"And Miss Aurora brought you back."

"You could have. I would have returned for you."

Lizzie shook her head. "Don't make plans. There's too much up in the air right now." She cleared her throat. "And on that note, I better go back. People are starting to leave, but we've got a good four hundred still in there."

"I love you, Lizzie."

She closed her eyes. Put her hands to her face. "Don't say that."

"I just found out that my father was going to let those murderers have Edward."

"What?" She dropped her arms. "What are you talking about?"

"He refused to pay Edward's ransom when he was kidnapped. Refused. He was going to let my brother die there. In fact, I think he wanted Edward to die."

Lizzie covered her mouth with her hand and closed her eyes. "So you did see him."

"Yeah."

"How . . . is he?"

When Lane sidestepped that one, she wasn't all that surprised: "You know," he said, "I've always wondered how Edward's kidnapping happened. Now I know."

"But why would anyone do that to their son?"

"Because it's an efficient way to murder a business rival and not have to worry about going to jail for it. You get killers to take him into the jungle and then refuse to pay the agreed-upon price. Coffin for one, please — oh, and then let us play the grieving, tortured father for sympathy in the press. Win/win."

"Lane . . . oh, my God."

"So when I ask you about going away, it's not just some romantic fantasy." He shook his head slowly. "I'm wondering if my brother wasn't onto my father . . . so the great William Baldwine didn't try to get rid of him."

Jesus, she thought, *if this was true, the Bradfords truly did take dysfunction to whole new levels.*

"What did Edward find out?" she wondered.

"He won't go into any of it." Lane's eyes narrowed. "He is, however, helping me get what I need."

Lizzie swallowed through a thick throat — and tried not to picture Lane as the victim of some "accident."

"You're scaring me," she whispered.

THIRTY-FIVE

Sutton blinked as her eyes adjusted to the dim interior of William Baldwine's business center. "I'm surprised you're so cavalier about this."

William shut them in together and turned on the lights. "We're competitors, but that doesn't mean we can't be seen together."

Glancing around, she decided that the circular reception area definitely reminded her of the Oval Office — and wasn't that typical of the arrogance of the man. Only Baldwine would demote such a national icon to a place where he kept people waiting.

"Shall we proceed into my office?" he said with the smooth smile of one of those men who did Cialis ads on TV: older, grayer, but still sexy.

"I'm happy to do it here."

"The papers are in my desk."

"Fine."

As they proceeded toward the glass cage of his executive assistant, Sutton found herself wishing that they weren't alone. Then again, for this, they were both going to want privacy.

And then they were in William's space.

Which, dear Lord, was kitted up like something out of Buckingham Palace, all kinds of royal purple damask, gold-leafed mirrors and tables, and throne-like chairs making one wonder how the man accomplished anything in such an over-the-top environment.

"Would you mind if I lit a cigar?" he said.

"No, not at all." She glanced back and found that he'd left the door open — which might have made things a little less creepy had there actually been anyone else around. "So . . . where are the papers."

Over at his huge desk, he opened a mahogany humidor and took out what was undoubtedly a Cuban. "I would offer you one, but these are not for a lady."

"Good thing my money doesn't wear a skirt, right?" As he glanced at her, she smiled sweetly. "Shall we sign the papers?"

"Would you care to go to the track with me? My wife is unwell." He cut the butt of the cigar off. "So she will have to stay at home."

"I'm going with my father, but thank you."

William's eyes went down her body. "Why have you never married, Sutton?"

Because I'm in love with your son, she thought. *Not that he has ever cared.*

"I'm committed to my work and it is a jealous husband. It is rather an eighties concept, perhaps, but also the truth when it comes to me."

"We have so much in common, you know." He picked up a heavy crystal lighter and kicked up a flame. "We are both responsible for so much."

"My father is still running the Sutton Distillery Corporation."

"Of course he is." William leaned into the lick of fire and puffed up. "But that is not going to last long. Not with his illness. Is it."

Sutton stayed quiet. The family was not yet prepared to announce her elevation to chairman and CEO, but Baldwine was not wrong. Her father's Parkinson's had been controlled for the last three years, however the disease was progressing, and very soon the medications and their careful timing to hide the symptoms were going to become an insufficient mask. The sad thing was that her father's mind was as sharp as ever. His physical stamina was starting to lag, though, and helming a company like Sutton Distillery was a grueling endurance test on a good day.

"No comment?" William said.

As another puff of blue smoke rose above his head, the tobacco's dirty-sock stench reached her nose and made her sneeze.

"God bless you."

She ignored the platitude, well aware the bastard had lit up precisely because it would irritate her. He was the kind of man who exploited weaknesses at that kind of level.

"William, if the papers are here, I'll sign them now. If not, call my office when you're ready."

The man bent at the waist and opened the long, thin drawer in the middle of his desk. "Here."

With a toss, the sheaf skated across the blotter — and the fact that it was stopped by a framed picture of Little V.E., his wife, seemed apt.

"I believe you will find everything in order."

Sutton picked up the packet. Reviewing page one, she went on to the next . . . and the third . . . and the —

Her head jerked up. "I know that is not your hand on my waist."

William's voice was close to her ear.

"Sutton, you and I have so much in common."

Stepping away, she smiled at him. "Yes, you're the exact age of my father."

"But I'm not in his kind of shape, am I."

Well, that was true. William filled out his suit better than men decades younger.

"Do you want this done now?" she said sharply. "Or sometime next week with my lawyers."

The way he smiled at her made her feel like she had turned him on. "But of course. All business, as you stated."

Sutton deliberately sat in a chair against the wall, and she did not cross her legs. About ten minutes later, she looked up. "I'm prepared to execute this."

"See? I made the changes you required." He coughed a little into his fist. "Pen — or do you insist on using your own?"

"I have that covered, thank you." Dipping in to her purse, she then used her thighs as a desktop, and signed her name above the notary public's testament that was already filled in. "And I'll be taking a copy with me as I leave, thank you."

"As you wish."

She got to her feet and crossed the carpet. "Your turn."

William took a Montblanc out of the

inside pocket of his pale blue suit jacket, and he signed on another page, above another previously executed notary public's attestation.

"After you," he said, indicating the way out with his arm. "The copier is next to the first conference room. I don't use the Xerox machine."

Of course, you don't, she thought. *Because like cooking and cleaning, you figure it's woman's work.*

As she took the document from him and walked for the doorway, a shiver went down her spine. But then she realized that there was another piece to all this, namely a transfer of funds only she could initiate.

So there was nothing she had to fear from him.

At this particular moment.

She was just passing by the executive assistant's desk when something caught her eye and made her hesitate. It was something down on the floor, sticking out from under the desk's flank . . .

It was a piece of cloth.

No, it was a collar. To a coat sleeve.

"Something wrong?" William asked.

Sutton glanced over her shoulder, her heart pounding. "I'm . . ."

We are not alone, she thought with panic.

■ ■ ■ ■

From his position squeezed into the well of the desk, Edward knew the instant Sutton somehow became aware of his presence.

As her voice trailed off, he cursed to himself.

"What is it?" his father asked.

"I'm" — she cleared her throat — "feeling a bit faint."

"I have brandy in my office."

"Fruit juice. I need . . . some fruit juice. Chilled, please."

There was a pause. "Anything for a lady. Although I must confess, this is considerably out of the realm of my usual duties."

"I'll stay here. And take a seat."

As his father came by and then walked off, Edward heard coughing that gradually grew softer. And then he got a boatload of Sutton's voice, hushed, but strong as steel.

"My concealed weapon is pointed at you and I am prepared to pull the trigger. Show me your face, *now.*"

Fainting spell my ass, Edward thought. But at least she'd sent his father off on a little errand first.

Edward grunted as he leaned out from his hiding place.

Sutton gasped and covered her mouth with the hand that was not on her gun.

"If I'd known our paths would cross again," Edward said smoothly, "I would have brought you your purse."

"What are you doing here?" she hissed as she put her palm-sized gun back into her pastel-pink Derby suit.

"What are you? What did you just sign?"

She looked up. "He's going to come back at any moment."

"The question, of course, is what are you going to do about that?"

"What is wrong with you —" Instantly, she snapped to, shooing him with her hand. And just as he retucked himself, Sutton said, "Oh, thank you, William. That is just what I need."

Wincing as his bad leg spasmed, Edward prayed that she kept protecting him. Also wished he'd greeted her with something other than a reminder that they'd had sex the night before for the first time — although only because he'd assumed she was a prostitute that he'd bought and paid for for the sole reason that he needed a woman who looked like her or he couldn't get it up.

"No, orange is best." There was a pop as if a cap had been opened. "Mmm . . . good."

His father coughed again. "Better?"

"Much. Let's go to the copy machine together, shall we?" she said. "Just in case I need help."

"My pleasure," William drawled.

"You know," Sutton said more dimly, as she led the way out of the office, "you shouldn't smoke. That stuff will kill you."

Edward closed his eyes.

"Oh, the lights," Sutton murmured. "Here, allow me. Once we get the copies, we should return to the party."

"So eager to enjoy better bourbon than you produce?"

Everything went dark. "Yes, William. Of course."

As the pair of them went off together, Edward listened to the prattle of their talk — and prayed, for his father's sake, that the man kept his hands off Sutton. Watching that little show by the desk had required a kind of discipline he had not been connected to for quite a while.

What the hell kind of business deal were the pair of them executing?

God, he never thought he'd think like this, but he hoped Sutton wasn't making any investment in the BBC — or trying to acquire it. She could well be pouring good money into a black hole.

Because, yes, even before he had started to get into those most recent files, Edward had suspected what his father was doing. He had never understood the why of it . . . but he did know where to look and exactly what he was going to find.

Some moments later, he heard Sutton say, "Well, I think this benefits us both. I'll execute the wire transfer first thing on Monday morning."

"Care to seal this with a kiss?"

Edward curled up a fist and thought of what his brother had said about Chantal.

"Thank you, but a handshake is more than sufficient — and even that, I don't require. I'll let myself out."

A door opened and closed.

And then his father came back, the heavy footfalls striding in Edward's direction making him wish he'd brought his own gun.

Lane knew where he was, however. If he didn't make it out of here alive, Lane . . . would know.

Closer . . .

Closer . . .

Except his father just walked right by the desk and into his own office — where he turned on a light, pulled open a drawer and put the papers that had been signed back inside. Then he closed things up and took a number of puffs on his cigar, as if he were lost in thought.

When a coughing fit ensued, Edward rolled his eyes. His father had been an asthmatic all his life. Why anyone with that condition, even if it was just a mild case as William had, would ever smoke anything was a mystery.

As the man took out a handkerchief and covered his mouth, he also retrieved his inhaler and briefly replaced the cigar butt with the drugs. After a quick huff, he put the cigar back in place, turned off the light, and . . .

. . . proceeded by his assistant's desk.

Edward didn't move. Continued to hold his breath. Waited for the sound of one of the French doors opening and closing.

None of that came.

THIRTY-SIX

As Lizzie stood before him looking shaken, Lane wanted to take it all back. He wanted to return to the time when it was only his family's wealth and social position . . . along with his lying, baby-killing, adulterous, soon-to-be ex-wife . . . who came between them.

Ah, yes, the good ol' days.

Not.

"I'm sorry," he whispered. And that was true about so damned much.

"That's all right."

"Not really."

When they fell silent, he found that the sound of the party annoyed the crap out of him — especially as he thought about all that money that his father had "borrowed." He had no idea exactly what the costs of the brunch were, but he could do the math. Six or seven hundred people, top-shelf liquor, even if they got it wholesale, food that was out of a Michelin three-star restaurant? With enough parkers and waiters to take care of the entire city of Charlemont?

A quarter of a million, at least. And that didn't include the boxes at the track. The tables in the private rooms at Steeplehill Downs. The ball that his family sponsored afterward.

It was a million-dollar event that lasted less than twenty-four hours.

"Listen, you better go." He didn't want her to see Edward. Mostly because he was guessing Edward wouldn't want to be seen. "I'll come to your place, even if I can't spend the whole night."

"I'd like that. I'm worried about you. Lot going on."

You have no idea, he thought.

He leaned in to kiss her, but she ducked away — which was probably the right thing to do. A couple of groundsmen in a golf cart were coming up the lane from the lower part of the estate, and no one needed to see that.

"I'll get there when I can," he said. Then he leaned in. "Know that I'm kissing you right now. Even if it's only in my mind."

She blushed. "I . . . I'll see you. Tonight. I'll leave the door unlocked if you go late."

"I love you."

As she turned away, he didn't like the look on her face. And it was impossible to hide the fact that he desperately wanted her to say those words back — and not because she was being polite, but because she meant them.

Because her heart was on the line . . . just as his was.

With his world so off-balance, Lizzie King certainly seemed like the only secure, steady thing on his horizon —

The sound of the door opening behind him ripped his head around.

Not Edward.

Not. Even. Close.

His father, not his brother, came out of the rear door of the business center, and Lane froze.

The first thing he did was look at the man's hands — and he expected to find blood there. But no. In fact, the only thing on them, or in one of them, rather, was a white handkerchief that was pressed to his mouth as if he were discreetly covering a cough.

His father did not look over, but didn't appear stressed. Preoccupied, yes. Stressed? No.

And the bastard walked right by the back end of the old truck, the lack of social position associated with such a vehicle putting the F-150 and whatever owner or passenger might be standing with it beneath his radar.

"I know what you did."

Lane wasn't aware of speaking until the words came out of his mouth. And his father stopped and turned around immediately.

As one of the garage doors began to trundle up in the background, William's eyes narrowed and he tucked the handkerchief inside his jacket.

"I beg your pardon," the man said.

Lane crossed the distance between them and met his father eye to eye. Keeping his voice low, he said, "You heard me. I know exactly what you did."

It was eerie how much that face looked so like his own. Also eerie that nothing in it moved . . . William's expression didn't change in the slightest.

"You'll have to be more specific. Son."

The cold tone suggested that last word could have been replaced by "waste of my time" or perhaps the more colloquial "asshole."

Lane gritted his teeth. He wanted to lay it all out, but the reality that his brother was still inside that business center — or at least, hopefully remained in there alive — coupled with the fact that his father would just redouble efforts to cover his tracks, stopped him.

"Chantal told me," Lane whispered.

William rolled his eyes. "About what? Her demand that her rooms be redecorated for the third time? Or is it that trip to New York she wanted to take — again? She's your wife. If she wants these things, she needs to discuss them with you."

Lane narrowed his stare, tracing every one of those features.

"Now, if you'll excuse me, Lane, I'm going to —"

"You don't know, do you."

His father indicated an elegant hand to the Rolls-Royce being pulled out of the garage. "I'm going to be late — and I don't play guessing games. Good day —"

"She's pregnant." As his father frowned, Lane made sure that he enunciated his words clearly. "Chantal is pregnant, and she says it's yours."

He waited for the tell, waited for that single pinpoint of weakness to show . . . used all his experience in poker to read the man in front of him.

And suddenly there it was, the admission spoken in the subtle twitching under the left eye.

"I'm divorcing her," Lane said softly. "So she's all yours, if you want her. But that bastard child is not living under my mother's roof, do you understand? You will not disrespect Mother like that. I will *not* have it."

William coughed a couple of times, and re-outed the handkerchief. "A piece of advice for you, son. Women like Chantal are as truthful as they are faithful. I have never been with your wife. For godsakes."

"Women like her aren't the only ones who lie."

"Ah, yes, a double entendre. The conversational harbor for the passive aggressive."

Fuck it, Lane thought.

"Fine, I know about your affair with Rosalinda, too, and I'm very sure she killed herself because of you. Considering you have refused to speak to the police, I'm assuming you know that fact as well and are waiting for your attorneys to tell you what to say."

The flush of rage that rose up from the French collar of his father's pressed and monogrammed shirt was a red stain that turned his skin ruddy as a tarp. "You better realign your thinking, boy."

"And I know what you did to Edward."

At that point, his voice cracked. "I know you refused to pay the ransom, and I'm pretty sure you had him kidnapped." Steering away from anything further about the financial issues, Lane continued, "You always hated him. I don't know why, but you always went after him. I'm only guessing you finally got bored toying with him and decided to end the game on your terms, once and for all."

Funny, over the years, he had often pictured himself confronting his father — had played out all kinds of different scenarios, tried on all sorts of righteous speeches and violent yelling.

The reality was so much more quiet than he would have imagined. And so much more devastating.

The Rolls-Royce came to a stop beside them, and the family's uniformed chauffeur got out. "Sir?"

William coughed into that handkerchief, his gold signet ring gleaming in the sunlight. "Good day, son. I hope you enjoy your fiction. It is easier to contend with than reality — for the weak."

Lane grabbed the man's arm and yanked him around. "You are a bastard."

"No," William said with boredom. "I know who both my parents were — a rather important detail in one's life. It can be so dispositive, don't you agree?"

As William ripped out of the hold and walked toward the car, the chauffeur opened the suicide door to the backseat and the man slid in. The Drophead was off a moment later, that handsome profile of its passanger remaining forward and composed as if nothing had happened.

But Lane knew better.

His father clearly hadn't been aware that Chantal was pregnant — and the man was very, very definitely in the running to be responsible.

Likely in first place.

Dear Lord.

Lane returned to Mack's truck, and resumed his casual, I'm-not-waiting-for-anything waiting.

Under more normal circumstances, he would probably have been ranting about the fact that his wife and his father had consummated some kind of a relationship.

But he didn't even care.

Focusing on that still-closed door of the business center, he just prayed his brother was okay. And wondered how long he needed to wait before he broke in.

For some reason, he heard Beatrix Mollie's voice in his head, back from the day before when the woman had been loitering outside Rosalinda's office.

It comes in threes. Death always comes in threes.

If that were true, he prayed his brother wasn't the number two . . . but he sure as hell had some recommendations for the universe on who should be.

Edward's body was screaming by the time he heard, off in the distance, the rear exit open and close.

In spite of the pain, he waited another ten minutes just to make sure the business center was empty.

When there were no further sounds, he gingerly shifted his feet out from under the desk and bit his lower lip as he tried to straighten his legs, move his arms, get himself unkinked. And he made it far enough to have to shove the office chair out of his way — thank God the thing was on rollers.

But that was it.

He tried to stand up. Over and over again: With all manner of grunting and swearing, he attempted every conceivable strategy of transitioning back to the vertical, whether it was gripping the top of the desk and pulling, sitting back on his hands and pushing, or even crawling like a child.

He made little to no progress.

It was like being stuck at the bottom of a thirty-foot well.

And to top it off, he had no cell phone in his pocket.

Further curse words ricocheted through his head, the f-bombs landing and making craters in his thought patterns. But following that period of air strikes, he was able to think more clearly. Stretching over as best he could, he grabbed hold of the phone wire that ran from the wall up through a hole in the bottom of the desk.

Good plan, except the trajectory was wrong. When he pulled it, he was only going to move the handset farther out of reach.

And he had to call Lane — not just because he wasn't going to be able to make it to the exit. If he didn't reach his brother soon, the man was liable to get impatient, break down the damn door and blow their cover.

Bracing himself, Edward rocked forward once . . . twice . . .

On three, he heaved his torso up, drawing on some reserve of strength he didn't know he had.

It was ugly. His bones literally rattled together under his skin, hitting one another hard without any buffering of muscle, but he did manage to snag the receiver from its cradle — and drag the rest of the phone forward on the desk until it fell off the edge and landed in his lap.

His hands were shaking so badly that he had to dial a couple of times because he kept messing up the sequence, and he was near to blacking out when he finally put the handset up to his ear.

Lane answered on the first ring, bless his heart. "Hello?" the guy said.

"You need to come and get —"

"Edward! Are you okay? Where are —"

"Shut up, and listen to me." He gave his brother the code and made Lane repeat it. "I'm behind the desk in Father's assistant's office."

He hung up by slapping the receiver around its base until it found home, and then he closed eyes and sagged against the drawers. Funny, he'd been laboring under the misconception that sweeping out the barn aisles regularly meant his stamina and mobility had improved. Not the case. Then again, his pretzel-under-the-desk routine might have been a challenge for anyone.

As he heard the rear door open and shut for a second time, he had a sudden urge to re-try the whole get-to-his-feet thing, just so that he and Lane could be spared the embarrassment that was about to come. But the flesh was unwilling even as his ego got up on its high horse.

A moment later, he cut Lane off before the man spoke even a syllable. "I got it," he said roughly. "I got what we need."

He had to salvage his pride somehow.

Lane's knees cracked as he crouched down. "Edward, what happened —"

"Spare me. Just get me up into that chair. I need to log out or we'll be compromised. Where has Father gone? I know he left out the back."

"He got in his car with the driver and I watched him leave. He's off to the track."

"Thank God. Now get me up."

More ugliness, with Lane grabbing him under the armpits as if he were a corpse and dragging him off the imperial purple carpet. When he was finally seated, a sudden drop in blood pressure made him light-headed, but he shook that off and turned on the monitor again.

"Go to his desk," he ordered Lane. "Top drawer in the middle. There's a sheaf of papers in there. Don't bother reading them, run to the Xerox machine and get us a copy. He just signed them." When Lane only stood there, as if he were wondering whether he had a medical emergency to deal with first, Edward slashed his hand through the air. "Go! And put them back exactly where they were. *Go!*"

When Lane finally got his ass in gear, Edward refocused on the computer screen. After transferring one final document, he began signing out of the network carefully, closing everything that he had opened.

Lane hightailed it back no more than a second after he was finally finished.

"Get me out of here," Edward said roughly. "But set the phone back up here first."

It was the height of impotence that he required his strong, able-bodied younger brother to put things back in order and then heft him to his feet and shuffle him out of the office like he was a geriatric.

And what do you know, Lane gave up trying to help him walk just as they came across that family crest in the carpet. "I'm going to have to pick you up."

"Whatever you must."

Edward turned his face away from his brother's shoulder as his weight was popped off the floor. The ride was a rough one, his pain level ramping up and shifting to all kinds of new places. They made better progress, however.

"What was the paperwork for?" Edward demanded as they moved fast down that hall of conference rooms and offices.

"You're going to have to walk once we get outside."

"I know. What was the paperwork about?"

Lane just shook his head as they came to the back door. "I need to put you down."

"I know —"

The grunt of pain was nothing he could hold in, much as he would have preferred to. And he had to wait to be sure that his legs accepted his weight, his hand biting into Lane's forearm as he used his brother's steady body to help stabilize himself.

"You okay?" Lane asked. "Are you good to get over to the truck?"

As if he had a choice.

Edward nodded and pulled the baseball hat down lower over his face. "Check outside first."

Lane popped the door and leaned out. "Okay, I'm taking your arm."

"How chivalrous."

God damn him, but Edward got his legs moving toward that truck like the business center was on fire and that old F-150 was the only shelter he had: No matter how much it hurt, he just gritted his teeth and made it happen.

When he was finally stuffed into the passenger seat with the door closed, his stomach rolled so badly, he had to close his eyes and breathe through his mouth.

Lane jumped in beside him and cranked the engine. There was a grind of protest from under the hood as things were put in gear, and then they . . .

When there was no forward motion, Edward glanced across. "What?"

In slow motion, his brother's head turned toward him, a strange reserve hitting Lane's too handsome face.

"What's wrong?" Edward demanded. "Why aren't you driving us out of here?"

Releasing his seat belt, Lane said, "Here, read this. I'll be right back."

As the set of documents fluttered over Edward's legs, he barked, "Where the hell are you going?"

Lane pointed at the papers and got out. "Read."

When the driver's-side door was slammed in his face, Edward wanted to throw something. What in God's green earth was Lane thinking? They had just broken into their father's —

For some reason, he glanced down at what was on his lap.

And saw the words "Mortgage" and

"Instrument."

"What . . . ?" he muttered, gathering the pages up and putting them in order.

When he was finished reading them, he closed his eyes and let his head fall back. In exchange for the good and fair consideration of "$10,000,000 USD or ten million US dollars" to Mrs. Virginia Elizabeth Bradford Baldwine . . . Sutton Smythe had an income stream of sixty thousand dollars a month until the full sum was repaid to her.

The kicker, of course, was the default clause: If the monthly interest wasn't paid on time, Sutton could foreclose on the entire Easterly estate.

Everything from the mansion, to the outbuildings, to the farmland would be hers.

Not a bad risk profile, considering at last valuation about four years ago, the place had been thought to be worth about forty million dollars.

Edward cracked his lids again and riffled to the signature page. It had been previously notarized — regular practice at BBC on the QT. And William Baldwine had signed on the line that was marked Virginia Elizabeth Bradford Baldwine with his own John Hancock and three letters: POA.

Power of attorney.

So even though his mother's name was

the only one on the deed, and she no doubt had no knowledge of the agreement, and wasn't going to see a penny of the money, everything was nice and legal.

Damn it.

When the door on his side of the truck opened, he cursed and shot a glare at Lane —

Except his brother wasn't the one who'd done the duty with the handle.

No, Lane was standing off to the side, under a magnolia tree.

Miss Aurora had lost weight, Edward thought numbly. Her face was the same, but far leaner than he remembered. Then again, that was true for the both of them.

He couldn't meet those eyes of hers.

Just couldn't.

He did look at her hands, though, her beautiful dark hands, which trembled as they reached for his face.

Closing his lids, his heart thundered as the contact was made. And he prepared himself for her to make some comment about how horrible he looked — or even say something in a tone of voice that told him exactly how mortified she was at what he had become.

She even took off the baseball cap.

He waited, bracing himself —

"Jesus has brought you home," she said hoarsely as she cradled his face, and kissed him on the cheek. "Precious boy, He has returned you to us."

Edward couldn't breathe.

Precious boy . . . that was what she had always called him when he was little. Precious boy. Lane was her favorite, always had been, and Max she had tolerated because she'd had to, but Miss Aurora had called him, Edward, precious.

Because she was old-school and the firstborn-son thing did matter to her.

"I prayed for you," she whispered. "I prayed for Him to bring you home to us. And my miracle has come finally."

He wanted to say something strong. He wanted to push her way because it was just too much. He wanted . . .

Next thing he knew, he had leaned in to her and she had wrapped her arms around him.

Much later, when everything had changed and he was living a life he couldn't have imagined on any level, he would come to recognize . . . that this moment, with his head in Miss Aurora's hands, with her heart under his ear, with her familiar voice soothing him and his brother watching from a discreet distance, was when he began to truly heal: For a brief instant, a split second, a single breath, his pilot light flicked on. The spark didn't last long — the flare died when she finally stepped back a little.

But the ignition did, in fact, occur. And that changed everything.

"I prayed every night for you," she said, brushing his shoulder. "I prayed and I asked for you to be saved."

"I don't believe in God, Miss Aurora."

"Neither does your brother. But like I tell him, He loves you anyway."

"Yes, ma'am." Because what else could he say to that?

"Thank you." She touched his head, his jaw. "I know you don't want to see me —"

He took her hand. "No, it's not that."

"You don't have to explain."

The idea that she felt she was somehow a second-class citizen made him feel like he'd been shot in the chest. "I don't . . . want to see anyone. I'm not who I once was."

She tilted his face up. "Look at me, boy."

He had to force himself to meet her dark stare. "Yes, ma'am."

"You are perfect in God's eyes. Do you understand me? And you are perfect in mine as well — no matter what you look like."

"Miss Aurora . . . it's not just my body

that's changed."

"That is in your hands, boy. You can choose to sink or swim based on what happened. Are you going to drown? Pretty stupid now that you're back on dry land."

If anyone else had said that bullshit to him, he would have rolled his eyes and never thought about the statement again. But he knew her background. He knew more than even Lane knew about what her life had been like before she had started to work at Easterly.

She was a survivor.

And she was inviting him to join the club.

So this was why he hadn't wanted to see her, he thought. He hadn't wanted this confrontation, this challenge that was clearly being offered to him.

"What if I can't get there," he found himself asking her in a voice that broke.

"You will." She leaned in and whispered in his ear, "You're going to have an angel watching over you."

"I don't believe in them, either."

"Doesn't matter."

Easing back, she stared at him for a long while, but not in a way that suggested she was taking note of how much older and thinner he looked.

"Are you okay?" he asked abruptly. "I

heard you went to the —"

"I'm perfectly fine. Don't you worry about me."

"I'm sorry."

"About what?" Before he could reply, she cut him off with her more typical, strident voice. "You don't be sorry for taking care of yourself. I'll always be with you, even when I'm not."

She didn't say good-bye. She just brushed his face one more time and then turned away. And it was funny. The image of her walking over to Lane and the pair of them talking together under the heavy dark green leaves of the magnolia tree was something that was going to also stick, as it turned out.

Just not for the reasons he thought.

THIRTY-SEVEN

The rain that was not forecasted started just after five p.m.

As Lizzie folded up the last of the tables under the tent, she smelled the change in the air and looked out to the ivy on the brick wall of the garden. Sure enough, the trefoil leaves were dancing, their faces shining up to the grey sky.

"It isn't supposed to rain," she muttered to no one in particular.

"You know what they say about the weather around here," one of the waiters retorted.

Yeah, yeah, she knew.

Where was Lane? she wondered. She hadn't heard anything from him since she'd seen him by that truck, and that had been six hours ago.

Mr. Harris came up to her. "You'll tell them that it's all to go into the staging area?"

"Yes," she said. "That's where the rentals

always go afterward — and before you ask, yes, silverware and glassware, too."

As the man lingered next to her, she was tempted to tell him to grab hold of the table and help her hump it across the event deck. But it was pretty clear he wasn't a hands-dirty sort of fellow.

"What's the matter?" she asked, frowning.

"The police have arrived again. They are trying to be respectful of our event, but they wish to interview me anew."

Lizzie lowered her voice. "Do you want me to take care of things out here?"

"I'm afraid they're not going to let this be."

"I'll make sure it's done right."

The butler cleared his throat. And then, God love him, he gave her a bit of a bow. "It would be most appreciated. Thank you — I shan't be long."

She nodded and watched him go. Then she got back to work.

Jerking the table off the deck, she strode across the now-cavernous interior and proceeded out into the open air where a sprinkling of that rain dusted her head and shoulders. The staging tent was way off by the opposite side of the house, and Greta's German accent emanated from it as twin streams of servers, one filing in with party debris, the other emerging with empty hands, moved with speed.

Lizzie waited along with the rest of them, inching her way closer and closer to the drop-off.

The larger of the two tents would be taken down in about twenty minutes — and the sweep-up crew was already working the floor, picking up crumpled napkins, errant forks, glasses.

Rich people were no different from any other herd of animals, capable of leaving a trail of detritus behind them after they abandoned a feeding station.

"Last table," she said as she once again went under cover.

"Good." Greta pointed to a stack. "It goes there, *ja*?"

"Yup." Lizzie jerked the weight up to waist level and slid the length on top of the pile. "Mr. Harris has to take care of some business, so I'll be manning clean up."

"We have all in order." Greta motioned for two young men with six crates of glasses apiece to the other corner. "Over there. Make sure under cover, *ja*?"

"I'm going to check in with the kitchen."

"We'll be finished out here in an hour."

"Right on schedule."

"Always."

And Greta was right. At six o'clock on the dot, they were finished, the big tent down, the house and gardens cleared out of anything rented, the backyard reset sure as if it had had its Ctrl+Alt+Del hit. As usual, the effort had been tremendous: As the staff filed off, most of them were heading downtown to drink off the aches, pains, and OMGs of the day, but not Lizzie — or her partner. Home. They were both going home — where she would wait for Lane, and Greta would get treated to a meal cooked by her husband.

As the two of them walked down to the staff parking area together, they didn't say a word, and at their cars, they shared a quick hug.

"Another in the can," Lizzie said as they pulled apart.

"Now we get ready for the Little V.E. birthday party."

Or Gin's wedding reception, Lizzie thought.

At least it wasn't going to be Lane's wedding anniversary.

"I'll see you tomorrow?" she said.

"Sunday? No." Greta laughed. "Not a soul will be stirring, not a martini nor a mouse."

"Right, right, right. Sorry, my brain is fried. See you Monday."

"You all right to drive home?"

"Yup."

After a wave, Lizzie got in her Yaris and then joined the lineup of cars and trucks proceeding out the staff lane.

As she took a left on River Road, what had started as sprinkles turned into an actual rain, and the deluge made her think of the race — shoot, she'd missed it. Reaching for the radio, she turned the thing on and futzed with the dial to find the local station. By the time she found the recap, she was out of spaghetti junction and heading over the Ohio.

But she didn't follow the reporting and not just because she didn't follow the sport.

Frowning, she leaned into her steering wheel. "Dear God . . ."

Up ahead, the horizon was filled with tremendous black clouds, the rolling thunderheads looming high in the sky. Worse? There was a green tinge to it all — and even to her untrained, naked eye, the stuff appeared to be rotating.

She checked over her shoulder. Behind her, there was nothing much going on weather-wise. There was even a stretch of blue sky.

Shoving her hand into her purse, she took out her phone and dialed Easterly. When that clipped English voice answered, she said, "Weather's coming. You're going to need —"

"Miss King?" the butler said.

"Look, you need to batten down the pool area and the pots —"

"But there is no 'weather,' as you called it, due. In fact, the weathermen have made it clear that a spot of rain is all we shall have this evening."

As a flash of lightning licked its way across the underside of that cloud front, she thought, well, at least she'd gotten along with the man for almost an hour. "Screw the Weather Channel. I'm telling you what I'm looking at right now — there is a storm bigger than downtown Charlemont heading across the river, and Easterly's hill is the first thing it's going to run into."

Crap, had she remembered to shut her windows at her farm?

"I was unaware of your skills as a meteorologist," Mr. Harris said dryly.

You are a dick, sir. "Fine, but then you can explain the following after it goes through: One, why the awning by the pool blew off. Two, why the four porch pots on the west side of the terrace have fallen over and need to be replanted. Three, where the lawn furniture ended up — because unless you make sure it's in the pool house, it's going to drag through the flower beds. Which brings me to number four — namely when the ivy, tea roses, and hydrangea will be fixed. Oh, and then you can follow all that up with writing the family a seven-thousand-dollar check to cover the new plant material that will be required."

Tick. Tock. Tick. Tock —

"What was the second . . . issue?" he said.

Tallyho, big guy.

Lizzie ran through the whole protocol, which was the result of her and Greta having worked with Gary McAdams for years storm-proofing the grounds in the spring and the fall. The thing was, it didn't take an EF5 dropping directly in Easterly's backyard to create a mess. Some of the generic storms were more than capable of doing a lot of damage if they had straight-line winds.

It was one of the things she'd had to learn fast when she'd moved down to Charle-mont —

As if on cue, she drove into a blistering wall of rain that hit the windshield so hard it sounded like a team of tap dancers rocking out to "The Star-Spangled Banner."

Cranking up her wipers, she took her foot off the accelerator because the Yaris was capable of hydroplaning on the highway with even the slightest amount of water under its tiny tires.

"You got it?" she said. "Because I need to hang up and drive through this."

"Yes, yes of course . . . oh, my God," the man whispered.

"So you see the storm?" *Have fun with that,* she thought. "Better get moving."

"Indeed. Quite."

Lizzie hung up and tossed her phone back into her purse. Then it was a case of hunch over the wheel, hold on tight . . . and pray that some idiot show-off in an SUV didn't run her off the road.

Things got even worse, fast.

And jeez, after a day as long as the one she had put in, the last thing she needed were torrential bands of water that cut her visuals down to five feet, along with teeth-rattling thunder and lightning, but the weather seemed determined to parallel what was going on at Easterly — almost as if the drama at the house was affecting even the weather.

Okay, that was hyperbole.

But still.

It took her five hundred years to reach her exit. And then another seven or eight to get to her driveway. Meanwhile, the storm had turned into storm*S* — with a big capital "S" on the end: Lightning crackled and sizzled, seeming to target her car, and thunder roared, and she got pelted with a round of hail you could have hit out of Fenway Park. White-knuckled, frankly pissed, worried about Lane, and sore all over, when she finally made it to her home, she was a hot mess of —

The finger of God.

That was the only thing she could think of.

One moment, she was just about to pull into her spot by her house. The next? A jagged bolt of lightning licked out of the sky — and nailed her big, beautiful tree right at the top.

Sparks flew like it was the Fourth of July.

And she screamed, "No!" as she hit the brakes.

The Yaris's tires were iffy on dry pavement. On a wet, muddy dirt road? It was greased-pig time.

And that was how she learned Lane was already at her house.

Because she plowed right into the back of his Porsche.

Lane had been sitting at Lizzie's kitchen table reading BBC financial reports for about two hours when the storm hit. As the first wave of rain and noise and flashing rumbled through the house, he didn't bother to look up from her laptop, even as the old-fashioned glass in the windows rattled and the roof beams creaked.

The volumes and volumes of data were overwhelming.

And he was panicked that he only understood a fraction of it all.

Then again, it had been pretty damn naive of him to think he could get a handle on his father's dealings with any kind of alacrity. Aside from the crushing numbers of files, he just didn't have the extensive accounting background that was going to be required to sort everything out.

Thank God Edward had been prepared for something like this, setting up those shadow accounts and passcodes and emails. Without all that, it would have been impossible to export the information without triggering some internal alert.

Maybe that would still happen, though.

He didn't know how much time they had before their father tweaked to the fact that there had been a major leak.

Taking a break, he sat back and rubbed his eyes — and that was when the second wave of storms hit. And whether it was the forced TO thanks to his burning retinas, or the fact that this T-cell really was kicking it up huge, he became very aware that Lizzie's home was suddenly under siege.

Getting to his feet, he went around and shut all the open windows, downstairs and up. As he jogged from room to room, lightning strobed in crazy bursts, casting fast, hard shadows over Lizzie's floorboards, her furniture, her piano. With the sky nearly dark as midnight and all the jagged licks nailing the farmland, he felt as though he were in a war zone.

He'd forgotten how rough these eastward-moving spring storms could be, the collisions of hot and cold fronts given free rein over the miles and miles of flat, tilled fields in the midwest.

Back on the first floor, he glanced out at the front porch and cursed. The wicker rockers and side tables were milling around, animated into nervous agitation by the countervailing gusts of wind.

When he went to open the door, the heavy weight blew in at the slightest turn of the knob, and he had to drag things shut behind himself as he stepped out. Grabbing hold of anything he came in contact with, he moved Lizzie's stuff around the corner of the porch, out of the worst of the gale.

He was coming back around to tackle the

final lounge chair when he saw headlights turn in off the main road. It had to be her — and he was glad she was home. He'd meant to call, text . . . send up smoke signals or a homing pigeon, but his head had been locked in a —

Everything happened in a weird combination of slo-mo and speed of sound: The blast of lightning that came out of the sky right above the house. The explosion of noise and the bomb burst of illumination.

That tree limb that was the size of an I beam cracking free of the trunk and falling to the ground.

Right as Lizzie pulled up under it.

The crunching sound of metal getting crushed stopped his heart in his chest.

"Lizzie!" he screamed as he went airborne off the porch.

Rain pelted him in the face, and the wind was like a pack of dogs tearing at his clothes, but he bolted across the puddled ground at a dead run.

Death comes in threes.

"No!" he hollered into the storm. "Nooooo!"

The Yaris had crumpled under the weight, its roof mashed down flat, its hood caved in — and his own life flashed through his mind as he skidded to a halt in his bare feet.

Branches with bright green, new spring leaves were everywhere, compromising his vision as much as the rain and the wind — and still lightning flashed and thunder carried on as if nothing important had happened.

"Lizzie!"

He dove into the wet mess of the leaves, clawing to get through, get around, get over. Even with all the wind, he could smell the gasoline, the oil, and hear the hiss of an engine that had been mortally wounded.

Maybe all the damp would stop a fire from igniting?

Lane changed tactics and began to climb up and over — until he worked his way around and onto the front of the car. Finally, he felt something slick and wet under his hands, and he knocked on it, wanting her to know he was there. "Lizzie, I'm going to get you out!"

With frantic jerks, he tore through the leaves and branches — until he found the spidered, bowed-out glass of the front windshield. The panel was still intact — but that didn't last long. Squeezing up a fist, he punched through and all but shoved himself into the opening.

Lizzie was laying sideways, her head in the passenger seat, her arms flopping around as if she were trying to orient herself. Both air bags had blown, and the chalky dryness in the air was at odds with the storm's tremendous humidity.

"Lizzie!"

At least she was moving.

Shit. There was no way he could get any of the doors opened. He was going to have to pull her out.

Reaching forward, he touched her face. "Lizzie?"

Her eyes were fluttering, and there was blood on her forehead. "Lane . . . ?"

"I got you. I'm going to get you out. Are you hurt? Your neck? Your back?"

"I'm sorry I hit . . . your car . . ."

He closed his eyes for a split second, and said a prayer. Then he snapped back into action. "I'm going to have to drag you out."

Fighting his way further into the interior, he somehow managed to reach the seat belt release, and then he grabbed ahold of her upper arms —

And stopped.

"Lizzie? Listen to me — are you sure you're not hurt? Can you move your arms and legs?" When she didn't reply, he felt a fresh surge of alarm. "Lizzie? Lizzie!"

Thirty-Eight

Back in Charlemont, Edward was not paying any attention to how his remaining horse did in the Derby. He wasn't even at the track.

No, he was trying on a new role.

Stalker.

Sitting behind the wheel of a Red & Black Stables truck, he glanced through the passenger window at the enormous brick mansion he was parked in front of.

Built in the early 1900s, the great Georgian pile was even larger than Easterly — which had been the point. The Suttons had been the interloping upstarts for almost a century at that point, and as that family's fortune finally overtook the Bradfords', they had constructed the house as a trophy to their triumph. With some twenty or thirty bedrooms and a village of staff quarters under its massive roof, the manse was nearly a city unto itself — on the second-best rise in town with the second-best view of the river and the second-best garden.

But yes, they had Easterly beat on size.

Just as the Sutton Distillery Corporation was bigger by thirds than the BBC.

Edward shook his head and glanced at the crappy watch he'd taken to wearing. If Sutton stayed true to her usual schedule, it would not be long now.

At least nobody in a uniform with a barking German shepherd at his side was harassing him to leave. Sutton Smythe's family estate had security that was every bit as tight as Easterly's, but he had two things going for him. One was the logo on his vehicle: the R&B trademark was like a royal warrant, and even if he had been a serial killer parked in the downtown lobby of the courthouse, there was every possibility that the police would leave him alone with that thing in place. The second gimme he had in his favor was the Derby. Undoubtedly, everyone was still talking about the race, settling up bets, reliving the glory.

Soon. She would be home soon.

After Lane had gotten him back to the farm, he had taken some of his meds and had a drink. Then he had reread the mortgage papers . . . and lasted about ten more minutes before he'd picked up

Sutton's evening purse and limped out to one of his trucks.

Moe and Shelby and the rest of the stable-hands were down at the track with the trainers and the horses. As he'd driven off, he'd thought it was a shame to waste the peace and quiet at the farm — but this was something he needed to handle in person.

Rain began to fall, first as a few drops; then as a drizzle.

He checked his watch again.

Thirteen minutes. He was betting she would be home in thirteen minutes: Whereas most of the two hundred thousand people at Steeplehill Downs were going to enjoy a long trek back to wherever they had left their cars, followed by a further gridlock as they attempted to get on the highway, folks like the Bradfords and the Suttons had police escorts that got them in and out the back ways fast.

And he was right.

Some twelve minutes and a number of seconds later, one of the Sutton family's black Mulsannes pulled up in front of the house, the driver popping out from behind the wheel and triggering an umbrella as he went to the rear door. A second security man did the same on the other side.

Sutton's father emerged first and needed

the arm of his chauffeur to get to the house.

Sutton, on the other hand, uncoiled slowly from the vehicle, her eyes trained on his truck. After speaking with the driver, she took the umbrella from the man and walked over, heedless that she was ruining her high-heeled shoes.

Edward put the window down as she approached — and tried to ignore the scent of her perfume as she came up to him.

"Get in," he said without sparing her a glance.

"Edward —"

"As if I'm going to discuss what you signed with my father in your own house? Or even in your front yard?"

She let out a very unlady-like curse and then marched around the front of the truck. With a grunt, he tried to reach over as a gentleman should and open her door, but she got there first — and besides, his body wouldn't let him stretch that far.

As she settled into the seat, she froze as she saw her purse.

Putting the truck in gear, he muttered, "I figured you'd want your driver's license back."

"I have to be at the ball in forty-five minutes," she said as he started down her hill.

"You hate going to those things."

"I have a date."

"Do you. Congratulations." A quick fantasy of kidnapping her and keeping her from going at all played out in a very Lifetime Movie sort of way — said fantasy culminating in her going Stockholm syndrome and falling in love with her captor. "Who is he?"

"None of your business."

Edward took a left and just kept driving. "So you're lying."

"Check the society pages tomorrow morning," she countered in a bored tone. "You can read all about it."

"I don't get the *Charlemont Courier Journal* anymore."

"Look, Edward —"

"What the *hell* are you doing? Mortgaging my goddamn house?"

Even though he wasn't looking at her, he could feel her icy stare nailing him in the face. "Number one, your father approached me. And number two, if you take that tone with me again, I'll foreclose just on principle."

Edward shot a glare in her direction. "How could you do that? Are you really that greedy?"

"The interest rate is more than fair! And

would you have preferred he go to a bank, where it would be recorded for the public? I'm going to keep everything private, assuming the payments are made."

He jabbed a finger at the documents on the seat between them. "I want you to make that go away."

"You are not a party to this, Edward. And apparently your father needs the money or he wouldn't have come to me."

"That is my mother's house!"

"You know, if I were you, I'd be thanking me. I'm not sure what's going on under that roof of yours, but ten million should be nothing for the likes of the grand and glorious Bradford family!"

Edward took a hard left and pulled into one of the public parks that dotted the Ohio River. Crossing the empty parking lot, he stopped when he got to the boat launch and put them in park. By now, the storm was really heating up, and the bursts of light from the sky fueled the anger inside of him.

Wrenching around in the seat, he swallowed a groan at the pain. "He doesn't need the money, Sutton."

It was a lie, of course, however the last thing the family needed was talk: As much as he was frustrated with Sutton, he knew he could trust her, but there had to be other people involved on her side. Lawyers, bankers. At least she could refute their conversation if it came up.

"Then why did he sign that document?" she demanded. "Why did your father go out of his way to divert me from a business meeting and put this on the table."

As she confronted him, he had a quick mental image from the night before of her straddling his hips, riding him, being gentle with his broken body.

Then he remembered his father reaching for her in the office.

Could this get any messier, he wondered as hatred for William Baldwine surged.

Edward focused on her lips and thought about his brother's wife. "Has he ever kissed you?"

"Excuse me."

"My father. Has he ever kissed you."

Sutton shook her head in disbelief. "Let's stick to fighting about the mortgage on Easterly, shall we?"

"Answer the goddamn question."

She threw up her hands. "You saw me in his office with him. What do you think."

So he had, Edward thought on a surge of fury.

"Look," Sutton said. "I don't know what's going on in your family, or why he wanted to do this. All I know is that it's a good deal for me . . . and I thought it would help you out. Stupid me, I thought the fact that I would keep this discreet might actually benefit you."

After a moment, he muttered, "Well, you're wrong. And that's why I want you to rip that up."

"Your father has a copy, too," she pointed out dryly. "Why don't you go talk to him."

"He made that deal with you because he hates me. He did it because he knows damn well that the last person on earth I would *ever* want my family to be indebted to is you."

At least that wasn't a lie, he thought as she gasped.

God knew he already felt like half a man around her anyway . . .

As Edward's words sank in, Sutton jerked in her seat — and couldn't catch the reaction in time to try to hide it.

Pride made her want to hit back at him hard, but the angry words log jammed in her head, and all she ended up doing was staring out at the choppy, muddy river.

The windshield wipers were on, and periodically, they made a swipe that gave her a momentarily clear view of the opposite shore. And it was funny, life was a bit like that, wasn't it. You went along, doing your thing, not really seeing the full landscape of where you were for all the daily minutiae you had to take care of — when suddenly, things crystallized and you got a brief picture that left you going, *Ah, so I am here.*

Sutton cleared her throat — but it didn't really do much, because as she spoke, her words were hoarse, "You know, I don't think I'll ever understand why you think so little of me. It's really quite . . . it's a mystery to me."

Edward said something, but she talked right over him. "You must know that I fell in love with you a long time ago."

That shut him up.

"You must know it. How could you not? I've been following you around for years — is that why you hate me?" She glanced over at him and couldn't see much of his eyes because of that baseball cap — probably a good thing. "Do you look down on me for that? I always figured you strung me along because you assumed my feelings could be useful to you at some point — but is it sicker than that? I know I despise myself for the weakness." She nodded at the papers. "I mean, that document there is a perfect example of how pathetic I am. I wouldn't have done a deal like that, under the table, for anyone else. But I suppose that's my problem, not yours, isn't it."

She went back to staring out the windshield ahead of her. "I know you don't like to talk about what happened to you in South America, but . . . I didn't sleep for the entire time they had you, and for months afterward, I had nightmares. And then you came back to Charlemont and wouldn't see me. I told myself it was because you weren't seeing anyone, but that isn't true, is it."

"Sutton —"

"No," she said sharply. "I'm not going to let you all out of that mortgage. That would be just another part of this stupidity I have going on with you."

"You have it all wrong, Sutton."

"Do I? I'm not so sure. So how about we end this right now — you can fuck off, Edward. Now, take me home before I call the police."

She expected him to argue with her. After a moment, though, he put the truck in reverse and turned them around.

As he headed back out to the road, she measured his grim profile. "You better pray that father of yours makes those payments in a timely fashion. If he doesn't, I will not hesitate to put your family out on the street

— and if you think that's not going to get people in this town talking, you're out of your goddamn mind."

That was the last thing either of them said on the return trip to her house.

When he pulled in front of the mansion, she made sure to get her purse and take it with her this time — and the truck barely rolled to a stop before she leaped out.

She was pretty sure he said her name one last time as she took off, but maybe not.

Who cared.

As she ran through the rain to her front door, the butler opened things up for her.

"Mistress!" he exclaimed. "Are you all right?"

She hadn't bothered with the umbrella, and a quick glance in the antique mirror by the door showed that she looked as worn-out and worn-down as she felt.

"Actually, I'm not feeling well." No lie there. "Will you please let Brandon Milner know that I've taken ill and am going to bed? I was supposed to go to the ball with him this evening."

He bowed. "Shall I call for Dr. Qalbi?"

"No, no. I'm just exhausted."

"I'll get you a tray and some tea."

That sounded perfectly nauseating. "How lovely, thank you."

As the man strode off for the kitchen wing, she went over to the elevator's paneled doors. Fortunately, the car was on the first floor and she was able to take it up right away. The last thing she needed was to run into her father or her brother.

Getting out, she took off her shoes and padded down the long hallway, slipping into her bedroom and closing the door behind herself.

Shutting her eyes, she kept hearing Edward's voice over and over again in her head.

He knows damn well that the last person on earth I would ever *want my family to be indebted to is you.*

Unbelievable.

And it was funny. Even with all the money she had, all the position and the authority, the respect and the adulation . . . she was still capable of being reduced to a devastated child.

All it took was being in an enclosed space with Edward Baldwine.

For ten minutes.

No more, she vowed. This unhealthy obsession she had going on with that man needed to stop right now.

In the back of her mind, she had sometimes wondered if he might be fighting an obsession with her of his own, their centuries-old family competition keeping him from making a move. But that had clearly been an unfair projection on her part, some kind of romantic fantasy born out of her own feelings.

The only nice things he'd said to her were when he'd thought she was a prostitute that he had bought and paid for.

Reality had now been clearly established, however: He had just put up a billboard in her proverbial town square. Set her straight with no room for misinterpretation.

She might be pathetic.

But she was not stupid.

Thirty-Nine

Punched in the head.

As Lizzie slumped to the side in the crushed cabin of her Yaris, she felt like she'd been punched in the head.

By a combination of Wolverine, The Rock, and maybe Ahnold from back in the day.

And as a result, nothing was processing well, not her having run into the back of Lane's car, not the fact that there was water in her face, not the loud noise —

"Lizzie!"

The sound of her name cleared some of the cobwebs away, and she looked around, trying to figure out why God suddenly sounded a lot like Lane.

"Lane?" she said, blinking hard.

Why was he coming through her windshield? Was this a dream?

"— hurt anywhere?" he was saying. "I need to know before I move you."

"I'm sorry . . . about your car —"

"Lizzie, y'all gotta tell me if you're hurt!"

Boy, when he got anxious that Southern accent came back thick, didn't it. Then she frowned. Hurt? Why would she be —

And that was when she saw all the greenery.

In her car.

Okay, this had to be a bad dream — and she might as well go along with it: Testing her arms, her legs, taking a deep breath, moving her head . . . everything checked out.

"I'm all right," she mumbled. "What happened?"

"I'm going to pull you forward — help me if you can, 'kay?"

"Sure. I'll —"

Wow. Ow!

But she was determined to participate in the effort. Even as things got stretched out of place and threatened to pop from sockets, she shoved her feet against anything she came in contact with, pushing as Lane pulled, twisting to keep going forward.

Rain on her face, in her hair, on her clothes. Scratches. Wind blinding her.

But he got her out.

And then she was in his arms, up against his chest, feeling him tremble.

"Oh, God," he said hoarsely. "Oh, praise

God, you're alive . . ."

Lizzie held on to him, still not understanding why they were sitting up in a tree. How had the cars gotten up in her —

The lightning bolt streaked out of the sky and landed so close to them, her ears exploded in pain.

"We have to get inside," Lane barked. "Come on."

Sometime in the process of tripping and falling to the ground, her brain came back online — and what she saw nearly paralyzed her.

Half of the beautiful tree that grew beside her house had crushed her car.

She hadn't hit his Porsche, after all.

The crunching had been her tiny sedan taking the brunt of all that tremendous weight.

"Lane . . . my car —"

That was all she got out before he took her up into his arms and ran for her house. As he jumped onto the porch, she pushed herself from his hold and refused to go any farther. Lifting her hand to her mouth at the sight of her car, she —

Blood. There was blood . . . all over her.

A sudden lightheadedness washed over her, making her sway as she looked down at herself. "Lane . . . am I hurt?"

"Inside," he demanded, moving her bodily to the door.

As he shoved her into her house and put his whole strength against the panels to re-shut them, her heart began to pound as she got a good look at her savior: He was a bloody, wet mess, too.

But what did it matter?

The two of them embraced in such a rush that their dripping clothes slapped together, their bodies reconnecting, sharing warmth, holding on hard.

"I thought I'd lost you," he said into her ear. "Oh, Christ, I thought I'd —"

"You saved me, you saved me —"

They were both talking a mile a minute, tripping over words, buzzing from the near miss. And then he was kissing her and she was kissing him back.

Except she stopped all that, pulling away. "I think you're the one who's bleeding."

"Just scratches —"

"Oh, God, look at your arms — your hands!"

He was totally torn up, his exposed skin streaked with cuts from his having fought through the branches to get to her — and there were further contusions on his face and his neck.

"I don't care," he said. "You're all I'm

worried about."

"Do you need a doctor?"

"Oh, please. The tree fell on you, remember?"

And that was when the lights went out.

Lizzie stilled for a moment . . . and then she started to laugh so hard that her eyes burned. It was just too much emotion about too many things for her to hold in — and before she knew it, Lane was laughing, too, the pair of them holding each other and letting out the ridiculous afterburn of everything from the problems with his family to the stress of the brunch . . . to that freak accident with her tree.

"Shower?" she said.

"I thought you would never ask."

Ordinarily, she'd have fussed over the wet footprints across her living room and up the planks of the stairs, but not now: The memory of that weight landing on her car was a prioritizer and a half.

"I swear, I thought I hit your car," she said as they came up to the second floor.

"It wouldn't have mattered if you had."

Ah, the joys of being a Bradford, she thought. "You have a backup Porsche, I'm sure."

"Even if I didn't, it wouldn't have mattered as long as you're okay."

Squeezing together, they made it through the jambs of her bedroom and into her bath — and then, as she turned on the shower, he went for her clothes, unbuttoning things, releasing zippers, shedding her second skin's worth of wet and cold and clingy.

Goosebumps tickled her arms and thighs, but that was more from the heat in his eyes than the chill in the air. And then Lane was taking off his own clothes, leaving them where they landed in a tangled mess with hers.

"Under the water," she groaned as he nuzzled into her throat, kissing his way to her mouth.

He cursed as they stepped into the warm, gentle spray — and as the blood washed off, she was relieved. Just cuts on him, nothing serious . . .

And that was the last thought she had as his big hands traveled over her slick breasts, and his mouth came down hard on hers, and that familiar erotic urgency sprang to life between them.

I love you, she thought inside her head. *I love you all over again, Lane.*

Sometime later, after the power came back on, and Lane had made love to his Lizzie twice in the shower and once more in her bed, after they had gone down and had the last of that frozen lasagna and most of the peach ice cream in her house, after they had returned upstairs and gotten into her bed again . . . all the problems of the day came back to him.

Fortunately, Lizzie was asleep and it was dark, so whatever expression he didn't have the energy to hide was a non-starter.

Staring at her ceiling, his mind pulled a churn and burn over it all, and the next thing he knew, light was glowing at the edge of the horizon. A quick glance at Lizzie's alarm clock and he was surprised to find that he'd blown the whole night.

Sliding out from under the sheets, he got to his feet and went into the bathroom. His clothes were unsalvageable; he picked them up off the floor and put them into her trash. The only thing he saved? His boxers.

Better than driving home buck-ass naked on the Lord's day.

Back out in the bedroom, he went over to Lizzie. "I gotta go."

She came awake on a jerk, and he soothed her until she put her head on the pillow again. "I've got a date with a beautiful woman that I can't miss," he said.

Lizzie smiled in a sleepy, fuzzy way that made him want to stare at her forever. "Tell her I said hello?"

"I will." He kissed her on the mouth. "I'm bringing you dinner tonight, by the way."

"Will it be frozen?"

"No, hotter'n'hell."

The smile she gave him went right through to his blood, cranking him up even though there was no time to do anything about it.

"I lo—" Lane stopped himself, knowing she wasn't going to like that good-bye. "I'll see you at five o'clock tonight."

"I'll be here."

He kissed her one more time and then strode for the door.

"Wait, what about your clothes?" she called out.

"They can't arrest me. The naughty bits are covered up."

Her laughter escorted him down her stairs and out of the house. And the sight of half that tree on top of her car made his heart skip a beat.

As he took a deep breath, his first instinct was to take out his phone and call Gary Mc-Adams to remove the limb and get that crushed tin can of hers off to a scrapyard. But he stopped himself. Lizzie was not the kind of woman who would appreciate that sort of maneuvering. She would have her own contacts, her own idea of how to handle the problem, her own plan for the Yaris.

Knowing her, she would try to get it back on its feet.

Shaking his head, he walked over to his car. The Porsche had very nearly been destroyed, too, the 911 missed by only a couple of feet. After clearing some leaves off the hood, he got in, juiced the engine, and made his way slowly down the lane, steering around the fallen branches and the divots in the dirt that were full of water. As soon as he hit the asphalt, he made up for lost time, speeding toward Charlemont, ripping across the river, gunning his way up Easterly's hill.

He was halfway to the top when he had to slow because another car was coming down.

It was a Mercedes sedan. Black S550.

And behind the wheel, in huge dark sunglasses and a black veil like she was in mourning, was his soon-to-be ex-wife.

Chantal did not look over at him even though she knew damn well who she was passing.

Fine. With any luck, she was relocating and they could let the lawyers take it from here. God knew he had enough other stuff to worry about.

Leaving the Porsche out front, he went in

through the main entrance and paused when he saw the luggage in the foyer.

It wasn't Chantal's. She had matching Louis Vuitton. This was Gucci, and marked with the initials RIP.

Richard Ignatius Pford.

One asshole leaving, he thought. *Another coming in.*

What the hell was Gin thinking?

Oh, wait. He knew that answer. For a woman with little formal education and no professional skills, his sister had one unassailable talent: taking care of herself.

Spooked about money, she had gone along with their father and latched onto the wealthiest sap in town so that no matter what happened to the family, her style of living wouldn't be affected. He just hoped that the cost to her didn't prove to be too high. Richard Pford was a nasty little SOB.

Not his circus, not his monkeys, however. As much as it saddened him, he had long ago learned to give Gin her head and just let her go — there was no other strategy to deal with his sister, really.

Jogging up the stairs, he went to his room and showered, shaved, and seersuckered. It took him two tries to get the bow tie right.

Man, he hated the things.

He took the staff stairs back down, cut

through the kitchen, and went to Miss Aurora's door. As he had when he'd come to see her earlier, he checked that everything was tucked in, buttoned properly, and as it should be before he knocked.

Except then he stilled. For some reason, he had an abject fear that she wouldn't answer the door this time. That he would rap his knuckles, and wait . . . and do it again, and wait some more . . .

And then he would have to break down the panels as he had with Rosalinda's office — and he would find another dead —

The door opened, and Miss Aurora frowned at him. "You're late."

Lane jumped out of his skin, but recovered fast. "I'm sorry, ma'am. I'm sorry."

Miss Aurora gave him a grunt and patted her bright blue church hat. Her outfit was as brilliant as a spring sky, and she had matching gloves, matching shoes, and a perfectly coordinated pocketbook that was the size of a tennis racquet. Her lipstick was cherry red, her earrings were the pearl ones he'd given her three years ago, and she was wearing the pearl ring he'd gotten her the year before that.

He offered her his arm as she shut her door, and she took it.

Together, they walked out through the

front of the house, passing Mr. Harris, who knew better than to say anything about which door they were using.

Lane escorted Miss Aurora to the Porsche's passenger seat and settled her in the car. Then he went around, got behind the wheel, and restarted the engine.

"We're going to be late," she said crisply.

"I'll get us there on time. Just watch me."

"I don't abide by no speeding."

He found himself looking over at her with a wink. "Then close your eyes, Miss Aurora."

She batted at his arm and glared at him. "You are not too old to spank."

"I know you want a seat in the front pew."

"Tulane Baldwine, don't you dare break the law."

"Yes, ma'am."

With a sly grin, he hit the gas, shooting the 911 down the hill — and as he passed a quick glance in her direction? He found that Miss Aurora was smiling to herself.

For a moment, all was right in his world.

FORTY

The Charlemont Baptist Church was located in the West End, and the bright white of its clapboards stood out among the blocks and blocks of lower-income housing units that surrounded the place. Talk about pristine, though. From its carefully tended-to grounds to its freshly surfaced parking lot, from the flowering pots by the double front doors to the basketball courts out back, the place was as polished and cared for as something from a 1950s postcard.

And at twenty minutes of nine on a Sunday morning, it was teeming with people.

The instant Lane pulled in, the greetings came so fast and so many that he had to slow the car to a crawl. Putting both their windows down, he took hold of hands, called out names, returned challenges for pickup games. Parking in the back, he went around and helped Miss Aurora out; then he led her over to the sidewalk that ran down the side of the church's flank.

Children were everywhere, dressed in flouncing gowns and little suits, the colors as bright as crayon boxes, their behavior better than that of a lot of the grown-ups who came to the parties at Easterly. Everyone, but *everyone,* paused and spoke to him and Miss Aurora, checking in, catching up — and in the process, he realized how much he had missed this community.

Funny, he wasn't a churchgoer, but whenever he was home, he never failed to come here with Miss Aurora.

Inside, there were easily a thousand people, the rows of pews filled with the faithful, everyone talking, hugging, laughing. It was too early for the fans to get broken out, but they would come, usually in June. Down in front, there was a band with electric guitars, drums and basses, and next to them were the risers that would hold the gospel choir. And behind all that? The incredible organ pipes — the kind that could blow the doors and the windows and the very roof wide open — rose as if connecting the congregation directly to Heaven.

Max should be here, Lane thought. That brother of his had sung in the choir for years before he'd gone off to college.

But that was a tradition that was lost, seemingly forever now.

Two rows from the front there was space for them, a family of seven squeezing in to make room.

"Much obliged," Lane said, as he shook the father's hand. "Hey, aren't you Thomas Blake's brother?"

"Am, yes," the man said. "I'm Stan, the older. And you're Miss Aurora's boy."

"Yessir."

"Where you been? We haven't seen you here for a while."

As Miss Aurora cocked a brow to him, Lane cleared his throat. "I've been up north."

"My condolences," Stan said. "But at least you're back now."

"There's my nephews." Miss Aurora pointed across the aisle. "D'Shawne is playing for the Indiana Colts now. Wide receiver. And Qwentin beside him is center for the Miami Heat."

Lane lifted his hand as the two men caught Miss Aurora's eye. "I remember when they were playing in college. Qwentin was one of the best centers the Eagles have ever had, and I was there when D'Shawne helped us win the Sugar Bowl."

"They're good boys."

"All your family is."

The organ cranked up, and the band started to play, and from the narthex, the bloodred robed choir strode in, fifty men and women walking together, singing the processional. Behind them, the Reverend Nyce followed with his Bible to his chest, the tall, distinguished man meeting the eyes of his flock, greeting them with honest warmth. When he saw Lane, he reached out and shook hands.

"Glad to have you back, son."

When it was time for everyone to settle back in their seats, Lane had the strangest feeling come over him. Disturbed, he reached over and took Miss Aurora's palm.

All he could think of was that tree limb falling the night before. The sight of Lizzie slumped in her car. The electric fear he'd felt as he'd dragged himself over those branches in the storm, screaming her name.

As the band struck up his favorite gospel song, he looked at the cross above the altar and just shook his head.

Of course it would be this one, he thought.

It was as if the church itself was welcoming him home, too.

Getting up to his feet with Miss Aurora, he started moving with the crowd, back and forth, back and forth.

He found himself singing along: *"I want you to know that God is keeping me . . ."*

An hour and a half later, the service ended and the Bubba hour started, the congregation going to the lower level for punch, cookies, and conversation.

"Let's go down," Lane said.

Miss Aurora shook her head. "I gotta go back. Work."

He frowned. "But we always —"

He stopped himself. There was nothing that needed tending to at Easterly. So the only explanation was one that made him want to call 911.

"Don't look at me like that, boy," she muttered. "This is not a medical emergency — and even if it was, I'm not dying in my church. God wouldn't do that to this congregation."

"Come on, take my arm again."

They were very nonchalant as they went against the crowd — and man, he really would have preferred to throw her into a fireman's hold and defensive lineman his way out of there. And then halfway to the door, he had to stop to talk to Qwentin and D'Shawne — along with seventeen other members of Miss Aurora's family. Ordinar-

572

ily, he would have loved the conversation . . . not today. He didn't want to be rude, but he was very aware of how much Miss Aurora was leaning on his arm.

When they finally got out of the church, he said, "You wait here. I'll bring the car around. And no, I'm not arguing about it, so just stop."

He almost hoped she put up a fight, and when she didn't, he fell into a jog, heading for the very far reaches of the parking lot.

Coming back with the Porsche, he nearly expected to find her passed out cold.

Nope. She was talking with a very regal, slender woman, who had a face like Nefertiti, a modest suit that was black, and a set of rim-less glasses over her sharp eyes.

Oh . . . wow, he thought. *Talk about a blast from the past.*

Lane got out. "Tanesha?"

"Lane, how are you." Tanesha Nyce was the reverend's oldest daughter. "It's good to see you."

They embraced and he nodded. "Good to see you, too. You a doctor yet?"

"In residency here at U of C."

"What are you going into?"

"Oncology."

"She's doing the work of the Lord," Miss Aurora said.

"How's Max?" Tanesha asked.

Lane cleared his throat. "Damned if I know. I haven't spoken to him since he went out west. You know him, always a wild card."

"Yes, he was."

Awkward. Moment.

"Well, I'm going to get Miss Aurora back home," he said. "Nice to see you."

"You, too."

The two women spoke in hushed voices for a moment, and then Miss Aurora allowed him to escort her down the steps and to the car.

"What was that all about?" he asked as he drove them off.

"Choir practice next week."

"You're not in the choir." He glanced over when she didn't say anything. "Miss Aurora? Do you need to tell me something?"

"Yes."

Oh, God. "What."

She took his hand and didn't look at him. "I want you to remember what I said to you before."

"What's that?"

"I got God." She squeezed hard. "And I got you. I am rich beyond means."

She held his hand all the way back to Easterly, and he knew . . . he *knew* . . . she was trying to get him ready for what was coming. Realized, too, that that was why he had insisted on Edward seeing her yesterday when his brother had been at the house.

If only there were a way to get ahold of Max.

"I don't want you to go," Lane said roughly. "It's too damn much."

Miss Aurora stayed silent until they got to the base of Easterly's hill. "Speaking of leaving," she said, "I heard that Chantal moved out."

"Yes, I'm ending all that."

"Good. Maybe you and Lizzie will finally get on track. She's the one for you."

"You know, Miss Aurora, I agree. Now I just have to convince her."

"I'll help."

"I'll take it." He glanced over. "She said to tell you hello, by the way."

Miss Aurora smiled. "Was that when you left her this morning?"

As Lane sputtered and turned red as that Mercedes he'd bought her, Miss Aurora laughed at him in a kind way.

"You're a bad boy, Lane."

"I know, ma'am. That's why you have to stay here and keep me straight. I keep tellin' you that."

Instead of stopping in front, he went around to the back, because it was closer to her quarters. Pulling up to the rear door, he hit the brakes, cut the engine . . . and didn't get out.

Looking over at her, he whispered, "I'm serious. I need you to help me here, on earth — in this house, in my life."

God, it was impossible to ignore the fact that three days ago she had been barking at him that she wasn't going anywhere, but now, something had changed. Something was different.

Before she could say anything, the garage door went up and the chauffeur came out with the Phantom, that five-hundred-thousand-dollar car proceeding by them as it headed around to the front of the house.

"He is evil," Lane said. "That father of mine . . ."

Miss Aurora lifted her palms. "Amen."

"Where the hell is he going this morning?"

"Not to church."

"Maybe he's going after Chantal."

The instant he spoke the words, he cursed.

"What are you talking about?"

Lane shook his head and got out. "Come on, let's get you inside."

Not the way it went. When he went over and opened her door, she just sat there with her purse in her lap, and her gloved hands folded one over the other. "Tell me."

"Miss Aurora —"

"What did he do to you?"

"This is not about me."

"If it's about bringing back that horrible wife of yours, you bet your fanny it's about you."

Lane fought the urge to bang his head on the Porsche's hood. "It really doesn't matter —"

"I know she got rid of your baby."

As those dark eyes stared up at him, he cursed again. "Miss Aurora. Don't do this. Leave it. There are so many other things worth worrying about."

All she did was cock that eyebrow.

Lane sank down on his haunches. God, he loved her face, every crease and crinkle, each curve and all the straightaways. And he loved how she was as lady-like as they came, but strong as a man.

She and Lizzie were so alike.

"There are some things that aren't worth knowing, ma'am."

"And others you shouldn't keep to yourself."

For some reason, he found himself dropping his eyes, as if he had done something he should be ashamed of. "She's pregnant, Miss Aurora. It's not mine."

"Whose is it," she demanded.

The rest of the story was communicated silently — and the funny thing was, she didn't seem totally shocked.

"Are you sure?" she asked in a low tone.

"That's what she said. And when I confronted him? It was in his face."

Miss Aurora stared straight ahead, her brow furrowed so low, he could no longer see her eyes. "God will punish him."

"I wouldn't hold your breath for that." He rose up and offered her his hand. "It's getting hot out here. Come on."

Miss Aurora looked back into his eyes. "I love you."

It was her way of apologizing for what she knew they had all been through with their father. Not just this Chantal ugliness, but those decades of what had gone before, back when they were children.

"You know," he said, "I've never thanked you. For all those years of being there, I never . . . you held us together, me especially. You were always there for me. You *are* always there for me."

"God gave me that sacred job when he crossed my life with y'all's."

"I love you, Momma," he choked out. "Forever."

FORTY-ONE

The sound of the chainsaw in Lizzie's hands was so loud, she didn't hear the car approach. And it wasn't until she let up on the gas and the thing's engine fell to a mutter that a very sexy male voice announced she was no longer alone:

"You are the hottest woman I have ever seen."

Twisting around and looking down, she found Lane leaning back against his Porsche, arms crossed, feet planted, expression intense.

From her vantage point on the mangled roof of her Yaris, she lifted the chainsaw over her head and pumped it a couple of times. "Hear me roar."

"Hear me beg."

She had to laugh as she jumped off to the ground. "I've made some good progress, don't you think —"

Lane cut her off by putting his mouth on

hers, the kiss getting so hot, so fast, that he ended up bending her nearly backward. When he finally let up a little, they were both panting.

"So . . . hi," he said.

"Did you, by any chance, miss me?"

"Every second." He straightened them up. "God, I love y— I love the way you handle that chainsaw."

It was impossible not to catch his slip — and she had to stumble in her own mind as an instinct to float out an ILY struck her as well.

Lane covered up the awkwardness with aplomb, however. "So I really did bring dinner. Takeout from the club. I got you that salad you hopefully still like, and a crap load of tenderloin — you know, just in case we need it to recover."

"From what," she drawled as she put her chainsaw down.

"Oh, you know what." Except then he frowned. "Unless you're . . . you know, sore from last night."

Lizzie shook her head. "No."

"Pity."

"Excuse me?"

Coming in close, his mouth lingered on hers and he licked at her lips. "I was thinking I could kiss it and make it better."

"You can do that anyway."

As he pivoted her around and eased her against his car, she felt her heart start to soar — and figured, what the hell, she might as well let herself go. A tree had killed her car, her front yard was a mess, and there was a small forest of limbs down all over her property . . . but Lane was here, and he'd remembered she liked that Cobb salad, and damn it, he was the best kisser on the planet.

Tomorrow, she would put her game head back on. Tomorrow, she would remember to watch herself —

Lane eased back. "Tell me, how do you feel about sex in the open air?"

She nodded over at the three cows who were standing by her porch. "I think our audience is going to double when my farmer buddy discovers those nice ladies have gone exploring again."

"Then we're heading into the house right now before I go insane."

"Far be it from me to stand between you and mental stability."

He'd even brought an overnight bag, she thought as they carried everything in.

"So I have news," he said as he closed her front door.

"What's that?"

"Chantal moved out this morning."

Lizzie stopped and looked at him. He was dressed in his casual, warm weather uniform of Bermuda shorts and an IZOD, the Gucci loafers on his feet, and his Ray Bans, and that Cartier watch making it seem like he'd walked out of an Instagram picture entitled Handsome & Rich. Even his hair was slicked back, although that was because he was fresh from a shower and it was still wet.

Her heart fluttered with a momentary fear because, looking as good as he was, he seemed like the poster boy of someone you shouldn't trust, especially about women who were like Chantal —

As if he could read her mind, Lane took his sunglasses off and showed her his eyes. In contrast to everything external about him, they were clear, steady . . . calm.

Honest.

"Really?" she whispered.

"Really." He came over and turned her toward him. "Lizzie, it's done. That whole thing with her is done. And before you say it, it's not just for you. I should have put a bullet into that marriage long ago. My mistake."

Looking up into his face, she cursed under her breath. "I'm sorry, Lane. I'm sorry that I doubted you, it's just —"

"Shh." He silenced her with his lips. "I don't live in the past. It's a waste of time. All I care about is where we are now."

Wrapping her arms around his neck, she bowed her body into his. "Soooooo . . . I wasn't able to make the friends thing stick, was I."

"And that is *perfectly* okay with me."

"That was quite possibly the best dinner I have ever had."

Lane glanced across the sofa and watched as Lizzie sank back into the cushions and put her hand on her belly. As her eyes began to drift shut, he pictured her up on that tree limb like an avenging angel, wielding that chainsaw, cutting the crap out of those branches that had killed her car.

Even though they'd spent the first hour of the visit getting all over each other, his erection thickened up again.

"It's a miracle," he murmured.

"That I liked the tenderloin so much? Not really."

"Being here with you, I mean."

Those blue eyes reopened slowly. "I feel the same way." As he laughed deep in his throat, she stopped him by putting her palm up. "No, you may not spike the dishes in victory."

Putting his napkin aside, he prowled up her body, mounting her. "I have other celebratory options, you know."

Rolling his hips, he felt a stab of lust as she bit down on her lower lip like she was ready for some more of him.

"You want me to demonstrate one for you?" he said as he nuzzled at her throat.

Her hands stroked up his back. "Yes, I do."

"Mmm —"

The sound of ringing on the coffee table made him jump forward and grab his phone. "Not Miss Aurora. Please not Miss Aurora —"

"Oh, my God — Lane, is she —"

As soon as he saw the call was from a 917 area code, he sagged in relief. "Thank God." He looked up. "I have to take this. It's a friend of mine from New York."

"Please."

He accepted the call and said, "Jeff."

"You miss me," his old roommate said. "I *know* that's why you left me that voice mail."

"Not even close."

"Well, I'm not FedExing you those cinnamon rolls you eat morning, noon and night —"

"I need to know how much vacation time you have."

Total. Silence. Then, "The World Series of

Poker isn't being played right now. Why are you asking me this?"

"I need your help." Absently, he eased back against the cushions and positioned Lizzie's legs over his lap. She'd changed into shorts after their shower, and he loved running his palm up and down those smooth, muscled calves of hers. "I've got a real problem here."

Jeff dropped the smartass. "What kind of problem."

"I need someone to tell me if my father is embezzling from the family company. To the tune of over fifty million dollars."

Jeff whistled softly. "That's a lot of cabbage, my friend."

"My brother managed to get me access to . . . Christ, it's about five hundred pages worth of spreadsheets and financial disclosures, but I have no idea what I'm looking at. I want you to come down and tell me what happened, and it has to be now — before he figures out I'm onto him and gets rid of anything that incriminates him."

"Listen, Lane, you know I love you like the long-lost Waspy brother I never had, but you're talking about forensic accounting. There are people who specialize in that — for a reason. Let me find you someone you can trust —"

"That's my point, Jeff. I can't trust anyone with this — it's my family we're talking about."

"We can blind all the documents. I can help with that — so that whoever it is won't know —"

"I want you."

"Oh, for fuck's sake, Lane."

Thanks to having known the guy for years, Lane was very aware that his job was now to shut up and let Jeff grumble his way down the rabbit hole. Nothing was going to sway the guy; there was no persuasion to be brought to bear, and if you did try to mouth off, sometimes it worked against you.

Instead, Lane knew if he kept quiet, all their years together were going to take care of the problem.

Bingo:

"I'm going to insist someone check my work," Jeff muttered. "And fuck you — that's non-negotiable. I'm not going to be responsible for screwing this up just because you have some romantic notion that I'm brilliant with numbers."

"But you are."

"Damn you, Baldwine."

"I can't send a plane for you. It would create too much attention."

"That's okay. One of my family's is on the

East Coast. I'll get on it tomorrow morning — and no, I can't come sooner. I'm going to have to shift some things around at work."

"I owe you."

"Damn straight you do. And you can start repaying me tomorrow night. I want free booze and loose women if I'm going to do this."

"I'll take care of everything. I'll even pick you up at the airport myself, just text me your arrival time."

Jeff was muttering obscenities as the guy hung up without saying good-bye.

As Lane put his own phone down, he blew out a breath. "Thank God."

"Who was that?"

"Guess you'd call him my best friend. He was the one I was staying with up north. Jeff Stern. Brilliant finance guy. If anyone can make sense of the money trail, he will. And after that . . ." Lane rubbed his eyes. "God, I guess I should go to the police? Maybe the SEC? But I'd really rather handle it quietly."

"What if your father's broken the law?"

A sudden image of William Baldwine in an orange jumpsuit made him relieved, in a sick way, that his mother was so out of it. "I'm not going to get in the way of the

587

authorities. What I'm worried about is that he's used Mother's power of attorney to drain her accounts, but I don't have access to those records — they're all at Prospect Trust."

"If the police or the FBI get involved, they can find that out."

Lane nodded, remembering the sight of that body bag leaving Easterly. "If Rosalinda committed suicide over this, my father has someone's blood on his hands. He needs to be brought to justice."

"You know, usually I try to look on the bright side of things, but . . ." She took his hand. "Well, no matter what happens, I'm with you, okay?"

Looking over at her, he said gravely, "That's all I need. No matter where this all goes . . . if I have you —"

The phone rang again, and he laughed as he picked it back up. "He's having second thoughts. No, Jeff, you can't back out of it —"

"Are you near a TV?"

Lane sat up. "Samuel T.?"

"Are you?"

"No. What's going on?"

"I need you to come to my house right away. The police are looking for you, and when you weren't at Easterly, Mitch called me."

"What — what are you talking about?" Then he thought, *Oh, shit.* "Look, I realize Edward and I technically entered the business center under false pretenses, but the goddamn facility's on the property, for one thing. And as for the documents we —"

"I don't know what you're talking about, and right now I don't care. Chantal went to the emergency room first thing this morning all beaten to hell and gone. She told the authorities you did it to her when you found out that she was pregnant after you filed the divorce papers. They're placing you under arrest for first-degree domestic assault, and they might have enough to lift it to attempted murder."

"What!" Lane jumped to his feet. "Is she insane!"

"No, what she is is in surgery. They're resetting her jaw at the moment."

"I never touched Chantal! And I can prove it! I wasn't even home last night —"

"Just get to my house. I'll broker an intake in the middle of the night so there are no pictures of you going in — and we'll bail you —"

"This is *bullshit*," Lane spat. "I'm not playing this game with her —"

"This isn't a game. And unless you make an appearance down at that jailhouse, you're going to be considered a fugitive."

Lane looked over at Lizzie. She was sitting up, in full alarm, braced for bad news.

All at once, he remembered passing Chantal in that Mercedes as she had left Easterly. Her face had been covered with the glasses, that black veil.

For all they knew, she'd pulled a *Gone Girl* and done the stuff to herself. He hadn't put the woman in true pathological territory before, but maybe he'd underestimated the crazy.

"Okay," he said. "I'm coming in. I'll be at your farm in twenty minutes."

Hanging up the phone, he heard himself say, "I have to go."

"Lane, what's happening?"

The dishes from their nice dinner were still on the table, the cushions of the sofa still dented from his having laid back and stroked her legs.

And yet those moments, which had happened mere minutes ago, were gone, gone, gone.

"I'm going to take care of it," he told her. "I'm going to make it all go away. She's lying. Once again, she's lying."

"What can I do to help?"

"Stay here — and don't turn on your radio. I'll call you as soon as I can and explain everything." Marching back over to Lizzie, he took her face in his hands. "I love you. I need you to believe that. I need you to remember that. And I'm going to take care of this, I swear on my momma's life."

"You're scaring me."

"It's all going to be okay. I promise."

With that, he left her house.

At a dead run.

FORTY-TWO

As Lane's Porsche roared off into the gathering darkness, Lizzie sat where he'd left her for a time. All she could think of was that none of them should be surprised. Chantal Baldwine was as tough as they came, and there was no way that woman was going to lose her social status and access to that Bradford lifestyle without putting up a tremendous fight.

So whatever this was might well just be an opening salvo.

Getting to her feet, she picked up their plates and thought, wow, not how she'd expected the evening to end.

But maybe he would still be back. He'd left his bag.

Damn you, Chantal.

Back in the kitchen, she put everything in the sink, pumped some dishwashing soap on top of the mess, and fired up the hot water.

She was about to get her hands wet when her cell phone rang over on the counter.

"Thank God," she said, leaping across the tile. "Lane? Lane, can you tell me what —"

"Lizzie? Are you home?"

"Greta?" There was a whirring noise over the connection, like the woman was behind the wheel of her car. "Greta? I'm having trouble hearing you?"

"— home?"

"Yes, yes, I'm home. Are you all right?"

"— on my way" — *buzz, chirp, whrrrrr* — "there in ten minutes."

"Okay, but I don't want to finish working on that limb now. It's nearly dark, and honestly, I'm not in the mood —"

"— off your phone."

"What?"

The metaphorical seas parted and the German's voice came through loud and clear: "You need to turn off your phone."

"Why? And I will not." Lane might call. "Look, I'm not really in the mood for company and —"

There was a loud chirp and the connection cut out entirely.

"Great."

Putting the phone in her pocket, she went back to the sink, washed the dishes and the silverware, dried the lot of it, and put everything away.

She was out in the living room, sitting on the sofa again, nervously thumbing through the latest issue of *Garden & Gun,* when headlights flashed across the front of the farmhouse and the cobblestones of her drive crackled.

Getting to her feet, she pulled her shirt down and double-checked her hair wasn't tangled. No sense looking like she'd rolled out of bed with Lane.

Especially because most of the sex they'd had had been on the rug in the hall. And on the stairs. And standing up in the shower.

Opening the door, she —

As her partner got out of the Mercedes station wagon, Lizzie could see Greta's face was ashen and her shoulders bowed. And she looked like she was wiping away tears under those tortoiseshell glasses of hers.

"Oh, my God," Lizzie said. "Is it one of the kids?"

The other woman didn't answer, just came up on the porch and walked right into the house. Lizzie followed, closing them in.

"Greta?"

The woman paced around. Then finally stopped. "Were you with him last night?"

"Excuse me?"

"Lane. Just . . . were you with him? For

the whole night?"

"What are you talking about?"

"Chantal is accusing Lane of beating her up badly enough to put her in the hospital."

"WHAT."

And that was when it came out: Chantal. The hospital. The police. The media.

Lane.

When Greta finally fell silent, Lizzie threw out a hand blindly as she backed up and fell into a chair. "I . . ."

"That man is a lot of things," Greta said, "but I've never known him to raise a hand to a woman."

"Of course not. God, no. Absolutely not."

"Was he here last night?"

"Yes. I came home into the storm, and he was here. And he didn't leave until the morning to take Miss Aurora to church." She leaped up. "I've got to help him! I've got to tell the police he was with me —"

"There's something else."

"Can you drive me? I'm so scattered, I don't think I should be —"

"Lizzie."

At the sound of her name, she stopped, a cold fear gripping her chest. "What . . . ?"

Now Greta's eyes started welling up. "I'm sorry."

"What! Will you just get it all out before

my head explodes —"

"Chantal's pregnant. And she told the police . . . it's Lane's."

Lizzie blinked as everything came to a crashing halt: her thoughts, her heart, her lungs . . . even time and the laws of physics.

"She says that's why he beat her. When she told him. She says he was furious."

A wave of vicious nausea nailed her in the gut — except no. She couldn't be reliving what had happened before. She couldn't possibly be in this exact same situation with Chantal and Lane again.

I've already done this, she thought. *I've lived through this nightmare already.*

God, no. Please, no.

"When . . ." Lizzie cleared her throat. "When did she go to the police?"

"First thing this morning. Around nine or ten."

If you were hurt badly, you wouldn't wait to get medical attention, Lizzie thought.

If the woman was pregnant, and she told him when he got back to Easterly . . . he could very well have —

With a horrible lurch, Lizzie skidded her way down the hall — and barely made it to the bathroom before she threw up all that tenderloin.

■ ■ ■ ■

By the time Lane pulled up to Samuel T.'s farm, he was mad enough to chew tin and spit nails.

Punching his foot into the brake, he skidded to a stop in the front of the man's mansion and nearly left the engine running as he got out.

Samuel T. opened the door before he even made it around the car. "I called Mitch. He's going to be here in forty-five minutes with an unmarked. They don't want to wait to take you in, but we're going to go in through the impound entrance. No one with a camera can get back there, so you'll be all right."

Lane brushed past the guy. "This is a total fucking lie! She's batshit crazy and is going to —" He stopped and frowned at his old friend. "What? Why are you looking at me like that."

By way of answer, Samuel T. reached out and took Lane's arm. "How did you get these scratches all over your hands. Your arms. Your neck and face."

Lane glanced down at himself. "Jesus Christ, Sam, these are from last night. I went out to Lizzie's and this limb fell on her car." When his friend just stared at him, he snapped, "She'll testify in court if she has to. I pulled her out of her goddamn Yaris. I thought she was dead."

"Are you seeing her again?"

"Yes, I am."

"And you think she's going to want to help you when she finds out Chantal's having your baby? Again? Didn't you two try this drama out a couple of years ago?"

Lane felt ninety percent of his blood leave his head. "It's not mine, Sam. I told you when I signed those papers — I haven't been with Chantal since I left."

"Not what she's telling the police. She says that she's been back and forth to Manhattan for the last year, working on your relationship."

"It's not mine." He lowered his voice, even though there was no one around. "It's my father's."

Now it was Samuel T.'s turn to be stunned. "Your . . . father's."

"You heard me."

"Are you sure?"

"Yeah, I've spoken to both of them about it."

Samuel T. coughed into his fist. "You know, your family is something else."

"That's what people tell me." Lane

crossed his arms over his chest. "I'll take a lie detector test. I'll swear on a Bible — hell, they should check under her fingernails. They won't find any part of me on her — or in her. I didn't touch her, Sam."

"She says she has a witness."

"Ha! In her dreams. Hell, she must have done it to herself —"

"It's a maid? Someone named Tiffany?"

Lane recoiled. "Maid? Tiff— wait, you mean, with a 'p-h-a-n-i-i?' "

He pictured the one with the towels, who'd introduced herself to him with that look in her eye.

Samuel T. shrugged. "I don't know how she spells it. I'm getting this on the QT from Mitch. But the woman says she overheard you and Chantal fighting, and you were threatening to, and I quote, 'beat the shit out of her.' "

"I never said that!"

"You were standing in the second-floor hallway, and the maid walked in on the conversation."

"She's lying —" Lane stopped and shook his head, the memory coming back. "Wait, no, no. Not about — no, I said that because Chantal disrespected Miss Aurora. I was pissed off at her. I didn't mean it literally."

Samuel T. looked down at the cuts on his

arms. "I'm going to be honest here. You seem to have a lot of convenient answers —"

"It's the truth! I'm not making this shit up!"

"Listen, I don't want to fight with you —"

"Samuel T.," he said in a level voice. "Have you ever known me to get violent. Especially toward a woman?"

Samuel T. stared at him for a long time. Then the guy put his palms out. "No, no, I haven't known you to be like that — and I want to believe you, I really do. But even if everything you're telling me is the God's honest, we have two problems here, a legal one and a PR one. The legality stuff will take care of itself assuming Lizzie will vouch for you, and there's no forensic proof on Chantal's body or yours. The PR problem? That is going to be so much harder to handle. This is big news, Lane — especially if you're right and your *father* is having a *kid* with your *wife.* Hell, this is nationwide news — and you've got to know that the press never lets the truth get in the way of a good story. And even though it shouldn't, this kind of scandal will have an effect on things like stock prices and the perceived value of the products your family's company sells. I'm not saying this is right, but it is reality. You *are* the Bradford Bourbon Company. Your family *is* the Bradford Bourbon Company. I might have been able to erase your sister's trip through the system, but this one . . . I can't un-ring this bell. It's already on the local news."

Lane paced around the man's front hall. Then he looked over at his buddy. "Speaking of my family, do you have any bourbon in this house?"

"Always. And I only serve the best so it's Bradford."

Lane thought of Mack and the fact that the stills had been shut down. And then of his father . . . and everything the man had done.

"We'll see for how much longer," Lane muttered.

FORTY-THREE

Six hours later, as Lane sat in an interrogation room down at the county jailhouse, he tried Lizzie's cell phone for the sixth time — and decided that she must have found out about the situation. Maybe someone had called her? Or maybe she'd turned on her radio, after all? She didn't have a television.

Hell, maybe somebody had put up a neon sign in downtown Charlemont and she could see it all the way in Indiana.

"We're almost done here," Samuel T. said as he came back in the stark grey room. "The good news is that you've been downgraded to a person of interest, but things are going to be in limbo until the investigation is concluded. At least you can go home now, though, and there's no mug shot."

Lane ended the call and rubbed his aching eyes. They'd given him his phone and his wallet back about fifteen minutes ago, and the first thing he'd done was try to get ahold of Lizzie again.

Given the way he'd left her house, there was no scenario where she wouldn't have picked up his call if she'd wanted to speak with him.

Clearly, she had no interest in hearing his side of things.

"How much longer?" he said as he rubbed his aching head. "Can I leave now?"

"Almost. They're just checking with the DA — who happens to be a hunting buddy of mine." Samuel T. sat down. "I know it's politically incorrect, but thank God the old boys' network is alive and well in this town — or you'd be getting strip searched right now."

"You're a miracle worker," Lane said numbly.

"It helps that Chantal's story had some holes in it. She obviously was operating on her own when she came up with this bright idea. Who the hell takes a bath right after they're attacked — and is careful to clean under her broken manicure? Makes no damn sense. And then there was the happy little fact that she called both the paper and two TV stations — from her ER bed."

"Told you." He checked his phone in case

Lizzie had called back and he'd somehow not heard the ring. "She's ruining my life, that one."

"Not if I have anything to do with it."

Lane tried Lizzie a seventh time. Put the phone back down. "What did she look like? You know, Chantal. When she got to the hospital."

"You sure you want to see the photographs?"

"Yeah, I need to know how bad it is."

Samuel T. got up again. "I'll see what I can do."

As the interrogation room door opened and shut once more, Lane fiddled with his phone. He thought about sending a text, but doubted that was going to make any difference at all.

Unbelievable. He literally could not believe this was happening to him again — same two women, same vocabulary . . . as for the outcome?

He was shit terrified he knew the answer to that one already: Lizzie had locked him out once. Clearly, this was the way she intended to handle him again.

Samuel T. came back ten minutes later with a manila envelope. "Here you go."

Lane took the thing and opened the flap. Sliding out four glossies, he frowned at the top one.

Two black eyes. Bruises on the sides of her face. Ligature marks around her throat.

"This is bad," he said roughly. "Jesus . . ."

There was no love lost for him when it came to Chantal, but he didn't like to see anyone in this condition — especially a woman. And no, he thought, there was no chance she had done this to herself. Someone must have hit her — repeatedly and hard.

Had she paid somebody? he wondered.

The second and third photos were close-ups. The fourth was —

Lane went back to the third one. Leaning in close, he studied a detail of her cheek — a cut in her skin under her eye.

Suddenly, he dropped the images on the table and sat back, closing his lids.

"What?" Samuel T. asked.

It was a long while before he could speak. But eventually, he turned the photo around and pointed to the bleeding cut on Chantal's skin. "My father did this to her."

"How do you know?"

With god-awful clarity, Lane remembered once again that terrible New Year's night, back when he'd been a kid and his older brother had taken a beating for the rest of them. "When he used to hit Edward, his signet ring would leave the exact same mark. My father hit her back handed, across the face . . . the gold makes the cut."

Samuel T. cursed under his breath. "Are you serious?"

"Dead. Serious."

"Hold on, let me bring the investigator back in. They're going to want to know about this."

As Lizzie drove in to work at the crack of dawn, she couldn't help thinking about the trip in from a couple of days ago, when that ambulance had passed her and proceeded up Easterly's hill.

She had the same feeling of foreboding now. And the same dread at seeing Lane.

No radio today on her commute. She didn't want to run the risk of the local NPR station cutting in with the big news that one of Charlemont's most prominent men had put his pregnant wife in the hospital. Further details about the situation weren't going to change the story, and she was feeling badly enough already.

Proceeding past the BFE main entrance, she went down to the staff road and traveled by the fields and the greenhouses, up to the parking lot. Thanks to her coming in so early, there was no one else around, not even Gary McAdams.

She'd planned it that way.

On autopilot, she turned off her truck and reached across for her purse. "Crap."

She'd left the thing at home. Which meant no sunglasses, no sunscreen, no hat.

Whatever. She wasn't driving back now.

And it was probably a good thing that she didn't have her phone. Lane hadn't stopped calling her — as early as four a.m. this morning he'd still been ringing her.

The walk up to the back door of Easterly took her a good long time, and she told herself it was a simple case of exhaustion. After Greta had finally left her house around one a.m., she had stayed up to watch the sunrise over the wreck in her front yard.

Nice little metaphor for her life.

Entering through the kitchen, she found Miss Aurora at the big stove. "Good morning," she said in what she hoped was a halfway normal voice. "Have you seen Mr. Harris?"

Miss Aurora flipped the eggs in her skillet with a spatula. "He's in his suite of rooms. I had no family orders this morning, so I'm making this for you and me and anyone else who's around. I'll have it in the break room in ten."

"I'm so sorry. I have to —"

"See you in there."

Lizzie took a deep breath. "I'll try to make it."

"You do that." Miss Aurora looked over her shoulder, her black eyes gleaming. "Otherwise, I'm going to have to come find you and talk to you about how you shouldn't believe everything you hear or read."

Ducking her eyes, Lizzie pushed her way out of the kitchen and went across to Mr. Harris's door. Before she knocked on it, she glanced back at Rosalinda's. A CMP seal had been put on the panels, and caution tape had been run between the jambs.

Yet another crime scene in the house, she thought. *Wonder what Chantal's bedroom looked like.*

The butler opened his door and jumped back. "Miss King?"

Lizzie shook herself. "Oh, sorry. Listen, I need to speak with you."

Mr. Harris frowned, but something about her affect must have reached through his haughty attitude. "Do come in."

Predictably, the decor was proper English, all kinds of leather-bound books, antique chairs, and garnet-colored Orientals filling out the space. Beyond the sitting area, there was a galley kitchen, and similar to Miss Aurora's quarters, on the far side there was a closed door she guessed led to his bedroom and bath.

It smelled good, lemony and clean, not stuffy.

"I'm giving my notice," she said abruptly. "Two weeks. I would have told Rosalinda, but . . ."

Mr. Harris stared at her for a moment; then he went over and sat behind a carved desk that had paperwork but no computer on it. "This is a surprise."

"It's in my contract. I only have to give two weeks."

"May I ask why?"

"Just a change of focus. I've been thinking about it for a while."

"Have you." He steepled his hands. "So this has nothing to do with the reports that came out last night?"

"I'm very sorry that the family is having to deal with such ugliness."

Mr. Harris cocked a brow. "Is there nothing I can do to convince you to stay?"

"My mind is made up, but thank you."

She left it at that, returning to the hall and shutting the door behind her. Standing by herself, she blinked away tears, tilting her head back while praying that her nose didn't start to run.

Of all the ways she had imagined leaving

Easterly, it had never been like this. But there was no going back. She had come to her decision to quit with Greta while they had polished off a half gallon of chocolate chip ice cream, in between her first crying jag and her second.

At the end of the day, she didn't actually believe that Lane could have hurt Chantal like that — it just didn't seem possible. But that wasn't the point.

It didn't even matter whether or not the woman was pregnant — or whose it was if she were having a baby.

The simple truth was that after nearly a decade with the family, Lizzie had come to realize that they were different from her in a fundamental way — and not because the Bradfords had more money than she would see in several lifetimes. The thing was, where she came from, people got married and had children; they contributed to their 401ks; and they went on one family vacation a year, to a place like Disney or Sandals. They paid their taxes on time, and celebrated marriages and births with potlucks, and they didn't cheat on their wives or their husbands.

They lived dignified, modest lives unmarked by the kind of crazy drama that went on with the Bradfords.

And the thing was, as much as she was attracted to Lane — hell, maybe she was drawn to the very insanity that also repelled her — she simply didn't have the energy or the wherewithal to keep going with him in any capacity. She fell too hard, too fast for him — and just as before, what he brought to her life was nothing but a pit in her stomach, more sleepless nights . . . and a feeling of profound depression.

Some risk pools you couldn't volunteer for. Whether it was certain cancers, or bad accidents, or other kinds of tragedies, you couldn't always reduce your chances of getting hurt — because you were alive and that was the reality for all the living things on the planet.

Other problems, issues and dangers, however, you were free to step out of, step away from — and when you were a responsible adult, who wanted to lead a halfway healthy existence, it was incumbant upon you to take care of yourself, protect yourself . . . nurture yourself.

Clearly, she couldn't be trusted to keep her head on straight around Lane Baldwine, so she was going to solve the problem of her lack of self-control . . . with a lack of proximity.

Time to leave.

Like an addict who was going cold turkey, she was just taking off — and no, she didn't want to talk to him about any of it. That just seemed like a junkie wanting to enter into a deep-and-meaningful with a syringe of heroin. Undoubtedly, Lane was going to have his side of things, but no matter what that was, it couldn't change the fact that her heart was broken all over again and her decision to quit her job was not subject to negotiation.

And now . . . she was going to do her best to get on with her day.

Heading down to the greenhouses, she went into the first one she got to and was more than ready to work on the seedlings — which were now not seedlings at all. But before she went over to the supply station to gather her pruning shears, she stopped and took out her phone.

What she did next took no more than a moment.

And was probably a stupid thing to do.

But she transferred seventeen thousand, four hundred, eighty-six dollars, and seventy-nine cents from her savings . . . to her mortgage account.

Paying off her farm.

Yeah, it was likely not the smartest move, considering she would be selling the thing.

Pride, however, made the transaction necessary. Pride, and a sense that she needed to feel that she had achieved the goal she had started with when she'd bought the place.

She had always wanted something that was her own in the world, a home that she established and paid for and maintained without help from anyone else.

The fact that she now didn't owe a red cent on the land was a counterbalance to everything else she was feeling.

Proof positive that she hadn't completely failed to look after herself.

Lane returned to Easterly as soon as he was released.

Well, minus the trip back out to Samuel T.'s to pick up his Porsche.

He entered his family's property via the back way, driving past the fields and the greenhouses for two reasons. One, because there was press at the main gates; and two, because he wanted to see whether Lizzie was on site.

She was. Her maroon farm truck was parked in the lot along with the other vehicles of the staff.

"Damn it," he exhaled.

Continuing up to the garages, he parked his car under the magnolia tree and went directly to the rear entrance of the business center. After he entered the code Edward had had him use, he yanked open the door and stalked his way to the reception area, passing those offices, that conference room, that dining room.

Men and women in suits looked up in alarm, but he ignored them.

He didn't stop until he was inside the glass office of his father's assistant. "I'm going in to see him now."

"Mr. Baldwine, you can't —"

"The hell I can't."

"Mr. Baldwine, he's —"

Lane threw the door open and —

Pulled up short. His father was not behind that desk.

"Mr. Baldwine, we don't know where he is."

Lane glanced over his shoulder. "What?"

"Your father . . . he was supposed to be traveling this morning, but he never showed up at the airport. The pilot waited for an hour."

"You called the house, of course."

"And his cell phone." The woman put her hand over her mouth. "He's never done this before. No one has seen him in the mansion."

"Shit."

Dear Lord, now what?

As Lane bolted out of there, the assistant's voice called after him, "Please tell him to call me?"

Back in the morning sunshine, he fell into a flat-out run for Easterly's kitchen entrance. Busting through, he ran past the stainless-steel counters and punched open the door into the staff hallway. He took the back stairs two at a time, nearly plowing into a maid who was vacuuming her way to the second floor.

Down the hall. Past his room. Past Chantal's.

To his father's.

Lane skidded to a halt in front of the door, and thought that he really wasn't ready to have a Rosalinda, Part II, with his own father — but not because he didn't want to see the dead body of one of his parents.

No, it was more because if the man was going to need a coffin, Lane was going to damn well be the one who put that bastard's head on the tufted pillow.

Lane threw things open. "Father," he barked. "Where are you."

Marching in, he listened for a response and then shut the door behind himself — just in case the man was alive: He was going to hurt the sonofabitch, heaven help him, but he was so going to hurt him.

Chantal might be a slut and a liar, but a woman should never be hit. No matter the circumstance.

"Where the fuck are you," he demanded as he opened up the bathroom.

When he didn't find the man hanging in the glass shower enclosure, he doubled back and went into the wardrobe room.

Also nothing.

No, wait.

His father's suitcase, the monogrammed one he used so often, was open and partially packed. But . . . packed badly. The clothes were messy inside, hastily thrown in by someone who had little to no experience in doing the duty for himself.

Rifling through the contents, Lane found nothing of note.

But he did notice that his father's favorite watch, the Audemars Piguet Royal Oak, was missing from the lineup inside the velvet-lined watch case. And his wallet was gone.

Heading back into the bedroom, he surveyed the furniture, the books, the desk, but had no idea if there was anything out of place. He'd been in here only a handful of times . . . and not for at least a good twenty years.

"What are you up to, Father," he asked

the quiet, still air.

Following an instinct, he went out, reshut the door, and jogged back down the staff stairs to the first floor. It took him less than a minute to get out to the garages and once inside, he counted the cars. The Phantom was still there, but two of the Mercedeses were missing. Chantal had obviously been in one.

His father had to have taken the other.

The question was . . . where.

And when.

FORTY-FOUR

"Y'all can't be doing this again. Come on, now, wake up."

Edward batted at the hand that pulled at his arm. "Lea . . . me 'lone."

"The heck I will. It's cold in here, and you're not up to this."

Edward opened his eyes slowly. Light was coming through the open bay at the end of the stable, catching swirls of hay dust and the profile of one of the barn cats. A mare whinnied across the way, and somebody kicked their stall — and off in the distance, he caught the low-pitched growl of one of the tractors.

Holy shit did his head hurt, but it was nothing compared to his ass. Funny how a part of the body could be both totally numb and in pain.

"Y'all need to get the hell up . . ."

All the chatter made him curse — and try to focus.

Well, what do you know. There were two Shelbys talking at him: His newest employee was standing over him like a disapproving teacher, her hands on her lean hips, her jeans-clad legs and booted feet braced as if she were considering soccer-balling his head.

"I thought you didn't curse," he mumbled.

"I don't."

"Well, I believe you just said a bad word."

Her eyes narrowed. "Are you getting up, or am I sweeping you out of here with the rest of the debris."

"Don't you know that 'hell' is a gateway word? It's like marijuana. Next thing you know, you'll be dropping 'fuck' bombs left and right."

"Fine. Stay there. See if I care."

As she turned and walked off, he called out, "How was your date the other night?"

She pivoted back around. "What are you talking about?"

"With Moe."

At that, he struggled to get himself up off the cold concrete floor of the stable. When he couldn't manage it, she lifted a brow. "You know, I do believe I *will* leave you there."

Above his head, Neb snickered like the stallion was laughing.

"I didn't ask for your help," Edward gritted out.

Without warning, his hand slipped and his body slammed down to the concrete so hard his teeth clapped together.

"You are going to kill yourself," she muttered as she marched back over.

Shelby picked him up with all the care one might offer to a fallen pitchfork — but he had to give her credit. Even though she came up to only his breastbone, she was more than strong enough to get him down the aisle, out of the bay, and across the lawn to his cottage.

Once they were inside, he nodded to his chair. "Over there would be —"

"Y'all hypothermic. That's *not* going to happen."

Next thing he knew, she'd sat him down on his toilet seat and was starting the bath.

"I'll take it from here," he said, leaning to the side and letting the wall catch him. "Thanks."

He was just shutting his eyes when she slapped him in the face. "Wake up."

The sting did bring him around, and he rubbed his cheek. "Did you enjoy that?"

"Yes, I did. And I'll do it again." She shoved his toothbrush into his mouth. "Use that."

It was hard to talk around the damn thing, so he did what he was told, working the left side, the right, the front, the under parts. Then he bent over and spit in the sink.

"It's not that cold," he said.

"How would you know. You're saturated drunk."

Actually, he wasn't — and that was probably part of the problem. For the first time in how long, he hadn't had anything to drink the night before —

"What are you doing?" he said as her hands went to his fleece.

"I'm getting you undressed."

"Really."

While she worked his clothes, he looked at her body. It was hard to see much of it, what with her sweatshirt, and he decided to reach for her to test out that waist.

She stopped. Stepped back. "I'm not interested in that."

"Then why are you taking my clothes off."

"Because your lips are blue."

"Turn that off." He pointed to the faucet. "I'll take it from here."

"You'll drown."

"So what if I do. Besides, you don't want to see what's under here."

"I'll be waiting out by your chair."

"And doesn't that give me something to

look forward to," he said under his breath.

She shut the door behind her with a clap — and he didn't follow through on anything. He just went back to leaning against the wall and looking at the steaming water.

"I don't hear any splashing," she said from outside.

"It's not deep enough for me to swim in yet."

Knock. Knock. Knock. "Hop to it, Mr. Baldwine."

"That's my father. And he's an asshole. I go by Edward."

"Shut up and get in the water."

Even through the fog of his stupor, he felt a flare of something for her. Respect, he supposed it was.

But who cared —

Boom, boom, boom!

"You are going to break that door down," he yelled over the noise. "And I thought you didn't want to see me naked."

"Water. Now," she clipped out. "And I don't, but better that than you being dead."

"Matter of opinion, my dear girl."

And yet he decided to do what she said. For some insane reason.

Bracing his arms on the sink and the back of the old-fashioned toilet, he hefted his body up to his feet. His clothes were a pain in the ass, but he got them off . . . and then he was in the tub. Strangely, the warm water had the opposite effect that it should have. Instead of heating him up, it made him feel freezing cold, and he began to shiver so badly, he created chop on the surface of the bath.

Crossing his arms over his chest, his teeth rattled together, and his heart skipped beats.

"You okay in there?" she asked.

When he didn't answer, Shelby said more loudly, "Edward?"

The door burst open and she jumped into the bathroom like she was prepared to go lifeguard and save him from twenty-four inches of water. And it was horrible . . . as she looked down at him, all he could do was stare into the messy water — and hope that it covered up his spindly legs, his flaccid sex, his white skin with its purple scars.

He was pretty sure she gasped.

Smiling up at her, he said, "Pretty, aren't I. But believe it or not, I'm fully functional. Well, Viagra helps. Be a darling, would you, and bring me some alcohol — I think I'm detoxing and that's why I'm shaking like this."

"Do you . . ." She cleared her throat. "Do you n-n-need a doctor?"

"No, just some Jim Beam. Or Jack Daniel's."

As she simply stared at him, he pointed through the open door behind her. "I'm serious. What I need is alcohol. If you want to save me, get me some. Now."

When Shelby Landis backed out of that bathroom and shut the door, she fully intended to get Edward what he'd asked for.

After all, she had a lot of experience with alcoholics — and even though she didn't approve of any of it, she'd brought her pops his booze a thousand times, and usually in the morning, too.

At least that was her plan. In reality, however, she couldn't seem to move, to think . . . even to breathe.

She had not been prepared for the sight of that man in there, his dark head bowed as if he were ashamed of his too-thin, mangled body, his man's pride as shredded and unhealed as his flesh. He had once been a great force; her father had told her the stories of his dominance in business, on the track, in society. Heck, she had heard about the Bradfords since she was young: Her father had refused to drink anything but their No. 15 — and so had most of the horse people she knew.

Putting her hands to her face, she whispered, "What did you do to me, Pops?"

Why had he sent her here?

Why . . .

"Shelby?" came the demand from inside the bathroom.

God, it was just like her father: The way Edward said her name with that hint of desperation . . . it was exactly the way her Pops had when he'd needed the drink bad.

Closing her eyes, she cursed out her breath. Then felt guilty. "Forgive me, Lord. I know not what I say."

Looking across the space, she found a lineup of full liquor bottles in front of one of the shelves of silver trophies, and the idea of delivering that poision to him made her want to be sick. But he would just come out here himself — and probably fall and hit his head on the way. And then where would they be? Plus, she knew the way things worked. That terrible trembling wasn't going to stop until the beast inside was fed what it needed, and his body looked so frail to begin with.

"Coming," she called out. "What kind do y'all want?"

"It doesn't matter."

Blindly heading for bottles, she picked up

some gin and went back to the closed door of the bathroom. She didn't bother to knock, just walked right in.

"Here." She cranked the top off. "Drink from it."

Except with the way his hands were trembling, there was no way he could handle the bottle himself without spilling it everywhere.

"Let me hold it for you," she muttered.

There was a moment of hesitation from him, and then he lifted his mouth like a newborn foal who had been left by its mother.

He took two or three deep swallows. And another. "Now, that's warm."

Putting the gin by the side of the tub so he could reach it if he wanted, she took a full-sized bath towel and submerged it in the water behind him. When it was soaked and dripping, she draped it over the protruding ridge of his spine and the strips of his ribs. Then she went to work on his head with a washcloth, getting his hair wet, slicking it back.

Without him asking, she brought the gin bottle up again and he took from it, nursing from the open mouth.

Washing him with the soap and the shampoo reminded her of caring for an animal not long rescued. He was flinchy. Mistrusting.

Half dead.

"You need to eat," she said in a voice that cracked.

I don't have this in me, Lord. I can't do this again.

She hadn't managed to save that miscreant alcoholic father of hers. Losing two men in one lifetime seemed more than enough failure to go around.

"I'm going to make you breakfast after this, Edward."

"You don't have to."

"Yes," she said roughly. "I know."

FORTY-FIVE

"So are we doing this again?"

At the sound of the male voice, Lizzie stopped in the process of transferring yet another *Hedera helix* spine into a fresh pot. Closing her eyes, she took a breath and ordered her hands not to shake or drop anything.

She had been waiting for Lane to come and find her. It hadn't taken long.

"Well?" he said. "Are we back at this thing where you hear something you don't like and shut me out? Because if that's the script we're running here, and it sure as hell looks like we are, I guess I should just hop back on a plane to New York and call it quits now. So much more efficient and I don't have to run up a phone bill leaving messages on your voice mail."

Forcing her hands to keep going, she put the root system into the hole she'd dug in the pot and began to transfer fresh soil in to fill things up.

"Something I didn't want to hear," she repeated. "Yes, you could say that finding out your wife is pregnant — again — is a news flash I would have preferred not to hear. Particularly because I learned about it right after I'd had sex with you myself. And then there was the happy news that you were being arrested for putting her in the hospital."

When he didn't say anything after that, she glanced over at him. He was standing just inside the greenhouse, by the workstation Greta would have been at had Lizzie not told the woman that she needed some time by herself.

"Do you honestly think I'm capable of something like that?" he asked in a low voice.

"It's not up to me to decide anything of the sort." She refocused on what she was doing and hated the words she spoke. "But the one thing I will say is that the best clue to future behavior is the way someone has conducted themselves in the past. And I can't . . . I can't do this with you anymore. Whether or not any of it is true isn't the issue for me."

After patting down the new soil, she reached for her watering can and tilted the thing over the ivy's feet. In another three months, the plant would be ready to move outdoors to one of the beds, or to the base of a wall, or to a pot on the terrace. They had great luck with this variant on the estate, but it was only good planning to have backups.

Wiping her hands off on the front of her potting apron, she turned to face him. "I'm leaving. I gave my notice. So you don't have to worry about going back to New York."

She had no trouble meeting his eyes. Looking him in the face. Squaring off at him.

It was amazing how clear you could become with others when you knew where you stood yourself.

"You really think I could do that to a woman," he repeated.

Of course I don't, she thought to herself. But she stayed silent because she knew that if she really wanted him to leave her alone, the insinuation would hurt his male pride and that, sadly, would work in her favor.

"Lizzie, answer the quesiton."

"It's not any of my business. It just isn't."

After a long moment, he nodded. "Okay. Fair enough."

As he pivoted and went for the door, she had to admit she was a little surprised.

She'd expected some long, drawn-out thing from him. A torrent of persuasion she was going to have to deflect. Some kind of *I love you, Lizzie. I really do love you.*

"I wish you well, Lizzie," he said. "Take care."

And that . . . was that.

The door eased shut of its own volition. And for a split second, she had an absolutely absurd impulse to go after him and yell in his face that he was a colossal fucking asshole to have seduced her like he had, that he was a reprobate, that he was exactly who she feared he was, a user of women, a lying, cheating elitist sadist who wouldn't know —

Lizzie forcibly pulled herself back from the brink.

If that good-bye was anything to go by, whether she was in or out of his life didn't seem to matter to him in the slightest.

Good to know, she thought bitterly. *Good to know.*

Here was the thing, Lane thought as he got behind the wheel of his 911. There were times in life when, as much as you wanted to fight for something, you just had to let it go.

You didn't have to like the failure.

You didn't have to feel really fucking great

about the way things turned out.

And you certainly didn't walk away from the shit scot-free, without being seriously damaged by the loss, crippled even.

But you needed to let that stuff go, because expending the energy wasn't going to get you anywhere, and you might as well get on with getting used to the loss.

It was the one lesson his relationship with his father had taught him. Would he have loved having a male figure he could look up to, make proud, feel respected by? Hell, yeah. Would it have been awesome to not grow up in a house where the sound of loafers on marble flooring or the whiff of cigarette smoke didn't make him run for cover? Duh. Could he have used some fatherly advice, especially at a time like this?

Yeah. He really could have.

That wasn't the way things had worked out for him, however — and he had had to get used to it or go insane negotiating with a failure he was never going to be able to change or improve.

By the same token, if Lizzie King truly believed there was even a possibility, however slight, that he could have taken his hand to a woman like that? That he could have lied to her face about Chantal? That whatever baby the woman was carrying was actually his? Then there was no hope for the two of them. No matter what he said to her or how he tried to explain things . . . she didn't really know him, and more to the point, she didn't really trust him.

The fact that it was all bullshit? The fact that Chantal had cheated him, once again, of the woman he loved?

Tough breaks.

Whaaa-whaaaa-whaaaa.

Go ask Santa for a new father. Get the tooth fairy to bring you a new ex-wife.

Whatever.

Leaving Easterly in the dust, he hopped on the highway and doubled the speed limit on his way to the Charlemont International Airport — not because he was in a hurry or going to be late, but because, what the hell. The car could handle it — and at the moment, he actually was sober at the controls.

The entrance for private arrivals and departures was the first exit off the concourse that circled the enormous facility, and he shot onto a narrow lane that led to a separate terminal. Parking right in front of the double doors, he got out, leaving the engine on.

Jeff Stern was just walking into the luxurious space, and even though it had been mere days, it seemed like a century since

Lane had played that poker game and become annoyed by that bimbo — and gotten to his feet to go answer his phone.

Unsurprisingly, his old roommate was dressed like the Wall Street man he was, with his structural glasses, and his dark suit, and his crisp white shirt. He even had a red power tie on.

"You could have worn shorts," Lane said as they clapped hands.

"I'm coming from the office, asshole."

That accent, at once foreign and familiar, was exactly what he needed to hear right now.

"God, you look like hell," Jeff said as his luggage arrived on a cart. "Family life clearly doesn't agree with you."

"Not mine at any rate. Tell me, is your plane still here?"

"Not for long. It's refueling. Why?" When Lane just looked out at the runways, his friend cursed. "No. No, no, no, you did *not* drag me down here south of the Mason-Dixon just to cry wolf and want to go back to Manhattan. Seriously, Lane."

For a moment, Lane stood with one foot on each side of the divide: Stay, just to screw his father to the wall on multiple levels; leave, because he was sick and tired of the bullshit.

634

Guess he and Lizzie had something in common after all.

They both wanted away from him.

"Lane?"

"Let's go," he said, tipping the redcap and picking up his old roommate's two leather suitcases. "When was the last time you were at Easterly?"

"Derby, a million years ago."

"Nothing has changed."

Outside, he popped the hood of the Porsche and put the luggage in; then he and Jeff were off, speeding around the airport, shooting out onto the highway.

"So, am I going to meet this woman of yours, Baldwine?"

"Probably not. She's quitting."

"Well, that de-escalated quickly. I'm very sorry."

"Don't pretend you haven't seen the news."

"Yeah, it's everywhere. I think you are personally responsible for resurrecting the printed newspaper. Congratulations."

Lane cursed and sped around a semi. "Not an award I was looking for, I assure you."

"Wait, quitting? You mean she works for your family? Is this a Sabrina thing, old man?"

"Lizzie's the head horticulturist at the estate. Or was."

"Not just the gardener, huh. Makes sense. You hate stupid women."

Lane glanced over. "No offense, but can we talk about something else? Like maybe how my family is losing all its money? I need to be cheered up."

Jeff shook his head. "You, my friend, lead one hell of a life."

"You want to trade? Because right now, I'm looking for a way out of all of it."

FORTY-SIX

That night, Lizzie arrived home to no tree in her front yard.

Getting out of her farm truck, she looked around. The Yaris was still where it had been crunched, the mangled little car with its busted-out windows and its soaked and leaf-riddled interior looking like something out of a video game. But the limb was gone, nothing but fresh, sweet-smelling sawdust sprinkling the ground in its place.

Don't you dare, Lane, she thought.

Don't you fricking dare try to take care of me now.

She glanced up high and saw that the ragged wound from where the tree had split had been cut with care and sealed up so that it would heal and the magnificent maple would survive the damage.

"Damn you."

At least he'd left the car where it was. If he'd taken that, too, she would have had to contact him to find out where to reclaim the body, so to speak.

She should have known better than to assume it was over between them.

Marching up to her front porch, she talked at him the entire way —

Lizzie stopped with her foot on the first step. On her screen door, a note had been taped to the wooden frame.

Great. Now what. Some kind of, *Now that cooler heads prevail, blah, blah, blah.*

He was a sick man.

And she was doing the right thing leaving. As much as it was going to kill her to go, she had to get away from him, from Easterly, from this bizarre stretch of her life that could be described only as a bad dream.

Forcing herself into gear, she went up and tore the paper off the door. She wanted to throw the thing out, but some sick, pick-at-the-wound impulse made that impossible. Opening the note up, she read —

Howdy, neigbor. Cows out n all over yur yard. Ruined beds out back. No good with flowers so took care of yur tree. The wife made you a pie. Left on yur counter.

— Buella 'n Ross

Exhaling, she felt a wave of exhaustion

wash over her, and instead of continuing into the house, she went across and sat down on her porch swing. Kicking the floorboards with her foot, she listened to the crickets and the creak of the steel chains that were bolted into the ceiling above her head. She felt the soft, warm breeze on her face and watched the waning sunlight thicken into a peach wash that created long shadows across the good earth.

She needed to plant her porch pots —

No, she really didn't.

Hey, at least she had good dessert tonight — Buella made pie that was out of this world. Maybe it would be peach. Or . . . blueberry.

Lizzie found herself wiping her eyes and staring at the tears on her fingertips.

It was a horrible thing to have to save herself by leaving all this — rather like, she supposed, having to cut off a diseased limb.

She'd been doing so well, she thought.

And then Lane just had to come back down here and ruin everything.

"That's as much as Edward took out of there," Lane said as he paced around the guest room Jeff had been given.

It was the best of the suites, looking out over the back garden and the river, and it also had a desk big enough to qualify as a kitchen counter. In fact, back a million years ago, the set of rooms had been his grandfather's private quarters, and after the man's death, nothing had been touched except for regular cleanings.

Jeff's comment when he'd walked in had been stereotypically dry. Something about whether the Civil War had been commanded out of the space.

Predictably, though, the second the guy had accessed the financial data, the smartass qualifiers had dried up and the man had become all business.

"Anyway, it's almost time for dinner." Lane looked at his watch. "We dress here. Well, everyone except for me. So your suit should be fine."

"Bring me something up here," Jeff muttered as he yanked off his tie, his eyes never leaving his computer screen. "And I need some legal pads and pens."

"You mean you don't want to see me and my father glare at each other across the soufflé?" Yeah, 'cuz Lane was *really* looking forward to that himself. "You could also meet my sister's fabulous new fiancé. The guy's about as charming as cancer."

When Jeff didn't respond, Lane walked across and peered over the guy's shoulder.

"Tell me that makes sense to you."

"Not yet, but it will."

Right man for the job, Lane thought when he finally left.

Out in the hall, he found himself staring at his mother's door. Maybe Edward was right. Maybe if everything went *poof!* his mother wouldn't notice: All those drugs kept her cocooned and safe in her delirium — something that, for the first time, he was coming to understand.

On that note, how about some bourbon.

Heading for the front stairs, he decided he was going to skip dinner himself. He still wanted to punch the hell out of his father, but with Jeff in the house, he had, hopefully, a much better way of taking the man down.

And then he was going to follow Lizzie's lead and get good and gone with all this.

It was just too much here, too Byzantine, too polluted.

Maybe he would go back to New York. Or perhaps it was time to cast a wider net. Take off to somewhere overseas —

Lane stopped halfway down the grand staircase.

Mitch Ramsey and two CMP officers were standing in the grand foyer below, their hats off, their faces like something out of a textbook on criminal justice: no expressions. At all.

Shit, Lane thought as he closed his eyes.

Guess Samuel T. had been able to work the old boys' network only so far.

"I'll go get my wallet," Lane called out. "And I'll call my lawyer —"

Mitch looked up just as Mr. Harris came bustling in from the dining room.

"Oh, Mr. Baldwine," the butler said. "These gentlemen are here to see you."

"I figured. I'll just grab my —"

Mitch spoke up. "Can we talk somewhere privately?"

Lane frowned. "I want my lawyer present."

When Mitch just shook his head, Lane glanced at the other officers. Neither of them were meeting him in the eye.

Lane descended down to ground level and indicated with his hand. "The parlor."

As the four of them proceeded into the elegant room, Mr. Harris closed the double doors into the foyer — and by tacit understanding, nothing was said until the man came around to the other side of the room and closed those panels as well.

Lane crossed his arms over his chest. "What's up, Mitch. You looking for a trifecta? Gin, then me — and now how about my father —"

"It is with profound regret that I inform you that —"

A cold shot of fear rocked through his body. "Not Edward, oh, God, please not Edward —"

"— a body was found in the river about two hours ago. We have reason to believe it is that of your father."

The exhale that left Lane's lungs was slow and strangely even. "What . . ." He cleared his throat. "Where was it found?"

"On the far side of the falls. We need you to come down and identify the body. Next of kin is preferred, but I never put a wife through that if I can avoid it."

By way of answering, Lane went over to the bar cart and poured himself a measure of Family Reserve. After tossing it back, he nodded to Mitch and the other two members of law enforcement.

"Give me a moment. I'll be right back."

As he passed by Mitch, the man reached out and grabbed his shoulder. "I'm very sorry, Lane."

Lane frowned. "You know, I can't say that I am."

FORTY-SEVEN

Lane told no one where he was going or why.

When he came back down from his rooms, he had his cell phone with him and his wallet, and he was careful to stay out of eyesight of the people who were eating and conversing quietly in the dining room.

No, he wasn't telling anyone anything. Not until it was certain.

Getting into the back of Mitch's sheriff's SUV, he closed himself in and stared out the front windshield.

When the guy was behind the wheel, Lane said, "Does anyone know?"

"We've kept it quiet so far. The body washed up into a boathouse slip about a quarter mile from the falls. The people who called it in are good folk. They were shaken up and don't want a lot of media attention or reporters on their property. It's not going to hold forever, though."

The ride down to the morgue was a bizarre one, time slowing to a crawl, everything too bright, too clear, too loud. And once they were inside the dull, utilitarian building, all that got worse until he felt like he was tripping, the surreal quality like something out of a Jerry Garcia cartoon.

The only thing he could do, the only thing he was tracking, was following Mitch wherever the guy went — and before long, Lane found himself in a private waiting room that was about the size of a pantry.

In the center of the wall ahead of him was a curtain that was pulled into place over what he assumed was a large glass window. Next to the setup was a door.

"No," Lane said to Mitch. "I want to see him face-to-face."

There was an awkward moment. "Listen, Lane, the body's in bad shape. It went over the falls and might have even tangled with a barge. It'll be easier —"

"Not interested in easy." Lane narrowed his eyes on the deputy. "I want in there."

Mitch cursed. "Give me a minute."

As the sheriff disappeared through the door, Lane was glad the guy hadn't fought him any harder than that — because he didn't want to admit to the guy that the reason he needed to get up close and personal in this situation was that he had to be sure his father was really dead.

Which was stupid.

Like all these cops would waste their time making this shit up?

Mitch came back and held the door open. "Come on in."

Walking into the tiled space was something Lane was going to remember for the rest of his life. And Jesus, it was just like the movies: In the center of the room, on a stainless-steel rolling table, was a body bag.

Absurdly, he noted that it was the exact same type as the one Rosalinda had been put into.

Off to the side of the gurney, a woman in a white coat stood with her gloved hands clasped in front of her. "If you're ready, sir?"

"Yes. Please."

She reached up and clasped the zipper. Pulling downward about two feet, she spread the opening wide.

Lane leaned in, but the smell of water and rot made him recoil.

He hadn't expected his father's eyes to be open.

"That's him," Lane choked out.

"I'm sorry for your loss," the coroner said as she started to rezip the bag.

When she'd finished the job, he supposed

they wanted him to leave, but he just stood there staring down at the body bag.

All kinds of images coughed their way into his thoughts, a jumble of things from the past and the present.

No more future, though, he thought. *There was going to be nothing further with the man after this point.*

God, of all the ways he'd envisioned things ending between them . . . this quiet moment, in this cold medical room, with Mitch Ramsey on one side of him and a total stranger on the other, was so not it.

"What now?" he heard himself ask.

Mitch cleared this throat. "Unofficially, and do not hold me to this, we're pretty sure it was a suicide. Given everything that has been . . . well, you know."

"Yes. Clearly." And law enforcement wasn't even aware of the missing money.

What a fucking coward, Lane thought at his father. *Creating this huge mess and then opting out by throwing yourself off a bridge.*

Asshole.

"We'd like your consent to do an autopsy," Mitch said. "Just to rule out foul play. But again, that's not what's on our minds."

"Of course." Lane glanced over at the deputy. "Listen, I need some time before this gets out in the press. I have to tell my mother, my brothers, my sister. I don't even know how to get in touch with Maxwell, but I do not want him hearing about this on the six-o'clock news. Or worse, TMZ."

"Law enforcement is committed to working with you and your family."

"I'll be as quick as I can."

"That would make it easier on everyone here."

A clipboard came out of nowhere, and he signed a variety of things. As he gave the pen back to the coroner, he thought, *Shit, they were going to have to plan a funeral.*

Although, to be honest, the very last thing he had any interest in was honoring his father in any fashion.

"I'm not hungry."

As Edward sat in his chair in his cottage, he was fully aware that he sounded like a four-year-old refusing dinner — but he didn't care.

The fact that the smells coming out of that galley kitchen were making his mouth water was beside the point.

Shelby, however, had selective hearing. "Here you go."

She put the bowl of stew on the table next to his bottle of . . . what was he drinking now? Oh, tequila. Well, wasn't that going to go swimmingly with the beef gravy.

"Eat," she commanded — in a tone that suggested he either did the job himself or she was going to puree the stuff and force feed it to him through a straw.

"You know, you can leave anytime you like," he muttered.

For godsakes, the woman had been in his house all day long, cleaning, doing laundry, cooking. He'd pointed out to her a couple of times that she had been hired to take care of the horses, not the owner, but again . . . her hearing was very spotty.

Damn, that's good, he thought as he took a mouthful.

"I want to make an appointment for you with your doctor."

The sound of a car driving up was a welcome intrusion. Especially as he struggled to remember what day it was — and hoped it was somehow Friday once again: He rather liked the idea of her seeing a prostitute come to service him. Hell, she could watch if she cared to, not that it was much of a show —

For a split second, he recalled the feel of Sutton straddling him, moving up and down, looking into his eyes.

A sharp pain through his chest made him eat faster just to get rid of the sensation.

The knocking was loud.

"Would you mind doing the honors?" he said to Shelby. "If it's a woman, invite her in. If it isn't, tell them to get the hell off my property — and use the word 'hell,' will you? We both know it's in your vocabulary."

The glare she shot him probably would have blown him off his feet if he hadn't been sitting down already.

But she did go to the door.

Opening it up, she said, "Oh. My."

"Who is it," Edward muttered. "Your fairy godmother?"

Except, no. It was Lane.

As his brother came into the cottage, Edward started shaking his head. "Whatever it is, you've gotta go somewhere else with it. I told you, I'm not going to help you anymore —"

"May we speak in private."

Not a question.

Edward rolled his eyes. "It doesn't matter what you say."

"This is family business."

"Isn't it always." When Lane didn't budge, Edward cursed. "Whatever it is, you can say it in front of her."

If anything, hopefully Shelby's presence in the little room would speed things along.

Lane glanced at the woman. Looked back.

"Father's dead."

As Shelby gasped, Edward slowly lowered his spoon back to the bowl. Then he said in a rough voice, "Shelby, will you please excuse my brother and me for a moment? Thank you kindly."

Funny how the manners came back out of him in times of crisis.

After Shelby scuttled out the door, Edward wiped his mouth on his paper napkin. "When?"

"Sometime last night, they think. He threw himself off the bridge, most likely. The body washed up on the other side of the falls."

Edward sat back in his chair.

He intended to say something. He really did.

He just . . . couldn't remember what it was.

Lane evidently felt the same way, because his youngest brother went to the only other chair in the room and sat down. "I told Mother before I came out here. I don't think . . . she has no idea what I said to her. She's not tracking at all. Also told Gin. Her reaction was just what yours is."

"Are they sure," Edward asked, "that it's him."

For some reason, that seemed vitally

important. Although how could a mistake of this magnitude be made?

"I was the one who identified the body."

Edward closed his eyes. And for a brief moment, that pilot light of his flickered on again. "That shouldn't have been you. I should have done that."

"It was fine. I didn't . . ." Lane took a deep breath. "I don't seem to be having any reaction to it at all. I'm sure you heard about yesterday."

Edward looked over at his brother. "What about yesterday?"

Lane laughed in a hard burst. "Sometimes not having cable television is a good thing, no? Anyway, it doesn't matter. It really doesn't."

They sat in silence for the longest time, and later, Edward would realize it was because he was waiting for some kind of an emotional reaction of his own. Sorrow. Hell, maybe joy.

There was nothing. Just a resonate numbness.

"I've got to find Max," Lane said. "Law enforcement is going to keep a lid on this until we're ready to make a statement, but that respite won't last forever."

"I don't know where he is," Edward murmured.

"I'll keep trying the number I had from two years ago. I sent him an e-mail, too, at his last known. I think he might be really far off the grid."

More quiet.

"Is Gin all right?" Edward asked.

Lane shook his head. Then swung his eyes over. "Are any of us?"

Sadly, Edward thought . . . *the answer to that is no.*

FORTY-EIGHT

The next morning, as Lizzie went up the back stairs with a bouquet in her hands, she gave herself a pep talk.

It was all well and good to hide in the greenhouses, but come on. She had thirteen days left of employment at Easterly and she was not going out on a shirker note. She always did the flowers for the bedrooms. She had her schedule, and she was going to goddamn well do her job.

Up on the second floor, she squared her shoulders and went down to the best guest room. Mr. Harris had told her they had an unexpected houseguest — and also that there was no need to refresh flowers in Chantal's room anymore.

Good to know, Mr. Harris. Thanks so much.

At least that was one person off her Don't Need To Run Into list.

Too bad the number-one spot was still under Easterly's roof.

"Thirteen days," she said under her breath. "Just thirteen days."

At the broad door, she knocked and waited. After a moment, a male voice said, "Come in."

Pushing the panels wide, she saw a man sitting at Lane's grandfather's desk across the way, his back bent into a comma as he scrummed down over a laptop. Next to him, a printer was spitting out pages marked with columns, and at his feet, wadded-up balls of yellow legal paper dotted the floor.

He didn't look up.

"I'm just here with some flowers," she said.

"Uh-huh."

Beside him, on the window shelf, was a tray of empty breakfast dishes. As she put the vase down on an antique bureau, she offered, "May I take that down for you?"

"What?" he muttered while still focused on the screen.

"The tray?"

"Sure. Thanks."

He had to be here to look at those files, she thought. *The ones Rosalinda left behind.*

Not her business, she reminded herself.

Going around the desk, she saw two expensive suitcases, one of which was open and rifled through — and yet she had the impression the man hadn't changed since whenever he'd arrived. His white shirt was wrinkled everywhere, and so were his pants.

Also not her business.

Picking up the tray, she —

"Oh my God."

As he spoke up, she almost didn't glance over at him, figuring he'd found something in whatever he was going through. But then she realized he was staring at her.

"What?" she asked.

"You're Lizzie. Right?"

Recoiling, she glanced around. But come on, like there was someone standing behind her?

"Ah, yes."

"Lane's Lizzie. The horticulturist."

"No," she said. "No, not his."

The man stretched his arms over his head, and as all kinds of cracking happened, she noticed that he was very good-looking, with dark hair and dark eyes that might have been brown, might have been blue.

The accent was very definitely New York.

"Wow," he murmured. "I thought you were made-up."

"If you'll excuse me, I have some work to do."

"And now I understand why he didn't go after anyone else for two years."

Don't ask, Lizzie told herself. *Don't* —

"I'm sorry?" she heard herself say.

Crap.

"For two years, nada. I mean, look, we went to college together, so I saw firsthand how he earned his reputation. But for the last two years, he didn't go near a woman. I thought he was gay. I even asked if he was gay." The man put his palms out to her. "Not that there's anything wrong with that."

Wasn't that a line from Seinfeld? she thought.

"I, ah . . ."

"So at least now I get it." The man smiled in a totally non-creepy way. "But he says you're leaving? It's none of my business, but why? He's a good man. Not perfect, but good. Wouldn't suggest you play poker against the guy, though. Not unless you have money to lose."

Lizzie frowned. "I, ah . . ."

"I didn't even know he was married, by the way. He never talked about her, I certainly never met her — and now, come to find out, it was about you all along. Well, anyway, back to work."

Like the guy hadn't just dropped a bomb in the middle of the room.

As Lizzie's heart started to pump at double speed, she said, "I'm sorry. Did you say . . . you never knew he was married?"

The guy looked back over at her. "No, he never brought up the woman. Not once in the two years he was sleeping on my couch. I didn't find out until he called me a couple of days ago."

"But you must have met her, right? When she visited him."

"Visited him? Honey, he never had any visitors — and I would know because he never left my place. We'd play poker all night, and I'd go to work, only to come back and find him on my sofa in exactly the same position I'd left him in. He didn't see anyone. Didn't accept phone calls. Never came back down here. Never traveled. Just locked himself in my apartment and drank. I figured his next stop was a dialysis unit."

"Oh."

The guy cocked an eyebrow as if he wanted to know if she needed any more information.

"Thank you," she said.

"Thank you for the flowers. I've never had a woman bring some to me before."

And then he was back to work, frowning at that screen.

Lizzie walked out of the room in a daze and had to remind herself to kick the door shut in her wake.

After standing there for a moment, she swiveled her head and looked down the hall to Mr. Baldwine's room.

No visitors. No phone calls. Two years up in New York on some old friend's couch.

And Chantal was supposedly pregnant.

With Lane's baby.

Lizzie wasn't consciously aware of deciding to move. But before she knew it, she had put the tray of dishes down on the runner outside of the guest room and was tiptoeing over the carpet. When she got to Mr. Baldwine's room, she put her ear to the panels.

Then she knocked quietly.

When there was no answer, she slipped inside and shut herself in.

There was something eerie about the room. Then again, she was essentially trespassing, as she had no valid reason for being in there.

Well, no valid reason tied to her job.

Glancing around to make sure she hadn't missed someone else in the bathroom beyond, she quickened over to the large bed that was made up with military precision.

Lowering herself down to her knees, she craned under the side table, under the bed frame itself.

The wisp of silk was still there, on the floor.

Lizzie stretched out her arm —

Knock, knock, knock. "Towel service, Mr. Baldwine."

With a frantic lunge, Lizzie threw herself under the bed skirt, just tucking her legs in as the maid opened the door and walked into the room.

A soft whistling and softer footsteps on the thick rug tracked the woman's progress as she went into the bathroom.

Please, don't clean, Lizzie thought as she lay still in the darkness. *Just drop those towels and keep going.*

Drop the towels.

Keep going.

God, her heart was pounding so hard it was a wonder the maid didn't hear the damn thing.

Moments later, a miracle happened and those footfalls backtracked and the door was re-shut.

Lizzie sagged and closed her eyes. Right, okay, she was taking cat burglar off her list of possible next careers after she left Easterly.

Locking a hold on the lingerie, she stuffed the thing into the waistband of her khakis and covered it up by untucking her polo shirt. Then she shuffled out from under, got to her feet, and brushed herself off.

Back at the door, she heard . . .

Shoot, the vacuum cleaner running right outside in the hall.

Down in Miss Aurora's quarters, Lane was struggling to get through his bacon and eggs.

"You don't have to finish that," she said next to him.

"Didn't think I'd ever hear that coming from you."

"The rules are suspended for today."

Sitting back in the Barcalounger, he glanced over at her little galley kitchen. All the dishes were done, everything drying in the rack. The sponge was in the dish. The dish towel was folded neatly over the oven's long handle.

"Do you think Reverend Nyce will do the service?" he asked. "At Charlemont Baptist?"

Miss Aurora looked at him sharply. "Really?"

"That's my church. Edward's and Gin's and Max's, too." He looked at her. "You were the only one who ever took us to worship."

"I think he would be honored."

"Good. I'll call him."

As they fell silent, Lane stared straight ahead, seeing nothing, focusing on nothing. There wasn't anything in his brain, either. He was numb from the floor up, an empty vessel reacting to the world around him rather than actually living in it.

"I'm not going to give you my blessing."

He shook himself and glanced back across at her. "I'm sorry?"

"I'm not going to tell you it's okay to leave."

Lane frowned and opened his mouth. Then shut things up.

Funny, he hadn't been aware of speaking that out loud, but then she knew him better than anybody. "Things didn't work with Lizzie. Again. Father's dead. Edward's moved out. Mother is — well, you know. Gin's going to marry that idiot and probably take Amelia with her. This whole era, it's over, Miss Aurora. And what's more, I don't know that the future holds any of us on this land anymore. Easterly . . ." He moved his hand around, thinking of the estate and all the people and buildings on it. "Easterly's part of the past, and you know, I can't live in that. It's poisonous. This family, this house, the way of life — it's just poisonous."

Miss Aurora shook her head. "You're looking at it the wrong way."

"I'm really not."

Miss Aurora sat forward in her chair and reached for his hands. "This is . . . your time, Lane. God has provided you with a sacred duty to keep this family together. You are the only one who can do it. This is all falling into place because it is your destiny to bind the blood once again. It happens every couple of generations. It's happening now. This is *your* time."

Lane stared down at their fingers, the white and dark intertwined. "It was supposed to be Edward, you know."

"No, or he wouldn't be where he is right now." Miss Aurora's voice gathered strength. "I raised you better than to be a coward, Lane. I raised you better than to leave your duty at the exit door. If you want to honor me when I'm gone, you will do it by taking this family and moving them forward — together. I did my sacred job with you — and you, son of my heart, are going to do it with them."

Lane closed his eyes and felt a sudden weight settle all over his body, as if Easterly's walls and roof had caved in and landed on him.

"You will do this, Lane, for me. Because if

you don't, everything I put into you means nothing. If you don't, I have failed in my job."

Inside, he was screaming.

Inside, he was already on a plane, going anywhere away from Charlemont.

"God does not give us more than we can handle," she said grimly.

But what if God doesn't really know us, Lane thought to himself. *Or worse . . . what if God was just plain wrong?*

"I don't know, Miss Aurora."

"Well, I do. And you are not going to let me down, son. You simply are not."

FORTY-NINE

The true definition of eternity, Lizzie decided, was when you were stuck somewhere you shouldn't be.

With a camisole that wasn't your own, shoved down your damn shorts.

When the sounds of people in the hall finally quieted, she waited another five or ten minutes before she poked her head out.

Lunchtime, she thought. *Thank God.*

Jumping into the middle of the hallway, she let the door close behind her and stayed where she was, listening.

Next stop was going down past Gin's room and knocking on Chantal's door.

No answer. Then again, the woman had left, right?

Sneaking inside, she shut herself in —

"Oh, God," she muttered, fanning in front of her nose.

The stench of fancy perfume was enough to make her eyes water, but she had bigger fish to fry, as they say. Hightailing it into Chantal's walk-in closet, she faced off at a wardrobe big enough to rival an entire Nordstrom's women's department. Or Saks. Or whatever high-end place folks like Chantal got their clothes from.

Jeez, was she actually going to do this?

It was probably a really dumb idea, she decided as she began rifling through the hanging sections, breezing past all manner of silk and satin and lace. Then came the suits, the jackets, the dresses, the gowns.

"Where is your lingerie, Chantal . . ."

Of course. The dresser.

In the middle of the room, like an island of organization, there was a built-in stretch of double-faced drawers, and she started pulling them open at random.

Okay, this is stupid, she thought. Did she really think she was going to find the bottoms —

She was third drawer from the bottom of the left side on the north-facing part when she found what she was looking for.

Sort of.

In the midst of a line-up of carefully folded and tissue-paper-separated slips and matching panties, she found . . . a purple camisole that was identical to the one she had taken from behind William Baldwine's bed.

Just to make sure she wasn't seeing things, she took the peach one out and put them both side by side on the thick white carpeting. Same size, same maker — La Perla? — same everything except for the color.

Lizzie sat back on her butt and stared at the two.

And that was when she saw the stain on the rug.

Over in the far end of the room, there was a make-up vanity that was lined up in a windowed alcove that overlooked the gardens. It was the perfect place to do your makeup — or have it done — in natural light.

And under the ivory legs, in the corner, there was an unsightly yellow stain in a circle.

It was the kind of thing you'd find in a house with dogs.

Except Easterly had no dogs.

Crab walking over, she wedged herself under a second piece of furniture and patted at the discoloration. It was dry. But as she brought her fingertips to her nose — yup, that was the source of the perfume smell in the air.

Frowning, Lizzie rose up onto her knees.

"Oh . . . God."

The glass-covered surface of the vanity had a crack down the center. And the mirror was smashed in a starburst pattern.

With blood in the center.

Time to get out of here, she thought to herself.

Going back to the lingerie she'd laid out, she returned the purple one to where it had been. And then on a lark, she used the peach silk to clean her fingerprints off the drawer pulls.

All of them.

The last thing she needed was for the police to come in here and find out she'd been sniffing around, so to speak —

Lizzie froze at the sound of a man's voice. Except it wasn't in the wardrobe with her. It was next door — Gin's room, she realized.

Two people were talking. Loudly.

Going over, she put her ear to the wall beside a painting of a French woman who was mostly nude.

"I don't care," came Gin's voice with greater clarity. "It's just at the courthouse."

"Your father is dead."

Lizzie recoiled, bringing her hand to her mouth. *What?*

Richard Pford continued, "We will wait to

be married until after the funeral."

"I'm not mourning him."

"Of course not. That would require having a heart, and we both know that the absence of one is an anatomical anomaly of yours."

Lizzie backed off. Stumbled. Fell into the dresser.

After a moment, she continued with the wipe down and then went back to the door into the hall. Her heart was beating so loudly, she couldn't hear well enough and decided, screw it. If she got caught, what were they going to do to her?

She could just tell anyone she was checking for flowers.

But no one was out there.

Blindly heading for the staff stairs, her mind was racing, her thoughts slamming into one another, splintering, falling to pieces.

At the core, though, she came to one, inescapable conclusion.

She had made a terrible mistake.

The kind for which forgiveness was going to be next to impossible.

Down on the first floor, she stopped dead in her tracks. And realized that, of all the places to stall out, she had picked Rosalinda's office.

William Baldwine was dead, too.

How? she wondered. *What had happened to him?*

In a series of flashes, she saw Lane standing in the greenhouse, his face shut down, his voice flat as asphalt. Then she heard his friend telling her that, contrary to happily banging Chantal on the side, Lane had seen no one, done nothing.

And then the bomb burst in that mirror upstairs. And the lingerie.

Her last image was of Chantal out by the pool that morning when the woman had insisted on a refresher on her lemonade.

At the time, the fact that she had been wearing a silk wrap hadn't seemed especially significant. But now . . .

She'd been pregnant and just starting to show. Which was why she had asked for a virgin — no alcohol.

Chantal had been sleeping with William Baldwine. Cheating on the son with the father. And she had become pregnant.

She must have told William, Lizzie thought. *After the Derby.*

And the man had lost it. And hit her up in that dressing room.

Then he had kicked her out of the house. Or something like that.

Shaking her head, Lizzie put her hands to

her hot face and tried to breathe.

Her one and only thought was that she had to make it right with Lane. She had condemned him based on her own fear of being hurt again . . .

. . . when in reality there was a very, very strong possibility that, in fact, he'd had nothing to do with any of it.

Dropping her arms, she knew words were not going to be enough. Not for this one.

When the solution came to her, she checked her watch. If she hurried . . .

Breaking out into a run, she flashed through the kitchen, and Miss Aurora looked up from the stove.

"Where you going?" the woman asked. "What's on fire?"

Lizzie skidded into the door out to the garages. "I've got to go to Indiana. If you see Lane, tell him I'm coming back. I'm coming back!"

Fifty

It was actually pretty nice out here, Lane thought as he took a seat in the garden.

Looking around at the ivy-covered walls and the orderly flower beds, across the sparkling blue pool and the French doors of the business center, he imagined all the work that it took to maintain this "natural" beauty.

It was impossible not to picture Lizzie out here, but he shut that down quick.

No reason to bother with those kinds of things.

Bowing his head, he rubbed his eyes. Samuel T. had called about the situation with Chantal, and he knew he had to call the guy back. Mitch had also left a message, likely about the preliminary results of the autopsy. And meanwhile, up on the second floor, Jeff was going through all the financial stuff.

There were funeral arrangements to be made.

He had no energy to deal with any of it.

Damn it, Miss Aurora, he thought. *Let me go. Just let me get out of this.*

He loved that woman so much. He owed her even more. And yet even with his momma kicking him in the can, he just wasn't in this fight anymore.

Raising his eyes to Easterly's incredible white expanse, he stared at the mansion as a real estate appraiser would. Sutton Smythe's mortgage notwithstanding, they could probably clear most of the debt with Prospect Trust by a sale of the place.

Hell, with his father dead, maybe he could just go to Sutton and ask her not to send the money and rip up that mortgage?

Edward, he thought. *He would send Edward to do that one.*

Or maybe not. Maybe he would simply let it all go.

Maybe instead of trying to fly this broken aircraft they were all in, he would let the goddamn thing crash into a mountainside.

He might die a coward who had let his momma down, but at least it would be over with faster than trying to yank at the controls and attempt to land on some airstrip far, far below —

Lane?

He closed his eyes. Great. He was starting

to hallucinate.

Like Lizzie would actually come find —

"Lane?"

Jerking around on the stone bench, he saw that . . . well, hypothetically, he saw that she was standing a couple feet away from him.

And what do you know, in the light of the very late afternoon, she was as beautiful as she had always been. Natural, lovely, with her bright blue eyes and her sun-streaked hair, and that Easterly uniform that really shouldn't have been sexy, but which was on her.

"Lane, can I talk to you?"

He cleared his throat. Sat up straight like a man.

Apparently, he hadn't imagined this.

"Yes, of course. What do you need? If it's a reference, I'll have the butler —"

"I'm sorry." As her voice cracked, she took a shuddering breath. "I'm so, so sorry."

What was she —

"Oh, my father." He shrugged. "I guess you overheard something. Yes, he's gone. Funeral in a week. Thanks for the kind words."

"I'm not talking about that. Although, well, I am sorry that you lost your father. I know that wasn't a good relationship for you, but it's still hard."

"Well, I happen to excel at relationships that are not good. I'm quite facile with them."

Even to his own ears, his voice sounded fake, the words not ones he would normally use, either.

Edward, he thought numbly. *He sounds like Edward.*

Lizzie came forward, and then he was more than a little surprised to find her kneeling before him. And she was —

"Why are you crying?" he asked. "Are you all right —"

"God, how can you ask that? After what I did —"

"What are you talking about —"

In their typical fashion, they were speaking over each other, and because he didn't have the energy left to decipher anything, he shut up in hopes she would do some explaining and clarify things.

"I was wrong," she choked out. "I'm sorry I didn't believe you. About Chantal. I just — I didn't want to get hurt again, and I jumped to conclusions, and oh, God, I know your father was the one. I *know* he was the one. He was the one who hit her, he was the one who got her pregnant. I'm so sorry."

Tears streamed down her cheeks, falling

like rain from her face, landing in the bluegrass at his feet.

Lane blinked. It was all he could —

Jesus, his brain wasn't able to process any of this. He literally couldn't understand what she was saying —

Reaching behind her back, she pulled out something. A sheaf of papers? That was folded in half?

"Sorry isn't enough," she said. "I've hurt you too badly for that. So . . . I need to do something concrete, something to prove that I'm really with you, that I love you, and I'm . . . I'm really with you."

She held the pages out to him. "I need to show you, not tell you."

Lane shook his head. "Lizzie, I don't know what —"

"Take it," she said.

He did as she asked only because he didn't have the brains to think of a reason not to. Opening the crease, he looked at . . .

A whole bunch of letters. Followed by some numbers.

The second sheet was a map?

"It's the deed to my farm," she whispered. "I know compared to everything you have, it's not much. But it's all I have in this world."

"I don't understand?"

"With the kind of money problems you're facing, it won't help with that kind of debt. But it's worth enough to pay for good lawyers, for people who can help you sort everything out." She tapped the document. "I paid it off yesterday. I don't owe anything on it. And I've been approached to sell it before. It's good land. It's valuable. And it's yours."

His breath left his body.

His heart stopped.

His soul broke in half.

"I love you, Lane. I'm sorry I doubted you. I feel . . . God, you have no idea how badly I feel. Let me make it up to you the only way I know how. Or . . . throw the papers in my face if you want. I won't blame you. But I had to do something that mattered. I had to . . . offer you everything I am and everything I have —"

Lane wasn't aware of reaching for her.

But he knew the moment she was up against his chest.

Wrapping his arms around her, he lost his shit completely, the dam cracking open, everything coming out in sobs.

And Lizzie, with her strong body and her big heart, held him for as long as it took.

"It's going to be okay," she told him. "I promise you . . . somehow, it'll be okay."

When he finally had it together enough to pull back, he had a quick urge to reach between his legs and make sure he was still a guy. But Lizzie didn't seem to care about him being weak.

He wiped her face with his thumbs and kissed her.

"I love you, Lizzie." Then he shook his head. "But I don't know about God."

"What?"

Lane took a shuddering breath. "It's just something that Miss Aurora always told me."

"What's that?"

He kissed his woman again. "I don't know if I have God . . . but I'm sure of this. I have you . . . and that makes me wealthy beyond means."

Bringing her back against him, he held on to her and stared up at Easterly.

To hell with flying into a mountain, he thought.

As of this moment . . . he was now the head of the family, such as it was.

And he would be damned if things went to hell and gone on his watch.

ACKNOWLEDGMENTS

Thank you so much to everyone at NAL, especially my wonderful boss, Kara Welsh, and Leslie Gelbman. Thank you also to Team Waud, and to my family and friends.

About ten years ago, I moved down South, and I have to say, I honestly love it. It took a while to get used to everything, but now that I have a profound passion for college hoops (#L1C4), a number of tremendous friends, and a house that feels like home, it is clear that this Northerner has embraced everything about living in the Derby City. To say that this book wouldn't have been possible without this town and all the people I know here is a vast understatement. And for the first time ever, there are some loose connections between certain folks in the book and people whom I know — with these kinds of characters, how can you not write about them?

To that end, I would like to thank the following in no particular order: Leonard, my daughter, my mom, Nomers & Jonah, my pup and TatSon, my bffle & her kids, my Papa, Bob Melzer, Nique & Clarke, Mr. Henry Camp a.k.a. Uncle Stank, Dr. Michael "Bad Boy" Haboubi and his family, Dr. and Mrs. Gary Edlin (chief, your nickname will stay on the QT in this public forum), Chuck Mitchell and the lovely Renee & Cya, Mr. & Mrs. Ballard & Gracie & SophSoph, my adopted godson, Jacob (Who's the man?!), my niece, Polly, and nephew, William (Go Cards!), and their parents, Aunt Betsey & Uncle Bob, and all their family, Grandmother Sue & Geegaw, my FIL Padre & Granny Gray, Granny & Aunt Lee, Little Lee and the twins, Dr. & Dr. Fox, the Norton Family, the incomparable Roderick Hodge & his whole family, Kathy Cary, the Robinsons (esp. the Mrs. who breaks out the good stuff for me), both sets of Ronalds (the ones by me and the ones by my mom), all of the members of the Brown family on whom absolutely, positively none of this is based (and I really do mean that), Sandra Frazier, the Fellons, Ghislain & Nicholas, Karl & Elizabeth, Steph & Robert & BOB, The Leslie & Andy Hyslop, and so many more.

And in closing, I have to acknowledge my

wonderful husband Neville's grandmother, Mrs. Neville Blakemore, who will remain in my heart forevermore as the ultimate Southern Lady.

I've tried not to leave anyone out, if I have, my apologies.

ABOUT THE AUTHOR

J. R. Ward is the author of more than twenty previous novels, including those in her #1 *New York Times* bestselling series, The Black Dagger Brotherhood. There are more than fifteen million copies of Ward's novels in print worldwide, and they have been published in twenty-five different countries around the world. She lives in the South with her family.

The employees of Thorndike Press hope you have enjoyed this Large Print book. All our Thorndike, Wheeler, and Kennebec Large Print titles are designed for easy reading, and all our books are made to last. Other Thorndike Press Large Print books are available at your library, through selected bookstores, or directly from us.

For information about titles, please call:
(800) 223-1244

or visit our Web site at:
http://gale.cengage.com/thorndike

To share your comments, please write:
Publisher
Thorndike Press
10 Water St., Suite 310
Waterville, ME 04901